COURTING CASSANDRY

COURTING CASSANDRY

JOYCE DiPASTENA

Also by Joyce DiPastena

Poitevin Hearts
Loyalty's Web (Book 1)
Illuminations of the Heart (Book 2)
Loving Lucianna (Book 3)
Dangerous Favor (Book 4)

Stand alone titles
The Lady and the Minstrel

Short Stories
An Epiphany Gift for Robin: A short prequel scene to The Lady
and the Minstrel (1)
The Girl by the River: A short prequel scene to The Lady and the
Minstrel (2)
"Caroles on the Green," in Timeless Romance Anthology: Winter
Edition (2012)
A Candlelight Courting: A Short Christmas Romance

Non-fiction
Name Your Medieval Character: Medieval Christian Names (12th-
13th Centuries)

Copyright 2016 Joyce DiPastena

Sable Tyger Books
Sabletygerbooks@gmail.com

Cover art by Roseanna White Designs
Sable Tyger Books logo by The Write Designer

Sable Tyger Books
sabletygerbooks@gmail.com

ISBN: 978-0986239663

112023

An unknown author once said, "Not all wounds are physical."

This story is dedicated to all who have suffered the wounds of emotional abuse. May you, too, find light on the other side of the trial.

Acknowledgments

It is impossible for any writer to be a completely objective reader of their own work. One day we think we've written gold, the next day the worst drivel on the planet. It takes both aspects of a writer's personality to ultimately succeed. Without those days when our writing feels like it sings, we'd never have the courage to share it with others. And without those moments of intense self-doubt, we'd never grow humble enough to seek out, listen to, and put into action well thought out criticism from objective and supportive fellow writers.

Therefore, it is with the deepest gratitude that I thank the following people for helping to improve my story with their kindly worded but honest suggestions, while also buoying my confidence in dark moments when I needed people who believed in me:

My wonderful critique group, Tina Scott, Joan Sowards, and Valerie Ipson, whose suggestions for the early chapters of *Courting Cassandry* were invaluable.

My beta readers, Shaunna Gonzales, Donna Hatch, Laura Miller, Heidi Murphy, and Laura Walker, who gave of their time to read my manuscript in its entirety and offer insightful feedback and encouragement.

And my editors at Eschler Editing, Heidi Brockbank and Michele Preisendorf, who gave this story its final shine.

This story is better because of each of you. Thank you to you all!

Cast of Characters

Fictional Characters
(in alphabetical order)

Antony de Reymes – Cassandry de Reymes's deceased husband

Aveline Follet – Gerolt's deceased wife

Cassandry de Reymes – former ward of Gerolt de Warrenne; widow of Antony de Reymes

Egelina de Reymes – daughter of Antony and Cassandry de Reymes

Emma Cook – head cook in Gerolt's kitchen

Fleur de Warrenne – Gerolt's deceased daughter

Garin – a squire of Gerolt's household

Gerolt de Warrenne – a wealthy baron; known as the Hero of Iconium

Herleve d'Aufai – Samson de Curzon's wife

Hyll – a physician

Lora – maid to Cassandry and Egelina

Marion – daughter of Samson de Curzon and Herleve d'Aufai

Rauffe de Warrenne – son of Gerolt and Aveline de Warrenne

Samson de Curzon – a knight who grew up with Gerolt; Gerolt's best friend

Sir Edward – a knight of Gerolt's household

Sir Fithian – a knight of Gerolt's household

Sir Ingram – a knight of Gerolt's household

Sir Owen – a knight of Gerolt's household

Sir Patrick – steward of Cassandry de Reymes's lands

Sir Payne – a knight of Gerolt's household

Sir Tobias – a knight of Gerolt's household

Pronunciation note:

The "g" in Gerolt and Egelina (Gelli) are both pronounced with a "j" sound; Garin is pronounced with a hard "g"

Chapter 1

England 1201

She curtsied as gracefully as he remembered. Twenty-four years and nothing had changed. Her tawny gown, with its sprinkling of embroidery beneath a modestly rounded neck, hugged her still-slender figure before it flowed into wide folds at her hips. Gerolt had come upon her unannounced as she'd crossed the great hall of Rengrave Castle before his footsteps had turned her about just short of the stairs. She had dispensed with a matron's veil, allowing her long dark hair to hang in two thick plaits over her shoulders.

"We were not expecting you, my lord," she said in the cool, familiar tone he had once held so dear.

He held out his hand as she rose, requiring her to place her fingers in his grasp. The blue sapphire from her wedding day still winked there, alongside a ruby he did not recognize, which graced her little finger. He bowed and brushed his lips against skin still smooth and white. He had not prayed for such a moment as this to come, but now that it had, excitement fluttered in his stomach. Just for an instant, he felt as bashful as a squire.

"My apologies, Lady Cassandry. I am returning from business

at Glinfield Manor, and I could not pass Rengrave without telling my men that I must stop and pay you my respects." Such visits to her castle had once been common until all communication with her had ceased two years after her marriage.

Even after so long a time, he hoped she would welcome him. Instead she cast a doubtful glance over his shoulder. None of his men had followed him into the hall. He would not inflict his retinue on her before he was certain they would not be intruding. Rengrave had always been the smallest of her late husband's fortresses.

She withdrew her hand, and he observed the way she tried to conceal the nervous trembling of her fingers against the folds of her gown.

"How many have come with you?" she inquired. "I will send word to the kitchen that we will have guests for dinner."

"I ride with a small party," he said, trying to reassure her. "Five men only. Samson, Ingram, and Fithian are with me, along with two young knights unknown to you."

A smile curved her lovely mouth. "And does each of these knights bring a squire? Have you brought pages, too, and grooms? Perhaps a herald to bear messages for you and a huntsman should you decide to pause and chase a few deer along your way?"

Gerolt felt his lips twitch upward in response. She knew him too well. "A falconer, not a huntsman," he said. "The skies have been unusually fair this spring. Perhaps you will join us for some hawking while we are here?"

Her smile faded and her brow furrowed with worry. "Antony sold our last gyrfalcon before he died. The mews have stood empty for three years. I fear your falconer will find sorry accommodations for your birds." Her hands came together beneath her breast, twisting together in ill-concealed anxiety. "I will speak with Sir Patrick, our steward. Perhaps he can make the mews more hospitable. I will have chambers prepared for your men as well.

You are all most welcome, of course." She dropped another curtsy. "If you will excuse me? Invite your men in, and I will send up refreshments while—"

He was not fooled by her attempts to appear at ease. He stopped her with a hand on her arm, ignoring the pang of disappointment that momentarily dimmed his excitement at being near her again after so long a time apart. He had hoped for a few days to reacquaint themselves before he made his proposal, but her apparent dismay at his suggestion of an extended visit swiftly changed his mind. Or perhaps it was the fact that she had not asked after his health, or that of the men she had once known, or after the affairs at Lyonstoke Castle, or any of the small questions that passed between people who had once been as close as they had.

He swallowed his regret and said in an attempt to soothe her evident worry, "I do not mean to overwhelm you with our company. We will not be staying the night."

"You said you would be here long enough to go hawking," she reminded him.

"A whimsy," he said lightly. "I would we could stay a few days, but it is a two-day ride to Lyonstoke, and I cannot tarry longer than I already have. My men would undoubtedly welcome the refreshment you speak of, but . . . is there someplace private we might speak while they partake?"

To his surprise, she hesitated. Surely she was not afraid to be alone with him?

"My solar," she said. "If you will follow me?"

It was as they passed the midday light slanting through one of the narrow, arched windows of the hall that he saw his mistake. She *had* changed. A few silver threads—only a few—sprinkled through her dark braids, and a faint web of lines had gathered at the corners of her eyes. It did not dull his ardor. Only this morning he had engaged in a sober study of his own graying brown hair and the deeply tanned face, which years spent in the sun and the joys and sorrows of life had creased. They were both past the years of youthful courtship. But not, he hoped, past courtship itself.

She paused to speak to a gray-haired knight she encountered at the head of the stairs, bidding him see to the welcome of their guests, before leading Gerolt on to the solar. He took a moment to take in the room before he spoke again. The intimate feminine space was not so different than his wife's had been, save that this room was smaller. Tapestries had been hung to warm the walls during winter; a wide, arched window allowed for a streaming flood of morning light; two baskets filled with embroidery threads sat near a pair of cushioned chairs; and another pair of baskets with neatly folded squares of sewing and embroidered cloth sat just beyond those. He did not remember Cassandry being so tidy with her stitchery as a girl, but it was natural that marriage and motherhood would have taught her discipline.

He motioned her to one of the chairs, then arranged the other so that he might sit to face her. "I have not even asked after your welfare. You are well? And Egelina? You were both understandably subdued when last I saw you." Three years ago, just after Antony's death.

"Our lives are quiet here, but we are content enough," she said. "You were generous to allow Egelina to remain in my custody after her father died. You must know how very grateful I am to you." Her voice trembled a little.

"Did you think I would take her from you, Cassandry?" he said, surprised.

He noted how carefully she avoided his gaze. "You are our liege lord and now her guardian. If you wished to raise her in your own household, it would have been your right."

"As I raised you? But she still has a mother. You had no one but my father, who most inconveniently died when I was but nineteen and left your care to me."

The ten years between them had felt like a lifetime then. How swiftly those years had narrowed when she had entered her teens, and now the span felt no more than days. At least to him. He removed the round cap he wore and ran a hand through his hair, pretending to smooth it down but in fact trying to discern again the ratio of coarsened gray to the softer brown. Was it too late? Would he always be too old?

He moved the conversation into pleasantries, asking after her now-fifteen-year-old daughter, telling her of his seventeen-year-old son who had been but fourteen when she had come to Lyonstoke to pledge her fealty for her dower lands and the lands Egelina had inherited from her father. When it came to his own daughter, Fleur, he assured Cassandry that the wound of her death had healed. It had not, of course, but he did not want any shadows hovering about him on this day.

The exchange appeared to relax her at last, and she began to inquire after people she had known in his household during her childhood and youth.

"Did you say Sir Ingram and Sir Fithian are with you? And . . . and Sir Samson? I must speak with them all before you leave. Why, Sir Fithian was still a page when I left you."

"He is three-and-thirty now and, alas, has never overcome his lisp. But he has the best sword arm among my men, and there are none who dare mock him now."

She smiled and bent forward to retrieve a piece of unfinished embroidery, thus averting her face. "Sir Samson still rides with you as well? Has ill befallen his inheritance?"

"Alas, many ills have befallen Sam since last you saw him. Aye, he still resides under my roof. But that is not why I have come to speak with you today."

She straightened in her chair, the embroidery cloth crumpling a little beneath the tightening of her fingers. "It is of Egelina, is it not? I know she is of an age to marry now, but—"

"No, Cassandry, I have not come to speak of Egelina. I have come to speak of you."

"Me?" She blinked at him for a moment, then the cloth slipped out of her grasp and fell at her feet. "Oh!"

The dread in her face was so stark it drove him to his feet and to the window. This was not the reaction he had hoped for. But then, he had hardly made himself clear.

He clasped his hands behind his back and gazed down on the dovecotes below. Antony may have closed the mews, but at least he had not robbed her of this comfort. The birds' sweet, mellow cooing floated upward on the air and into the silence of the solar.

Gerolt glanced over his shoulder and saw her sitting with her hands locked tightly in her lap.

He turned back toward her but did not return to his chair. "Have you not thought of your own future, Cassandry? Antony has been dead three years. Do you intend to mourn him forever?"

Her gaze fell to her laced fingers. "You wish me to marry again?"

"Are you not lonely? Aveline has been gone but a year, and while I sorely miss her . . . Lyonstoke Castle is in need of a woman's touch. I found other positions for Aveline's ladies after she died, and we have become a bachelor household, but I cannot remember to order the rushes to be swept, or restore the spices in the kitchen, or wrap Rauffe up when he is ill, or—" Oh, blazes! What kind of proposal was this, to make it sound like he had come in search of a servant rather than a wife? "What I meant to say was—"

"It is different for men," she interrupted. "Poor Sir Patrick was so miserable when his wife died that I encouraged him to marry again, even though it had scarce been six months. Now he is no longer glum and short-tempered with our bailiffs but treats them fairly as he did before, and our lands prosper for it." She paused. "Your lands prosper for it. Forgive me, my lord. I've spoken presumptuously. My dower lands are most comfortable. If you wish me to retire to them, I shall willingly do so. Only—only may I keep Egelina with me just a while longer?"

"I do not wish you to retire to your dower lands," he said, an edge to his voice. What a fumble he was making of it! It did not help that she kept calling him "my lord," as though he had not known her since she was nine. "I thought . . . It occurred to me after Aveline died that you might like . . . That is, I thought it might please you to come back to Lyonstoke."

She stared at him unblinkingly now, the blank look in her dark eyes shaking him almost as much as her former dread had. Was it so incomprehensible to her that he should offer—

"You wish me to marry one of your knights?" She rose so swiftly she knocked over the embroidery basket next to her chair. Her laced hands began to wring one another. "My lord, I beg you, I am quite content as a widow. Do not—Of course, if you command me I must obey . . . but I pray you will not—"

"Command you? When did I ever command you to do anything, Cassandry? And when did you cease to call me Gerolt?"

She bit her lower lip before she replied. "When I became wife to your vassal, Sir Antony. Things are not what they were between us, my lord. They can never be so again. Too much time has passed. We both know that. I am your devoted servant." She curtsied, her hands still moving with distress against her tawny gown. "And I must do as you . . . request. But I have no desire to marry again."

Disappointment pierced his chest. He stepped forward, ignoring the sudden urge to move within arm's reach of her. Even as she stood rejecting him, he still felt the charge of desire for her.

"None, Cassandry?"

She did not look away this time but gazed with so much earnestness into his eyes that the hopeful fluttering in his stomach turned to a leaden ball.

"I should not change my mind if you asked me to wed yourself. I am too old to be a wife again, my lord. This knight of whom you speak—no, please do not tell me his name—I wish to remember all of them fondly, without awkwardness should we meet. Whomever he is, he deserves a younger, merrier woman than I."

'Twas the first time he observed it, the loss of merriment in her eyes. She had been so bright and cheerful at Lyonstoke, her spirit so warm, her nature so sweet and trusting. But she'd had a joyful future waiting to embrace her then. He supposed a woman who had loved as fervently as she had would be a woman who would mourn the loss of that love to her final days.

He resolutely clamped down his hurt, as he had the day he had given her hand to Antony. He had lost enough years with her. Awkwardness was the last thing he wished between them now. He had hoped for a favorable response, but a part of him had been braced for failure. Nevertheless, he did not intend to let her simply slip out of his life again as she had two years after her marriage. If he could not bind her to him as his wife, he would bind her to him another way.

"Very well," he said. He set a hand on her shoulder and pressed her back into her chair, then returned to his own. "It shall be as you wish. We shall not speak further of it. I've another proposition for you, however. And this one does involve the Lady Egelina."

He watched Cassandry's cheeks pale as though waiting for a blow. *Have I become so great a stranger to you as that?* He cinched the hurt down still tighter.

He crossed his legs, determined to appear as calm as she was rigid. "As you say, your daughter is fifteen and of an age to marry. With four castles to her name—your two and Antony's—she is quite the little heiress. She is pretty and lively, and with you as her mother, I have not the least doubt she is well mannered and sensible as well. I believe she would make an excellent match for my son."

This had been his original plan for their children. He had been preparing himself to speak of it to Antony just before Antony died. But the death of Gerolt's daughter had distracted him from approaching Cassandry about the matter, and then Gerolt's wife had died, opening an unexpected pathway to Cassandry's hand for himself. But now that that hope had failed, he resorted to his first design.

"You wish to betroth her to Rauffe?"

"Have you any objections?"

As Egelina's liege lord and guardian, he did not need to take her mother's feelings into consideration in this matter, but he was not a man who enjoyed imposing his will on others, and he had his arguments marshaled to win an agreement from Cassandry, however reluctant she might be.

"Oh, Gerolt, you do not know how that relieves my mind!" Cassandry blushed. "I mean, my lord—"

"The idea pleases you?" He had not been prepared for an immediate capitulation.

"I knew Egelina must be married and that you have likely been considering the best alliance for her since she turned twelve. I have been in dread of your decision. Not that I thought you would choose poorly for her," Cassandry added quickly, "but marriage is such a . . . weighty matter, and she has so little experience with men. Almost none, in fact, since Antony kept so few knights here at Rengrave Castle, and those he kept were old enough to be her grandfather. I hoped you would choose someone gentle and patient with her, but . . . oh, I never dared hope it would be you!"

She leaned forward on the words, startling him when she reached out and grasped his hands.

"*I* am not marrying her," Gerolt said. Oh, heavens, how had he fumbled this, too?

She smiled again. "Of course not. She will marry Rauffe. I only meant that I know she will be safe with you. You will see that she is happy. How could she not be, married to your son? I never knew a kinder, more patient man than you, and Rauffe is certain to be the same." She rose, squeezing his hands as he followed her to his feet. "Thank you! I have worried for her ever so much, but now I will be at peace."

He felt another wave of yearning as he held her hands in his. Perhaps he had accepted her rebuff too quickly. He cast about almost wildly for some way to rescind the words he had just spoken. Once Egelina and Rauffe were wed, Church law forbade marriage between their parents. Gerolt would lose Cassandry forever . . .

You have already lost her. You lost her the day you gave her to Antony. Her heart remains with him.

Still, he answered himself stubbornly, *if I insisted, she would have no choice. We were friends once. We could be so again.*

Friends only, his head warned his heart. *Do you really want another "dutiful" marriage?*

No. He did not.

He released her hands. "Then it is settled. You will bring her to Lyonstoke a fortnight hence—"

"A fortnight? You are not thinking of marriage already? She is only—Rauffe is only seventeen! When I wished to marry Antony, you insisted that he wait for his twenty-first birthday."

Gerolt hated to see the alarm return to her face. And he hated it more that this time he could not reassure her. "I cannot wait that long with Rauffe. His health has been poor all his life. He falls victim to the slightest chill, has a paltry appetite, and now these headaches. As he is my only heir, I cannot risk—" *his dying.* Gerolt could not speak the harsh word and replaced it with the softest one he could. "I cannot lose him before he gives me a grandchild. I still pray he will outgrow his weaknesses, but I am too clear-eyed to count on it." He strove for a lighter note he was far from feeling when he thought of his son. "Rauffe is not tottering at the edge of the grave yet, however, and I would like them to have an opportunity to know one another before they wed. I am suggesting a betrothal, with marriage in a year—when Egelina is sixteen, your own age when you married Antony. I think you cannot object to that?"

She looked as if she wanted to object very much indeed, but she paused in what he sensed was a battle to hold her tongue. He wished he could offer her more, but with Rauffe's health so tenuous . . .

"As you wish, my lord."

He cursed the return of her formality, then held his breath as she caught his hand again, the stiffness once more dropping away from her.

"I would fight you on this if you wished her to marry anyone else. I would, Gerolt. But I know you will care for her and be kind and that Rauffe will be kind to her as well."

Because he is your son. She did not speak the words, yet he read the thought in the brief, wistful smile she gave him. *There is my Cassandry.* A longing to sweep her off her feet and carry her and that smile back to Lyonstoke Castle shook him to his core, but the moment was fleeting, her smile already gone.

"A year, then," she said. "But when they are wed, may I ask of you a boon?"

"You need not wait a year for that," he replied. "When did I ever deny you anything you wished?"

Her brows gave a small twitch over the bridge of her nose. "Perhaps you should have been more strict."

"I might have, had you not been so sensible. You never asked anything of me the least untoward—except to marry Antony when you were fourteen. Mad as you were for each other, he was far too ramshackle to be a husband yet. Was I not right to make you wait?"

Did she hesitate before she nodded? Nay, surely it was only the shift of a cloud against the sunlight.

"We have lingered overlong," she said. "Your men will be thinking me the worst hostess in the world that I have not greeted them yet. Are you sure you will not stay to dine?"

He strolled with her toward the exit. "I do not wish to inconvenience you—"

"Heavens, it is no inconvenience. You took me unawares with your arrival; we are so unused to visitors. But a table is easily laid. We eat simply here, but your men will not go away hungry. I will have Egelina join us so that you may study her good manners."

She spoke in a light, bantering tone, almost teasing him the way she used to. Did she tweak him for praising her daughter for virtues she knew his limited acquaintance with Egelina could only allow him to guess at?

He smiled in response. "Will you tell her of the betrothal before we dine?"

Cassandry cocked her head to the side in thought. So she had not lost the habit that had prompted him to laugh and call her "Sparrow" when she had been but nine years old.

"I think I will wait until you are gone. She has had no thought in her head of marriage. I know I should have been preparing her for this day . . . that is, I *have* prepared her to be a wife. You need not fear for that. She will see that your rushes are swept and your spices replenished and that Rauffe does not go out without his cloak. But we have not spoken of marriage coming so soon."

Many women wed at Egelina's age, but clearly Cassandry had thought that because Gerolt had delayed her own marriage he would do the same with Egelina. Had Fleur lived long enough to give him a grandchild, he might have afforded her more lenience.

But his daughter had not, and much though Gerolt wished Rauffe was older, fate had not left him with easy choices.

"I thought you might wish for time to prepare her," Gerolt said. He lifted the tapestry in the doorway to allow Cassandry to pass beneath it. "Will a fortnight be enough?"

"Oh yes. Thank you."

"You will accompany her, of course, and I trust you will stay at Lyonstoke until she has settled in? A month or two at least—"

"So long? I do not know. We shall see. I trust she and Rauffe will strike a friendship quickly and she will have no need for me to linger. I'm afraid I have grown to enjoy the quiet here too much."

Her lips moved as though they intended another smile, but the upward curve he expected failed to fully form. She paused and touched his arm as they stopped just short of the top of the stairs that would take them back to the hall.

"You will not forget about the boon?"

"You will not tell me what it is now?"

She shook her head. "In a year, when Egelina and Rauffe are wed. That will be time enough to speak it."

He was about to remind her that she had never kept secrets from him before when her words came back as a bitter reminder: *Things are not what they were between us. They can never be so again.* He cursed his own generosity, which had given her to another man and lost him the comfort of her companionship for twenty-four years. But no longer. She had no children save Egelina. Gerolt intended to make sure Cassandry remained deeply involved in her daughter's life, even after her marriage. And perhaps, in time, friendship would grow between them again. It was not what he had hoped for when he had arrived, but it was far better than losing her a second time.

"You promise me you will grant it?" she said, her hand now pressing into his arm.

"This mysterious boon of yours? As long as it is a sensible request."

"It is most sensible. You will not find me to have grown into an impulsive, irrational woman since I left your house."

"I am very relieved," he said. "I'd feared perhaps Antony may have taught you to be capricious and wayward. What a high-strung fellow he was. I'd never have let him marry you had I not seen how deftly you steadied him. He loved you more than I'd ever seen any man love a woman." A self-protest tried to rear itself, but Gerolt thrust it relentlessly down to where he had buried his hurt. He laid his fingers over the hand that still rested on his arm. "I am sorry it has been so difficult since you lost him."

"Thank you. And my sensible boon?"

He did not need more time with her to recognize once again that the sweet, confiding child he had loved was gone, replaced by this remote, self-contained woman who turned aside his sympathy as though it were some invasion of her privacy. Yet, still, he could not imagine her so changed at her core as to find any reason to deny her.

"Whatever you ask is yours."

"Then you have made me twice happy this day. Now come. I must greet your men."

She swept ahead of him down the stairs, leaving him awash in regret as he followed her.

Chapter 2

"I will not marry him," Egelina declared for what must surely be the hundredth time. "You cannot make me!"

Thank heavens Gerolt was not here to see Cassandry's "well-mannered and sensible daughter" with her hands on her hips and her lower lip thrust out. Egelina had behaved prettily enough for Gerolt and his men. Cassandry knew Gerolt had ridden away well pleased with the alliance they had agreed to. She had not told Egelina of the betrothal until the following morning. There had been nothing but shouting and tantrums and sulking for a week and a half since then. Three years a woman in the eyes of the Church, Egelina nevertheless continued to cling to a childishness that tried her mother's endurance.

"I am not making you do anything," Cassandry pointed out, determined to cling to her thin-growing patience. "It is the decision of Lord Gerolt. He was your father's liege lord and is your legal guardian. If he chooses to marry you to his son, there is nothing either of us can do in the matter."

Egelina stamped her foot, her blue eyes as stormy as her late father's when his temper overflowed. Cassandry felt a slight tremor at the sight but quickly reminded herself of her duty to raise a temperate, responsible daughter and not a mercurial waif who could make life as miserable as she could delightful for all around her.

"I hate Lord Gerolt! I hate Lord Rauffe! And I hate you!"

Egelina whirled, clearly intending to flounce from the solar, but Cassandry stepped swiftly before the tapestry draped over the entryway and blocked her escape.

"I think not, Egelina. Do not make me call you 'child,' for you are old enough to wed. Not that I would consent to that yet, and Lord Gerolt has not asked it. It is only a betrothal, not marriage. You need not wed until you are sixteen."

Cassandry regretted failing to persuade Gerolt to wait longer. Whatever the law declared the age of adulthood, she had lived to lament her own immaturity at sixteen and, still worse, her husband's at twenty-one. She knew now what she had not known then, that, emotionally, boys matured much slower than women—and some men, she reflected bitterly, never. But Rauffe was not Antony, and he would have a cool, judicious, steady-eyed father to guide him.

Egelina glowered at her mother, her pretty, fair face again reminding Cassandry painfully of Antony. Her husband three years dead, Cassandry just turned forty, and still she struggled with her shattered trust in the beautiful illusion love had been. It was why she accepted, even welcomed, this arranged marriage for her daughter. Three years ago Rauffe had been a shy, quiet boy. If he proved an unexciting husband, all the better, so long as he also proved a kind one.

"Lord Gerolt would not be demanding anything," Egelina said, "if you had only asked his consent to my request a year ago when I begged you to let me enter Elstow Abbey. He would not have dared deny a holy calling."

Cassandry barely smothered an inelegant snort. "I can think of no one less suited than you for a nunnery. These temper tantrums of yours would never be tolerated by the abbess."

Her daughter's petite foot stamped against the floorboards again. "I should have nothing to be angry *about* were you not so unreasonable. If Lord Gerolt is so desperate for Papa's lands, why does *he* not marry *you*? The lands would have no heir if I were in a nunnery, and when you die the lands will be his, and when he dies the lands will be Rauffe's, and everything will fall out exactly the way he wants without him having to torment *me*."

"Egelina!"

Egelina looked suddenly stricken and ran forward to throw her arms around her mother's neck. "Oh, Mamma, I did not mean it that way. I never, ever wish you to die! Only I do not wish to marry. I wish to go to the nunnery so that I may learn to write."

Cassandry sighed as she embraced her daughter. Egelina had always had a quicksilver nature, but she had never been sullen, and her cheerfulness had far outweighed her doldrums—until she had turned thirteen. Since then she seemed constantly irritable and moody, with only occasional bursts of her old, familiar buoyancy.

Cassandry led her daughter to the window seat that spanned the wide embrasure beneath shutters open wide to the sun of this bright spring day.

"It would be different if you could teach me," Egelina said with a whine that, as with her tantrums, too frequently threaded through her voice. "But where else am I to learn if not in a nunnery?"

"The written word is dangerous, Gelli," Cassandry said. "I have told you that. And so is this silly poetry of yours. If you cannot stop it from filling your mind, then it is best to allow the words to vanish harmlessly into the air and hope they vanish from your memory just as quickly. You have no idea of how men can twist a woman's words to her detriment." *Like your father did mine.* She hastened to add when Egelina looked slightly alarmed, "But I remember Rauffe as a mild-tempered boy. I am sure he will treat you kindly, and I expect you, Egelina, to treat him the same."

Egelina sat quietly for a few moments while Cassandry worried what she might be thinking.

"If I agree," Egelina said at last, "and I give Rauffe an heir and then he dies, do you think Lord Gerolt would let me enter a nunnery then?"

"All this talk of death!" Cassandry exclaimed. "Gelli, whatever makes you think Rauffe might die?"

"After Papa's funeral, when we went to Lyonstoke Castle for you to repeat Papa's fealty to Lord Gerolt on my behalf, Rauffe spent the entire time wrapped in warm cloaks, even when we sat before the fire. Sir Samson said he has been sickly from birth and doubted he would live long enough to marry." She appeared to miss her mother's frown at Sir Samson's name. Egelina's voice turned cross. "I wish he hadn't. Then you and Lord Gerolt would not be persecuting me this way."

"That is a wicked thing to say, Egelina. And it is hardly a persecution to wish you to wed and rear a family. Children are a blessing, not a curse." Cassandry tucked a stray coil of gold behind her daughter's ear. "I cannot bear to think what my life might have been had I not had you to brighten it."

Indeed, there had been too many days in her own turbulent marriage when only Egelina's young needs had kept Cassandry functioning instead of curled up in a weeping ball of despair.

"This is not the same," Egelina said. "You cannot know what it is like. I have words forever tumbling about in my head, and I do not *wish* for them to vanish. I wish to keep them forever and ever, but I am afraid someday I will have so very, very many of them that they will all spill out and dissolve away like the mist. *Please*, Mamma."

Even her daughter's speech, which had once chirped as cheerfully as a robin on a beautiful spring day, had turned overly dramatic these last two years. When Cassandry shook her head, she did so braced for Egelina to burst into tears.

Egelina did so. "Th-then I shall s-simply have to g-go mad!" she sobbed. "I promise you I will d-do so if you do n-not let me learn to wr-write. My head will explode and I may die. How can you be so cr-cruel?"

She bounced up from the seat and fled the solar, unhindered this time by her mother.

Cassandry moaned and thrust her hands into the hair at her temples, setting the white veil on her head askew. She was too old to deal with such volatile behavior again. Evidence of her advancing years stared back at her from her small hand mirror every morning, reflecting the lines at the corners of her eyes. As if those were not bad enough, she had plucked three gray hairs from her sleek, dark locks this morning. 'Twas a wonder she had not gone gray ten years ago. She had hoped for peace after Antony's death. She had almost found it for a year, but then her dear, sweet-tempered Egelina had woken up one morning inexplicably demonstrating all of her father's worst traits.

Or so it had seemed to Cassandry. Perhaps there had been signs of gradual moodiness as Egelina had approached young womanhood. And perhaps that was all it was—a young girl's struggle to find her way into adulthood. Cassandry did not remember suffering such mood swings when she was Egelina's age, but she recalled little enough of her parents and whether they had been as volatile as Egelina's father or as merry-tempered as Cassandry before marriage had crushed her into a joyless abyss.

Air. She needed air. This narrow-walled castle of Antony's had ever oppressed her spirits. Only the solar admitted any meaningful light. But the rest of it—its narrow galleries, its gloomy chambers with narrow window slits, its cramped storerooms, even its great hall, which stretched more long than wide, its vaulted ceiling dwarfed by the spacious one she remembered at Lyonstoke

Castle— reminded her of how trapped she felt. She should have removed to one of her own castles after Antony's death, but she barely remembered them from her early childhood, and her spirits had felt so beaten down she could not summon the energy it would have required to uproot herself and her daughter.

Antony had not liked her riding out about the manor and had never allowed it without at least two solemn gray-haired knights escorting her. It was a constant battle to remind herself that she might now ride where she pleased, when she pleased.

She stood up, determined once again to enjoy her freedom while she could. Once she asked her boon of Gerolt, there would be no more unhurried spring days, no sun on her face, no wind blowing through her hair. But there would be peace at last. Nunneries were not for young, lovely, spirited girls like Egelina. They were for old women like Cassandry, places to withdraw and contemplate and perhaps, she prayed, at last find forgiveness in her heart. She hoped contentment would follow, and even someday serenity. She vaguely remembered the latter, as a young girl in Gerolt's house, smiling, laughing, falling asleep feeling secure and loved. But it had been so long ago that sometimes she feared she had only dreamed it.

"Sir Patrick," she called as she exited the solar.

The gray-haired knight whose face had again become ruddy with vitality since he had married a young widow, came swiftly up the steps from the hall below.

"My lady?"

"Saddle my mare. I wish to ride."

"Shall I escort you, my lady? Or if you prefer it, my wife would be glad to accompany you."

"Nay, I will be safe enough on our own lands, and I prefer to ride alone."

Sir Patrick looked displeased. Her husband had trained him to keep her under his eye. *As though there was anyone here who might remotely prove a threat to you, Antony. What, did you think I would seduce the reeve or the hayward?* But Antony was gone, and the only one with authority to countermand her orders now was far away at Lyonstoke.

Once clear of the castle, Cassandry removed her veil, unpinned her braids to allow them to spill down her back, tucked the pins carefully inside the veil, which she then tucked inside her girdle, and flicked the reins, sending her mare into a frolicsome canter through the woods that bridged the manor. She followed the path she and Antony had marked out when they had first been married and had ridden together nearly every day. Free from her husband's judgmental knights, she set her mare to gallop hard. The wind whipped her braids from her face and stung her eyes. She knew every twist and turn by heart. Ecstasy once. Now merely mindless respite as she allowed the drumming hoofbeats to drown out all thought. The trees blurred, her braids snapped behind her, and all emotion whipped away, leaving a wonderful emptiness of feeling.

But reality always flowed back as her mare sailed over the trunk of the fallen chestnut tree, signaling to Cassandry that it was time to turn back. She slowly reined in the mare, easing her into a canter once more, and then a trot before bringing her to rest alongside the stream that gurgled through the woods. While her mare drank, Cassandry pinned her braids back up and restored her veil, knowing she could not fully repair the damage done by the wind. Without a comb and mirror, some renegade strand always floated against her cheek when she returned to Rengrave Castle, bringing frowns from the knights who had once served her husband. At least none of them dared chide her for it, though she always entered the castle with a quickened heartbeat, as though not yet convinced that Antony would not be waiting with a blistering rebuke.

She was halfway up the path leading to Rengrave's gatehouse when she saw the rider trotting over the drawbridge. The sun shone in her eyes so that she could not make out the rider's features until he was almost alongside her.

"What are you doing here?" she said, her voice as stiff as her back. "Is Gerolt with you?"

"Nay," the rider replied. "He sent me to escort you and your daughter to Lyonstoke."

Cassandry struggled to subdue a scowl. Of an age with Gerolt, Sir Samson de Curzon's close-cropped curls of wiry brown showed but the faintest sprinkling of gray. In another ten years Cassandry's would be the color of lead; she was quite certain of it. Fortunate the man who had no obstinate daughters to deal with. Or had he? She realized she did not know if Sir Samson had ever married or sired any children. She had not asked Gerolt when he visited, and she had spared as few words as politely possible in conversing with Sir Samson himself.

"I will provide my own escort to Lyonstoke. There are three days yet before Egelina and I need depart. Return to Gerolt and tell him we did not require your services." She trusted her icy tone made his dismissal clear.

"Really, Cassandry," Sir Samson protested, "it has been over twenty years. I never thought you so vindictive as to hold a grudge for half the span of your life."

"There is no grudge," she said. "But though I be twenty-three years older, my wits have not deserted me, and I am quite sure I do not recall giving you leave to call me by my given name then or now."

"'Tis true Gerolt never allowed us to call you anything but *Lady* Cassandry, even when you were a child," he replied, appearing unruffled by her rebuke. "Very well, it shall be as it pleases you, my lady." A too-familiar gleam slipped into his eyes. "For now."

She flicked the reins, moving her mare forward again. "Did you ask Gerolt to send you? If so, it is too late for apologies."

Sir Samson reached for her bridle, bringing her to a stop again. Though he was only slightly taller than she, his shoulders strained at his dusty tunic and his muscles bulged beneath his sleeves, reminding her of the strength with which he had wrestled every knight of Gerolt's household to the ground, save Gerolt himself, when they had been young.

"Aye, I asked Gerolt to send me because you scarce spoke two words to me when I was here with him. I wished to offer you my condolences. A few years too late, perhaps, but I lost my ability to count the hours during my interminable imprisonment by the infidel. All these years later the days still slip by like sand. But I am sorry for Antony's death."

His words took her aback. "Infidel?"

He released her bridle. Her mare fidgeted, but Cassandry quieted her.

"Gerolt did not tell you?" Sir Samson said.

"Gerolt and I ceased our communications during my marriage." She would not give Sir Samson the satisfaction of adding *Thanks to you.* "I had no private conversation with Gerolt when I brought my daughter to swear fealty for her inheritance after Antony died. We did not speak again until last week when he proposed a betrothal between our children. I did not ask him about your well-being." Egelina's reminder that Cassandry had found Sir Samson discussing Rauffe's health with her daughter during their visit to Lyonstoke two years ago did nothing to thaw the frosty note in her voice.

"How cold you have grown," Sir Samson murmured. "This is not how I remember you, my lady."

"You never knew me at all, Sir Samson, else you would never have shamed me before my husband as you did."

"'Twas but a jest. Antony must have known I never meant it seriously."

A jest? He had ruined everything. Her marriage, her lifeline to Gerolt . . . She snapped her reins more briskly now, setting her mare to a trot.

Sir Samson did not try to stay her again but urged his own mount to match her pace. "I was ever restless in those days," he said. "I grew quickly bored with married life. Did you know that I married Lady Herleve d'Aufai?"

She shook her head. Antony had cut her off from the world, and with it all news of the people she once had loved, after Sir Samson's "jest."

"She was pretty, but her querulous nature grew tedious, and as events were to prove, she was tragically inept. I did not know the latter when I left her. I merely thought it would be a grand adventure to take up the Cross and join the crusaders in the East. So I left my wife and three young children, and off I rode." He swatted at a fly that buzzed past his ear, his casual expression abruptly darkening. "There were far too many of these accursed things in the desert. I do not like the memories they bring."

Cassandry could not imagine Antony abandoning her and Egelina, even for a holy cause. He had been too jealous of Cassandry and too adoring of his daughter. Cassandry chided herself for wondering, however briefly, how different her life might have been had he done so.

"I journeyed all the way to the kingdom of Jerusalem," Sir Samson continued, the unruffled note back in his voice, "and thought I found the excitement I was looking for in the conflict that had fallen between its Christian rulers. They settled their differences quickly, however, when word arrived that Saladin had united the infidel against us. We marched to battle against their forces, but we were outnumbered, and soon the Saracens surrounded us near a place called Hattin. I will spare you the unpleasant details of our defeat. Suffice it to say that 'adventure' quickly lost its allure for me. Our army was slaughtered, but a fortunate few were taken prisoner. I, my lady, was one of them."

Again, a dark shade fell over Sir Samson's face. This time it startled Cassandry into guilt. However difficult their marriage, she would never have wished such a fate on Antony or on any Christian man—not even Sir Samson.

"I am glad you lived," she said, her voice softening. "How did you find your way back home to England?"

He gave his shoulders a slight shake, as if to shed the flitting gloom. "After a year of humiliating imprisonment, my masters agreed to release me in return for a sizeable ransom, if I could raise it. Where could I turn but to Gerolt? Two years passed before he at last came for me—but he did come, my lady. He will forever hold my debt for that."

Despite these words, something in Sir Samson's tone drew Cassandry's brows together. She could not tell what it signified, the inflection was so subtle, but it left her feeling vaguely unsettled.

"I thank heaven for your safety," she repeated. "It does not change the past between us, but I will trust that you learned a hard and painful lesson. There will be no more grudges between us, Sir Samson."

She drew up her mare again and this time held out her hand to him. What else could she do after such a story? To deny him compassion would condemn her own Christian heart. Before, she had noted only how lightly his hair had grayed. Now she saw the deep lines in his face and the grooves alongside his mouth that she observed, albeit softer, in her own mirror every morning. The imprint of bitterness.

Sir Samson took her hand. She let her fingers lie against his gloved palm as he finished his tale.

"When I returned to England, I learned not only that my wife had died but that my lands lay in ruin. What little fortune I had once had was gone. During my absence, my wife proved herself a spendthrift. She sold off my jewels and silver while her mismanagement depleted my fields. My children scarcely knew me. To this day they look upon Gerolt more affectionately than they do upon me, for he took them into his own house when he saw how my wife frittered away their inheritance. The years have not worn lightly upon me, I fear, and what I once counted a boon—my freedom—I now find an empty phantom." His gaze had drifted over her shoulder during his memories, but it returned now to her face. "Are you lonely, Cassandry? Do you miss Antony?"

She drew her hand away again. She did not like the look in Sir Samson's eye. Just so had he looked at her after her marriage, before he had begun the "jest" that had ruined everything.

"Gerolt asked me the same question when he came." Was it possible he had been speaking on Sir Samson's behalf? She let the distant coolness steal back into her voice and continued with some emphasis, "As I told Gerolt then, I am content in my widowhood. I have a beautiful daughter whom I must prepare to be a wife and a comfortable dower to sustain me when her husband takes command of her lands. I am sorry for your losses, Sir Samson." She used the plural, reflecting his multiple misfortunes. "But I am content as I am and trust you will not speak what I fear that gleam in your eye portends."

She remembered her relief at how quickly Gerolt allowed the subject to drop when he had queried her about marrying again. As her late husband's liege lord and guardian of her daughter's inheritance, Gerolt could have demanded Cassandry marry whomever he chose, even Samson. The silence between them had stretched so many years, their conversation so stilted after Antony's death, that she honestly had not known if Gerolt had come to Rengrave Castle to issue exactly such a command. Instead, he had inquired after her desires and accepted them with such familiar gentleness that she had wept on a flood of memories after he had gone.

"You mourn him so greatly, then?" Sir Samson said.

She started in her saddle, thinking for a moment that he spoke of her friendship with Gerolt.

"I had never seen two people more in love than you and Antony. Save, perhaps, for Gerolt and Aveline."

Gerolt had married Aveline Follet a year after Cassandry had married Antony. She was glad to hear that Gerolt had been happy. No one deserved happiness more than the dear, generous man who had raised her. *You were not only my guardian but my closest friend. Even my love for Antony could not fill the loss in my life when I left you, and then when he made me sever my last connection with you—* For a moment, she felt again the wrenching pain of that blow and the void it had left.

She had come into Gerolt's wardship in her ninth year, after the death of his father. Gerolt had only been nineteen and had been traveling France, Venice, and Florence with Samson, when his inheritance and his sudden guardianship of Cassandry had called him back to England. She had not understood then how young he was, though now, of course, she knew how awkward being called upon to raise the young, orphaned daughter of one of his vassals must have been. He had indulged her every whim, calling her a generous-hearted, levelheaded lass who would not ask for foolishness. The only impulsive thing she had ever done was fall in love with Antony, and even that Gerolt had not denied her.

He thought he had dealt her a gift accorded to few women by allowing her to marry for love. Too many years of silence had passed for her to ever tell him the truth. The past could not be mended now. She had pushed the pain down to that place where the years had eventually dulled it, that nearly-lost corner of her being where she had locked away the girl she once had been.

"The day is growing late," she said. Sir Samson's presence raised too many disquieting memories. She had let him speak his piece. Now she would have him away from her. "There is an abbey up the road that extends its hospitality to travelers for the night. You will find more jovial company there, for my daughter and I are accustomed to dining quietly and retiring early. Tell Gerolt my daughter and I will arrive on Wednesday as we agreed, with an escort of my own knights. Now good day to you, Sir Samson. I shall pray for your continued good fortune."

This time she did not give him her hand. He looked for a moment as though he intended to argue, but then he simply bowed in the saddle. "I shall see you at the betrothal, then. I hope your daughter and his son find as much happiness in wedded bliss as did you and Antony."

She watched him ride down to the forest road, then nudged her mare yet again up the path toward the drawbridge. She felt the tightening of her lips as she bitterly considered his remarks. Sir Samson was not the only one who had learned a hard and painful lesson. Bliss in marriage was a fiction. Gerolt's offer to unite their children had come as a relief, for Cassandry had devoted much time and mental energy to plotting how she might prevent her impulsive daughter from repeating her mistakes. Guardian or no, Cassandry would have fought Gerolt with everything in her had she not believed Egelina could learn to be happy with his son. But passionate? Nay! They would learn to be fond of each other, no more. And Cassandry would never, ever give Egelina the means to bring Rauffe's distrust and anger upon her head, as Gerolt had unknowingly done with Cassandry.

Chapter 3

Gerolt slowly counted under his breath to ten. It was a trick his mother had taught him as a boy to help him learn to think before he spoke rashly. The counsel had stood him in good stead through the years, earning him the respect of both his vassals and knights for his calm and judicious temper. But these days, counting to ten failed to adequately control his exasperation, so he continued . . . *Eleven, twelve, thirteen* . . . all the way to twenty before he finally spoke.

"You are *not* wearing that to your betrothal," he stated.

Rauffe glanced down at his garish ensemble of yellows and reds and blues and greens. "What's wrong with it?"

"You look like a strutting peacock." Or he would if not for his perpetual slouch. *Twenty-one, twenty-two, twenty-three* . . . "Stand up straight. I know you are self-conscious about being so tall, but you will find it a benefit one day. You'll not stand beside your betrothed slumping for all the world as if you hold her in dislike."

As was too often the case of late, his father had to strain to hear his answer.

"I barely know her," Rauffe mumbled. "How can I know whether I like her or not?"

They stood in Rauffe's bedchamber. Cassandry and her daughter had arrived an hour ago and were dressing for the betrothal. Experience had warned Gerolt that he had better check his son's attire, for Rauffe had a habit of dismissing his servant while he chose his wardrobe, almost always with the same outlandish outcome as the mismatched colors he wore now.

"You met her three years ago, just after her father's death. You will be kind and patient with her, Rauffe, and you will speak clearly and smile at her and ask her pleasure at the dinner table—I saw that."

Rauffe had scrunched up his face while simultaneously rolling his eyes at his father's lecture. His angular features fell sulky again.

Twenty-four, twenty-five, twenty-six . . . "Lady Egelina and her mother will be ready anytime now. Change into something less gaudy. Those yellow hose are so bright they will blind our company. And if you wish to wear green, find a less garish color than that surcote. Did you hear me?" Gerolt said when Rauffe rolled his eyes again.

Rauffe mumbled something and hitched his drooping shoulders in a motion very near a shrug.

Blazes. Gerolt knew he should be more forbearing. His son was still pale from the headache he had suffered all night. But this obstinate muttering and slouching and eye rolling combined with his stubborn refusal to accept any counsel on his taste in clothing was beyond unacceptable, no matter how sickly and cosseted he had been from the cradle.

All further counting flew out of Gerolt's head. "I beg your pardon?" he said in the forbiddingly level tone he sometimes used with his knights but had never directed at his son before these last two years.

"I said, 'yes, sir.'" Rauffe said it on a growl.

Saints, what had happened to the inquisitive, even-tempered boy who had once trailed all day at Gerolt's heels and battered him with questions about how he had become the Hero of Iconium?

Lady Egelina will think he's become a hunchback if she sees him standing stooped like that. Gerolt had not forgotten his own awkwardness when he too had grown taller than his companions by Rauffe's age, but his father had taught him to stand proudly in spite of it. But he had never been so thin as Rauffe, nor had he spent so many years as a sickly boy that Gerolt had feared he might be left without an heir.

"Do not dally," Gerolt said, trying to soften the impatience in his voice. "I will send Sir Owen up to help you select something a little more . . . subdued."

Rauffe scrunched his face again, but he refrained from rolling his eyes, at least until his father had left his chamber. Gerolt should not have allowed his wife to coddle Rauffe so. They had argued over it many times, especially when Gerolt had forced his son to pick up a sword and train with his fellow squires only to have his mother call him in as soon as Gerolt's back was turned and wrap him in a thick, fur-lined cloak and press a goblet of warm, mulled wine between his bony hands.

"I have been robbed of three children," she'd said when Gerolt rebuked her. "I will not be robbed of the only one left to us."

One son stillborn, the other taken by heaven at less than a month old, and finally Fleur, their beautiful, loving Fleur, lost two years ago with her first babe in childbirth. The reminders always caused him to let Aveline have her way. Gerolt might scold Rauffe a bit too roughly at times, but the Hero of Iconium who had ridden with blazing boldness into battle against a heathen enemy flinched at the prospect of experiencing more grief when he had not yet fully healed from the loss of his beloved Fleur.

Sir Owen, one of Gerolt's young knights with hair the color of ripe wheat, mingled in the hall with the other knights and vassals

Gerolt had assembled to witness his son's betrothal. Sir Owen's easy manner had won Rauffe's trust. When Rauffe listened to Gerolt as though he possessed a head full of wool between his ears, Sir Owen always seemed to know how to win a reluctant smile from the boy. Gerolt maneuvered through the crowd and tapped Sir Owen on the shoulder.

"Sir Owen, would you mind checking on Rauffe? See that he's donned something suitable for the ceremony."

Sir Owen responded with one of his willing grins. "Certainly, my lord. No yellow hose?"

"No yellow hose."

Sir Owen nodded and disappeared up the steps Gerolt had just descended.

Gerolt moved among his vassals, thanking them for their attendance, bowing over the hands of their wives, and inquiring after their families, until he at last found himself at Samson's side. Sam, as his friend preferred to be called. He hated his biblical name for which his fellow squires had teased him mercilessly as a youth given his burly, muscular stature. Unable to abide their snickering, he had clipped his hair short and had worn his wiry curls thus ever since.

"You've chosen well for the boy," Samson said. "The Lady Egelina is a little beauty."

"Aye, she is a lovely girl and seems to have pretty manners. I would expect no less from a daughter of Cassandry's."

His friend nodded. Here, with Samson at his shoulder, where Sam had stood almost as long as Gerolt's memories stretched, a little of the tension that a lifetime of training had taught him to conceal eased just a fraction. Sam knew him as no other man. Fostered as a page to Gerolt's father, Samson had become as a brother to Gerolt. They had enjoyed a great many rough-and-tumble adventures together, and though of vastly different temperaments, no sword had ever rung truer at

Gerolt's side or in quicker defense of his back than had Samson's.

A stirring turned Gerolt's attention toward the stairs. Cassandry was sweeping down them with her daughter. Gerolt knew the sudden silence that fell across the hall was for Egelina, a vision in blue and white, but Gerolt barely spared her a glance as his gaze riveted on Cassandry. The dark gray gown she wore, with its modest embroidered scrollwork, appeared designed to keep her an unobtrusive foil for the younger girl's beauty.

Samson must have heard Gerolt's soft catch of breath.

"She is as graceful as ever," Samson murmured, nodding toward Cassandry. "Her hair is still sleek—I suspect one would have to search those dark tresses deeply to discover a silver thread or two—and her complexion remains nearly as smooth as her daughter's. But the light has gone from her eyes, Gerolt."

Gerolt bristled. "You are a thick wit if you fail to see their luster."

"I do not quarrel with their beauty. But look for yourself."

Gerolt watched her weave through the hall greeting old friends and introducing them to her daughter—Sir Ingram, who had allowed Antony to drag him too eagerly into a great many scrapes as a squire, and Sir Fithian, no longer a frightened, lisping page but a seasoned knight undaunted by his continued speech impediment. Sir Payne, Sir Edward, Sir Tobias—all of them swarmed around her, as did many of Gerolt's vassals, some with too reminiscent a gleam in their eyes. All had known her as a child and young woman, and more than a few of them Gerolt still suspected of having hoped to win his consent for her hand when she came of marriageable age. Even Samson, he recalled, had looked warmly upon her in those days. He darted a glance at his friend, but Samson's gaze was fixed not on Cassandry but on Gerolt.

"She smiles," Samson said. "She is polite and gracious to them all. But surely you can see, even from here, that there is no joy in her countenance."

Gerolt looked back at Cassandry. No joy. Just as he had found her after his father died. While caring generously for her physical needs, his widowed father had spared little attention for his eight-year-old ward's emotional welfare. When Gerolt inherited Cassandry's guardianship alongside his father's lands a year later, he discovered a nine-year-old orphaned girl still grieving for her parents, so shy she barely spoke. It had taken Gerolt months to learn how to tease a smile from her, and then a few words.

Eventually he had not only coaxed her from her bashfulness, but he had found himself the confidant of her youthful chatter. It did not occur to him until he'd inadvertently cajoled from her the secret of her love for Antony de Reymes that she viewed him not as the potential mate he had gradually grown to hope and wait for, but as a trusted brother.

Three years and she still grieves too deeply for Antony to even see me.

"I know how you wanted her," Samson said, "how you grieved for her loss when she wed Antony. I saw what no one else took time to observe afterward—the long hours you sat gazing into the hearth fire, the way you ceased riding the hills and vales when she was no longer here to ride with you. I saw your hope when you married Aveline and how she disappointed you."

"She did not disappoint me," Gerolt said sharply. "It was not her fault the babes died, that Rauffe was born sickly, that Fleur died so young."

"I was not speaking of the children," Sam replied. "I, alas, married an inept spendthrift, you an efficient, dutiful wife. But you cannot deny there was a coolness to Aveline's nature, as different from Cassandry's liveliness and warmth as the moon is from the sun."

She is cool now. Gerolt had not confided to Samson his true reason for visiting Cassandry a fortnight ago. Something had changed in Sam since Gerolt had brought him back from the East. Samson had not talked of what happened during his imprisonment, but something—a stiffness, a distance—that had never been there before now stood between them. Yet as he felt Samson's gaze still fixed on him, he knew he did not have to tell Sam of his recent dashed hopes with Cassandry. Samson knew, just as he had twenty-four years ago.

"You were right to betroth Rauffe to her daughter," Samson said. "Lovely as she still is, Cassandry has passed her fortieth year. Even had she been willing, it would have been foolish to marry her now. She would be unlikely to give you more heirs, and, as I have told you before, it is unwise to pin all your hopes on Rauffe . . . Nay, do not glower at me. It is simple prudence to seek a few more."

"I am not marrying your daughter, Sam." Gerolt's gaze drifted to the pretty, slender young woman with whom Sir Tobias had turned to converse after Cassandry had moved past him. Her dark hair was a few shades lighter than Cassandry's and the green eyes that raised to meet Gerolt's as if instantly aware of his regard were lit with an animated glow.

"She is not like Aveline," Samson pressed. "Marion is a good, obedient girl with a sunny temper and has proven her worth by the sons she bore her first husband. You'd not be troubled with them; their grandmother has taken them into her care. Marion would be completely devoted to you and would bring cheerfulness to your house again."

As Cassandry once had. Gerolt knew she was lost to him. The betrothal would seal that. But marry another?

"I have an heir," Gerolt repeated as he did every time Samson raised this subject, "and pray heaven I will have a grandson ere long. I've no need for another wife. If you wish a new husband for your daughter, I will provide a second dowry, as I did with the first. Now excuse me. I must see what is keeping Rauffe."

He moved away from his friend, grateful to leave the subject of Marion behind—at least for now.

The hall had not changed much since Cassandry had left Lyonstoke Castle. Even with Gerolt's crowd of vassals and knights assembled, the wide walls and vaulted ceiling lent the room a pleasing spaciousness. Old, familiar tapestries mingled with new ones on the walls. The massive stone fireplace, reflective of Gerolt's wealth, graced the west wall with its familiar carvings of lion-headed, fishtailed sea lions beneath arched hearthstones. The chaplain awaited the betrothal couple on the dais, for the chapel would not hold all the guests Gerolt had summoned. Cassandry noted that the chaplain's hair, salted with gray when she had known him, had now gone completely white. Curious, how the years had concurrently dragged and flown since she had stood here twenty-four years ago, exchanging her vows with Antony.

Cassandry drew Egelina into a small pocket of space near one of the narrow, arched windows. She tugged at Egelina's veil not because it was crooked but because Cassandry was nervous. Egelina was so young to be bound to a youth she did not know, even if he was Gerolt's son, yet she trusted in a fair future for her daughter. *But how I will miss you. I do not know how I will bear it at Rengrave Castle for another year before I ask my boon of Gerolt, without your bright spirit there to cheer me. Aye, I will miss even your sulks and your pouts and your tantrums. Oh, Gelli, if you knew how much I love you.*

Cassandry did not say any of it aloud, but her eyes grew misty. She straightened the modest gold circlet that held the veil in place, arranged Egelina's gilt curls to fall prettily over her shoulders, adjusted the knot in her girdle . . . Oh, dear, in another moment she would be openly crying. Cassandry needed a distraction. She glanced about the chapel and saw it in Gerolt.

"Sir Fithian," she said to the knight who stood near, conversing with Sir Patrick, "would you mind attending my daughter while I have a word with Lord Gerolt?"

She might have asked one of her own retainers who had escorted them to Lyonstoke, but she wished Egelina to begin to know the friends of her past, to whom she was entrusting her daughter's care almost as much as she was to Gerolt.

"It would be my pleathure, my lady," Sir Fithian lisped with a smile for both her and Egelina.

Cassandry ignored Egelina's look of alarm at being left with a stranger, thanked Sir Fithian, and moved across the floor to Gerolt, who was standing with Sir Ingram at the foot of the stairs. When he saw Cassandry, he paused, then said to Sir Ingram, "See what is keeping them."

Sir Ingram first greeted Cassandry with the boyish grin he had apparently never outgrown.

"Lady Cassandry, how unfair that you must spend the betrothal feast on the dais. I've half a mind to disguise you as some lady-in-waiting to one of Lord Gerolt's vassals so that you might sit next to me instead."

Gerolt cut him off with a thrust of his elbow to the man's ribs. "Enough from you, you rattler. Go."

Sir Ingram did so, but not before he laid his hand to his heart and gave Cassandry a dramatic bow.

"He is not much changed," Cassandry said.

"He was a great admirer of your husband," Gerolt replied, "and Antony always did things with a flourish. I never saw him moderate himself for anyone but you."

Unlike the pages and squires Cassandry had grown up with, Antony had not come to train for knighthood with Gerolt until he was seventeen. The novelty of him, along with his dashing face and almost-immediate attraction to Cassandry, had swept her normally level head into a whirlwind of emotion. They had shared so much, their courtship so intense. How could she have known him so little?

"Perhaps this is not a good time to speak," Cassandry said, choosing to avoid Gerolt's remarks about her husband. "Lord Rauffe will be joining us any moment . . ."

"He was having a little trouble with his wardrobe this morning, I fear. Sir Ingram will straighten it out. Nothing would delight me more than to pass the time conversing with you, my lady."

His formality stung, but she knew she deserved it, having so persistently referred to Gerolt as "my lord." She had not dared do otherwise, not when her heart had leapt so confusingly at seeing him in her hall at Rengrave. She thought she had overcome the pain of his loss, but when she looked up that day and saw him, her first impulse had been to run into the familiar embrace of his arms, bury her face against his strong, reassuring chest, and burst into tears. The temptation had so shaken her that formality had been her only defense. She thought Antony had stripped her of everything, including her pride, but it had reared up strongly on seeing Gerolt. How she had pleaded and wheedled and, yes, even whined with him to get her way. She could not bear for him to know what a fool she had been.

She glanced at Egelina listening politely to whatever Sir Fithian was saying to her. Cassandry let down her guard enough to confess, "I was afraid I was going to cry. You cannot know what it is like to lose a daughter—Oh, Gerolt, I am sorry!"

Her thoughtless words horrified her. Her hand went to his arm, the gesture still so natural that she could not stop it.

Gerolt laid his strong fingers over hers, squeezing them a little. "Do not mind it. Aye, I miss Fleur. I missed her when she married, too. Aveline seemed more proud than sorrowful when she wed. 'I have done my full duty to you now, sir,' she said to me. 'Your daughter is honorably married and shall soon give you grandsons, for I raised her to be a dutiful daughter.' I fear she did not think Rauffe would live to see his tenth year, much less his seventeenth. We neither of us expected to lose Fleur and our first grandchild all in one blow."

He gazed over Cassandry's head, his eyes blurring at the memories. "She was not only a dutiful daughter, she was warm and loving. She and I continued to exchange letters after she married, as you and I once did. When they ceased—" He blinked, his gaze focusing again as he gazed down at her. "I will take good care of her, Cassandry." He nodded toward Egelina. "And you are always welcome here. This was once your home. If you wish to make it so again, if it pains you too much to part from her . . ."

She shook her head and withdrew her hand. "She would never learn to be chatelaine if I were always hovering over her. I have taught her everything she needs to know to be a good wife and will be an excellent mistress of Lyonstoke Castle. But I must go in order for her to learn her own strength." *And perhaps find my own again.* Contemplation, meditation, prayer—these would fill the remainder of Cassandry's years, her mind at rest knowing that Egelina was safe in Gerolt's keeping.

"But you will not go yet," Gerolt insisted. "Would you make the break so quickly? It will not hurt to linger a month or two, to help her learn the workings of Lyonstoke."

She studied her daughter from across the room. "I wish that we might wait. They are both still so young."

"And life is precarious, as we both know. Fleur was gone before she was twenty, and Rauffe—I must have an heir, Cassandry. I will wait a year, as promised, but a grandchild I must have."

She nodded. As much as she worried for Egelina, she would much rather leave her in Gerolt's care than hazard the mistake of giving her to a man she entirely misread, as she had misread Antony.

Rauffe will be a good husband.

But her confidence was sorely shaken when Rauffe finally joined them in the hall. He had been a painfully thin boy of fourteen when last she had seen him. He still looked little more than skin and bones, his cheeks gaunt, his bony nose jutting from his face like a blade, his surcote of red silk hanging loosely on his rawboned body while emphasizing the pallor of his cheeks. Rauffe's grasp on life looked as "precarious" as Gerolt feared. Enough vitality lingered in the boy's eyes to suggest a stubborn grasp of living yet, but a man of Gerolt's wealth must have an eye to his inheritance.

"I will ready Egelina for the ceremony," she murmured and hasted back to her daughter's side.

She "straightened" Egelina's veil again, shook her daughter's skirts into graceful folds, then, with no other excuses for delay, urged Egelina to join Rauffe and the chaplain on the dais while Cassandry and Gerolt took up their positions behind the young couple. Cassandry's concerns for the boy's health spiked when she saw how he stood with his shoulders slumped. To have so little energy he could not stand up straight!

"Wilt thou, Rauffe," the chaplain intoned, "promise to have this woman for thy wedded wife . . . ?"

Cassandry's worry veered from Rauffe's health to Egelina's rebellion and back to Rauffe, who listened to the words of the betrothal vows then, while the chaplain paused for him to utter a reply of future consent, mumbled something Cassandry could not understand.

An abrupt clearing of a throat from where Gerolt stood jerked the boy's shoulders up, and he answered hoarsely, "I will."

"Wilt thou, Egelina . . ."

Cassandry wished she were not forced to stand at Egelina's

back. Were her blue eyes flashing with resistance, or would the sudden swooping of Rauffe to a height that nearly matched his father's intimidate her into answering with a becoming maidenly meekness? A pause hung in the air when the chaplain finished. Cassandry saw Egelina's hand plucking nervously at her gown, disarraying the lines of the skirts her mother had so carefully arranged, until her fingers vanished amidst the mussed folds. Cassandry waited, her nerves stretching tighter and tighter until she was nearly ready to shout her daughter's assent herself.

At last Egelina's young voice floated across the silence with a surprisingly cheerful chirp. "I will."

Relief washed over Cassandry, and some of her tension slipped away. Egelina's body rocked gently from side to side, undoubtedly bored as the chaplain repeated the lengthy terms of the dowry and dower Cassandry and Gerolt had agreed to. Rauffe must have grown bored too, for it took another clearing of Gerolt's throat to jar him into another hoarse confirmation when the chaplain eventually fell silent once more.

And then it was time for the ring and the betrothal kiss. Cassandry heard a soft, "Ow!" and a muffled, "Sorry." as Rauffe apparently shoved the ring too forcefully over Egelina's knuckle. The young couple turned their profiles sufficiently for Cassandry to see them gazing doubtfully at one another then. At last—after a sharp cough this time from Gerolt—Rauffe ducked down and dropped a swift kiss on Egelina's cheek, one that turned both their faces fiery red. Rauffe's shoulders fell into a slump again after the necessary salute.

The chaplain intoned a final invocation upon the couple, and then Cassandry moved to her daughter's side in the same moment Gerolt reached his son and dealt a light thump of approval upon his shallow shoulder.

"Must we stay any longer?" Egelina whispered.

"Just long enough to receive the company's congratulations,"

Cassandry said as the knights in the chapel broke into stomping and clapping and shouting, none of their words identifiable in the cacophony. "Smile, love."

Egelina did so, thinly. Rauffe's face looked as strained as his wife's-to-be. Sir Fithian lisped his felicitations to the couple. Sir Ingram heaped dramatic exclamations of Egelina's beauty and Rauffe's good fortune upon their heads. A young knight with bright, wheat-colored hair kissed Egelina's hand, and even a red-haired squire managed to squeeze forward to bow to her.

Gerolt broke in at length. "I think we will not overwhelm them with too many more formalities."

Egelina and Rauffe sagged with almost identical relief when the crowd of vassals and ladies dispersed at their lord's command.

"May we please go *now*?" Egelina whispered to her mother.

"Yes, love." To the crowd, she said, "Excuse us, everyone, but my daughter must change her gown for the feast."

"How horrid!" Egelina exclaimed when they were alone with their maid, Lora, in the bedchamber. "I did not know Rauffe should have to *kiss* me."

Lora unlaced the back of her surcote while Cassandry removed her daughter's veil. She had specifically requested Egelina share her chamber until she became more comfortable in her new home.

"Well, he shall not have to kiss you again for a very long time," Cassandry said. "You must be kind to him, Egelina. As you saw from the way he slumped, he is not well."

"Oh, he did not slump because he is ill."

Egelina stepped out of her surcote so that Lora could place it in the pretty, painted wooden wardrobe from Cassandry's child-hood. Cassandry pushed away the flood of memories that again swept over her much as they had when she'd crossed the threshold to discover her former bedchamber still so unchanged from her youth.

She moved behind her daughter to begin untying the laces of her undertunic as Egelina rattled on. "He was trying to appear shorter than he really is. Hob the stableboy did the same thing when he shot up to tower over the other boys his age. He slouched about horribly until Janeta the goose girl caught his eye and he began trying to win her interest. Then he stood ever so straight, but it did no good, for she fell in love with Clim the cowherd. You remember, Mamma, you gave them permission to marry two years ago."

Cassandry hesitated, surprised by her daughter's insightfulness. She finished with the laces and handed the undertunic to the maid, then stood a moment gazing at her daughter. Egelina looked so young and vulnerable in her flowing white chemise. Like an angel Cassandry wished she could keep and protect forever. She breathed a small prayer of gratitude that if Egelina had to grow up, she would do so in the house of the man who had so gently raised Cassandry herself. How she sometimes longed for those days, when she had been able to lay all her cares on Gerolt's strong shoulders. He had made her feel not only safe but valued and trusted. *And good.*

She motioned to Lora, who brought forth the previously agreed upon soft azure silk from their traveling trunks. "This blue will look charming on you, my dear," Cassandry said.

"But I just wore blue," Egelina protested.

"Embroidered in white for purity, appropriate for your betrothal. These gold threads will gleam beautifully beneath the torchlights of the hall, while the blue beneath them will still bring out the hue of your eyes. Oh, it will not be long before the entire court is smitten with you, including young Rauffe."

Cassandry bit her tongue. Smitten? 'Twas the last thing she

wanted for her daughter! But she did not want cold indifference in her marriage, either. A gentle affection between her and Rauffe— Aye, that would be the answer to her mother's prayer.

"He can be smitten out of his mind for me and I will not care because I am not going to marry him."

If they were going to argue again, it would not be in front of the maid. Cassandry signaled to Lora to leave them alone. Just hearing Egelina's declaration again made Cassandry's head ache. Lora had set the new blue silk on the bed, so Cassandry retrieved a fresh undertunic. She shook out a cream-colored silk with red roses embroidered on the cuffs.

"Do not be absurd," she said. "You have just spoken the betrothal vows. Of course you must marry Rauffe now."

"No, I shan't because . . ." The rest of the words were lost in the folds of the tunic as Cassandry slid it over her daughter's golden curls. Egelina continued talking beneath the cloth, ending with, ". . . so you may as well just take me home," when her head popped out again through the neckline.

Wishing to preserve her daughter's youth forever was one thing. Acknowledging reality was quite another. "I have heard enough of this nonsense. Of course I am not going to take you back to Rengrave. *This* is your home now, here with Rauffe and Lord Gerolt. I shall stay until you are settled—a fortnight, perhaps two— but you must resign yourself to your future, Egelina. You've spoken the vows. You are bound to him now."

"But I did not mean it when I spoke them."

Cassandry so lost her patience that she pulled the laces at the back of the tunic too tightly and forced a little *oomph* of air from her daughter. She quickly relaxed the pressure and tied them into place.

"Nevertheless, you spoke them and they are binding. You know that, Egelina." She turned her daughter to gaze firmly into her eyes.

Egelina shook her head. "I crossed my fingers when I said, 'I will.'"

Cassandry blinked, thinking she must not have heard right. "I beg your pardon?"

"I crossed my fingers and said in my head, 'I won't!' when I said out loud, 'I will.'"

"You crossed your fingers? Oh, Gelli, surely you cannot think that negates anything."

"But it does! I hid my hand in my gown and made the sign of the cross with my fingers to ward off God's anger for saying a lie out loud. He knows I do not want to marry Rauffe anyway. He would much rather I be a nun. Well, of course God would! And I shall tell Lord Gerolt so, even if his height does frighten me a little."

Cassandry did not know what to say. On the one hand, her daughter's gesture seemed absurd. But on the other, if she had made the sign of the cross . . . Cassandry could not dismiss that as lightly as she wanted to.

"What a dilemma you have cast me into. I shall have to tell Lord Gerolt. You and Rauffe will repeat the vows—this time with your fingers *un*crossed—but it can be done in private, to avoid embarrassment to us all."

"I won't!" Egelina's face went sulky again, too sulky for a young woman who dreamed of being a nun. "I should hate being Rauffe's wife. He is clumsy, and I could barely understand his mumbling. And I wish to learn to read and write!"

Cassandry sighed. "We will speak more of this after dinner. You *will* sit at Rauffe's side and smile and converse with him. I know I have indulged you in a great many things, but I did not raise you to be unkind, Egelina."

The sulkiness fled, though some defensiveness lingered on Egelina's now-softened features. "I will not be rude to him. But just because I try to be kind does not mean I will marry him."

That answer, at least, reassured Cassandry that they might make it through dinner peacefully. She slipped the blue surcote with golden threads over the cream-colored tunic and laced up the back, then began combing out the curls that had been mussed by the change of clothing.

"I can comb my own hair." Egelina took the pretty wooden tool from her mother's hand. "You should be dressing too. Shall I help you, or shall I call Lora to rejoin us?"

"I will call Lora. We will be late if we do not begin to hurry along. Be sure you get every last tangle out. I wish your hair to shine like spun gold. We shall allow it to tumble loose over your shoulders, with just a ribbon threaded through to match your eyes and gown. Oh, you shall be a vision, Gelli!"

Egelina blushed, for she had never displayed the least vainness about her loveliness. "You shall be a vision as well," she said, "if you will wear the pretty crimson you donned for Christmas last year. I saw you pack it, so do not tell me you left it at home."

Cassandry did not know why she had, except that Gerolt had praised its color on her when she'd worn it to dinner during his visit to Rengrave Castle. After years of dressing drably, it had felt so bold to don the crimson, and so very, very pleasant to have a man compliment instead of condemn her for it. She'd instinctively known that here, at Lyonstoke, she would not be judged for wishing to appear her best. She was much too old to ever be called a "vision" again, but she could look neat and comely, and if the shade flattered her, was that really such a sin?

Chapter 4

Cassandry passed a restless night listening to her daughter's breathing in the darkness, conscious of Egelina's every movement in the bed they shared. At least there had been no tears after dinner. Cassandry would hardly have blamed Egelina for another emotional outburst. Rauffe had scarcely spoken two words to her while they ate, coloring clear to his ears whenever Egelina sought, at the nudging of her mother's elbow, to draw him into conversation. They had at last fallen to eating in silence, even Cassandry having given up on the tongue-tied youth who so clearly uncomfortably shared his trencher with his betrothed. To Rauffe's credit, he had offered Egelina a dish or two, but since his choices had fallen to an insipid-looking barley soup and a mild chicken with rosewater sauce, Cassandry could not blame Egelina for declining.

Egelina huddled deeper into the blankets. She must be exhausted, Cassandry owned, for they had combined a lengthy ride, a stressful betrothal, and a long celebratory dinner all in one day. Today would be quieter.

She had dozed off a time or two after she heard the church bells chime midnight. She knew it because she had jerked awake, thinking herself still seated at the table on the dais conversing with

Gerolt on a dozen innocuous subjects while worrying about her daughter and fretting how to tell him their children would have to repeat the betrothal vows. She hoped his reaction would be as reasonable as it had always been her youth. But people changed through the years. Antony had taught her that. Surely it was too much to hope Gerolt had not changed too?

She did not realize her fingers kept threading through the hair she had pushed back from her forehead until a small hand reached up to cover hers.

"Can you not sleep, Mamma?" Egelina's drowsy voice carried in it a husky concern. "I have felt you tossing and turning for hours."

Cassandry pressed her daughter's fingers and laid them back on the bolster. "I had a dream, that is all. Do not trouble yourself. There are a few more hours before we must rise and break our fast. Go back to sleep, my love."

She leaned over and kissed her daughter on the cheek.

Egelina sighed a little but asked, "What kind of dream?"

"Nothing to worry you." Cassandry rolled on her back. She must lie very still so as not to disturb Egelina again. Only a few more hours before she would be able to act on her concerns. Waiting had always made her fidget. She preferred to be up and doing, to face a crisis head-on, and only when it was over to retreat into some mindless womanly task like spinning or weaving or embroidery. She could lose herself there, in the rhythm of the loom or the small, tedious details of setting stitches in cloth . . .

"Were you dreaming of Lord Gerolt?"

"What?" Her daughter's query took her by surprise.

"He is very tall."

"So he is." Egelina had mentioned Gerolt's height before. It had never intimidated Cassandry, but then, Gerolt's tall frame had been familiar to her as long as she could remember.

"And he has eyes like smoke."

Gray, Cassandry thought. She had never thought of them like smoke. They had always only been the eyes of her guardian, eyes that laughed with her, that listened patiently to her, that weighed her words with wisdom and discernment. Or so it had seemed through her seven years as his young ward. She supposed her dependence on him had allowed her to read too much in his steady gaze. He had not been so wise concerning Antony. *But Gerolt's laughter and patience—I did not imagine that.*

"I do not think he angers easily like Papa did." Egelina spoke with so much throaty sleepiness Cassandry wondered if she even knew what she said.

"He did not used to," Cassandry admitted. "But it has been a very long time since I lived with him. People change, Egelina."

"Rauffe was horrid tonight, mumbling and trying to feed me food so bland it curled my tongue, but his father never once scolded him, or me when I gave a great huff of disgust and repeated very loudly, 'No, thank you.' It made some of the diners stare at us, and Lord Gerolt frowned, but Rauffe did not look afraid of him. I think he would have if his father was like Papa, don't you?"

Cassandry raised herself onto an elbow and smoothed the hair at her daughter's brow. "Your father loved you, Egelina. He always called you 'sweetling.' If he sometimes snapped at you to leave us, he meant no harm. You know that, do you not?"

Egelina nodded. "I know he loved me. He loved you, too. I know he did, Mamma. I am sorry he hurt you sometimes."

"He did not hurt me, Gelli. You must never think that." As difficult as Antony had been, he had never raised his hand to Cassandry.

"I mean here." Egelina moved her hand to rest her palm against Cassandry's heart. "I am sorry, Mamma."

She gave another long, deep sigh, and then her hand grew slack as she slipped back into slumber.

Cassandry wound her arms around her daughter and pressed her face into the soft silk of her curls, grateful for the tumbling locks that hid her sudden tears.

At last, when the haze of dawn began to blush pink, Cassandry slept—so deeply that her daughter's rustlings beside her had failed to rouse more than a faint awareness from her. When her hand found empty space on Egelina's side of the bed, she did not at first register any concern. Only as the silence stretched on did worry begin stir in her. Her mind became quickly alert, flashing back to the aftermath of yesterday's betrothal. *I do not think he angers easily.* Oh, heavens! Surely Egelina had not gone in search of Gerolt to tell him she did not wish to marry his son!

Cassandry sat up swiftly, sleep flying from her eyes, but Egelina was seated on the cushioned stool Cassandry had once sat upon as a girl, combing out her gilded locks.

"How long have you been up?" Cassandry asked.

Egelina smothered a yawn behind her hand. "Only a little while," she said. "I sent Lora to bring us some bread and cheese. You are very pretty when you sleep, Mamma. Except that now you have circles under your eyes. Whatever kept you awake all night?"

You, child. What ever drove slumber from me save worrying about you or quarreling with your father?

"Something at dinner must not have agreed with me," Cassandry lied. "I am fine now, though." She tossed back the blankets and slipped out of bed.

"Shall I go to the kitchen and ask if they have any camomile?" Egelina asked. "To soothe your eyes before Lord Gerolt sees them. They are a little red, too."

Oh, heavens, to greet the day with bloodshot eyes and muddy circles would surely accentuate the lines that age had carved.

Cassandry retrieved the small hand mirror Lora had set on the table near the wardrobe the night before. 'Twas a tired, middle-aged woman who gazed back at her. Lines under her eyes as well as at the corners. The creases around her mouth seemed more etched too. And—oh!—how had she missed yet another silver hair? Had it been as noticeable yesterday when she'd greeted Gerolt? Had it glistened like a traitor in the torchlight of the hall at dinner? Why had she worn her braids knotted at the back of her head instead of covering them with a veil? She plucked the hair out with a savage vengeance, then felt her face warm when Egelina gave a giggle.

"Here, let me look." Egelina rounded behind her mother. Three sharp stings to her scalp betrayed the discovery of threads Cassandry could not see.

"How many more are there?" she asked in dismay.

"Only a few." Egelina patted the back of her mother's hair. "But they are pretty there, so truly you must not mind. Your veil will conceal them. Lord Gerolt has far, far more gray in his hair than this."

And more lines than Cassandry had in her face, but she found no comfort in that fact.

Egelina must have seen her mother's frown, for she said quickly, "I will go find some camomile."

Cassandry had begun cultivating the herb at Rengrave Castle to fade the frequent circles she awoke with in the mornings, for Antony had demanded she look her best even when she had stopped caring. *So why do I care today?*

Egelina selected a tunic that required no lacing up the back, pulled it over her head, belted it loosely about her slender waist, then opened the door. "Oh! But how pretty!"

Cassandry glanced up at her daughter's exclamation. Something dangled in Egelina's hand. She carried it across the room to show her mother. It was a thin, delicate seashell with alternating rays of white and reddish-brown spanning from the wide-rimmed edge to the dulled point, where someone had cut a hole and threaded it on a leather thong.

"Look, Mamma. It was lying just outside the door. Someone must have left it for—"

Cassandry was on her feet and across to the doorway before Egelina could finish. She glanced up and down the passageway, but whoever had placed the seashell there had vanished. Rauffe would not have left it. Even in his obvious shyness, he had no reason not to present a gift directly to Egelina.

"This is unpardonable," Cassandry muttered. "If one of Gerolt's men thinks it amusing to flirt with you—"

"It is just a seashell," Egelina protested. "And how do you know someone left it for me?"

"Who else would it be for?"

Cassandry glanced up the passageway again. Perhaps she made too much of it. As Egelina said, it was only a shell. It was just the sort of silly, prankish gesture an impulsive young squire might make. Cassandry thought of the red-haired youth who had pushed forward to bow to Egelina after the betrothal and of the young knight with the wheat-colored hair who had fixed his attention a little too frequently on Egelina during dinner. How had Gerolt introduced him? Sir Owen, yes, that was it. Or even, perhaps, Sir Ingram. She would not put it past him to tease Cassandry by teasing her daughter. Even when she had thought the sun revolved around Antony, his luster had always shone a little less bright when he and Ingram had resorted to some of their more foolish antics. And few antics could be more foolish—and dangerous for Sir Ingram's continued service in Gerolt's household—than playing coy games with the future wife of his lord's son.

She swung about on another thought. "When I left you in Sir Fithian's company yesterday, what did you and he talk about?"

"Nothing of any consequence." Egelina stretched out the

thong until the shell rested in the palm of her hand. "I do not think anyone would leave it for me. They all think I am betrothed to Lord Rauffe. Someone must have left it for you, Mamma."

"That is absurd, Gelli. No one would leave a token for me."

"But did you not have one like this once? One that made Papa angry?"

"That one was white and gray." Like storm clouds. Like Gerolt's eyes the day he had placed it around her neck. "How do you know it made your father angry?"

One of the few things she and Antony had agreed upon was not to allow their quarrels to spill over into Egelina's life.

"I had a nightmare one night when I was little and came to find you, but you and Papa were arguing in your chamber. You were wearing the seashell, and Papa made you give it to him. I saw you crying, so I went and found Lora instead. And I never saw you wear the shell again. Did Papa . . . do something to it?"

Cassandry could still hear the awful crunch of it beneath Antony's heel. "Your father lost it," she lied. "And I am certain I was not crying. The alder tree that grew outside our window made my eyes water day and night when it was in bloom."

She could not tell if Egelina believed her, but after a moment she simply held out the shell to her mother.

"Well, one of us must wear it," she said. "I think it should be you. It would go so prettily with your sunflower gown."

Cassandry was about to state flatly that neither of them would wear it when it occurred to her that she might catch a look of betraying surprise from the giver if he saw it around her neck, and thus she would know whom to rebuke. She took the shell from Egelina and set it alongside the comb and mirror on the table.

During yesterday's dinner, Lora had unpacked the gowns from their traveling chests and placed them in the wooden wardrobe. Before Cassandry pulled open one of the doors, she brushed her fingers along the wreaths of small white flowers encircling a cluster of purple blossoms—periwinkle and sweet woodruff. Gerolt had them painted there after he found her in the garden with her arms filled with the combined blooms when she had been ten years old.

"An heiress should have a prettier wardrobe than an old scuffed cabinet of pine, don't you think?" he had asked her with a twinkle in his eye.

Not long afterward, he had added the four panels of birds along the top—a red-breasted robin, a golden oriel, a blue swallow, and a starling, its black plumage speckled with white—altogether too prophetic of Cassandry's aging locks. And yet even that panel made her smile, for she remembered how Gerolt had taught her to pick out the calls of the four birds, even the mimics of the starling.

"I wonder what can be keeping Lora?" Egelina said. "I'm getting hungry."

"Go see if you can find her. I will choose our gowns for the day."

"Wear the sunflower one, Mamma," Egelina repeated. "It makes your hair look all glossy."

Cassandry pulled open the wardrobe as her daughter went out, but as soon as Egelina was gone, she returned to the table and picked up the shell again. The colors were different, but the memories rushed back all the same. Gerolt must have thought her quite silly to be delighted over so simple a token, but though she had inherited expensive jewels from her parents, the shell had been her very first gift from a man, even though at the time Gerolt had seemed quite old. Twenty-two to her twelve years. A part of her had wished the handsome new squire in the household, Antony de Reymes, had tied the token around her neck. But another part of her, the adoring part that idolized Gerolt as if he had been her own beloved brother, had cherished what it signaled between them, a bond she knew no handsome squire and no circumstance could ever break.

Antony had never liked how often she wore it. Cassandry had

thought his jealousy flattering before they wed. She refused other men's gifts to please him, but spurn them from Gerolt? That demand was too absurd. She had worn the shell proudly. She had teased Antony with it sometimes, just to assert her womanly power over him to make him frown or smile. But after they had married and his jealousy had turned from flattering to harrowing, she had hidden it, insisting she had lost it years ago. And then she had grown so lonely she had donned it again, tucking it inside her gown to nestle against her heart while praying Antony might not ask about the thong around her neck.

But of course he had. *So much anger and bitterness and hurt.* She ran her fingers over the ridges of the shell. She should throw it out the window and hurl the memory away with it. Instead she whispered, "I wish this was from you. Oh, Gerolt, I became so lost without you. Why did I not see what Antony was? Why did *you* not see?"

He should have. He should have known her marriage would be a disaster. She had trusted Gerolt with everything in her life, and in her most critical decision, he had failed her. She should be angry. She should be furious with him. But she could find no rage inside. Only the desolating emptiness Antony had left her with.

She drew her sunflower-yellow kirtle out of the wardrobe and set it on the bed simply because she did not have the energy to select something else. Besides, it always pleased Egelina when her mother followed her advice on her gowns.

She had just decided on a reddish-brown surcote with white decorative embroidery on the sleeves for Egelina when her daughter returned, entering the room with a skipping step alongside the maid, who carried a tray of bread and cheese and two goblets of watered wine.

"Ill news, my lady," Lora said as she set the tray on the table. "I am afraid Lord Rauffe awoke with a headache that all the castle says will keep him abed all day."

So that explained Egelina's cheerful look. Cassandry and Gerolt had agreed during yesterday's banquet that a stroll in the gardens today would give the young couple a chance to become better acquainted. Cassandry was not prepared to admit defeat until she knew more about Rauffe's condition.

"Who is attending to him?" she inquired. "Do you know what remedies they have tried?"

"A physician hired by his late mother by the name of Hyll," Lora said, handing one of the goblets to Cassandry. "I suggested some camomile tea, but they said in the kitchen that it never helps the boy."

"What about rosemary and lavender? They always ease Sir Patrick's head when he is ill."

"I am sure those will not help, either," Egelina said around a mouthful of cheese, "You'd best leave him to the physician, Mamma."

Cassandry pursed her lips. *So that he might be too sick to walk with you in the garden? Not if I can help it, my dear.*

"I do not know what kind of physician this Hyll can be," Cassandry said, "if he has been with Lord Rauffe for nearly seventeen years and the boy is still as thin as a rail." She took a sip of wine.

"They said in the kitchen that he administers a special draught to Lord Rauffe he insists will ease the headaches eventually."

"Eventually?" Cassandry repeated. "As in a few hours?"

Lora held out one of the plates to Cassandry. "Or days. So they say in the kitchen."

Days?

Egelina sat down on the bed, looking altogether too satisfied.

Cassandry swallowed a bite of bread before saying, "Lora, go gather some lavender and rosemary from the herb garden and make up a small pillow with them to set over Lord Rauffe's eyes. It can do him no harm and may do him much good."

"Oh, Mamma," Egelina protested. "I am sure you ought not to interfere with the physician."

Hmph! Cassandry thought. Lora curtsied to her mistress with an obedient, "Yes, my lady," and slipped out of the room.

By the time Cassandry and Egelina had finished eating their breakfast and changed into their gowns, Lora had returned with the news that the herb-scented pillow had worked such a wonder that Lord Rauffe would be joining them in the gardens after all.

"I wish you'd left Lord Rauffe with a headache," Egelina said with a scowl. "I do not wish to walk with him." She looked at Cassandry with a bit of trepidation. "Are you going to tell his father what I did?"

"You know that I must."

Egelina tossed her bright curls. "Then tell him about the nunnery as well."

"We will speak of this later," Cassandry said. Resuming their quarrel now would bring on a headache of her own.

She slipped on the seashell. Her eye would be keenly attuned to any glance of surprise from one of Gerolt's men when he saw Cassandry wearing the token.

Before she and Egelina could reach the garden, they had to enter and cross through the great hall. The room was already filled with men and women mingling to decide their activities for the day. One rumbling voice was attempting to put together a hunting party. Some of the women were eager to join the men, while others were buzzing over where the best light might be found to work on their embroidery. It would not be stitchery alone they would be engaged in, Cassandry knew, but gossip and news, for some of the vassals' wives had recently visited London.

Sir Ingram appeared in their path. "Lady Cassandry. Lady Egelina."

Cassandry remembered how he and Antony had made it a contest to see who could accomplish the most elaborate bow. Sir

Ingram removed his cap and flourished it not once but thrice before he bent over her hand and then Egelina's.

"Will you not join us?" he said. "Sir Fithian sighted a robust stag on his ride this morning, and we are off to see who among us can bring it down. Wagers are being set that it will be either Sir Payne or Lord Lionel. We need not linger for the kill if you are squeamish," he said, waggling an eyebrow at Egelina when she shuddered a little. "The fun is in the chase. A good, hearty ride would set a glow to your cheeks, my lady, although the wind would be hard-pressed to deepen the blush already there."

"That is because you are still clinging to her hand," Cassandry said. "Antony may not be here to knock you down as he did when you held my fingers too long, but if you do not release her, you may be sure that I will box your ears right here in the hall."

Sir Ingram released Egelina's hand, though he slid a roguish look at Cassandry. She waited, as she had when he had bowed to her, for his gaze to dip to the shell, but he gave it not a glance.

"Your daughter is altogether too charming. You cannot expect men not to pine for such a beauty, betrothed or not."

"And *you* should know better than to think you can play with fire by flirting with Lord Gerolt's future daughter-in-law. For goodness sake, Ingram, you are old enough to be her father! If you have learned no better sense than this in twenty-four years, I must ask Gerolt why he continues to employ you in his service."

Sir Ingram's audacity swiftly faded. "'Twas only a game, my lady. No harm intended, no harm done. I pray you will say nothing of this to Lord Gerolt."

Sir Ingram bowed again, this time without a flourish, and swiftly disappeared into the crowd.

"You were very harsh with him, Mamma," Egelina murmured. "I do believe he only meant to tease me."

She hoped Egelina was right. She did not like suspecting old friends, but Sir Samson had taught her not to take any man for granted. Sir Ingram had not shown any interest in the seashell, though.

Neither did Sir Fithian when they encountered him and he launched into an enthusiastic description of the stag. "The hunthman ith out quethting for it now. We're gathering a party for the chathe. Thome have thuggethted we make a picnic of it if the day runth long. Will you not join uth, my ladieth?"

"Another time," Cassandry said as she watched Egelina pucker her brow, no doubt in an attempt to mentally translate his speech. "Lord Gerolt is waiting for us in the gardens."

Sir Fithian laid a hand to his heart in a gesture that, though dramatic, bore an innocent playfulness. "Of courth, my lady. I would not athk you to keep the Hero of Iconium waiting."

That made Cassandry pause. "The Hero of Iconium?"

"Lord Gerolt, of courth. Have you not heard the tale? After he ranthomed Thir Thamthon from his Eathtern captor, he and Thir Thamthon fought with the emperor in a valiant attempt to recover Jeruthalem from the infidel. Lord Gerolt rethcued twenty Chrithtian knighth at the verge of thlaughter at a plathe called Iconium. Twenty, my lady! For that, he returned to England hailed by thothe men ath a hero."

Twenty Christian knights saved from infidel slaughter by Gerolt? Sir Samson had shared nothing of this story when he had come to escort her and Egelina from Rengrave Castle. What else had Antony's irrational jealousies cut her off from knowing about Gerolt's life when time had lain silent between them? She felt a flash of hot resentment, but the numbness that was now so much a part of her quickly extinguished it.

"Thank you for your invitation, Sir Fithian," she said, "but, truly, we must go."

She realized he had directed his tale toward Egelina, smiling in his sweet, amiable way, barely glancing at Cassandry and not at all at the shell. Cassandry hurried her daughter along. Twice more they were forced to stop. Someone pulled at Cassandry's skirts, and when she turned, she found the red-haired squire holding out a white ribbon.

"It is mine, Mamma," Egelina said. "It must have fallen out of my sleeve. I brought it along in case it grew warm in the sun and I wished to tie up my hair. Thank you, Garin."

Cassandry noted that the embroidery down the ribbon's center matched the pattern on Egelina's sleeves, which squelched any suspicion in her regarding the squire, though she did wonder aloud how Egelina knew his name.

"He served Rauffe and me at the table last night, and I heard Rauffe call him Garin."

"My ladies." Sir Owen of the wheat-colored hair appeared. "Some of us who care not for the hunt are putting together a game of blindman's buff. We thought the Lady Egelina—"

"That is *not* a game for my daughter, Sir Owen," Cassandry said in her sternest voice. Heavens! Blindfolded men pawing at her daughter trying to "guess" her identity? Gerolt had refused to let Cassandry play that game, even when she was twelve.

She shooed Egelina along again. Other men paused to bow and smile at the women. *At Egelina.* Far too many appreciative gazes at her daughter for Cassandry's peace of mind, but not one had she caught at the seashell.

Chapter 5

S am was wrong. Not all the light had gone out of Cassandry's eyes. Gerolt saw the loving glow whenever she gazed upon her daughter. So she had not lost all ability to love with Antony's death.

If Gerolt could only find some way to fan the embers that remained, to draw its direction toward himself . . .

He rubbed a weary hand against his brow. Saints, what was he thinking? By his own decision, it was now too late. He had just betrothed his son to her daughter, a contract that was nearly as irrevocable as marriage itself.

"Have you a headache too, my lord?" Cassandry queried as they strolled in the garden with the betrothed couple.

"Nay. I have not thanked you, by the way, for your assistance with Rauffe this morning. Were it not for whatever remedy you sent, he would likely still be sick in bed."

"I think the air will do him good," Cassandry said. "Did you not observe how much brighter his eyes have grown already?"

Gerolt had not, but now that he glanced at his son, who had stopped beside Egelina while she bent to admire a cluster of roses, there did seem to be more color in his face. If only the boy would stand up straight.

Although Rauffe had grown stronger as he had grown older, he still suffered from too many ailments—the headaches being but one too-frequent example—to be able to trust the future indefinitely to him. Gerolt must have a grandson—or he could marry again, as Sam suggested. But that counsel continued to ring hollow in his ears. After Cassandry had married Antony, Gerolt had tried to give his whole heart to Aveline. He had sought her hand because she had been so utterly different from Cassandry— fair instead of dark, short instead of tall, subdued instead of merry. He had thought her merely shy when she'd responded so meekly to his attentions, until after they were wed when she had thrown the word *dutiful* quite complacently in his face. She strove to be a good wife, as she had been a good daughter, not because she loved him—she disabused him of that notion too many times—but because she believed duty the shining crown of womanhood.

Gerolt's hand drifted too near Cassandry's. He caught himself just before he attempted to lace his fingers with hers. The temptation was almost more than he could bear, to have her so near after so many years of aching for what might have been between them. He locked his hands behind his back instead.

"I think we could not ask for a more accommodating morning for a budding courtship," he said. When she glanced at him, he nodded toward the two young people, who had resumed walking a few paces ahead of them. The sun cast its warming rays through the break in the clouds that had brought light showers earlier that morning.

Cassandry's gaze tilted to study the sky for a moment. "You are right, I hope. Oh, the day will most certainly be beautiful, but the courtship?"

Rauffe and Egelina had looked equally panicked when Gerolt had suggested they leave them to walk alone. He had seen Egelina tug on her mother's sleeve and whisper urgently and a bit too loudly, "What will we talk about? I could barely understand him last night. Please, *please* come with us!"

So they had started out, the four of them together. Cassandry had done her best to draw Rauffe out with questions about his interests, but Gerolt had been forced to clear his throat after each muttered reply before the boy repeated his answer clearly enough to be heard. Rauffe had dressed today in an absurd combination of all yellow shades, which only accented the pallor that lingered on his cheeks.

Gradually, Cassandry slowed her pace and Gerolt matched it. When Egelina threw a desperate look over her shoulder, Cassandry came to a complete stop and turned to study a stalk of hollyhocks.

"The two of you go ahead," she insisted. "Lord Gerolt is going to tell me how his gardener makes these grow so tall when they always shrivel and die at home."

"Take Lady Egelina's arm," Gerolt bade his son, "and show her the fountain. She will like to see the swans in the pond as well."

Egelina's eyes rounded with interest at the mention of swans, but she laid her hand gingerly on the lanky arm Rauffe held awkwardly out to her before they moved on down the graveled pathway.

Cassandry waited until they rounded a corner, then sank down on a carved stone bench near the hollyhocks. She left enough room for Gerolt to sit beside her, and, after a moment's hesitation, he did so.

"My gardener does not really need any advice," she confessed. "He said he'd solved the problem of the hollyhocks just last week." She gave him a smile that appeared to attempt to draw forth the old mischief in her, but it fell just short and turned strained instead.

Strained. He had never imagined anything but total trust and warmth could lie between them, but the years had clearly altered her in ways he had never conceived possible. *What happened after you left me? Why did all news of you fall silent?*

Her lovely face grew sober. "I have sought to do my best with Egelina, to teach her to be kind and good and thoughtful—and honest—as you taught me."

She fiddled with something around her neck. A seashell. Similar to the one he had given her when she was twelve, but these colors were different. Absurd to hope that she might have kept so inconsequential a token from him as a shell.

"Perhaps I would have been a better mother if I had had one myself," she said. "I remember so little of her. Your father was a widower and he too died when I was so young. I had only you to pattern parenthood on. I fear, perhaps, you were too lenient with me, and I have therefore been too lenient with Egelina."

Her words took him aback. "You used me as a pattern for parenthood?"

She nodded.

"Saints, girl! I was barely nineteen when your keeping fell to me. I knew nothing of raising children."

"But you were wonderful," she protested. "I thought you the wisest man I knew. Because you were always so generous to me, I taught Egelina that she should be generous to others. I encouraged her to find something to make her laugh when she was sad, just as you always taught me I should try to do. And when I grew angry, you taught me that I must count and count until I no longer felt hot and offended, and that I should strike my hands together when I was alone and say, 'I will not let you hurt me.' And then I must let my grudge go and remember that I was stronger than the pain."

To his surprise, she turned her face away.

"Only I wasn't. I wasn't strong. I have sought so hard that Egelina should never know how weak I truly was, but I must have failed because she did a dreadful thing yesterday."

Again he almost took her hand, but at the last minute he set his own lightly on her sleeve instead. "I cannot imagine any daughter of yours doing anything dreadful, Sparrow."

That brought her eyes back to his—was the glimmer in them a reflection of a tear?—and then a laugh that sounded almost genuine slipped from her lips.

"You stopped calling me that when I turned fourteen."

"Because that was when I saw the way you looked at Antony and knew you were readying yourself to fly away from me. I made you wait two more years—but perhaps I let you go too soon."

Again she averted her face. He suspected she had held in her grief so as not to burden her daughter with it. What else could have caused this change in her? For her own good, she had to share it. And as painful as it would be for him to listen to her reliving all the sweet, poignant memories of love between her and Antony, Gerolt would endure it if it would finally ease her heart. This time he pushed conscience aside and slid his hand to cover hers. How could she chide him for it? They had always sat, hands clasped, when she had poured out her heart to him.

"Will you tell me about it?" he asked softly.

She pulled her fingers from beneath his and stood up, walking several paces away before turning about again. Her eyes were shadowed but dry. "There is nothing to tell—save for what Egelina did yesterday. Her father overindulged her, and I clearly failed to counteract his permissiveness. I thought I had taught her better—truly, she has a good heart, Gerolt. But we have done nothing but quarrel since I told her of the betrothal. I was certain she would not dare defy us when she stood before your chaplain, but she said when she spoke the vows yesterday, she crossed her fingers."

"Crossed her fingers?" he repeated. "You mean for luck?" Well, any girl Egelina's age might be hesitant about marriage and send a prayer to the heavens for an agreeable bridegroom.

"No, because she spoke the vows as a lie. She said when she

repeated the words, 'I will,' she thought to heaven, 'I won't,' and crossed her fingers to confirm her unspoken vow."

Gerolt stared at Cassandry, then threw back his head and laughed.

"It is not funny," she said.

"No," Gerolt agreed on a chuckle, "it is not, but it is very much something that Antony might have done. That boy had the most reckless imagination. Oh, forgive me," he said in response to Cassandry's frown. "It is not a criticism, only an observation."

He did not mean to treat her revelation lightly, but how did one respond to such a ridiculous dilemma? And the deed done before his entire household! So Egelina resembled her father in more than just her beauty and golden curls.

Antony's tendency toward rashness had been why Gerolt had insisted they wait until Cassandry was sixteen and Antony knighted at twenty-one before Gerolt gave his permission for them to wed. He wished he could give Rauffe as much time to mature, or more, but he feared circumstances would not allow for that.

"Well," Gerolt said, "her act was not irrevocable. The vows can be said again in private—" He stopped, realizing with a tiny shock that Cassandry was watching him almost . . . warily? "Did you think I would be angry?"

"You would have every right to be."

"If I were, I assure you I would have counted long and hard before I said anything to wound you." He stood up. "What has happened to you, Cassandry? What has happened to us, that you would think otherwise of me?" It brought him no comfort when she took a step back from him.

"It is my fault," she said. "I should have taught her better."

"There is no blame here. Children do foolish things. Did you see the absurd clothes Rauffe chose to wear today? For all he and Egelina are of an age to marry, they are still imprudent and young. Rauffe is forever lying about groaning of headaches, and when he is well he is sulky and defiant. I am near my wits end to know how to deal with him."

"And I with Egelina," she said with such vehemence that it appeared to sweep away the constraint between them. "If she speaks to me of a nunnery one more time—"

"A nunnery?"

"A nunnery! Have you ever heard anything more absurd? All because I refuse to let her learn to read and write."

"Why do you refuse her that?"

"Because it is knowledge unfit for a woman. You should never have let me learn."

"But you begged me—"

"And you were supposed to be wise and to know better than I. But you are right. I understand now how young you were. I must have tried your patience sorely with all my pleading. I wish you had not heeded me . . . but I know you did it with that generosity you always showered me with. Forgive me. I did not mean to chide you for something you granted me in kindness."

Before he could respond, a footstep crunched on the graveled path. Gerolt turned as Samson joined them.

"The sky is darkening again," Sam said, "and Rauffe's servant confirmed he refused to don his cloak." He smiled at Cassandry. "The boy says he is tired of being coddled, but you will have noticed he is not at all well. I have told Gerolt that he should marry again and get himself another son or two. I flatter myself that he begins to look favorably on my daughter, Marion. She has proven herself a worthy wife. I trust, in time, she will woo him away from his grief for Aveline."

Gerolt frowned. Why would Samson say such a thing to Cassandry when he knew grief was not what held Gerolt back?

Samson glanced toward the turn in the pathway. "Have they gone on to the fountain? I will join them just long enough to see Rauffe warmly bundled, then I will leave you all alone again. I will take another exit from the garden, for I fear I've interrupted some sort of important exchange between you."

He ended with a nod and started down the path, then paused and bent to pluck some flowers. He turned and proffered them to Cassandry.

"Are these still your favorite?"

She hesitated, then stretched out her cupped hands. Samson dropped the periwinkle into her palms, then continued on to the fountain.

Gerolt silently cursed Samson for acting on the memory when Gerolt had not thought to do so. He said, so that she should not think he had forgotten, "And sweet woodruff. You always loved the color of one and the scent of the other. Do you remember the wreath I wove for you when you were fourteen?"

"I wore it for days," she said. "Partly because it was so pretty and partly because it made Antony jealous. I was so flattered when he railed at you behind your back, calling you a would-be seducer, when nothing could have been more absurd. You looked on me as a child and guarded me as dearly as I knew you would guard a true sister." She lowered her gaze to the purple blossoms in her hands. "Antony admitted later his suspicions were ridiculous, but to think that he believed I could tempt another man, as awkward and shy as I was—oh, I thought it the most marvelous jest at the time."

Ah, lass, you never had an awkward bone in your body. But Gerolt recalled how she had always doubted the natural grace and charm he had perceived in her from the first, until Antony's love had given her the confidence to bloom.

"This business of your daughter and a nunnery," he said, drawing them back to their former conversation. "If she feels she has a calling, I must not take that lightly. Nor do I wish to force a reluctant bride on Rauffe."

Cassandry frowned. "She is not reluctant. She does not truly wish to be a nun. She only says it to provoke me into letting her learn to write. You must not encourage her." Her gaze lifted to his with a severity she could only have learned from motherhood. "I have taught her everything she needs to know to be a good wife and chatelaine of your estates. But she does not need to know how to wield a pen for any of it. You will not be disappointed in her, I promise."

"And what will become of you?" he asked abruptly. "Do you plan to simply retire to your dower lands and fade away? There is too much life in you yet for that, Cassandry."

"If you are again asking me if I wish to remarry, my answer remains the same."

At the risk of another rebuff, he took her hand again, allowing some of the purple blossoms to scatter at their feet. How could she not feel his longing for her in his touch? His thumb swept lightly over her knuckles. "I cannot let you simply disappear again."

He prayed for some flicker of response, some light in her eyes, but her gaze, although pleading, remained distant.

"Perhaps that is what I wish to do. You say there is too much life in me, but the truth is, I am wrung dry. I have buried a husband. I have raised a daughter. I have done all life has required of me. I wish now to rest, but I can only do that if I know Egelina is safe with you. Please, you must give me your word that you will pay no heed to her pleas for a nunnery. By all the friendship I ever cherished between us, I beg you to marry her to Rauffe and to love her for me."

"Cassandry"—he heard the way his voice gruffened—"what if I found another husband for Egelina? Nay, I would not force her, but if she were to develop an affection for one of my knights—"

What was he saying? What would become of the grandson he needed, the heir for his lands? Did he wish to scramble haphazardly to find another wife for Rauffe? How would Rauffe interpret Gerolt shuffling one betrothed for another? What if

Cassandry still refused him? *But if she said yes . . . if she said yes . . . !*

"No." Cassandry spoke the word sharply, shattering his mad hope. "I will trust her to no one save you and Rauffe. You promised me, Gerolt. You promised you would care for her."

He clung to the dream for one more moment. "She will be in my household, among my knights, for a year before the marriage. What if she falls in love with one of them? What if she comes to me, as you did, and says—"

"You will tell her—nay, you will send her to me, and *I* will tell her that she has made a vow—for I promise you, she *will* speak the betrothal vows—and that she has a duty to abide by it. And she will do so, Gerolt. She will be a good wife to Rauffe, and she will be happier with him than she thinks she will be. I am confident of it, else I never would have agreed to your proposal for them to wed."

Gerolt shrank within when Cassandry spoke the word *duty*. Was that what he wished for Rauffe? A merely "dutiful" wife, as Aveline had been to Gerolt? How could he even contemplate such a thing for his son? If only Rauffe were stronger. If only there were time to let him grow to manhood and choose a wife of his own. At least then the mistakes would be his and not Gerolt's. But there was not time. He had to trust that enough of Cassandry lay inside her daughter that Egelina would someday make Rauffe as happy as Cassandry believed Rauffe would someday make Egelina.

He searched Cassandry's eyes as deeply as the shadows there allowed, then sighed and motioned back to the bench.

"Let us sit again while we wait for them to return."

She resumed her former place on the bench and appeared to contemplate the palmful of petals that remained in her hand. "It was generous of you to take Sir Samson back into your household."

The turn of subjects surprised him. "How could I do otherwise? His wife left his estates in ruins. But you do not know the story—"

"About his adventure in the East? He told me some of it when you sent him to escort Egelina and me to Lyonstoke."

Gerolt raised his brows. He had done no such thing.

"He said he went crusading," she continued, "and fell prisoner to the Saracens at the Battle of Hattin. They agreed to hold him prisoner in exchange for a very large ransom, but he said it took you three years to pay it."

"Because it took three years for one of the messengers to reach me," he said. "By then Jerusalem had fallen and another crusade had been called, but our King Richard was taking too long to raise the money to join it. Frederick Barbarossa, the Holy Roman Emperor, was already setting out, so I joined his troops. When I reached the East, I paid the ransom and Samson was freed."

"And then you and Sir Samson fought alongside the emperor as he sought to retrieve Jerusalem from the hands of the infidel. He failed, but you returned to England the Hero of Iconium." She smiled faintly as his brows shot up this time. "Sir Fithian told me that part."

"The title is exaggerated. I rescued a few of our knights who found themselves surrounded by the enemy and in danger of losing their heads to the Saracens' dreaded scimitars."

"A few? Fithian said you saved twenty men with your bravery and quick thinking. Twenty men who would be dead today, were it not for you."

Gerolt may have embellished the story to entertain Rauffe as a boy, but in truth, the title embarrassed him. "I was lucky in my aim. I struck one man down with a spear to his back, then startled the rest by riding recklessly into their midst. Sam was one of the encircled knights in danger of losing his head. I had not ridden thousands of miles to ransom him simply to see him die at the hands of an infidel. I disarmed three of the enemy, and each time I did, I flung their scimitars to one of our men. It was not long before Sam caught on to the trick and called it out to the others. They all quickly followed my lead, using our enemy's own weapons to drive them back, tossing each abandoned scimitar to another of our men, until our would-be executioners were outnumbered. They called me 'rescuer' and 'hero,' and the latter stuck, for all it took the entire lot of us to defeat them."

He stared at the hollyhocks that sprang up near the bench, but their brilliant colors faded, replaced by the vision of a young boy's eager face. "There was a time Rauffe could not beg me enough to repeat that story to him, his eyes round and shining like he possessed some great figure of legend for a father. But now all he does is slump about and growl and mutter when I speak to him. His health has been precarious since birth, but he has clung stubbornly to life for seventeen years. Everything I am wants to see him thrive and grow into a strong, healthy, happy young man, but I worry for him. Aveline always knew how to care for him. I have been at a loss to know how to deal with him."

He must give Aveline her due. If Gerolt had thought her scrupulous care of Rauffe bordered on overbearing at times, she had nonetheless successfully dragged him through all the ills of childhood.

"Perhaps I can help," Cassandry said after a moment. "I can do nothing about Rauffe's moods, of course, but I know how to oversee a kitchen. I fed my husband's household for twenty-four years and nursed some of his aging knights through their last days. If you would like me to examine Rauffe's diet, I should be happy to offer you what advice I can."

Gerolt was confident Aveline's judgment continued to be observed by his kitchen staff, but he confessed it would bring him comfort to have Cassandry second his late wife's decisions. Perhaps Aveline's observant eye had missed something? Perhaps

Cassandry would have some new, fresh idea that would bolster Rauffe's strength?

"Thank you," he said, hoping she could see the gratitude in his eyes. "I should welcome that."

She returned his gaze so long it made his heart skip, then she glanced away, down the path that led to the fountain.

"I am surprised they have been gone so long," she said. "Shall we see what they are about?"

Gerolt agreed, hoping the young couple's absence portended an amicable understanding between them. But as he and Cassandry drew near enough to hear the playful splashing of the fountain, he heard Rauffe's voice sound with surprising clarity from around the curve in the path.

"Well, I do not want to marry you, either. 'Gliding incantations of mythic moonlight—'"

"Incarnations, not incantations. Mystic, not mythic. You are too cloddish to be a husband." A sharp crackle against the gravel accompanied Egelina's rebuke.

Cassandry froze midstep, dismay stark across her face as she muttered under her breath, "Egelina, you did *not* just stamp your foot at Lord Rauffe!"

"'Mythic, mystic,'" Rauffe retorted, "they are both equally absurd. It should drive me to distraction to have to listen to such foolery as that all day."

Horrified by his son's rudeness, Gerolt strode forward, rounding the corner with a snap on his lips. "Rauffe!"

Rauffe whirled away from Egelina, his shoulders immediately hunching defensively. "She started it. She called me boorish because I laughed when she compared the swans to incantations and mythic moonlight. What sort of woman talks like that?"

Egelina's foot slammed down in the gravel, repeating the crunch Gerolt had heard before he and Cassandry had joined the youthful pair. Egelina rounded on her mother, her eyes flashing blue fire.

"He has not a poetic bone in his body. I will not marry him. I do not care what either of you says." Her stormy gaze now engulfed Gerolt as well. "If you try to make me, I will make his life as miserable as I can, and I will hate you both forever!"

Gerolt caught the sob that burst from Egelina as she ran between him and Cassandry and fled from the gardens.

"You heard her," Rauffe said, his own face flushed and angry. "She means to torture me by spouting silly verses in my ears. As if I do not have enough headaches without listening to *that*." He stalked after Egelina with so much offended dignity that he forgot to slump his shoulders.

Cassandry threw Gerolt a pleading, apologetic look before hastening after her daughter.

Well, Gerolt thought, at least his fears of saddling Rauffe with a "dutiful wife" were clearly groundless.

Chapter 6

Wake up, Mamma!"

Cassandry blinked sleepily at Egelina's cry. When had she fallen asleep? She had heard the bells toll matins from the village church but admittedly remembered little after that.

The last week had been wretched. Cassandry had spent every night tossing with frustration. Egelina and Rauffe had glared at each other through every meal, after which Rauffe always retired with a headache. Cassandry had examined all the dishes served from the kitchen but so far had been unable to identify anything that might be influencing the boy's poor health. To her horror, during Rauffe's absences, Egelina flirted outrageously with Gerolt's knights. She even batted her long fair lashes at the redheaded squire whose name Cassandry could never recall. Where had she learned such behavior? Certainly not at Rengrave Castle among her father's gray-bearded knights!

Cassandry had been certain she would not sleep a wink after another tempestuous evening alternately scolding and attempting to cajole Egelina into repeating the betrothal vows. Egelina had wept and stormed and stamped her foot, then flung herself into bed and pulled the covers over her head without capitulating to her mother's demands.

But this time exhaustion from multiple nights of sleeplessness overwhelmed Cassandry as she burrowed deep into the covers, longing to escape into oblivion, and she dropped off as soon as she joined her daughter in the bed.

"Mamma!" An impatient hand shook her. "Sit up. Look what I found outside the door."

Cassandry inhaled the familiar fragrance, flooding her with memories and emotions. She heard his dear voice calling her Sparrow again, tumbling her for one precious moment back to a time of sweet safety. How nearly she had spilled out all the pain in her heart when his hand had closed over hers in the garden. The warmth behind the gratitude in his eyes had startled her, a warmth she'd seen in Antony's gaze and even in Sir Samson's, but never before in Gerolt's. It had ignited a little quiver, a tiny flame she had long since thought dead.

Fool. She jerked the covers over her still-closed eyes. *You are imagining things. This is Gerolt. He still sees you as a sister, as his little sparrow. Go back to sleep until you can wake up sane.*

Someone snatched the covers away.

"Mamma, you must wake up and look!"

Cassandry rubbed the sleep from her eyes and reluctantly sat up. Egelina set something in her lap. Cassandry gazed drowsily at the cluster of purple flowers. Her senses sharpened. She blinked away the mist. 'Twas not a bouquet but a wreath of periwinkle woven together with white sprays of sweet woodruff. Before she could stop herself, she lifted the wreath to smell again the fragrance of the woodruff.

"Where did you get this?" she asked her daughter.

"Someone left it outside our door, just like the seashell. Lora found it when she brought up our breakfast. You slept very late this morning, Mamma. I thought you should never wake up for me to show it to you."

Cassandry glanced over at the platter of half-eaten cheese and bread set on the table beside the wardrobe. She saw that Egelina already wore a loose-fitting tunic over her chemise and had braided her hair. Egelina took the wreath and placed it on Cassandry's head.

"Oh, it is so pretty! It will look so well with your spring-green gown. You must wear the wreath all day."

"Me?" Cassandry pulled the wreath from her head. "No one leaves a gift like this for a woman my age. When I discover who is behind this—" She swung her legs out of the bed. "You must stop flirting with Lord Gerolt's knights, Gelli. I heard you reciting your poetry to the birds in our garden at home. Some of your verses were a great deal too romantic. I do not know where you learned such nonsense." *Or how to flutter your lashes as coyly as you did at the red-haired squire.*

Egelina looked unabashed at the rebuke. "From the minstrel who sang for us at Christmas when I was ten, and the other one Papa invited to sing to me on my eleventh birthday. Papa said he came all the way from France. Not for my birthday, of course, but he happened to be traveling through England, and Papa heard him in the village. He came and sang such charming verses to me about love. You remember, Mamma."

Cassandry did, and she had not approved, though Antony had found their daughter's blushes amusing. She had clearly been right to frown on the minstrels. She also recalled Gerolt's spoken fear that Egelina might fall in love with one of his knights before she married Rauffe.

"You must be more careful," Cassandry said. "Men are prone to misinterpreting a woman's friendship." She thought bitterly of Sir Samson. "You are young and inexperienced, Gelli, so you must trust me in this. I know you are angry with Rauffe, but he *will* be your husband. No. I will hear no more protests. You must take care how you smile at other men, how you speak to them, even how long you allow them to hold your gaze. You may think it an innocent game, but it may quickly become more serious than you can anticipate. I will not have you humiliate yourself or Rauffe."

She slid out of the bed and padded across to the hearth in her bare feet.

"What are you doing?" Egelina sounded alarmed.

"I am going to throw this into the flames."

"No!" Egelina ran and grabbed the wreath out of her mother's hands. "You will do no such thing! Besides, it isn't for me, it's for you. You have an admirer."

Forty-year-old women did not have admirers. "Nay, Gelli, that is the most absurd thing you have said yet."

"'Tis not absurd. These are your favorite flowers, periwinkle and sweet woodruff. You know that mine are roses."

'Twas true. Whoever had plucked them had chosen Cassandry's favorite blooms. Her thoughts flew to the day in the garden when Sir Samson had gathered some periwinkle for her. Oh, surely he would not be such a fool as to press his unwelcome suit for Cassandry's hand right under Gerolt's nose?

No, she was certain he would not. Gerolt had promised he would not press her to marry again/ Sir Samson would not dare defy him, not when he was living under Gerolt's own roof, hoping to marry his daughter to Gerolt. 'Twas merely a coincidence that the flowers were the same. Or, more likely, a hope by some man unfamiliar with Egelina's preferences that her tastes might mirror her mother's. Sir Ingram and Sir Fithian surely remembered that Cassandry loved sweet woodruff and periwinkle, as would all the other knights their age. And it would not be difficult for a younger member of Gerolt's household to learn of it, even a red-haired squire.

Well, whoever he was would not have the satisfaction of seeing

Egelina demean herself by wearing his outrageous token in front of the youth she was destined to marry. Cassandry swept the wreath away from Egelina and tossed it into the fire.

A burst of fragrance like fresh mown hay burst from the hearth, ever so briefly throwing Cassandry back to her fourteenth year. She cut off the thought and caught her daughter by the shoulders.

"Gelli, do you know who sent you this?"

Egelina shook her head, staring into the flames with her full lower lip thrust out and looking as though she might burst into tears. Someone had most certainly caught her eye.

"Was it Sir Ingram? What did he say to you while you played at draughts yesterday?"

"Only a lot of foolishness. My hair is as spun gold. My eyes as blue as a midsummer sky. He was as extravagant as the minstrels who came to Rengrave Castle, only for some reason all his compliments rang silly. I think it is because he is so old."

Cassandry bristled a little. Sir Ingram was only a little younger than Gerolt. But that made him old enough to be Egelina's father, and Cassandry could well imagine that Egelina might have been embarrassed by Antony behaving so flamboyantly. To his credit, at least Antony had outgrown such affectations.

But because Egelina thought Sir Ingram silly did not mean Sir Ingram viewed himself the same. Or Sir Fithian or Sir Payne or Sir Tobias. And there were the younger knights too.

"What about Sir Owen?" Cassandry said. "Did he also flatter you? And Gelli, what were you thinking to encourage that redheaded squire?"

"His name is Garin. And I didn't encourage him to do anything. It is just that he blushes so easily. I never knew I could make someone blush just by smiling at him." She pulled away from her mother and flounced across the room to sit on the bed.

Cassandry tried to follow her, but the fragrance from the

burning wreath held her rooted by the hearth. The present fell away again as she remembered something else: the traitorous way her heart had thumped when Gerolt had adorned her head with the blossoms. She had loved Antony since she was old enough to realize what love was. She had thought they shared one soul, their spirits so attuned they could finish each others' verses when they sat together composing poetry. And yet there had been something about Gerolt's touch that day, and his smile, that for one baffling moment had prompted her to wonder if his kiss might taste as sweet as Antony's.

She thrust the memory away and firmly locked it back up where it belonged—in the past. All illusions of love had died long ago save for the bright, shining child on the bed now pulling apart her braid with harsh, jerking movements. Cassandry understood Egelina's reluctance to confess who in Gerolt's household had caught her attention. Cassandry's feelings for Antony had felt like a sacred secret before Gerolt had guessed them and confronted her with it over twenty-six years ago.

"Whoever it is, Gelli," Cassandry said, "you must tell him to cease. No more tokens. You are not free to accept them."

Egelina opened her mouth, her eyes sparking a clear protest. Cassandry crossed to the bed and closed her daughter's lips with a firm thrust of her finger beneath Egelina's chin.

"You will listen to me. You have no idea how dangerous this game can be. We do not yet know Lord Rauffe's temperament. I trust that his father has taught him to count his anger off"— although he did not appear to do so in the garden, but then, neither had Egelina when Cassandry had taught her the very same trick— "but it is possible he takes after his mother, who I never knew at all. The thing is, Gelli, that you must learn to be very careful and very wise and never do anything to provoke Lord Rauffe to jealousy."

"Jealousy?" Egelina jerked her chin away from her mother's

finger, her lip quivering dangerously. "Lord Rauffe can barely bring himself to look at me. I do not care what you say, or Lord Gerolt either, I *will* be a nun, I *will* learn to write, and then I shall spend the rest of my life scribbling down all the words in my head. I will never, *never* be content to let them all vanish away!"

She left the bed to grab up the comb that lay next to the platter of food, sat down on the red, padded stool, and dragged the comb through her hair in swift, angry strokes while she glared at her mother.

Cassandry suddenly wished her head replete with gray hairs so she might relieve her frustration by pulling them out by the fist-fuls. Whatever was she to do with this exasperating child? Had Cassandry been as vexing at this age? If so, how had Gerolt borne so patiently with her? She should be reassured by Egelina's continued refrain of desiring a nunnery, but whether an unsuited religious life or an unsuitable suitor, both spelled disaster for her daughter's future if Cassandry allowed either to go forward.

Wearing the shell had revealed nothing. She had impulsively thrown the flowers into the fire. Now she would have to talk to Gerolt. She had hoped to avoid raising the issue with him. As imperturbable as she had thought him growing up, she had once seen the end to his patience. One of his knights had become drunk, fallen into a tavern brawl, and ended up thrashing his dicing companion, the tavern keeper, and one of the serving wenches. Gerolt had circled the knight, looking him up and down, a gleam of scathing disappointment in his smoky gray eyes. He had no use for intemperate drunkards in his service, he'd said, his voice level and cold. He'd dismissed the knight to find service elsewhere. Except that Gerolt's reputation for shrewd judgment of men was such that word of the knight's dismissal spread quickly and he had found himself scorned by other barons who might have employed him. Cassandry heard he had ultimately turned mercenary, gone to fight in France, and been struck down before his thirtieth year.

She did not wish to bring that same cold condemnation down upon any of the knights she remembered with fondness, but she could not allow this to continue. Surely a brisk rebuke by Gerolt would be enough to stop it. For if it continued, Cassandry had little doubt that Gerolt would feel obligated to dismiss the offender from his service. However he had spoken of Egelina falling in love with one of his knights, she did not believe for one moment that Gerolt would stand idly by and allow his son to be humiliated, as Rauffe would surely be if Egelina spurned him once they were truly betrothed.

Egelina flipped her hair over the opposite shoulder and resumed coming out her curls, rather too pointedly now looking way from her mother.

"Have you finished eating?" Cassandry asked.

"Yes. And you had better do so as well, before Lora comes back to take the tray away."

As though the maid would deprive Cassandry of her breakfast like some errant child. *I am not the one sitting pouting on the stool.* Though she was not particularly hungry, Cassandry nevertheless drank some of the watered wine and nibbled at a square of fresh, soft cheese. She knew she would need the sustenance. She had a feeling this was going to be a very long day.

Chapter 7

Egelina was still sulking about the wreath when Cassandry took her down to the kitchen.

"I do not *want* to prepare a dish for Rauffe. I am not—"

"—going to marry him," Cassandry finished for her. "It is not that simple, Gelli. But we will not argue about that again just now. You will marry someone someday—yes, my love, you will, for the nunnery remains out of the question. Your father always liked it when I prepared a special dish for him with my own hands. Your future husband—whoever he is—will be equally flattered that you made such an effort on his behalf."

Cassandry had discovered this truth quite by accident when she had been thirteen and suffering from a toothache. She had wandered into the kitchen seeking some remedy and became so entranced by the cook's preparation of an elderflower-cheese pie that she temporarily forgot her discomfort. The cook had succumbed to the young girl's curiosity and allowed her to assemble the dish herself, following the cook's instructions.

Cassandry had been surprised when, hours after Gerolt had dined with his knights, he had come to her chamber, where she sat curled up with a compress for her tooth, and thanked her for her thoughtfulness.

Having discovered a way to please him, she frequently visited the kitchen thereafter, learning all his favorite dishes, and when Antony had begun to court her, she had learned his, too. Having a special dish of her own making delivered to the dinner table had reestablished peace between her and her husband a few times after some particularly bitter quarrels between them. It was a trick worth trying to teach Egelina.

"My daughter and I would like to prepare a special treat for Lord Rauffe," Cassandry said to the cook. She was not the same woman Cassandry remembered from her girlhood. "Can you tell us a few of the dishes he favors?"

The cook dipped a respectful curtsy but replied, "You must know, my lady, that the boy's health is most delicate. His mother only allowed him to partake of mild dishes, such as barley soup, hen in unseasoned wine broth, and chicken in rosewater sauce."

Cassandry subdued the impulse to wrinkle her nose at this bland fare.

"I saw him look longingly at a dish of venison last night," Egelina said, sounding as though she begrudged confessing the observation.

The cook shook her head. "Lady Aveline said venison was too rich for him."

In Cassandry's opinion, a bit of good red meat might be just the thing to strengthen Rauffe's tepid blood, but she hesitated to counteract Gerolt's late wife's orders.

The cook added, "My lord is allowed to end his meal with a bryndon cake without the pepper, cloves, and mace. But my Lady Aveline always compensated for the spices with a double serving of nuts in the cake."

Cassandry realized just how little she knew of Lady Aveline. Had she prepared elderflower-cheese pies and pear comfits for

Gerolt as well as bryndon cakes for Rauffe? Had Aveline been beautiful? Kind? Had her love filled even the corner of Gerolt's heart that Cassandry had once thought belonged to her alone? *Antony never touched the corner where you dwelt in mine.*

She tried to push the thought away. It felt disloyal, no matter how dark a shambles her marriage had become.

"You taught me to make bryndon cakes, Mamma," Egelina said. "You always let me add extra honey, even though Papa said it made them too sweet. Rauffe made a wretched face when they were served to him yesterday and muttered some complaint that I could not quite catch. Perhaps he would like them if they were sweeter, too?"

"That is a splendid suggestion," Cassandry said, quick to encourage any generous thought that might pass through her daughter's mind concerning Rauffe. "We will begin by simmering some figs in wine."

"I know," Egelina said with a touch of impatience. "Then add the honey and bring it all to a boil. I remember how to do it, Mamma."

Egelina turned to the cook and began issuing instructions on the ingredients she would need for the sauce and dough, along with a bowl to assemble the latter and a pan to fry the thinly sliced cakes.

The cook looked surprised. "You mean to fry them yourself, my lady?"

"Yes, of course," Egelina replied.

"But my Lady Aveline never stepped foot in the kitchen or told me how to do my work." Surprise turned swiftly to affront.

Her words surprised Cassandry. Aveline had managed the kitchen from a distance? She spoke to soothe the cook's feelings. "It is just a little treat my daughter wishes to prepare for Lord Rauffe. We will have the server state clearly that it was made by my daughter when it is set before him. Any blame for Lord Rauffe's dislike will fall on her rather than you."

Egelina's face quirked as though offended at the suggestion that Rauffe might dislike her cakes. The cook stood in no position to deny a woman of Cassandry's rank, so she nodded, albeit curtly, and began gathering the ingredients. Cassandry watched silently for several minutes while Egelina simmered the figs, boiled the extra honey and wine, then added saffron, dates, currents, and then stirred in the figs.

Reassured by her daughter's ease with the recipe, Cassandry moved deeper into the room. What had Gerolt said? "I cannot remember to restore the spices in the kitchen." Sure enough, when she came to the spice shelf, she found the ginger and pepper woefully low and the cinnamon Gerolt loved in his dishes completely depleted. One day Egelina would be responsible for keeping track of such inventories, but for now it was a small service Cassandry could perform on her behalf. She wandered about the kitchen making mental notes of other low or missing items that needed to be purchased. 'Twas a shame the staff had proven so irresponsible since the death of their mistress.

"You cannot leave out the nuts, my lady," the cook objected from the other side of the kitchen. "Lady Aveline always insisted upon them."

Cassandry turned to see how her daughter would handle the rebuke. She would be mistress of this kitchen when she was wed and must not allow herself to be intimidated by the servants.

"But I do not think Rauffe likes them," Egelina said. "I saw him trying to pick them out at dinner yesterday, but you chopped them so fine he finally gave up."

"Nonsense," the cook scoffed. "Almonds are his favorite. Lady Aveline always said so."

A heap of almonds sat near the cutting board. The cook picked up the knife Egelina had used to cut the fruit and began swiftly chopping the nuts, then gathered them in her hand.

"I tell you, he does not like them," Egelina repeated and reached out to block their addition to the sauce.

The cook stood bristling for a moment, then slowly began to lower the fist that cupped the nuts.

"No doubt your daughter means to be helpful," a male voice spoke from behind Cassandry, "but Emma Cook is quite right."

Cassandry turned to see that Sir Samson had entered the kitchen.

"Lady Aveline took the greatest care with her son's health," he said. "If she thought nuts did him good, then we ought not to tamper with her prescription, don't you think?"

Cassandry could not blame Egelina for wilting in defeat at these words. It was one thing to contradict a servant, quite another a knight of Sir Samson's age. Egelina dropped her hand, and the cook tossed the nuts into the bubbling sauce. The sight made Cassandry cross. What was he doing in the kitchen, anyway?

"May we speak for a moment?" he asked.

Cassandry glanced again at her daughter, but Egelina had already handed the cook a spoon and instructed her to stir the sauce while Egelina began work on the cakes. Having won her victory with the nuts, the cook looked in a mood to cooperate with better grace. Cassandry drew Sir Samson back over to the spice shelf, far enough away that they could converse out of Egelina's hearing while still keeping the young woman in view.

"Gerolt sent me to find you," Sir Samson said. "I had forgotten how much time you used to spend in the kitchen until your maid told me to look for you here."

"I offered to review Rauffe's diet. Gerolt is understandably troubled that his son's health fails to improve."

Sir Samson's brows rose. "Have you found aught amiss with the food?"

"It seems rather bland. He must find the dishes served to him terribly dull. But no," she confessed, "I see no harm in Lady Aveline's choices for him."

Sir Samson allowed his gaze to rest on Egelina for a moment. "Gerolt told me of the trick your daughter played at the betrothal."

Cassandry's face warmed. "Has he told the entire castle?"

"Nay, he has too much regard for your feelings for that. But I overheard your daughter telling Rauffe that they were not truly betrothed when I took him his cloak in the garden. I asked Gerolt about it. You must know that he and I have never held secrets from one another."

She did know it. As long as she could remember, Samson had been Gerolt's closest friend, nay, more like a brother. And yet—

"You've kept one secret from him, Sir Samson. And it is for the love I know he bears you that I have kept it all these years, too."

His blue eyes glinted into hers. "Sometimes I wonder what he would do if he knew. Do you suppose he would sever me from his affection? Or would he sever you?"

Cassandry caught a shocked breath. It had never occurred to her that Gerolt could doubt her word in anything. But she saw in a flash the threat in Sir Samson's words. She may have been Gerolt's ward, but he had known Samson much longer—through all his boyhood years, through his adolescence, and through their shared manhood. They had traveled through distant countries together before their knighthoods, and when Samson's freedom had been at stake, Gerolt had journeyed all the way to the East, paid a fortune, and even risked his life for Samson. No, all the fondness Gerolt had shown her could not compete with that, especially when she was certain Samson would twist his actions to reflect poorly not on himself, but on her.

Gerolt could not dismiss her as he had the drunken knight. She would be mother to his heir's wife. But he could stare at her with that same cold look of disappointment in his eyes, and the vision of that made everything within her shrink. It should not matter what he thought of her. She meant to put the world and all its hurt behind her. And yet she prayed the prayer of a worldly coward. *Let Samson say what he will of me. Let him make Gerolt think the worst. But please, kind heaven, let him do it after I am gone, and let me never, never know!*

Sir Samson clasped his hands behind his back and rocked gently on his heels. "Gerolt asked me to consult with you on the festivities to follow dinner," he said, smoothly shifting the subject to his original mission. "He fancies a bit of dancing might throw the young couple together and give them a better opportunity to become acquainted with one another before he broaches the subject of betrothal again. I confess I have my doubts that Rauffe will live long enough to complete a marriage, much less sire a son. If you truly care for Gerolt, my lady—and I have full confidence that you do—you will encourage him to marry again. My daughter, Marion, would make him an excellent wife."

Cassandry had not missed the frequent glowing looks Lady Marion sent Gerolt during dinner every day. The young woman's face radiated with so much gaiety that sometimes Cassandry felt her heart twinge for the days when she too had felt so alive. Now all the energy she could drag from the depths of her numbness was spent quarreling with Egelina. Cassandry had wondered more than once if Gerolt gazed longingly back at Marion when Cassandry was too distracted with Egelina and Rauffe to notice.

It was none of her concern, she told herself. But Rauffe's health was.

"Rauffe is painfully thin, it is true," she admitted, "but there is fire in his eyes. If we could only identify the exact nature of his ailment..."

"Do you think his parents have not tried to do so for seventeen years? The boy has been sickly and weak all his life. His headaches are but the most recent manifestation that his health continues to worsen rather than improve. I fear even his vision has become affected. Have you seen the way he dresses? Either in a jumble of colors such as would embarrass a court jester to wear, or in pallid yellow shades such as he is wearing today. And now he is laid out on his bed yet again. How Gerolt thinks to prop him up long enough to join us at dinner is beyond my guess. If I were you, my lady, I would reconsider your daughter's desire to join a nunnery."

Cassandry stared at him. "How do you know of that?"

"She shouted it at Rauffe in the garden. 'We are not betrothed and we never will be. I *will* be a nun no matter what my mother says!' She had her hands on her hips and was leaning forward to glare at Rauffe when I rounded the corner on them. Rauffe looked so relieved by my interruption that he actually thanked me for his cloak. Usually he goes about without it just to irk his father."

"It is merely a silly whim she has taken into her head," Cassandry said, annoyed that Egelina had betrayed a private family matter to Sir Samson, of all people. "She merely says it to spite me, because—well, never mind. Tell Gerolt I think dancing is a splendid idea. Egelina has not had many opportunities to dance, but I saw that she was instructed in the steps all the same."

"I left Gerolt giving instructions to his musicians, but whether Rauffe will be well enough to stand up in a few hours, much less dance . . ." Sir Samson trailed off with a shrug.

Cassandry had no intention of relying on hope as Sir Samson bowed to her and left the kitchen. As soon as he was gone, she flew from shelf to shelf and jar to jar. At least the herb garden had not been allowed to go to waste. Cassandry filled a basket with every remedy she knew.

Emma Cook left Egelina's side to protest. "Hyll the physician is likely with Lord Rauffe now. You will only be in the way, my lady."

Cassandry ignored her. "Take care not to burn the cakes," she said to Egelina.

"Yes, I know, Mamma." She sent her mother a curious look, but Cassandry only added that she would be back soon and hurried away to see just how ill her future son-in-law truly was.

Rauffe lay in a darkened chamber, moaning upon his bed. Cassandry could make out little of the man who hovered over him other than that he was thin and held something in his hand.

"Just one more sip, my lord. Lady Aveline always knew what was best."

"I will be sick if I drink any more." Rauffe clapped a hand over his mouth to block what now showed clearly as a goblet in the light that slipped into the room behind Cassandry.

The man turned, looking startled by her footsteps. The same light that revealed the goblet glistened against a black, drooping mustache that ran down either side of his mouth and a small tuft of beard on his chin.

"I have come to see how he is," she said, "and discover if there is anything I can do to help. I am Lady Cassandry," she added lest he think her a servant and try to dismiss her.

"That is kind of you, my lady"—his voice carried a mournful rumble—"but unnecessary. Lady Aveline left strict instructions for her son's care."

"Lady Aveline's instructions? But are you not the physician, then?"

"Indeed I am, and we were always perfectly agreed in the best course of treatment for my lord."

"I won't drink any more of that," Rauffe muttered weakly from the bed. "Go away and leave me to my misery."

"Now, my lord, you know that your lady mother chose me to watch over you when you are ill."

"Go away—and take that dreck with you!" Rauffe groaned

again as though the exclamation had come at a heavy cost to his strength, rolled over on his stomach, and buried his face against the pillow.

"Pray, sir, go," Cassandry urged. "I have brought a few herbs that may bring him relief."

She could fairly feel the physician's glower in the darkness. "Forgive me, my lady, but I cannot—"

"That was not a request."

The physician thumped the goblet down so hard on the table beside the bed that Rauffe winced and moaned. *Physician, indeed! Prideful, insensitive fellow.* And apparently incompetent as well, if Rauffe remained so ill after his ministrations that the poor boy still sprawled prostrate in his bed.

"Please light a candle before you go," she bade the physician as he reached the door, "and set it over there in the corner so the light does not make his headache worse."

She must have some means of discerning one herb from another in the murky chamber.

When the man had done as she'd asked and was gone, she sat down on the side of the bed. It felt as natural to reach out a hand to lightly stroke the back of Rauffe's hair as it would to have stroked Egelina's.

"Just try to lie still," she said softly, "and breathe deeply. Nay, do not gasp like that. Just draw in a long, slow breath. There, now, let it out again. Now draw another . . ."

Rauffe obeyed, loudly and gulpingly at first. She felt his body shaking and feared he might be more ill than she had brought the means to address.

"Are . . . are you . . . g-going to t-tell Egelina . . . how p-pathetic I am?"

His shoulders shook again. Cassandry recognized the trembling tones—she had heard them too often in Egelina's voice. He was weeping, undoubtedly shamed to be caught in what he must feel a humiliating display for the young man he was striving to be.

"Of course not," she said. "I have seen men older than you cry with the pain you are suffering. Sir Patrick, my husband's steward, suffers such headaches whenever the weather changes. Do you think that might be what brings on yours as well?"

Rauffe rolled his head back and forth carefully against the pillow, as if wary of aggravating his own pain. "I have them . . . nearly every day. Sometimes they come on . . . after I go to bed at night and last till morning. I nearly always . . . have one . . . after dinner. They say . . . it is because . . . my constitution has always been weak . . . and because I am a feeble, worthless excuse for an heir."

This time he sobbed outright, though he tried to muffle it quickly by pulling the pillow tightly against his mouth.

Cassandry gasped in the darkness. "Who would dare say such a thing as that to you? Surely not your father." She could never believe such a thing from Gerolt.

Again Rauffe made a careful, negating motion with his head. "Not Father—though I am sure he thinks it."

"Nonsense," Cassandry said. "Your father is concerned for you, nothing more. Here, roll over and let us try some of these remedies I brought to see if they will ease your suffering."

After a few moments, he rolled slowly onto his back once more.

"My maid said the lavender-scented pillow she brought you gave you some relief yesterday. Would you like to try it again?"

"Anything, if it will stop this horrid pain."

His voice sounded thin and stretched out, as though he were reaching the limits of his endurance. She brushed a hand to his forehead, just to reassure herself that the headache did not stem from a fever, and was relieved to find his brow cool.

"Where did you put the pillow?"

"Hyll threw it out," Rauffe muttered. "He said Mamma would not approve. She always said that if I were to be a man someday, I must learn to ignore the pain—but I have tried, and I cannot."

"Of course you cannot." What foolishness! She could hunt about in the dark for a stray bit of cloth to make a new pillow, or she could tear a strip from her chemise to create a pouch for the lavender and rosemary petals she had brought from the kitchen. It was quicker to do the latter. She did so, tied the ends of the cloth together to hold in the petals, and laid the makeshift pouch across Rauffe's brow. "Lie still now, and just breathe in the fragrance. Slowly again. In . . . out . . . in . . ."

She waited patiently for the aromatic petals to take effect. After some time of listening to his slow, steadying breathing, she crossed the chamber to crack open the shutter just enough to try to judge the time.

"I do not think you will be well enough for dinner." Years of attempting to placate a volatile husband had taught her to conceal her disappointment, however strong, when she spoke. "I will explain to your father—"

"No!" Rauffe swung into a sitting position, then immediately dropped his head into his hands with a muffled groan.

"I assure you he'll not be angry," Cassandry said.

"I know he won't. He'll just be disappointed in me, which is even worse." Rauffe rubbed at his temples. "He has been ashamed of me ever since the headaches began. Mamma said so. She kept telling me that I must be a man so that he would be proud of me. I cannot bear it, Lady Cassandry. I wanted so much to be like him—the Hero of Iconium! But all I have done is humiliate him with this disgusting weakness I cannot overcome."

Cassandry was appalled. What sort of mother told her son his father was ashamed of him? Even Antony had never loosed his belittling tongue on Cassandry in front of Egelina. *He saved that for the endless hours of the night when we were alone in our bedchamber.*

She laid a hand on one of Rauffe's gaunt shoulders. "You misjudge your father. Perhaps you misunderstood your mother's words."

Surely that had been the case? There had been no sign of shame in Gerolt when he had spoken of Rauffe in the gardens, only worry and a man's helplessness in the face of his son's illness.

"I did not misunderstand," Rauffe muttered. "I heard her say it to Sir Samson when Papa brought him back from the East. 'A worthless, feeble excuse for an heir.' I never knew . . . I thought . . . I always thought she fussed so over me because she loved me— until then."

Cassandry jerked her hand away before it could tighten like a claw about Rauffe's shoulder. Shock held her speechless. Quarrels between husband and wife were one thing, but how could any mother say such a hurtful thing about her own child, even if she did not know he was listening?

"I will come to dinner." The rosemary and lavender must have eased Rauffe's pain to some degree, for though he spoke gruffly, his voice was more steady. "I am feeling better. Please do not tell Father I have been ill again."

Cassandry reached into her basket and pulled out a small linen towel she had knotted together at the corners. She untied the cloth and set it in Rauffe's hands.

"I will not tell him if you promise me you will eat this."

"What is it?" He sifted the contents through his fingers.

"Just a salad from the kitchen. Some borage leaves and parsley and sage, with some feverfew and pennyroyal leaves mixed in."

"Raw?" He sounded surprised. "Mamma always insisted that my greens be cooked."

Cassandry smiled. "I assure you it will not harm you to eat them thus. Raw feverfew and pennyroyal, like lavender, are helpful with headaches. While you eat that, I will return to the kitchen and make you some camomile tea to help you sleep."

"No tea. I will miss dinner if I sleep."

"Just for an hour," she assured him. "I will make an excuse to put dinner back that long without involving you. You will feel ever so much better when you awaken, and it will please your father to see you rested and refreshed, don't you think?"

"Well . . . my temples aren't throbbing as badly, but I still feel like a horse galloped over me. Father will know I have been sick again if he sees me now."

"Finish that," Cassandry said, "and I will bring up the tea."

Chapter 8

I am afraid dinner will be just a little late. I showed Egelina about your kitchen earlier and am afraid we distracted your kitchen staff."

Gerolt followed Cassandry as she swept up and down along the long tables in the hall, straightening the trenchers and spoons and knives. Aveline had kept all the eating utensils in perfect alignment too. He knew his household had become more casual after his wife had died and he'd dismissed her ladies, but he had not realized how haphazard the table settings had grown until he watched Cassandry whisk one after another into perfect order.

They were not completely alone. The pantler was setting out bread on a table near the door that led from the hall to the kitchen. The butler was giving instructions to the dispensers as to which wines to bring up from the cellar. Above the dais, a rebec, citole, and shawm were all being tuned to the soft trills of a trumpet and the subdued roll of a drum in the musicians' gallery.

"I am glad we have a few minutes to speak before your knights and vassals join us," she said. "There is something I must discuss with you."

Her tone suggested something serious. The noise from the musicians would keep any conversation between them private.

"What is it?" Gerolt asked.

She moved one of the goblets so that it would be in equal reach of the two diners who would share it, before turning to face him.

"I know you place absolute trust in the knights you surround yourself with, and I do not wish to accuse any of them unjustly, but . . . someone left a token at our door for Egelina this morning. Do . . . do you suppose it could have been Rauffe?"

"Rauffe, leave a token?" He laughed before he could stop himself. "You have seen him. He cannot string two words together to speak to a girl. I cannot imagine he would even know how to choose a token. When the minstrels sing in my hall of romance, Rauffe always nods off by the fire. What sort of token was it?"

She hesitated, then said, "Flowers. Just flowers." She moved on to neaten the next table setting. "Perhaps it was meant harmlessly. But she has never been around so many men; her head might be easily turned. Infatuation is not the same as love, and I am afraid at her age she is too young to know the difference."

You knew yourself in love with Antony at her age. But Gerolt agreed this was different. Cassandry had been flattered and indulged by all his men from the time she entered his household without her interpreting any of their actions as anything but friendship, save for Antony's. Egelina had only been at Lyonstoke Castle a little over a week and all his men were strangers to her. As was Rauffe. That was something he hoped tonight's entertainment would help to remedy.

"I have a few hot-blooded young knights and impulsive squires in my service. Perhaps one of them saw her cross her fingers at the betrothal and thought it gave him license to flirt with a pretty girl. I will look into it; you may set your mind at rest."

He took her hand, intending the gesture only as a promise of reassurance, but it instantly turned into something more for him. Oh, saints, how he longed to draw her to him, to pull her into his arms . . .

"Thank you," she murmured. "I should go change my gown and check on Egelina."

She dropped a curtsy and slipped away from him, vanishing up the stairs.

Gerolt's gaze lingered on his son's pale cheeks where he sat in glum silence next to Egelina. His eyelids drooped heavily, as though he had been roused prematurely from a deep sleep. As always, he picked lackadaisically at the unseasoned chicken set before him, eating no more than half a dozen small tidbits before pushing the rest away to sit in a lumpish collection at one edge of his trencher. Egelina sat as rigidly as Rauffe slouched. The few times they glanced at one another, there was naught but dislike in both their eyes.

Cassandry nibbled on a parsnip fritter. "He is looking better, do you not think?"

"Better than death warmed over, do you mean?" Gerolt speared his salt cod with his dining knife a little too forcefully.

"Oh, you must not jump to conclusions merely because he is pale. He is surely still angry with Egelina. She was terribly unkind to him in the gardens a week ago."

"I am his father, Cassandry. I know when he's been laid out cold with one of his headaches."

Gerolt saw Rauffe cast a narrow-eyed glance at him.

"Well, at least pretend you do not know," Cassandry said, lowering her voice. "He was hoping to conceal it from you. He is very anxious for your regard and believes his illness has made him a disappointment to you. He cannot help it if he gets headaches, you know."

"I have never said he could," Gerolt replied, surprised. "And I have never told him I am disappointed in him for doing so. Did he tell you I did?"

"No."

She paused and frowned a little. Gerolt stiffened, bracing for some absurd accusation his son had made and swiftly gathering a defense against it, but Cassandry offered nothing more, merely taking another bite of her fritter, followed by a sip of wine.

Gerolt returned to his salt cod. He slowly and methodically studied each of his knights and vassals as he ate. Which among them glanced a little too frequently at Egelina? Which ones were unguarded enough to smile at her outright? Sir Owen, the handsome young fool. Sir Ingram. Gerolt doubted that portended anything but one of his chivalrous gestures. He still fancied himself a splendid gallant, but he was no seducer. Sir Fithian. That surprised Gerolt. Fithian, of all his knights, had the most level head. Gerolt would sound him out later, nonetheless, as he would Sir Owen. Nor would he overlook Garin, the fiery haired squire who blushed at Egelina's word of thanks as he placed some braised stuffed beef on her trencher.

His scrutiny of the diners at last brought his gaze to Marion. She laughed at something her dining companion said, her face alight with animation. Gerolt had brought her and her brothers into his household after their mother died. In time, Gerolt had found advantageous positions for Samson's sons with two of his vassals. He had arranged Marion's marriage as well, and even paid her dowry from his own wealth. Aveline had attended to most of their care, for unlike when Cassandry had come into his ward, Gerolt had a wife to raise Sam's children.

"She is very lovely," Cassandry murmured from beside him.

Gerolt silently cursed that she had seen his gaze lingering on the young woman. "She was of an age with Fleur. They grew up almost as sisters. Marion is too young to remain long a widow. I should see about finding her a new husband."

"Yourself, perhaps?"

"That is a nonsensical daydream of Sam's. I am no more looking for another wife than you are another husband." He tried to imagine a future with the lovely, vivacious Marion, who clearly chose not to allow mourning to quench her light, but the only woman his heart quickened for was the quiet, sober, still-so-dear woman beside him.

At length, the squires who served the tables marched in bearing the sweet dishes that marked the end of the first course: strawberries in white custard sauce, pears in wine syrup, bread pudding with cherries . . .

"I am tired of bryndon cakes. Take them away."

Gerolt looked down the table to see Rauffe wave a bony hand at the squire who knelt before his place at the table.

"But, my lord," the squire said, "these were made by the Lady Egelina's own hands."

The glower on Rauffe's face smoothed out in surprise. "Is that true?" he asked Egelina.

Egelina blushed prettily and nodded. She slipped a glance at her mother before saying, "You did not seem to like them yesterday, so I added extra honey to these."

Rauffe used his spoon to scoop a few of the nuts out of the sauce, but from his sigh, Gerolt guessed they must be cut too fine for him to remove all of them.

"I told your cook you did not like nuts," Egelina added, "but she insisted on adding them anyway."

"Almonds were my mother's favorites," Rauffe replied. "She ate them at every meal and drank them ground up with saffron in her wine." He took another bite, chewed, and swallowed. "These are good. I like the extra honey."

Egelina gave a shy smile. "Perhaps you would like some of this braised beef as well?" She cut a slice off her own portion and placed it on Rauffe's trencher.

Gerolt regretted dousing the sparkle that sprang into Rauffe's eyes, but he nonetheless sharply cleared his throat to check his son's attack of the beef. Aveline had insisted red meat was too rich for Rauffe's blood. Women knew these things, especially mothers. No one had tended more assiduously to Rauffe's health than Aveline had. Whatever aloofness she and Gerolt had had in their marriage, Gerolt had to continue to trust in her judgment where their son was concerned. Had her diligence not sustained Rauffe for seventeen years?

A hand touched his arm. He glanced down into Cassandry's dark eyes.

"Let him eat it," she murmured. "It is only a little. He has scarcely touched anything else on his trencher all night."

"But Aveline always said—"

"And for you, my lady," a squire's voice broke in, "a custard tart with nutmeg and ginger and a generous serving of dates, just the way you like it."

He set a small golden-crusted tart on the table directly in front of Egelina.

"Oh!" Egelina said. Her formerly pink cheeks went red.

"Stay." Cassandry checked the squire when he would have bowed and moved away. "Who sent this tart to my daughter?"

Gerolt swept another glance over the diners, registering the truth a beat behind Cassandry's question. His household feasted on strawberries and pears and pudding, but the only tart in the hall sat before Egelina.

The squire looked flustered. "I do not know, my lady. The cook only said a request had been sent to the kitchen for a custard tart to be set before our lady guest."

"Whoever it was could not possibly have meant me," Egelina said. "Look! This tart is full of raisins as well as dates. I detest raisins as much as Rauffe detests nuts. But you love them, Mamma. This must be meant for you."

Egelina picked up the tart and plopped it down in front of Cassandry.

"That is nonsense, Gelli," Cassandry said. "Who would send *me* a tart?"

"You have an admirer, Mamma. The same one who sent you the wreath and the shell." Egelina gave a giggle, as though she found the thought a merry jest.

"Wreath?" Gerolt repeated.

Cassandry lowered her voice again. "The token I told you of. But that was left for Egelina."

"What sort of wreath?"

She hesitated before replying. "Periwinkle and sweet woodruff."

"Those are *your* favorites." Like the dates and raisins in the tart.

"It must be someone who knew me when I was a girl and guessed that Egelina should favor them, as I did. Gerolt, you cannot seriously think that any man would spare me a second glance at my age?"

He could far too easily think it, and did so. He narrowed his eyes, tightening his gaze as he looked yet again over the tables below the dais from one knight's face to another. He had assumed all the glances and smiles had been meant for Egelina. Might one of them have been directed at Cassandry instead? The squire's pronouncement must have attracted curiosity, for all of his vassals and knights were now staring at Cassandry and the tart.

"But perhaps it is best to pretend it is so," Cassandry murmured from beside him. "It is better than having my daughter made a spectacle of by one of your men." Then, more loudly to the squire, "Thank the cook, but return this to the kitchen. I cannot eat it."

"But, Mamma—"

"Hush, Egelina," Cassandry whispered. "You have drawn enough attention to this ill-judged indiscretion."

The scolding brought Gerolt's gaze back to the dais to view the pout of Egelina's full pink lips at her mother's rebuke. Egelina dropped her gaze to her trencher. Then he saw how Cassandry's eyes seemed to bore through the air directly in front of her before she followed her daughter's example and lowered her gaze. Gerolt shifted his own gaze to below the dais where Cassandry had so briefly focused. Surely it was mere coincidence that Samson sat just there?

"Did you send it?" Gerolt asked quietly as the musicians tuned their instruments for dancing.

Samson raised his brows. "Send what?"

"The tart to Cassandry. If you did, it displeased her mightily. I'll thank you not to embarrass her again."

They stood to the side with the rest of the company while servants cleared and removed the trestle tables to make room on the floor for the dancers.

"Ah," Samson murmured. "Or is it merely that you hope she was displeased because if you cannot have her yourself, you prefer that she remain as she is, a widow to the end of time?" He laid his hand on Gerolt's shoulder. "You cannot, you know. Have her. Even if she were not a hollow shell of the woman you remember, once the children are wed, it will be a sin to even want her, the mother of your daughter by marriage."

"I know that," Gerolt said curtly. The clamp of Samson's fingers had once comforted him. Now the gesture jarred.

From the flicker he caught in Samson's eye, his friend knew it. Samson dropped his hand, glancing away with one of those despondent looks that fell too frequently over his face since Gerolt had brought him back to England.

"Sam—"

Before Gerolt could soothe the hurt his defensiveness over Cassandry had caused, Samson said, "He is unlikely to make it to the altar, you know. Rauffe. It is impractical to place all your hopes on him. Look at him, already sitting a-slump in the corner with another headache coming on."

Gerolt followed the direction of Samson's gaze.

"The boy is useless to you. He will never make the husband you hope for, and Cassandry can never bear you another heir. I wish you would reconsider Marion. She is a good, obedient girl. The sons she bore her first husband are strong and healthy. She will bear you sons who are the same."

Gerolt bit back an irritable response, not wanting to offend his friend again, no matter how tiresome Samson's refrain had become.

He studied Rauffe, slumping on a bench pushed up along one side of the hall and said instead, "Did you see the way he ate the beef Lady Egelina shared with him? He wolfed it down as though he had not eaten in years. And the way he devoured the bryndon cakes—the sight gave me fresh hope before he began to droop again."

He paused as Cassandry appeared at his son's side with some sprig of greenery in her hand. She sat next to him, slid an arm around his hunched shoulders, and held the sprig beneath Rauffe's nose. Aveline had fluttered and hovered about him in his illnesses, but Gerolt had never once seen her embrace the boy as Cassandry was now.

"I will give it more time," he said. "Cassandry too is a mother. Perhaps she knows some tricks of healing Aveline was unfamiliar with."

Samson clicked his tongue disapprovingly, turning Gerolt's head back toward his friend.

"And what exactly did you hope to accomplish with the tart?" he asked. "Do you think to court her for yourself?"

Samson nonchalantly smoothed a hand down his sleeve. "She might not be as averse as you think, if I did. I always believed she and I might suit well."

Cassandry was a grown woman, more than capable of making her own choices, yet a coil of heat sprang through Gerolt at Samson's words. "She and Antony were made for each other from the first. She never spared you a glance, save as my friend. Three years and she still grieves for him. What have you to give her but this bitterness you brought back from the East?"

"Bitter? I? Because you left me to rot three years before you bestirred yourself to rescue me?"

Samson threw the complaint in Gerolt's face less frequently than he had during the first few months after his release from prison, but it still resurfaced from time to time. Gerolt counted to ten before he answered, forcing himself to remember that he still did not know all the details of Samson's ordeal between those prison walls.

"How many times must I tell you that I did not know? The first messengers you say you sent never reached me, and by the time one did, your captors had moved you. It took me time to raise the money for your ransom, time to travel to the East, and more time to track down your new location. I came for you, Sam, as soon as I could, and I saved your life again at Iconium. I held as true to our friendship as circumstance allowed me. Why you continue to hold this grudge—"

"There is no grudge. If there were, would I offer you my own daughter in marriage? Now, shall you dance with your future daughter-in-law, since Rauffe appears in no condition to take her hand?"

The dancers gathered in a circle for a familiar carole dance while the musicians played an introduction. Gerolt let go of his frustration with Samson. He started toward Egelina, but Sir Fithian reached her first. Egelina looked uncertain at the knight's invitation to partner her and cast a glance toward her mother for guidance, but Cassandry's attention was still fixed upon Rauffe. Gerolt caught Egelina's eye and gave an approving nod. Even if Sir Fithian harbored any inappropriate thoughts, which Gerolt could ill believe, he would scarcely act on it before the entire company. Egelina visibly relaxed, smiled, and allowed Sir Fithian to lead her into the circle that had formed in the center of the hall.

Gerolt glanced about at the other couples and discovered that all had found partners save for Marion. Much though he wished to pretend he had not seen her, courtesy forced him to ask her to dance with him. She moved through the steps competently enough to be able to converse with him as they joined hands and circled with the other dancers.

"You are well, my lady?" he inquired. "And your sons the same?"

"Oh yes," she answered, adding, "but it seems ever so strange to hear you call me 'my lady.' I hope you will call me Marion again. Returning to Lyonstoke, even just for Rauffe's betrothal, feels like coming home once more. Except, of course, that Fleur is not here."

The circle broke to allow each couple to turn together, hands laid palm to palm.

"It was heartbreaking to hear she had died," Marion continued. "But one cannot dwell in the past. I miss my husband, but my sons are full of mischief and energy. How can I mourn when they bring such happiness to my life?"

Gerolt caught sight of Egelina, her bright hair fiery gold in the light of the torches. He had seen Cassandry's mourning tempered by the fierceness of her love for her daughter. Perhaps that was why he himself clung so hard his to hope for Rauffe. To lose a second child after losing Fleur felt more than Gerolt could bear.

They rejoined the circle, skipping now to the left with the other dancers. Marion's dark braids, free of silvering threads, bounced in a manner that put him strongly in mind of another winsome lass who had danced more lightly, more gracefully, more buoyantly than the dexterous but somewhat heavier-footed young woman beside him.

How could he remember Cassandry's lithesome movements after all these years? Perhaps he did not. Perhaps he had fashioned memories out of the loneliness he had felt with Aveline.

Marion laughed beside him and threw him a twinkling glance. But he felt nothing as he danced with her other than a faint memory of fondness for her for Samson's sake. He did not need to marry again. Rauffe would wed Egelina and sire him a second heir. *He will. He must.* But as the circle turned him toward his slumping son, Gerolt felt the familiar panic constricting his heart.

When the dance ended, he handed Marion to Sir Owen before the young knight could whisk Egelina into the next circle. That left Sir Ingram bowing over Egelina's fingers. His flourishing kiss lingered briefly enough to convince Gerolt no harm lay there, so he crossed the floor to join Rauffe and Cassandry. Gerolt knew his son could not help the fits that came upon him, though never having suffered a headache himself or even the sniffles more than twice in his life, he could not quite comprehend a pain as disabling as Rauffe's appeared to be.

It was not impatience that roughened his voice when he spoke but fear. He had lost Fleur, then Aveline. The thought that Rauffe's affliction might be so serious that he might lose Rauffe, too—

"How ill are you?" he asked his white-faced son. "Do you wish to go to bed?"

"No, I do not *wish* to," Rauffe said without lifting his head from his hands. "I *wish* my head did not pound fit to explode. I *wish* my stomach wasn't flopping about like a fish. I *wish* I were the strapping, martial son you wanted instead of a pathetic invalid. But wishes are a crutch used by children, not by men, Mamma always said. So I *will* dance with Egelina"—he unexpectedly surged to his feet—"and I will *not* faint and embarrass you."

He wobbled precariously but shook off his father's hand when Gerolt reached for his arm. Rauffe staggered a few steps toward the circle where Egelina was laughing and skipping sideways with her hands in Sir Ingram's, then froze, his cheeks tingeing green. He clapped his palm over his mouth, whirled, and dove for the stairs.

"Oh, dear," Cassandry murmured. "I thought we had mastered his headache before dinner. Something set him off again."

Gerolt suspiciously eyed the sprig in her hand. "Perhaps it was whatever you held under his nose."

"This?" She waved it beneath his nostrils. "It is merely pennyroyal."

He recognized the strong minty smell.

"It helped him earlier, that and a few other herbs I tried. I should go to the kitchen and gather some more."

Gerolt caught her arm when she started to move away. "Nay. Hyll will see to him. Who will attend Egelina if you disappear now? I will cut short the dancing, as we've rather lost the point of it without Rauffe, but let my guests enjoy another round or two first." He glanced at the dancers as the pace of the carole picked up, the tune more vigorous than the first one. Impulsively, he took Cassandry's fingers in his. "Let us join them."

"Dance? Oh, Gerolt, at my age?"

"Aye, and at mine. We are not ancient yet, Cassandry. If you have forgotten the steps, then I will guide you."

"I have not forgotten," she said, then bit her lip, her forehead wrinkling. "I have not danced for over twenty years. Antony would not want me to start again now."

Gerolt could not bear to see such despondency in a face that had once been so lively and merry. Before he could catch himself, he bent down to whisper in her ear, "Antony is not here to stop you."

He tugged Cassandry firmly over to the circle before she could protest again. It took a mere tap on Sir Ingram's shoulder to let them in. The entire circle paused while they took their places.

"Take my hand thus," he said, "and place your other in Sir Ingram's. We take two steps to the left with this tune, then three steps to the right, then—"

"I remember," she said shortly, then glanced at Sir Ingram's startled face and blushed. "Forgive me, Sir Ingram. It has been a very long time since I've danced, and Lord Gerolt thinks I no longer recall how. We will show him, you and I, that he is wrong. Trade places with me, Egelina."

Gerolt felt dismayed as Cassandry's fingers slid from his. Egelina lingered, hesitant at Sir Ingram's side until Cassandry repeated her name, then moved with wide, rather doubtful eyes to let Gerolt take her hand in place of her mother's. Egelina lacked her mother's height by several inches, causing Gerolt to feel like he loomed over her. From the disconcerted look on her face, Egelina suffered the same sensation. Was this why Rauffe hunched so when he stood or sat near her? Surely Egelina would grow a few more inches before they wed? Both her parents were tall. But her grandmother, Cassandry's mother, had been small, like Egelina.

Gerolt had never thought, until their exchange in the garden, how difficult Cassandry must have found it growing up without her mother. He had engaged older women to teach her such womanly tasks as stitchery, of course, but they had proven overly deferential to the young heiress, conceding a great many details of her rearing to him when they saw how she constantly sought his company. It was Gerolt who had taught her to dance, holding her little ten-year-old hands in his large twenty-year-old ones while showing her how to step and skip to this tune, how to turn beneath his arm and let him lift her by the waist to that one. Just as he had sat in her chamber while she ate her dinner and taught her the rules of etiquette for when she grew old enough to join his household in the hall. He had shown her how to shoot her hunting bow and introduced her to her first horse when she was loath to leave her childhood pony.

He had naively imagined she would always be under his roof, his to dance with in the open when she came of age, his companion on the dais when they dined, his when riding side by side through the valleys and hills that surrounded his castles, hunting and hawking together . . . always his own Cassandry.

But she had not chosen him. Once she laid eyes on Antony de Reymes, she had danced and dined and ridden and hunted only with him. And now . . . now that she was free, she still chose to dance with another.

"My lord?"

With effort he dragged his gaze away from Cassandry—her graceful steps in the circle, her smiles for Sir Ingram—and looked down at her blue-eyed daughter. "Yes, my lady?"

"I—"

She darted a wary glance at his height, but there was nothing he could do about it. He was not an immature boy to hunch his shoulders in an absurd attempt to appear shorter than he was.

Egelina blinked twice, then appeared to attempt to summon some courage. "I must apologize for the way I spoke to Rauffe in the garden. It was unkind of me, no matter how provoking he was."

Gerolt's lips twitched a little at this rather artless admission. "Did your mother tell you to apologize?"

She blushed. "Yes," she confessed. "But she was right. There is never an excuse to be unkind. And . . . and I should not have said I hate you and Mamma for making me marry your son. It is not *your* fault we are so ill suited. Did—did she tell you about my crossed fingers?"

He nodded.

"I am meant for a nunnery, you see," Egelina said, her gaze dropping shyly. "Mamma is against it, but I am determined to hold out firm. So it is not that I truly dislike your son that I cannot marry him. I suppose he cannot help it that he has no poetry in him."

She paused to execute a skillful little double step that preceded the circle revolving in the other direction. He wondered if this were her first dance from the bright satisfaction that flooded her face.

"And I think you should let him eat beef," she added, presumably referring to Rauffe again. "And tell your cook to put extra honey in his bryndon cakes and leave out the nuts, for I can tell he does not like them at all. But he and I are not at all well matched, and I cannot sin against my conscience, so will you please tell Mamma she should let me join the nunnery?"

"Why do you wish to be a nun?" Cassandry was right; from what he had observed of Egelina thus far, she was far from such a holy calling. She had eaten the various dishes served her at dinner with entirely too much relish, glowed too much while dancing, and, despite her apology, possessed too temperamental a nature to bend easily to the austere life of a nun.

"So that I may learn to write, of course!"

Gerolt remembered his conversation in the garden with Cassandry on this subject. Her words had confused and stung him, but Egelina was not his daughter to raise. He said, "If your mother did not see fit to teach you, she must have had very good reasons. Perhaps you should trust her to know what is best."

Egelina's blue eyes fluttered up at him, then she burst into a giggling fit. "Mamma teach me to write? Of course she could not.

She does not know how herself!" Gerolt knew he'd made a mistake in abruptly pulling his gaze away from hers to stare at the center of the circle when she added in a quavering voice, "D-does she?"

He looked down at her again in time to see her send a furious look past Sir Ingram at her mother, but Cassandry was conversing with the knight as they danced as old friends and clearly missed her daughter's glare. Gerolt half feared a tantrum from the storm in Egelina's eyes, but she finished the dance with him, albeit in a rather frigid silence. But no sooner did the music draw to a close than she shook her hands free of his and swept directly in front of her mother.

"How *could* you?" Egelina hissed. "I will never, ever forgive you for this!"

She left her mother standing with utter befuddlement on her face, stiffly crossed the hall to the staircase, then ascended at an undignified run, leaving a sob floating on the air in her wake.

Chapter 9

Cassandry pulled her astonished gaze away from her fleeing daughter to demand of Gerolt, "What did you say to her?"

Instead of answering, Gerolt turned toward the dancers, half of whom were staring at the stairs, the other half at him and Cassandry.

"You must forgive the Lady Egelina," he said smoothly. "This was her first dance, and she was overcome by the heat. She has only gone to her chambers to rest. Let us have one more carole, and then we will dismiss our good musicians to retire as well." He lowered his voice again so that only Cassandry could hear. "And you will dance too, this time with me. It will calm everyone's alarm and curiosity. Your daughter will be the better for some time to cool her temper."

Cassandry knew that much was true. And she preferred to be armed with what offense she had supposedly committed before she faced Egelina again.

She joined him in the circle. Her free hand took Sir Fithian's, who danced with Samson's daughter, Marion, on his other side. Cassandry could not help admiring the young woman's dark, still-glossy braids. Comely and slim, Marion could warm any man's heart with her smile. Would she make Gerolt happy? If so, Cassandry ought to encourage the match regardless of Gerolt's spoken reluctance and the hollow way the thought made her chest feel. Men needed wives. Young, cheerful wives.

She allowed Gerolt to turn her slowly under his arm at the proper beat in the music, lead her three steps to the left in the circle, then set his hands at her waist to lift her off the floor. She almost forgot both Marion and Egelina as her fingertips brushed his wide shoulders, then slid down the muscles beneath his sleeves as he set her back on her feet. She had loved dancing once, with Antony, with Sir Ingram and Sir Payne, even with Sir Samson. But most of all with Gerolt. Antony had been too impetuous to keep time to the music. He liked to swing her too hard, laughing when she complained that he set her veil askew or twirled her until she was dizzy, which had been amusing only the first half dozen times. From her very first lesson at ten years old until their final dance on her wedding day, Gerolt had always guided her lightly through the steps, making her feel as graceful as a summer's breeze. That same litheness flowed through her now, flooding her with memories so poignant they almost brought tears to her eyes. *I should have stayed here with you where I was safe, where I was loved . . .*

As a sister. It was all Gerolt had ever seen her as, while she had been too young to envision him as anything but a brother. But Cassandry had learned another kind of love with Antony. To her dismay, a similar ember had stirred, faintly but undeniably, when she and Gerolt had walked in the gardens, then again when he had held her hand before dinner—and now.

"I am afraid I let it slip that you know how to read."

Cassandry had drifted so deeply into her thoughts that it took several minutes for Gerolt's words to penetrate the confusion swirling in her.

"In my defense," he continued, "you never specifically told me that she did not already know. I cannot be expected to help you conceal your secrets if you do not confide in me what they are." He spoke with a gentle chiding, the kind that meant "You can trust me with your troubles," and coaxed from her all her hidden thoughts and fears when she was a child.

But she was no longer a child, and her adult barriers now stood firm against his reproof.

"Why were you even speaking of such things?" she asked with a surge of vexation.

The rhythm of the tune quickened, and they moved sideways together with a swift hopping skip, both her hands clasped in his.

"Egelina apologized for saying she hated me in the garden."

He released Cassandry's left hand so that she could extend it to meet the other women's in the circle's center. They revolved around the circle with a slow marching step, the women's colorful gowns flowing like petals fanning out from a flower's disk. Or so Gerolt had described the step pattern when he had taught it to Cassandry so many years ago.

"She did so very prettily," he continued. "You would have been quite pleased with her."

"I do not see how that led to the topic of—"

He held up a finger on his free hand, curbing her impatience.

"She then proceeded to explain to me, again very prettily, why she could not marry my son. She said she was meant for a convent, so I asked her why she wished to be a nun—"

"I see." This time it was Cassandry who cut *him* off. When the music changed, she nearly snapped her hand away from the other women's she was so annoyed. "Now that she knows, she will plague me to death to teach her."

"Why haven't you?" Their hands came together again as the circle reversed direction. "You said it is knowledge unfit for a woman, but I witnessed no harm in it with you. You and Antony were always exchanging love notes filled with poetry, as I recall.

You told me it bound your hearts together more tightly than all the words of spoken love that vanished away like mist in the air."

"Poetry. Folderol better left to minstrels and jongleurs. I was young. I was foolish. I—"

"You were in love."

She bit her lip.

"I had never seen a lass more smitten than you or a youth more smitten with a lass than Antony."

Smitten. Infatuated. Besotted. Antony had consumed her every thought. And then he had consumed her.

"You should not have encouraged it, Gerolt."

The music changed again. Their arms encircled one another's waists while Gerolt's free arm arched over his head and hers spanned out again, this time into empty air. They spun to the tune together, a hop, a pointed toe, a hop, another pointed toe . . .

"You needed no encouragement, Cassandry."

A husky note stole into his voice. She glanced up into his eyes to try to decipher what had caused it and glimpsed something sober and sad before he blinked and it vanished.

A hop, a pointed toe, a hop . . .

"Exactly," she said. "What did I know of men or love? You were my guardian, my brother. You were supposed to have a care for me. Why did you not make Antony court me in the traditional way? With a matron or maid to sit between us, teaching us how to speak politely with one another, constraining our passion rather than letting us run together unhampered in your garden lost in silly, unrealistic dreams?"

"I was your guardian, aye, but not your brother." His rough tone startled her. "I did what I thought you wanted. Are you telling me you were not happy with him?"

How could she tell Gerolt that? How could she hurt him by telling him how badly he had failed her? Antony had cursed her, and belittled her, and humiliated her, and worse, he had cut her off from anyone who might have sustained her crumbling self-image. She had always trusted Gerolt to protect her, but when she had needed him most, he had been too lost in affairs of his own—his new wife—to come thundering after Cassandry to seek out the reason for her silence.

It was unreasonable to blame him. He had given her everything she had ever asked of him, including the means of the destruction of her marriage. How could he know? Of course he could not. And yet a quivering, wounded part of her could not forgive him for not knowing anyway.

Thankfully the music came to an end.

"I must go check on Rauffe," she said, "then try to make my peace with Egelina."

Gerolt caught her arm when she started to move away from him. "You have not answered my question."

Too many barbs suddenly clamored for freedom on the tip of her tongue. She dared not speak another word. She shook her head, pulled herself from his grasp, and swept wordlessly out of the hall.

Cassandry heard Gerolt's footsteps on the stairs behind her. It was all she could do not to snap over her shoulder at him to go away. She paused with her hand on the door to Rauffe's chamber and forced herself to meet Gerolt's gaze.

"He will not wish to see you," she said, hoping to deflect any suspicions she had roused during their dance.

"I am his father—" Gerolt broke off as she pursed her lips, then admitted, "No, he will not. But he is my son. I will linger here in the darkness of the doorway where he cannot see me. I need to know for myself how he fares, not content myself with some secondhand account. Not even from you, Cassandry."

She gave a curt nod and opened the door, but again he caught her arm.

"What did I say to anger you?" He spoke low, so that Rauffe might not hear.

It is not what you said, it is what you did—or did not do— twenty-two years ago.

"Nothing," she replied. "I am only anxious about Rauffe and Egelina. Please let me see how he fares."

His hand tightened around her arm for a moment, then dropped to his side. She slipped into the chamber, mindful that he lingered just outside the door and would be listening to every word that passed between her and Rauffe.

As before, Rauffe was not alone. Hyll the physician bent over his bed, his hand behind the youth's head, lifting it while he pressed a goblet to Rauffe's lips.

"Just one more sip, my lord. It will help you sleep."

"It will . . . s-set me to . . . r-retching again," Rauffe said on a moan. "T-take it away, or I'll soil that fine tunic of yours next."

The physician frowned as Cassandry joined him. Candles had been lit on the table next to the bed this time, allowing her to see the contents of Rauffe's supper in the chamber pot. She also observed that he had been stripped down to his smock.

"You may go, sir," Cassandry said. "I will attend him now." She held her breath for a moment, wondering if Gerolt would countermand her order.

The physician stiffened, as he had the previous time she had interrupted him. "Lady Aveline entrusted his care to me, my lady. She and I agreed completely upon his course of treatment. He would have expired years ago if not for me."

Ruffe plunged both hands into his hair. "I would . . . rather . . . expire than drink another d-drop of that. If I were dead, at least my head would stop pounding." He moaned again.

Cassandry felt a surge of the protective fire that had always roused her to Egelina's defense when every other interest in Cassandry's benumbed life failed to animate her. "If you call this 'caring for him,'" she told the physician, "you have done an abysmal job of it. Take this,"—she picked up the chamber pot and thrust it into his arms,—"and go."

Barely catching the pot before it clattered to the floor, he moved away with obvious reluctance, muttering under his breath but checking himself as he reached the open door. Cassandry tensed, again expecting Gerolt to protest and evict her instead of the physician, but he spoke not a word. He must have imparted some sort of communication, however, for the physician did not return.

She set the goblet on the table, her hand brushing against something that released its fragrance to her now that the chamber pot was gone. The makeshift pillow she had made from her chemise during her last visit.

"Here, let us try this again." She spoke soothingly, the way she did to Egelina whenever she was sick. Cassandry nudged Rauffe's hands away from his hair and draped the pillow over his brow. "Do you remember how I told you to breathe? Slowly . . . in . . . out . . . in . . . out . . ."

"It . . ." He inhaled, ". . . isn't . . ." exhaled, ". . . helping . . ." inhaled. "Oh, saints, I am going to be sick again."

He bolted upright, swung his legs over the side of the bed, but succumbed only to a series of dry heaves. She guessed he had nothing left in his stomach to lose. She sat down beside him and rubbed his back as the heaves ended on a gasping sob.

"It will be all right. Keep your head down . . . Aye, toward your knees like that. Now breathe again."

She looked up at the shadowed figure that had appeared in the doorway but signaled Gerolt to silence.

"I will send a servant for more pennyroyal and feverfew. They helped last time, did they not?"

"A-aye. B-but I do not think I c-can eat anything without b-being s-sick again."

"I saw some ginger in the kitchen." There had not been a lot. She hoped the cook had not used all of it for dinner.

"Cook m-makes gingerbread w-with it sometimes," Rauffe said, "b-but I am not allowed to have any."

Cassandry's toe twitched impatiently, sounding out a small *tap-tap* against the floor. She held increasingly little confidence in the efficacy of Lady Aveline's dietary strictures. "A little fresh ginger will help settle your stomach. Keep your head down and keep breathing while I send a servant to fetch some."

Before she could even rise from the bed, she saw Gerolt pivot and disappear from the doorway. She hoped he would also return with the feverfew and pennyroyal. She wished she had mentioned camomile tea before he had disappeared.

She left the bed so as not to rouse Rauffe's suspicions about her lingering. She moved to the table, picked up the goblet, and sniffed at the liquid. It smelled of wine and lemon balm. She sipped the wine and felt her tongue curl at its unexpectedly grainy texture.

"What is in this, do you think?" She murmured the query into the air, not expecting Rauffe to answer, but he tilted his head away from his hands to glance at the goblet before rolling his face back into his palms.

"Wine," he said in a muffled voice, "lemon balm, a little saffron, and ground almonds."

"Almonds? Why would anyone grind up almonds for wine?"

"It was Mamma's favorite food. She put them in everything. Soups, sauces, stews, sweets like bryndon cakes—she even made 'milk' out of it. And she drank some ground up in her wine every night before she went to bed."

From the way his words now flowed without a stammer, Cassandry assumed Rauffe's lowered head had eased the nausea somewhat.

"She said almonds were a symbol of divine favor. The staff of Aaron, Moses's brother, budded almonds by a miracle. Mamma credited almonds for her own good health and Father's, and insisted the divinity she believed lay in them would someday make me well. Only they never have, and I hate them. Oh!" He groaned and clutched his head as though a searing pain shot through it. "I should not have said that against something divine. No wonder I am sick all the time! I have lost God's grace, and—"

"Absurd boy." Cassandry sat down on the bed and rubbed his back again. "Of course you have not lost God's grace. Can you think of anything you did that might have brought your headache on this morning?" She was beginning to guess and pressed him when he shook his head. "Think hard. Did you eat or drink anything?"

He sat for a few moments in silence. "A little wine. Sir Owen brought it up. Father is always sending him to help me dress, which is just humiliating. I do not need a knight to help me choose my wardrobe, as if I were a child. He brought me a goblet of wine with him, from Hyll."

"With ground almonds?"

"Always with almonds. But I only sipped a little because it made me cross when Sir Owen wanted me to wear a wretched striped surcote when I wanted to wear the one with diamond shapes. I said he could not tell me what to do and I would wear what I wanted. But I did not want him to tell Father I was being petulant, so I agreed to drink a little of the wine to satisfy him. Then my head started to pound again, and the next thing I knew I was in bed with a raging pain, and Sir Owen called for Hyll, and Hyll tried to force more wine down my throat, even though my stomach was flopping, but then you came and sent him away and made everything better again."

He looked up from his hands, gazing into her face with eyes that might have shimmered from the candlelight—or from tears.

"Did you feel better during dinner?" she asked. "The way you picked at your food—"

"I am so *tired* of chicken," he said. "Mamma, and now Hyll, will not even let the kitchen salt it. It is the dullest food in the world, Lady Cassandry. My sister, Fleur, used to sneak me bits of beef and venison and salmon when I was little. I thought perhaps I really had died and woken up in heaven when Egelina gave me some of her beef. I have not tasted anything that heavenly in years, since Fleur left us to marry. And the bryndon cakes . . . I liked them so much more the way Egelina made them, with the extra honey. Except then—oh, I am so *pathetic*!"

"You began to feel ill again after you ate them, did you not?" It was all becoming clear now to Cassandry. "It is the almonds, Rauffe. They may be a blessing to other people, but they are a curse to you."

"Because I said I hated them."

She hid a smile at the panic in his voice. "I did not mean a real curse. My husband, Antony, could not eat any fish that came from the shell. It would make him break out in a terrible rash. Some foods do not agree with certain people. For you, it is almonds that bring on headaches. You must not eat them anymore."

"How am I to stop? They are in all the foods at the dinner table and in that wretched wine."

A shadow reappeared in the doorway. She looked at it and said very distinctly, "They will not be in your food anymore, nor will they be in your wine." She nudged him to lie back down. "There, now. The servant has come with relief for you. Close your eyes and try to rest for a moment."

Rauffe obeyed but with a little whimpering moan that attested to his continuing misery. She set the lavender pillow over his eyes, then crossed the floor, relieved when Gerolt placed a tray in her hands.

"Ginger," he said, "and a salad of feverfew and pennyroyal mixed with other greens I cannot remember—and camomile tea."

She looked into his shaded face, surprised. "How did you know?"

"I did not. But Emma Cook said you brought some up when Rauffe had a headache before dinner."

"Thank you." She did not know if he could see her smile against the darkness. "You heard what I said about the almonds?"

"Aye. I do not know if you are correct, but we will try it. No more almonds in any of Rauffe's food."

"Or in his wine."

"Heavens, no! Aveline tried to make me drink ground almonds in my wine, but I could not bear the gritty texture in my mouth. If I had known she was inflicting it on Rauffe I'd have stopped it, even if I hadn't known almonds made him ill."

"She thought she was helping him."

Cassandry hoped the words did not sound as grudging as they felt in her heart. She knew it was true, but how could Lady Aveline not have recognized what Cassandry had deduced in a week? Perhaps because she had been too busy dismissing her own son as "a worthless, feeble excuse for an heir."

"I must take this to Rauffe." Cassandry nodded at the tray.

Gerolt's fingers curled into her sleeve. "Aye, but when he has fallen asleep, come to me. We must talk."

Her heart hitched. Of what? She did not want to answer questions about her marriage, but she had been too careless during their dance, and she knew Gerolt had sniffed trouble there, as keenly as a hound sniffed out a fox.

"Not tonight. I must see to Egelina when I finish here."

His hand left her sleeve to cup her chin. He tilted her face up as if to try to read her eyes, but the torch down the passageway burned too far away, distanced, she guessed, so as not to aggravate Rauffe's sensitivity to light when his headaches came on. She trusted Gerolt could no more read her obscured expression than she could read his.

His thumb stretched up to lightly brush the hollow of her cheek, then his hand fell away. "Very well, in the morning, then." He turned to leave, then paused to look over his shoulder. "But, Cassandry, if you are wrong about the almonds—if Rauffe continues to fall ill—"

"Yes?" Did her voice shake as much as her body had at his touch?

"Well, we will talk of that tomorrow, too."

She leaned against the doorjamb as his footsteps faded down the passageway. An very unbrotherly glow warmed her skin where his thumb had skimmed along her cheek, while a very unsisterly wish stirred that it had lingered just a little longer.

Chapter 10

Cassandry did not know whether to interpret it as a good or bad sign that Egelina had left a candle burning for her. The flame cast a reddish glow over the golden lock that had strayed across Egelina's closed eyes where she lay curled in their bed. Cassandry stood a moment, gazing down on her sleeping daughter. Egelina looked so young, so innocent and vulnerable. All the passion and tantrums and tears when she was awake did not change the truth that she was still wonderful in so many ways. Cassandry remembered how mature she had thought herself at sixteen. Old enough to be a wife. In truth, she had been impulsive and naïve. Which was why she would protect Egelina at any cost from the mistakes of her own past.

Cassandry blew out the candle and slid beneath the bedclothes. A slit of moonlight fell across the pillows through a crack in the shutters. She reached from behind Egelina to brush the hair away from her daughter's eyes and realized Evelina's shallow breathing bespoke a continued wakefulness.

"Egelina—" she began, but Egelina cut her off with a bitter murmur.

"I knew you were insensitive and unfeeling, Mamma, but I did not know you were also a hypocrite."

Egelina shifted across the wide bed to escape her mother's touch and pulled the covers over her face.

Cassandry pressed a hand to her mouth, stung—and shamed. The bewildered yearning she had felt at Gerolt's touch shriveled in the hurt of her daughter's rejection. Curse him! Why had he not kept his tongue still? Now she would have to tell Egelina the cause of the rift between her parents. She rolled onto her back and stared into the darkness. Antony's voice roared again in her ear . . .

"What a fool I was. Thinking I was the only one. Believing you virtuous and faithful."

Cassandry's fingers wrapped around her throat, trying to choke off the painful lump that surged there. It only succeeded in slowing the flow of her attempted explanation, allowing Antony to rage on.

"'My heart's mate,' I called you. You fluttered those luscious lashes at me, and I fell at your feet. And all the while your perfidious heart beat a thousand different directions."

Nothing she had said had convinced him of her innocence, that she had always loved only him. He had passed beyond reasoning when he'd intercepted the letter. He had shouted her numb, his blue eyes flashing so wildly, his voice thundering so raucously in her ears, she felt as if she'd been swept away in the storm.

The words of the letter had been too passionate, too bold, suggesting responses she had never penned in the hopes of provoking her to surrender to the very infidelity she had stood so adamantly against.

"Tell him his harlot is no longer available for his pleasure."

She gasped as Antony's harshness bit up another notch. The

accusation thrust like a sword through her heart. "Antony! You know I came to you a maid."

He shook the intercepted letter in her face, the parchment crackling in his hand. "Not in your heart," he flung at her. "To think I have let him walk freely in my own hall, never suspecting your intent. How many more of these have there been?"

She had flinched when his fist soared toward her, bracing for a blow, but he'd only thrust the letter beneath her nose.

"Saints!" he swore. "I *have* been a fool. You have written to them all. 'Old friends,' you told me. Sir Samson, Sir Ingram, Sir Payne, and the others. Writing obscenities like this, luring them to visit you, to seduce you right under my nose."

"I have not!" She wiped her tears away on a fresh flood of anger. "I cannot help that they came with Gerolt when he used to visit us on his way to his manor in Hertfordshire."

Those visits had ceased four months ago, after Gerolt had married Lady Aveline Follet, but Cassandry had continued to correspond with him and many of his knights. She had always considered Samson as an innocent friend, like Sir Ingram and Sir Payne, until his letters had turned from affable to searing hot. But none of it was an excuse for Antony's lack of faith in her.

"How can you think . . . ? How dare you think I would betray you with any of them!"

He replied with a blasphemous oath, gripped her shoulders in a grasp that made her wince, and swiveled her toward the writing table he had permitted her to keep in her solar. The place she had composed such sweet poetry to him and sat, smiling, to read his replies—until Samson's wicked letters had begun arriving. She had burned every one of them in shock and indignation, but they had thrown her off balance. *Antony will understand your innocence if he learns of this*, she had told herself each time she'd held the parchment to the flame. But small, troubling memories broke through the glow of their marriage: Antony's ridiculous anger when Gerolt had woven a wreath for her hair. His absurd frowns whenever a dish she had prepared to please her guardian was set before Gerolt at the dinner table. The way he glowered when Gerolt acted upon his rights as her guardian to dance with her. All of it harmless. As though Gerolt could ever think of her as anything but a sister!

The indecent letters were not from Gerolt, it was true, but she had guessed aright that Antony would not limit his jealousy to her guardian alone.

"Here." He slapped a sheet of parchment down on the table, making Cassandry jump, along with the inkpot. "Take this"—he dipped a quill into the ink and thrust it into her hand— "and write what I bid you."

She traced out the first few words he dictated with a shaking hand, then stopped and exclaimed, "I will not write *that*. It makes me sound as guilty as he!"

"He could not have written such perverseness as that if you were not."

"Antony, I swear to you—" She started to rise, but he rammed her back into the chair so hard her teeth clattered together.

"Write."

Antony's glare lashed her so foreign in its rage, that she dared not refuse. Word by spirit-crushing word, she traced out the humiliating response he demanded to the unsolicited correspondence that had set her precious marriage on its fatal, teetering course.

Cassandry rolled over in the bed, her back to Egelina. How could she have any tears left to weep? She thought she had cried herself dry, but she felt them rolling down her face as she relived the memories she had sought to bury the day she had buried Antony. However humiliatingly done, it had been a relief to have finally quieted Samson. He had sent her no more correspondence after Antony had dictated that demeaning letter.

She had only minded a little when he'd cut her off from Gerolt's other friends as well, men who had treated her fondly but respectfully during her wardship. Antony had refused to let her correspond further with them and denied them hospitality thereafter at Rengrave Castle, as he once had freely granted them whenever they passed it on their way to some other destination.

Having eliminated these perceived threats from her past, Antony had slowly grown warm toward her again. But matters could not be quite the same between them as they had before Samson's letters, not after Antony had called her such foul names. The sweet verses they had exchanged from the beginning of their courtship ceased, both in written and spoken form. Struggle as she might, Cassandry found she could summon no more poetry from her depths. But their smiles gradually grew less strained. They even learned to laugh together again.

Then Antony had cast the second sword through her heart, one so shattering it sliced through her soul as well. Cassandry laced her hands together as though she might pray the memory away, but it pierced her like a blade's honed edge. She rolled her forehead against her knotted fingers and let the tears flow again.

"What is this?" Antony snatched the parchment from her hand. "I thought I had forbidden you to write to any of them."

"I have not," she said, surprised at his frown. "This one is to Gerolt. He is my guardian; you cannot possibly have meant to include him."

Antony's shoulders snapped stiffly in anger. To her horror, he crossed her solar and threw her letter into the fire.

She sprang up from her chair. "This is too much, Antony.

There was nothing you could object to in that letter. I asked only after Gerolt's health and that of Lady Aveline. And I thanked him for that pretty little mirror on a chain he sent me for Christmas." The one Antony had seized from her and thrown into the moat.

"*I* sent him thanks for that," Antony said with a scowl, "along with a request that he cease sending you any further gifts. That you have been writing to him behind my back! Doing so was against my express command, and you know it. Not that I expect the truth from you. You may make up whatever innocent tale you wish about its contents now that it's in the flames."

"Do not dare start that again," she said, her own temper flaring. "I have never betrayed you, whatever you may think. Not with Sir Samson, not with any of the men from Lyonstoke, and certainly not with Gerolt. You should be ashamed to think it. He knighted you with his own sword and gave you my hand when you asked it of him. You never had any reason to be jealous of him, and you have no reason now." She stretched her fingers to Antony, praying he would take them and cradle and kiss them tenderly as he had so often done through the first year and a half of their marriage. "Antony, I have never loved any man but you."

Antony's lips curled in a now familiar sneer. "Love . . . lust . . . do you even know the difference? If you think I have forgotten a single word of that vile letter Sir Samson sent you, you are not only contemptible, you are addled. You confessed you burned his letters to conceal them from me."

She dropped her hand, clenching her fingers into a ball. She had burned the letters in disgust, but before she could say so yet again, Antony threw a challenge at her.

"Have you burned Gerolt's as well?"

She knew her silence condemned her. But how could she tell Antony she had tied Gerolt's letters together with a crimson ribbon that had begun to fray from the many times she had unbound and rebound them? That she had read them over and over in the abyss of Antony's rejection, trying to forget the constant ache in her chest by reading about the simple normalcy of Gerolt's life in his familiar script? At first she had wanted to spill out all her heart's woes to Gerolt, as she had when she was a child. But it would have been disloyal to Antony and the marriage she still hoped to salvage once the crisis of Samson had passed. So she had kept her replies to Gerolt as innocuous as his were to her.

It had calmed her to see the strong strokes of his pen, to read of simple matters like the planting of the rye, the ripening of the fruit in his orchards, the repairing of the mill. She had even welcomed his praise of his new wife's deft touch with the servants. And she had wept for him when he had written of the stillborn death of his first son. But mostly she had simply devoured the letters again and again, hearing Gerolt's dear voice in every penned word, clinging to his continued presence in her life, comforted by the knowledge that if marriage to Antony ever crossed the bounds of bearing, Gerolt would be there to catch her as he had throughout her life.

"I told you to stop them all, Cassandry, and I meant *all*. You will write one last letter to Gerolt. You will say it is inappropriate of him to communicate with you further. You will tell him—"

"Inappropriate?" she repeated. "Gerolt? How much more absurd can you grow?"

A ruddy stain rose up in Antony's cheeks. "Tell him you have taken another lover, then," he snapped. "Say to him what you will, but the letters between you and Gerolt stop *now*."

She felt her own face flame, but she bit her tongue. After three years, Cassandry had finally found herself with child. The news had begun to bind her and Antony's hearts together again, so much so that she had begun to feel a long-buried flicker of hope inside. He had even been coolly courteous to Gerolt when he had surprised them with a visit three months ago on his way to his Hertfordshire manor. She had been so happy in her approaching motherhood that she knew she had given no sign that anything had ever been amiss in her marriage. How could Antony resume such horrid, hurtful accusations at a time like this?

"Now, Cassandry," he repeated, "or so help me, I will ride to Lyonstoke and confront him myself."

Antony swung toward the door when she hesitated.

"No, wait!" she cried. "You cannot think Gerolt will fight you?"

"Perhaps I will not need to make him. When I throw you and Sir Samson in his face, do you think Gerolt will still want you then?"

Her face went cold. "You would not tell him that lie."

But she saw in Antony's eyes that he still did not believe it was a lie, and in his outraged fury, she knew he would tell Gerolt all he believed and more. Gerolt would not believe him—he *could* not believe him! But it would lead to questions, the sort that might destroy his lifelong friendship with Samson. Whatever Samson had done to her and her marriage, Cassandry could not bear to be the cause of any heartache to Gerolt.

Still, she heard herself grind out between her teeth, "If you sever me from Gerolt, I will never forgive you."

"Go back to him, then, and take that brat with you. How do I know he has not visited you before when I was absent from the manor? How do I know that child is mine?"

She pressed the palm of her hand hard against her lips. She was going to be sick, and not with the child. "How can you do this? If you ever loved me, how can you treat me like this?"

"Prove that you still love *me*," he said, his gaze as relentless as his words. "If that child is mine, if you hope to heal our marriage, then sit at that table and write to Gerolt and make sure he knows you never want to hear from him again."

Shaking so hard she feared her knees might buckle, she walked to the desk and sank into the chair in which she had once found so much joy with her pen. She picked up the quill—Gerolt would know something was wrong if her words wobbled about like drunken men. She drew in breath after long, slow, aching breath until her fingers finally steadied. Then she dipped the tip into the inkpot and set it to the parchment.

But I will never forgive you for this.

After that, they had had peace again for a time. Antony had even held Cassandry in his arms as she wept after she'd sent the letter off with a messenger. Everything would be right between them again now, he'd promised. He had only needed to know that she loved him more than she had loved anyone else, including Gerolt. For weeks he'd grown tender and gentle with her again. He almost became her Antony once more. They began to rejoice together for the child she carried, to plan and to dream . . . until the pains had come too early. Much too suddenly, the child was gone. Antony withdrew into his own grief, and when she had most needed someone to comfort her, neither he nor Gerolt were there.

Cassandry listened dimly to the deepened breathing of Egelina, her precious, living child. How long since her daughter had fallen asleep? Cassandry had lost track of the time, hearing only dully the chime of the church bells through the night, tolling the passing of the hours. She tried to alter the course of her thoughts, to wrap them around Egelina and what she would say to her in the morning, but the night slipped away as the past continued to flood through her.

The return of Antony's churlish temper. The glares in which she saw his blame for the child's loss—though, surprisingly, he held his tongue on that matter. But it lashed her enough on other ones. She smiled too much at the young knights of his household. Useless to protest she only meant to be kind. One by one he'd turned the younger men out of his service until only his gray-headed knights remained.

"You dress to seduce," he said with a glower whenever she wore a color that flattered her.

"You dress like a hag," he told her when she resigned herself to dreary grays and browns and braided and pinned her hair.

She tried to quiet his irrational jealousy and win back his regard a dozen different ways. She embroidered him a tunic displaying a profusion of golden apples, the symbol of his house, but he'd tossed it aside, saying the shade of the threads was all wrong, which she would have known if she had a better eye for colors. She spent endless hours weaving him a tapestry of an apple tree, this time matching the threads so perfectly he could not possibly criticize the shade. He condemned the symmetry of the pattern instead, insisting he could not bear to gaze upon workmanship so shoddy.

Even Egelina's birth had not healed their rift. Though he doted on his new daughter, he remained cold to her mother. He must have sensed that despite her attempts at reconciliation, her vow to never forgive him had been true. Deep within her, she still clung to her pain and anger over the loss of Gerolt's support. She could not reach him even in her darkest hours, for Antony had burned all her parchment and destroyed all her quills, removed her writing table, and left strict orders that no letter from her hand should ever leave the castle again.

Occasionally Antony almost softened when she went to the kitchen and prepared a favorite dish for him. But then had come the dreadful day he had scorned it before their entire house.

"I'll eat no dish made by a strumpet's hands," he had announced loudly enough for all his men to hear.

Too late had she realized she had served him pears in syrup, a favorite Gerolt had enjoyed, as well as Antony, back in the days when the three of them had been in accord.

Only later that night, when Egelina had confessed she had slipped away from her nurse to sit on the stairs and watch the diners, then asked Antony what a strumpet was, had he looked ashamed. He'd flushed and made up a gentle lie. Thereafter he had ceased to humiliate Cassandry in public, but in private he continued relentlessly. If she defended herself, he called her shrew. If she wept, he called her overwrought. If she failed to smile when he wished it, she was sour. But her smiles offended him, too, for then he said she schemed.

He never raised his hand to her, but there were times she thought it would have been more bearable if he had: a slap, followed by an apology, answered with forgiveness, and then all forgotten in the kisses all the hurt had not quite washed from her memory, the love that had once burned so bright between them renewed, the future filled once more with hope . . .

"Oh, Gelli." Cassandry rolled over, suddenly acutely attuned to her daughter's presence. She feared to touch her shoulder more than lightly lest she wake her. "Forgive me. I cannot bear to lose you too."

But Cassandry would find a way to endure that pain if it would protect Egelina from repeating her mistakes. Pen and parchment had ruined Cassandry's life. Had she not known how to read Samson's wicked letters, had she not coveted the comfort of Gerolt's written words, she and Antony might have lived out the happy promise of their marriage.

She buried her face in her pillow and quietly wept.

Like before, Cassandry finally dozed toward dawn, and, as before, she awoke to find herself alone. This time, however, Egelina was not sitting nearby, combing out her sleep-tumbled curls.

Cassandry surveyed the empty room with apprehension. Her daughter's absence portended a stormy exchange.

She slipped from the bed and changed into a loose-fitting brown tunic so that she would not need to summon her maid for assistance. She did not bother to look in her hand mirror. She knew she looked the hag Antony had called her. She suspected even camomile would not erase the shadows undoubtedly bagging her eyes after another night of sleeplessness. Enough pride stirred in her, however, to comb the mats from her hair and plait her long tresses, then pin them up. She settled a modest veil over her hair, securing it in place with a ribbon, guided by years of experience to be assured the fringe gathered evenly across her brow.

She felt too ill with anxiety to break her fast. Even the most delectable dish would taste like ashes until she had spoken with Egelina and tried to make peace between them. Peace. Nay, she knew her daughter too well to hope for that this day. Perhaps tomorrow. Perhaps in a week. *Perhaps she will never forgive me, as I never forgave her father.*

A chill of despair stole down Cassandry's spine. *But I am still her mother. I may not be able to make her forgive me, but I can make her listen. I can try to make her understand.*

Cassandry drew a breath for courage, then pulled open the chamber door. In her haste to get the confrontation over with, she nearly stepped on the glinting object that lay in the passageway on the other side of the threshold. She bent to pick it up, then froze. Had some demon invaded her memories in the night?

From her fingers dangled a tiny round mirror on a chain, exactly like the one Gerolt had sent her at Christmas twenty-two years ago.

Chapter 11

The suspicion seemed absurd, but Cassandry could not dismiss the smug little smile that hovered on Samson's mouth when the custard tart had been served to Egelina. She waited until Samson dismissed the groom he had been speaking to in the stable doorway, then held out the mirror with its chain, her fist shaking with anger.

"Did you send this?"

Samson's brows rose, but nothing in his study of the dangling object gave his thoughts away. "To whom, dear one?"

"Do not call me that. Do not ever call me that. Did you send this to my daughter?"

"Why on earth would I send such a trinket to the Lady Egelina? She is betrothed to Gerolt's son, or soon will be. If you think I would serve him such a despicable blow as that behind his back and beneath his own roof, after all he and I have shared—"

"All you and he shared did not prevent you from trying to seduce me twenty-three years ago."

Samson darted a glance at the knights milling in the yard, then guided her around a corner of the stable where they were removed from public view.

His forehead knit a little as she shook off his hand. "That had nothing to do with Gerolt," he said. "As his ward, I would never have touched you. But you no longer belonged to him, and I had no allegiance to Antony. I had wanted you for a very, very long time, Cassandry." Samson's gaze flowed warmly over her loose-fitting tunic. "Nearly as long as Gerolt did. He was too honorable to take you when he had every legal right to demand your hand, however much you wanted another man. The fool. What did honor get him but an empty marriage?"

Cassandry found herself battling the memory of Gerolt's hand against her cheek last night. Surely she had mistaken his intent in the darkness?

"It is monstrous of you to suggest that Gerolt ever thought of me as Antony did, to say that he did not love his wife. His affection for her was in every letter he sent me. You told me yourself that he loved her."

Samson chewed his lip briefly, then shrugged. "I said it because Gerolt did not wish you to know the truth. He knew you were happy with Antony and wanted you to believe him the same with Aveline. In fact, he was miserable. Aveline was lovely. She was also dutiful and cold. He tried to hide it even from me, but I had known him too long, and in time I came to know her, too. I could not live that way. To stoically stand aside while the woman I burned for gave herself to another . . ." Too much meaning glinted in his eyes. "Such selflessness as that has never been in me, I fear."

Disdain curled her lip. "You proved that with those wicked letters you sent me. You wrote as though I were already your mistress. How could you think such obscene lies would ever gain you my favor?"

"You were no longer an innocent maid but a wife acquainted with passion. The heat of my words might have tempted you. Or they might have so angered Antony that he would spurn you, and you would turn to me."

Her breath caught. "You *wanted* Antony to see your letters?"

"I counted on it."

Before she could stop herself, her hand flew up to slap him. Samson's head swiveled at her blow, but when he looked back at her, it was with a grin.

"So at least half my plan worked. I presume that final letter you wrote me thanking me for the passion we had shared but warning me that Antony would have my head quite literally if one more letter crossed your threshold was the price of striking peace with your husband over your 'sin'?"

Oh, how she had hated Samson over the years! How could he stand there so dismissive of the tragedy he had wrought in her marriage?

She checked herself, appalled by the violent anger flooding through her. It had been so long since she had felt emotions this strong. She fisted her hands at her sides. She should not have slapped him. After all she had sought to teach her daughter of self-restraint.

She did not trust his denial about Egelina. Perhaps he toyed with her merely to annoy Cassandry. Or to court favor with Egelina in case some tragedy struck Rauffe. Had not Aveline complained of her son's uncertain health to Samson? Egelina stood heiress to considerable lands in her own right, and Samson's late wife had left his estates impoverished.

Gerolt might not believe Samson's designs so self-serving—he could not know what a scoundrel his friend was or he'd not have given him shelter beneath his own roof. But if Cassandry worded it right, convinced Gerolt that Egelina was taking Samson's "playful game" too seriously, he would surely see to it that the "game" stopped immediately.

But what if Egelina's regard had not been his intent? Samson might remember the shell Cassandry had worn as a girl, and surely remembered the wreath Gerolt had made her, which she had worn so proudly. He had even known she loved custard tarts.

The links of the chain bit into her palm as her fingers clenched still tighter around it. She held the chain out to Samson with more control this time. "You did not send this to me." She said it as a statement in the most frigid of tones.

"But it is such an elegant gift." He reached out a finger to trace the tiny diamonds studding the silver frame around the mirror. "Any woman would be flattered to receive something so delicate and rare."

"Neither my daughter nor I are susceptible to flattery, rare or otherwise," Cassandry said. "Take it back and give it to some other victim of your self-indulgent charm."

"So you do find me charming?"

She started to turn away in disgust, but he whirled her about, then abruptly pushed her up against the wall of the stable. She gasped as he flung back her veil to allow his mouth to nuzzle her ear. He leaned against her, pressing his breast to hers, trapping her arms beneath his so that her hand could not fly up to slap him again.

"There is still fire in you," he murmured, his voice a soft thrum. "My cheek still stings with it. We could set the world ablaze together, you and I. Who is there to stop us now?"

She pushed frantically against his waist. "Get . . . off . . . of . . . me!"

The only thing he moved was his head, so that he could kiss her roughly. "Three years a widow," he muttered against her lips. "You cannot tell me you have not missed this." He kissed her again. "And this," and again, "and this."

She finally managed to twist aside. "Sir Samson, I will scream. I swear I will." She would if she could find breath through the panic squeezing her chest. There were a dozen knights in the yard who would come to her aid. Or would they all believe they were merely intruding upon a lovers' spat?

"We could do it honorably this time, Cassandry. Marriage, you and I. Saints, but how lusciously you've aged! Waiting whets the appetite, and I have waited so very long."

His strength held her pinned against the wall. His hand caressed her face, not with the tenderness of Gerolt's touch last night but with the boldness of lust. If she tried to scream now, Samson could smother her in an instant.

Calm yourself, Cassandry. He will not ravish you here, where a groom might come around the corner at any moment.

"We need no one's permission to wed at our age, not even Gerolt's. We could run away this very hour. I swear I will make the night to come one that will live in your memory forever."

His words, his touch, repulsed her. How innocent she must have been not to see what a villain he was in her youth! His thumb lightly stroked her lips. However "logically" safe she knew herself, her throat constricted.

She choked out a desperate defense through her revulsion. "Gerolt . . . remains . . . my liege lord . . . for Egelina's inheritance. We cannot simply . . . run away."

"Then tell him you love me as you loved Antony." Samson's thumb teased the corner of her mouth. "He did not deny you then. He will not deny us now." It played against her trembling lower lip. "You cannot tell me, in all honesty, that my letters to you never once made you wonder what it might be like to lie in my arms?"

She shuddered, then opened her mouth and bit down on his thumb with all the frightened, angry force slamming through her.

Samson yelped and jerked his hand away, enabling her to break free from his slackened hold.

"Never once!" She scrubbed her hand across her mouth. She half feared his fury, but instead his eyes gleamed with amusement, even as he nursed his wounded thumb with his other hand. She flung the chain with the mirror at his feet, then backed quickly beyond his reach. "You are despicable. Stay away from Egelina. Stay away from me. For Gerolt's sake, I will try to be civil with you in his house, but if you come near my daughter or try to touch me again—"

"What?" he cut her off, his smile smug. "What will you do?"

"I will tell Gerolt everything. *Everything*, Sir Samson."

His smile widened. "And after I relate to him my version of those long ago events—and even of this tryst—he will believe you because . . . ?"

The lie flashed into her mind as he trailed off with a smirk. "Because I have evidence that *I* was not the one doing the seducing twenty-three years ago."

His smirk faltered, then vanished. "You saved the letters I sent you?"

He would not ask if he knew otherwise. "And you cannot threaten me with the same, since I never returned one line of encouragement to you. So who do you think Gerolt will believe now?"

She almost wept with relief at the alarm on his face. He would not look so dismayed if he had kept the final, humiliating, incriminating letter Antony had made her write.

"You will not tell Gerolt." An unaccustomed note of tension strained his voice. "I have no place else to go."

His consternation failed to rouse her pity. She dodged past him into the open yard. She had only taken a few steps when she saw Gerolt talking with Sir Ingram. Gerolt turned just as Samson joined her. They both paused so near the stable door she realized it looked as if they had just emerged from within.

Gerolt strode across the yard to greet her. "Good morning. Are you just back from a ride? You should have told me. Sam and I would have accompanied you. We are off to have a look at my fields—" Gerolt broke off. His too-perceptive gaze swept over her still heated cheeks. "What is amiss?"

Before she could speak, he set his cool palm to her forehead.

"She is not ill," Samson said, his voice once more cocky. "I said something to make her cross with me, that is all. It was only a small disagreement that heated her face against me, but she has promised to forgive me and be civil, so there will be no disruption in your house. Is that not so, Lady Cassandry?"

She tried to think of a civil reply, but since she was trembling inside with a fury that surpassed her former panic, she ignored him and said to Gerolt in a voice she knew came out too tight, "Have you seen Egelina this morning? She escaped from our chambers before I woke up."

Gerolt set one finger under her chin and lifted her face to the sun. She felt his gaze lingering on the pools of sleeplessness beneath her eyes.

"Was it a very bad quarrel?" he asked softly.

She knew he was not referring to Samson's words. "She was asleep when I came to bed. We have not spoken of the matter yet."

A glint caught the corner of her eye. She turned her head slightly to see Samson casually swinging the chain with the tiny mirror. It freed her from Gerolt's touch, which was just as well, as she had again suffered a disconcertingly pleasant tremor.

"I found her sitting beside Rauffe's bed when I went to visit him this morning," Gerolt said. "They appeared to have found some accord, for they were talking so low I could not hear their words, but Egelina was smiling. She rose when she saw me and gave me a very pretty curtsy and went off, she said, to find some cheese for breakfast."

"Then I will join her." Cassandry could not bring herself to speak to Samson. Later, she would be civil to him in public, but just now her palm wanted nothing so much as to slap him again. She started to leave, but Gerolt stopped her with a hand on her arm.

"When you are finished with Egelina, come and find me."

His parting words of last night burned again in her ears. *We must talk.* He meant to ask her about Antony and the last twenty-two years of silence between them.

It is none of your business, Gerolt. You did not come to seek the truth after I sent you that hateful letter telling you to stay away. How could you have thought I meant a word of it? You left me alone to fall and fall and fall into despair, and you think you can pick up the pieces now?

Unfair! the voice of reason chided her. *Your words were cold and hurtful. You left him no choice but to do as you bade him.*

It does not matter now, a third voice said. *The past cannot be changed. You have chosen your own future. Quietness and contemplation and finally, finally peace.*

The only thing that had kept her from slipping away to the solitude of a nunnery on the very day Antony died had been Egelina. Unlike her young, impulsive daughter who had still needed a mother's guiding hand, the events of Cassandry's life had fashioned her for the ultimate retreat, where numbness from earthly emotion would be counted as a blessing. She would not allow a thumb brush to her cheek in a candlelit chamber or a finger beneath her chin, or a dance that made her float once more like a summer's breeze pull her back into a world that held only heartbreak, disillusionment, and darkness.

She tried to drag the protective cloak of emotional deadness back around her, but the rage Samson had ignited roiled through her again. If she did not stare somewhere other than at Gerolt, he would see her sudden, deep awareness of him, of his height, his strength, the curve of his mouth, the gray of his eyes, the way their corners crinkled when he laughed, the worried cock of his brows when he gazed on Rauffe, the powerful flow of his movements when he trained with his knights . . . That last memory of long ago had been revived when her hands had embraced the muscles beneath his sleeves as he'd lifted and lowered her in yesterday's dance. She pointedly fixed her gaze on Sir Ingram, the feather in his cap dancing merrily on the breeze as he mounted a bay horse.

Fire churned in her stomach. *How dare you make me feel again? After you failed me so abysmally. You abandon me, then sweep back into my life as though you were never gone. But I will always be a child to you, your sparrow, when at this moment I want nothing more than to wipe away the taste of Sir Samson with your kiss on my lips.*

Her fury flowed so hot she almost gasped. No, it was not Gerolt. It was Samson who had lit this blaze, this horrible, consuming torrent of emotion. Feeding wretched lies to her about Gerolt wanting her as a woman, taunting her with the tokens of her past with him, Samson treating so lightly the destruction of her marriage, then assaulting her. None of it was Gerolt's fault, yet everything inside her hurt again as acutely as the day Antony had made her cut him off. *If you had only come after me. How could you not have come after me?*

She watched Sir Ingram ride out of the yard, then shifted her gaze to Sir Owen, who was crossing from the smithy toward the keep.

"Rauffe does not need help dressing," she said, aware of how utterly random it sounded, but the casual thought gave her time to try to compose herself before she looked Gerolt in the face again. "If he is old enough to be a husband, he is old enough to select his own wardrobe, however you might frown upon his choices."

"But you have seen his absurd taste in apparel." Gerolt sounded defensive. "Sir Owen's judgment is above reproach. I have only asked him to share a bit of advice with Rauffe."

"He does not like it. If you do not wish him to act as a child, then do not treat him as one." She dared a tentative glance at him, just quick enough to see him stiffen before her gaze flitted away again.

"This rebuke from the woman who refused to tell her daughter that she knows how to read and write when that daughter wants nothing more in the world than to learn how to do the same?"

Her head whirled to meet his gaze, which was lit now with some heat of his own. "Do not judge me, Gerolt. You know nothing about this matter."

"Because you refuse to confide in me." She saw a rare shade of impatience slip into his eyes. "I realize that you still grieve for Antony, but do you think I cannot understand your loss? I have lost my wife, two babes, and a grown daughter. I know how much it hurts, but this overlong mourning of yours is unhealthy." He reached out to take both her hands. His voice softened. "You never withheld any hurt from me when you were young. Why will you not let me in? Why will you not let me help you, Sparrow?"

Despite her anger, her fingers had clung to his at his touch, but she snatched them away when he called her Sparrow.

"I am not a child anymore, Gerolt," she said. "You cannot expect me to come running to you with every problem of my life. I have faced them alone for twenty-two years while you built a life of your own with Aveline."

"You did not have to face them alone, Cassandry," he replied. "Even married to Aveline, I was always here for you. Or would willingly have been, had you not cut me out of your life." His softened voice now took on an edge. "Do I not at least deserve to know what I did for you to shun me?"

She felt Samson watching them, which only fueled her anger anew. She struggled to keep her voice even. "You did not do anything. It was not about you, Gerolt."

"Then what was it about? Antony?"

She flinched inside as Gerolt struck too near the truth. His eyes widened when she did not immediately deny it.

"Saints, Cassandry! Did he do something to hurt you?"

"No," she said quickly, "of course not." In spite of all the bitterness, she would not have Gerolt or anyone think that Antony had ever struck her. But there were other hurts that thrust as deep, and in another moment Gerolt's keen eyes would see her lie. "I do not wish to speak of this," she said, knowing she sounded as petulant as Egelina. "My life is not your concern anymore, not my past and not my present. I must ask you to respect my privacy. Now, if you will excuse me . . ."

She curtsied, expecting him to step aside, but he remained squarely in her path.

"Cassandry," he said, very softly now. "I cannot let you just walk away from me. Not again."

"It is not your choice, Gerolt. It is mine."

"Sparrow—"

He reached for her hand again, but she snatched it away. "I am not your Sparrow anymore. But you are still my liege lord. Whatever you command me, I must obey. Is that what you require from me? Abject obedience?"

"Heaven forbid!" he whispered. "I want what we had before. Your trust, your friendship—freely given."

"I have trusted you with the most precious thing in my life. I am trusting you with Egelina."

"And I shall care for her as tenderly as though she were my own daughter. But—"

"I know you will," she cut him off, and suddenly, to her surprise, there were tears in her eyes. "Oh, Gerolt, I know you will. You will have my gratitude for that, and for so much more, forever. But do not ask more of me. The years have stretched too long. I am not your Sparrow, and you are not the brother I once gazed upon with girlhood adoration. Life has altered us both. It has altered *me*. Let me finish preparing my daughter to be a good and dutiful wife to your son. Then I will name the boon you promised me, and let us part again in peace."

He looked as though he were about to say something more, but Samson touched his shoulder, bringing his attention to someone they had not noticed approaching them in their focus upon one another.

"I hope I am not intruding." Marion curtsied first to her father.

Cassandry thought there was an odd stiffness in her salute, but the young woman's smile was warm as she dipped the same greeting to Gerolt.

"It is such a lovely morning," Marion said. "I thought, my lord, you might condescend to accompany me to reacquaint myself with the manor." Her rosy cheeks glowed as brightly as the spring sunshine.

The words flowed into Cassandry's mind: *She will make him a joyous wife.* However Gerolt had unknowingly failed Cassandry, he had also given her so very much she could never adequately thank him for. If Samson had spoken truly, if Gerolt's first marriage had been a disappointment, then she prayed with all her heart that he might find happiness with Marion. But as she took advantage of his distraction to walk past him toward the keep, she felt something she had thought buried too deeply inside her to ever stir again give a broken little crack.

Chapter 12

Gerolt hoped the curse he called down upon Marion's ill timing did not show on his face. He forced himself to stand and greet her politely when everything in him wanted to stride after Cassandry and demand the meaning of her parting words. What was this mysterious "boon" she had made him swear to grant her? He'd held confidence in the good sense he remembered in her not to name something outlandish, but that was before he had witnessed the fierce resolve in her eyes. She meant to leave him. When all this was over, when Rauffe and Egelina were safely bound, Cassandry meant to cut herself out of his life again, and without knowing how, he had unknowingly sworn to let her.

"Is it too much to hope I might find my former mare still in your stables?" Marion said, her voice lilting like a bird's merry song. "That would set the seal of contentment on my coming home again."

Samson interposed before Gerolt could reply. "We were off to view Lord Gerolt's fields. By all means, join us, Marion."

Gerolt barely suppressed a glare at his friend. Samson's persistence in advocating a marriage between Gerolt and Marion was ridiculous. He was old enough to be her father and had practically raised her as if he were. True, she had left his house a soft-faced girl of fifteen when she had married Sir Gregory Lindahl, and returned with the mature angles and curves of a woman. True, as well, that he had involved himself a good deal less in her young life than he had in his own daughter, Fleur's, a subtle difference that undoubtedly gave Samson hope that Gerolt could come to see her as a potential match. But Cassandry's stinging rebuke had reinforced his inability to see Marion as anything but an annoyance.

You are not the brother I once gazed upon with girlhood adoration.

Thank the heavens! The last thing he wanted was for Cassandry to view him as any sort of kin, even though he knew anything more than friendship would soon be forbidden them. But he would sooner take and hold tight to friendship with her than seek consolation in marriage with another woman.

But first he would have to persuade her to stay—for Egelina's sake, of course. He would pray that time would heal the rest between them. And change her mind about the boon.

"Forgive me, Lady Marion," he said. "I did, indeed, intend to go riding with your father this morning, but that was before I recalled a half-dozen duties I cannot escape." He deliberately avoided Samson's eye. "I am certain your father would be more than happy to accompany you."

Samson should thank him. His friend had been trying to reestablish an affectionate relationship with his daughter ever since he'd returned from the East. Marion had remained resistant, though, unwilling, apparently, to forget the way her father had chosen the adventure of a crusade over the tedium of raising a young family.

Samson held out a ready hand to her, but Marion's smile faded.

"Thank you, Father," she said with a coldness reserved only for Samson, "but I have remembered a few duties of my own that I should not neglect. I should spend some time with Rauffe now that he is feeling better." Her stiffened lips relaxed into a softer curve again for Gerolt. "Perhaps I can coax him into wearing a pair of hose that does not clash horribly against his tunic. The entire household was blinking at him in dismay yesterday. He's always had peculiar taste in colors, but I fear he has taken it to extremes since Lady Aveline's passing."

"If you can convince him to choose some more compatible hues, I shall be much in your debt, Lady Marion," Gerolt said in frank honesty.

Her smile widened again. "I am certain that I can. He was a stubborn child for always being so sickly, but he always listened to Fleur, and he viewed me as a sister, too. Truly, I am surprised Lady Cassandry has not dealt with him more firmly. She has seen him with the rest of us and spent hours with him yesterday nursing his headache. I should have thought she would have burned those atrocious yellow hose he wore to dinner. Lady Aveline would have. But Lady Cassandry is not his mother, and one can see from her daughter's unbecoming pouts and temper that her discipline is slack."

Marion extended her hand to Gerolt as he was still absorbing her impertinent criticism of Cassandry.

"I shall see you, then, at dinner, my lord."

He bowed over her fingers. Her smile was sweet as she dipped him a curtsy before withdrawing to the keep. If she had ever been subject to the emotional outbursts Egelina suffered from, he had never witnessed it. But then, Aveline would never have allowed such passion from any young woman in her care, including poor Fleur. His daughter had had to conceal her soaring joys and tearful disappointments until Gerolt had drawn her aside to listen to her heart, as he had once listened to Cassandry's.

As soon as Marion had gone, Gerolt turned with a frown to Samson. "What did you say to her?" he demanded.

"To Marion?"

"To Cassandry, to turn her face so red."

Samson shrugged. "She seems to be under the impression that I sent this to her daughter." He dangled a tiny mirror on a chain in front of Gerolt.

Gerolt felt a pang at the sight of it. The mirror twisted on the breeze so that he could not clearly catch the design, but he had given one very like it to Cassandry once.

"Why would I do such a thing, I ask you?" Samson queried.

The answer was so glaring, Gerolt nearly let out a harsh laugh. He and Samson might be friends, but Gerolt had never been blind to Samson's failings. He had hoped the crusade would impart some discipline in his friend. Instead, Samson had come home more unruly than he had been even as a youth.

"Perhaps," Gerolt replied, "because the Lady Egelina is the loveliest little flower you have seen in quite some while?" He added, very soft and very level, "Do I need to remind you that she is betrothed to my son?"

"No, you do not." Samson tossed the bauble he held into the air and caught it. "And for that reason, she remains as safe from me as an ancient crone would be. But even if I hoped to seduce her, I would hardly be fool enough to try to do it with this." He held out the mirror and chain to Gerolt.

Gerolt took them, then drew in a sharp breath. He could not mistake the silver frame with tiny diamonds studding the delicate filigree. "This belonged to Aveline."

"The gift you gave her during her first Christmas as your wife. Cassandry's second Christmas away from you. Did Aveline ever know you sent one very like it to your former ward?"

Gerolt shook his head. Samson had been with him when he'd bought both gifts at a fair. Aveline had been far from his mind when he had selected this mirror for Cassandry. It had seemed harmless, a small token to reassure her that his friendship stood firm no matter how far away from him she was. Samson had been right to remind him of his new wife, the one who smiled more obediently than joyfully, conducted her new household with vigorous efficiency, thought dancing unseemly, avoided the garden lest the sunshine spoil her pale complexion, and excused herself from hunting, hawking, and pleasure riding for the same reason. Samson had suggested a second mirror with a more modest sprinkling of pearls against an unetched setting for Aveline, but Gerolt's conscience would not allow him to give his wife the lesser gift. He had sent the simpler pearled mirror to Cassandry.

Had she understood its message? She could not have, or the light would not have gone out of her eyes.

"I'd say you have a thief in your house."

Gerolt looked up from the mirror, where his own reflection had blurred into Cassandry's distant, troubled face. "What?"

Samson nodded at the object in Gerolt's hand. "Someone left it in a manner for Cassandry to find and interpret as a gift, either for her daughter or herself. Where do you keep it?"

"In my chamber in an ivory box with Aveline's other jewelry. I put it all away with her clothes in a chest that sits in the corner. I wished Rauffe to choose some pieces before I gave her trinkets and gowns to Elstow Abbey for the poor, but he has been so unwell. I did not want to burden him with more grief for his mother until he felt stronger."

A year since Aveline's death, and that hope had seemed as far away as ever, until Gerolt had seen his son sitting up and smiling this morning, with so much healthy color in his face his father might have been looking at a stranger. Was it possible something as simple as almonds had been the source of Rauffe's illness all along?

"Aveline employed only the most trustworthy servants," Gerolt said. "Do you expect me to believe one of my own knights raided my chamber when I was not there?"

"I can think of none of your knights who would dare,"

Samson replied. "If one did, then he should be stripped of his spurs. But your castle is teeming just now with your vassals, summoned for the betrothal, and their servants and pages and squires. It could be well-nigh anyone. Have you kept your chamber door locked?"

"Nay, 'twould be dishonorable to distrust my own vassals, whom I know to a man. Their servants, and perhaps their young pages . . . you may have a point there. But I keep my own jewels and wardrobe locked, so nothing of significance is at risk."

He remembered he had not repaired the lock on Aveline's jewelry casket, though. It had broken just before she'd fallen ill, and Gerolt had been too consumed with worry for her and then with grief at her loss, to have given repairing the lock a thought.

He weighed Samson, but his friend was right. Sam would not have used a gift Gerolt would so easily recognize to try to seduce any woman.

"I will have to ask questions," Gerolt said grimly. "Awkward questions among my vassals, I fear. Whoever allowed his servant to steal this—it is not only theft but dishonor to my son."

"And a more dangerous dishonor against yourself, if one of your vassals succeeds in seducing the prospective daughter-in-law of his own liege lord. You cannot ignore an insult such as that, Gerolt."

No, he could not. The game was going too far. What fool in his household, from his highest born vassal to the grooms who mucked out his stables, would not know the danger Samson described? All of them would. Then who would be so daring as to risk Gerolt's anger? The last man who had done so had been forced to flee to France, so disgraced had Gerolt's displeasure left him among the barons of England.

But the gifts themselves. They had all been so oddly chosen. A shell, a wreath, a chain with a mirror . . . What had Egelina said at the dining table? "You have an admirer, Mamma!" Was it possible

Egelina had never been the target? Could some man of Gerolt's house be attempting to court Cassandry?

"You sent the tart to Cassandry at the dining table," Gerolt said abruptly. Samson might come and go from Gerolt's chambers as he pleased, and Gerolt would scarcely have questioned him. Samson's constant attempts to discourage Gerolt from the love—yes, love—he still felt for Cassandry took on a new, perverse possibility. "Did you also leave the wreath of periwinkle and sweet woodruff at her door? You knew them to be her favorite flowers, as well as I."

"I never said I sent her the tart."

Gerolt stared at him, surprised. "Of course you did."

Samson shook his head. "You asked, and I did not deny it, but I did not admit it, either. I was feeling bearish, as I sometimes do when memories of my long imprisonment in the East weigh upon me. I know you still desire her, or rather, you desire the woman she once was. In my doldrums, I found it amusing to tweak you a bit, just to see the jealousy in your face. But I am feeling sane today. I did not send her the tart or the wreath, and I certainly did not raid your chamber to give her Lady Aveline's chain."

Gerolt studied his friend, trying to discern the truth. Things had been so different between them since Samson's misadventure in the East. One day he would be the Sam Gerolt had always known, grinning and cocky but as devoted and as staunch as the boy and the man who had guarded Gerolt's back as closely as a shadow for over forty years; the next, a cynical, mirthless stranger.

One memory returned now that Samson could not deny. "You went to Rengrave Castle and told Cassandry that I had sent you to escort her and her daughter to the betrothal when I did no such thing. Why did you go, and why did you not tell me?"

"I did not think she should be traveling alone. Did you see those graybeards Antony left her with as guards? A swift attack by a handful of athletic young bandits would knock them all out of the saddle and leave Cassandry and her daughter at their mercy. I merely tried to anticipate a risk that had not occurred to you."

"I'd offered her a guard of my men, and she declined. She said she had faith in her knights' skill to protect her, despite their gray beards."

"Well, you did not confide that to me, did you? I should have told you what I intended, of course, but I hardly thought you would object to me offering her my escort."

"Of course I do not object. You do not need my permission to ride where you will, and the gesture was generous of you. Thank you, Sam."

A new distraction caught his attention. Egelina emerged from the keep with her hand tucked into the crook of Sir Fithian's arm.

"Your castle is very crowded," Egelina said, pausing to bob Gerolt and Samson a respectful curtsy. "I can scarcely move, there are so many people. Sir Fithian has kindly agreed to take me riding so that I might breathe some fresh air. You do not mind, do you, my lord?"

Sir Fithian had never shown himself anything but completely trustworthy in Gerolt's service. All the same, given the evidence of four clearly romantic tokens being cast either at Egelina's or her mother's feet, he deemed it only prudent to discourage a private ride between Egelina and any of his knights. He would not have Sir Fithian think himself under his lord's mistrust if his intentions were innocent, however. Gerolt found it easier to question Egelina.

"Have you permission from your mother?"

Egelina pushed her toe impatiently against the earth of the bailey, sending up a little cloud of dust. "I have not seen Mamma this morning, but she could not possibly object. She has known Sir Fithian forever. She says he is as harmless as a lamb."

"Only to pretty ladieth, like you," Sir Fithian protested.

"When fathed with my lord'th enemieth, I am accounted one of hith foremotht thowrdthmen, am I not, my lord?"

"Indeed, Sir Fithian," Gerolt agreed, "you have always been an exceptional swordsman. It is certainly not the Lady Egelina's safety I doubt with you, only her mother's approval that she go riding this morn with anyone."

"I promise you she will not mind," Egelina said. "She is busy in the kitchen reviewing the dishes being served for dinner to be certain no almonds slip into any of Rauffe's dishes. Sir Fithian and I will not be gone long. We shall only ride down to the—where did you say we would ride again?" she asked the knight.

"Down to the thtew pond."

"Yes, down to the stew pond," Egelina repeated, "to see the live eels. I have never seen a live eel, only the ones we eat at dinner. Do they really slither like snakes through the water?"

"Indeed they do, I told her," Sir Fithian replied before Gerolt could do so. "But she wanth to thee for herthelf."

Gerolt searched for an answer that would not offend either Sir Fithian or Egelina. "Then take a squire with you. In case you should like to bring some eels back with you for the kitchen. I promise you should not like to carry such slithery creatures, my lady, and I cannot ask my foremost swordsman to lower himself to act the fisherman. Garin!" He called to the redheaded squire, who looked to be on an errand to the blacksmith shop at the far side of the castle's bailey. "Accompany Sir Fithian and Lady Egelina down to the stew pond and assist them however they require."

"Yes, sir," Garin said.

The squire bowed with such an eager glance at Egelina that Gerolt belatedly wondered who would be chaperoning whom on their ride.

When the small party had vanished over the drawbridge, Samson asked, "Do you suspect Sir Fithian? He has always been abundantly loyal to you. But as you said, Lady Egelina is 'the loveliest little flower' to cross your threshold in years. I suppose even his level head might be turned at the sight of her. But seduce her with trinkets when he thinks her betrothed to your son? That does not seem to be in his nature."

"I should not like to believe it of him," Gerolt agreed. "I should not like to suspect any of my men. Even you." He smiled to cover the only half-teasing jab at his friend. "Not where Egelina is concerned. But if the gifts were meant for Cassandry . . ."

"It would have to be some man unworthy of her, else why not simply ask you for her hand? It is yours to give to whomever you will."

Gerolt began strolling toward the keep, and Samson fell in step beside him. "I would never force her to remarry. She knows that. You should too."

"You were ever too lenient with her. Still, she is hardly a romantic young girl anymore for her head to be turned by trinkets. Someone is most certainly attempting to seduce your future daughter-in-law."

"But the gifts. They have all been replications, or nearly so, of ones I gave to Cassandry in her youth. A shell—"

"A common first gift for lovers, especially from young men with little money in their purse. Shells are freely obtained by any man."

"But the wreath was made of Cassandry's flowers. None of my young squires or knights lived here when she was a girl. How do you explain such a coincidence?"

In a cordoned off part of the bailey, some of those squires now practiced their swordsmanship beneath the watchful eye of Sir Payne.

"Then we cannot rule out the older knights who knew her, some of whom, like Sir Payne, were squires when she was here," Samson said. "Many of them squander the wages you pay them and likely could not afford much more than a shell or a flower. The latter are as equally free from your garden as are the shells beside the river. He could not know Lady Egelina's own favorites, so he likely guessed they would be the same as her mother's."

"That is what Cassandry said."

"Trust a mother's wisdom and instincts. The same could be said for the tart."

Gerolt stood too far away to discern the squires' faces, but he saw one of the squires in training hit the ground, sent there by a strong blow from one of his companions. The youth rolled and sprang pluckily back to his feet. Gerolt silently applauded him, then paused and turned to face Samson again. "The first three gifts may have been innocent enough, but any way you look at it, the chain was pure theft. How do you propose to explain that away without casting irredeemable shame on one of my knights or vassals?"

"I cannot," Samson confessed. "Having failed to win the Lady Egelina's regard with the prior tokens, perhaps her would-be suitor grew desperate and thought a trinket of diamonds and silver would bring him more success. You realize what a prize she is, do you not? She stands heiress to both Antony's and Cassandry's lands. Can you think of anyone whose purse is so desperately empty that he might be tempted to dishonor himself to gain a rich wife?"

Only you, Gerolt thought, then rebuked himself for it. There was one way to narrow down the suspects. He would dismiss all his vassals in the morning to return to their homes. If the gifts ceased, then he would know one of them had been the source. If the gifts continued . . . well, none of his knights were rich men. They received free room and board along with a modest wage in exchange for their service to Gerolt. Most of them could not afford wives unless they conserved their pay for years. In general, they preferred to gamble their coins away to one another or lose them at the tavern in the market town. To attract a woman of Egelina's standing would require more status and wealth than any of them could aspire to—or to a cunning seduction.

The days ahead would tell the story.

Sir Payne's voice carried to Gerolt's ears as he stood reflecting. "That is enough for one day, my lord. You should be off to rest now."

"No. I am not tired yet. I almost got Thomas last time. One more round and I will—"

Gerolt swiveled on his heel. The young squire's voice was most certainly Rauffe's. He strode across to the training area just as Rauffe angled his sword over his arm, knees bent, and bounced lightly on the balls of his feet in anticipation of his opponent's strike, the way Gerolt had taught him to do when he was fourteen years old, before Aveline had come rushing between them to wrap their son in a fur-lined cloak and drag him inside to sit by the fire.

Rauffe caught his father's eye, straightened, and lowered his sword. A sulky flush rose to his face. Did he expect Gerolt to rebuke him? From the smirks that crossed the other squires' faces, they appeared to anticipate the familiar coddling of their lord's son. Rauffe looked winded and tired—his stamina could not be great after spending so many hours in bed with his headaches—but his eyes gleamed with a determination that made Gerolt's heart swell with pride. It did not matter how many times an opponent knocked one down as long as he rose to fight again.

Sir Payne saw Gerolt and said quickly, "I was about to send Lord Rauffe in, sir."

"Why?" Gerolt asked. "He's asked for another round with Thomas. Let him take it."

Sir Payne looked surprised, as did Rauffe and the other squires, but the knight commanded the two combatants to resume their places. Their swords clashed together in a reverberating flurry of strikes. Feet scuffled, bodies whirled and dodged, and a few minutes later, Thomas lay in the dust.

Chapter 13

Even with the crowd of vassals gone, Egelina managed to elude Cassandry for over a week. It did not help that Cassandry's mornings were taken up in the kitchen, ensuring that almond-free dishes be served to Rauffe. Emma Cook proved reluctant to acknowledge that her former mistress could possibly have been wrong about the prescription for her son's health. Even as vigor returned to Rauffe's body, Emma Cook grumbled each time Cassandry told her to her remake a dish she had tried to slip some of the nuts into, and muttered dire warnings about the ill effects of such rich meats as venison, goose, and pork when Cassandry insisted all three should be added to Rauffe's diet.

Each day when Cassandry sat down to dine, Egelina pointedly ignored her and chattered incessantly to Rauffe. He looked dismayed at first by Egelina's attentions but gradually lost his awkwardness and began to respond to her. Cassandry hoped their growing camaraderie bode well for the betrothal that, technically, still needed to be repeated.

"They seem to be getting along well now. Is she ready to speak the vows?" Gerolt asked from his place beside Cassandry at the table, echoing her thoughts. "My chaplain could preside over a private ceremony. We need only a few witnesses. Sir Samson and Sir Ingram—Ah," he added as Cassandry felt her brow pucker, "Sir Fithian, then, if you are still out of sorts with Sam."

Out of sorts was putting it mildly. Except when they dined, Cassandry had avoided Gerolt almost as studiously as Egelina was avoiding her. She did not want to talk to him about Antony or Samson or even the tokens. Especially not the tokens. She hoped her silence had convinced him that the inappropriate gifts had ceased with the departure of his vassals when, in fact, there had been two more—a silk ribbon and a wooden hairpin carved into a delicate swirling pattern. She had discovered each outside her chamber door in the morning, as before, but these last two had each arrived with a bit of parchment attached bearing a name: *Cassandry*. The neatly drawn letters gave her no clue as to their author, but she immediately suspected Samson. She knew his handwriting, of course—his script was burned into her memory alongside her humiliation—but she presumed he preferred to conceal his identity lest she show the parchment to Gerolt.

It was all she could do not to scowl at him where he ate with the other knights below the dais, but that would only further stir Gerolt's curiosity.

"I have not spoken to Egelina yet," Cassandry confessed. She took a bite of roast beef drenched in garlic-pepper sauce. "She has been evading me ever since you told her I was a hypocrite."

"I told her no such thing," Gerolt objected. "Why do you not talk to her now? There is no one on the dais to hear but us, and her answer concerns all of us, even Rauffe."

"Do you think I have not tried?" Cassandry said, exasperated. "Each time I attempt to draw her attention, she chirps, 'Just one moment, Mamma, I must finish my story to Rauffe,' and turns away from me again. She will not let me work a word in edgewise when we dine. When I look for her in the gardens, I am told she is in the kitchen. When I look in the kitchen, I am told she has just left to watch Rauffe train with your squires. By the time I reach the training field, she is riding through the gate with Sir Ingram or Sir Fithian or Sir Owen, with that red-haired squire in their train."

"Do you wish me to forbid her to ride? I thought with the threat removed from whichever of my misguided vassals was trying to win her attention—"

"No, no, there is no harm to it." Cassandry prayed there was nothing in her eyes that would betray the continuation of the tokens. "Antony kept us both confined much to the castle. This will be her new home; I do not wish her to feel a prisoner here."

Gerolt appeared to study the bit of beef speared on the tip of his dining knife before saying, "Perhaps you will have more luck when you both retire to bed tonight."

"She is just as elusive there. Somehow she always manages to slip into bed and fall asleep—or at least pretend to—before I join her in our chamber. I try to lie awake to catch her in the morning, but, to my disgust, I always doze off just as it begins to get light, and when I jerk awake, Egelina is dressed and gone again."

"Even you must sleep sometime, Cassandry," he said with a small smile.

"Oh, Gerolt, I am too old to care how many circles I have under my eyes."

"But I am not."

The bite of roast beef she had just slipped into her mouth suddenly turned to ash. Had she shamed Gerolt, as she had Antony, with the toll that sleeplessness took on her? Gerolt would never call her 'hag'—but did he think it?

"I hate seeing you in such distress." The vehemence that shook his lowered voice made her turn her head to gaze at him. "As much as we love them, children can sometimes be the very devil. If you would like me to shake Egelina for you, I should be happy to oblige."

His impatient glance shot at her daughter rather than at the shadows Cassandry knew hovered beneath her eyes.

"Oh, Gerolt, we must not say such things."

He sighed. "No. But do you not think it sometimes? There have been many times I have wished to shake Rauffe when he mumbles the same answer ten times, or continues slumping after my dozenth rebuke, or comes to dinner wearing something like that *again*."

Cassandry followed his gaze to the youth. Rauffe's hose were a subdued shade of yellow tonight, but he had overlaid a blazing red tunic with a surcote of intense blue covered in embroidery of a screaming shade of green.

"I took your advice and refrained from sending Sir Owen or anyone else to encourage him to show more sense with his wardrobe," Gerolt said. "The strategy has done no good till now, anyway."

"You must remember to count when he irks you so."

"Do you remember to count when Egelina irks you?"

Cassandry hesitated, then allowed the corner of her mouth to quirk up. "Sometimes."

Gerolt's gaze shifted back to her face. His eyes suddenly grew so warm she almost felt herself embraced. "There you are," he murmured.

She gazed back at him, baffled while at the same time feeling something begin to glow inside her. "What do you mean?"

"That smile. I feared I had lost it forever."

She dropped her gaze to her trencher in confusion. Had she smiled? She could not deny that she was beginning to feel different. More engaged, first with her care of Rauffe, then during her mornings managing the kitchen. She had not realized how much she had continued to merely go through the motions of tending to the requirements of Rengrave Castle, even after Antony's death. But Rauffe's needs had thrust her back into the details of life.

Long-buried emotions had begun to stir again. She had felt rage once more with Samson, while Gerolt had roused feelings—tender and yearning—she had never thought she would experience toward any man again.

She lifted her gaze to Marion, who was seated beside her father. The young woman watched Gerolt with a desire she no doubt thought safe from observation, for she blushed when she caught Cassandry's eye and quickly returned to her meal.

"You have my deepest gratitude, you know." Gerolt took her hand and drew it beneath the tablecloth, pressing her fingers. "I confess I had given up hope of ever seeing Rauffe well enough to hold a sword, much less do respectable battle with it. The last few nights he has come to my bedchamber to rehearse to me the blows he's dealt his fellow squires, as well as the falls he's taken from them, speaking with so much enthusiasm that he's forgotten to mumble. He has even forgotten to slouch of late. Have you noticed?"

She nodded. She'd only briefly observed Rauffe on the training field when she'd gone in search of Egelina, but she had seen him stand proudly there, still thin but straight and determined, as his father always stood when he held a sword. Rauffe was improving so quickly Gerolt had dismissed the physician Hyll, giving explicit instructions to the kitchen staff to obey Cassandry's every command.

"They were merely headaches," she said. "Miserable, crushing headaches when he suffered them, but they would not have been fatal. They put off his appetite, as did the insipid dishes the kitchen served him—"

"You mean that Aveline served him," Gerolt interrupted. "Look how he eats now. As though he's been starved for years! Which, perhaps, he has been. I do not doubt Aveline's love for Rauffe, but I see now that she was not as wise as I trusted her to be."

Cassandry bit her lip. Loving mothers did not call their sons worthless. She withdrew her hand so that she could resume eating, fixing her attention again upon her meal so that Gerolt might not see the flash of anger in her eyes. If Gerolt remained ignorant of what his wife had said, it was not her place to reveal it.

"Walk with me in the gardens," Gerolt cajoled when the meal ended and Egelina had flitted away on Rauffe's arm before Cassandry could attempt to stay her. "I wish to show you something."

"What is it?" she asked suspiciously as he drew her to her feet.

"Something you will like, I promise. I will ask you no uncomfortable questions," he added, too easily reading her doubts. "Just take one turn with me."

She cast an uncertain glance at Marion, who stood behind her chair watching them both with a frown. Sir Samson leaned down to whisper something to her. She whisked her head away as though he had said something distasteful.

"Poor Sam," Gerolt murmured. He must have followed Cassandry's gaze. "I do not know that he would have made a good father if he had stayed in England rather than going off on crusade when his children were young, but he would not have been a stranger to them. He pretends not to care how they cut him now, but I know him . . . or I did once."

Gerolt drew her hand through his arm so absently that she allowed it to rest there as he led her out of the hall.

"I know he did or said something to inflame you. For whatever it was, I apologize." Gerolt kept his gaze straight ahead as they walked, but his voice grew subtly pleading. "He was a good friend to me when we were young, Cassandry. Wild, yes, occasionally reckless; perhaps even at times unprincipled. But to me he was always loyal and faithful."

Through her own bitter memories Samson's words returned to her. He had not acted on his desire for her until after she had ceased being Gerolt's ward and become Antony's wife. It did not excuse the terrible blow Samson had dealt to her marriage . . . but even with all his lax, deplorable morals, he had not betrayed Gerolt. Nor, as the two tokens with Cassandry's name attached had proven, had he attempted to toy with Egelina while he believed her betrothed to Gerolt's son. For twenty-three years she had questioned how Gerolt could be so blind to Samson's faults. He had not been. She saw it now in the bleak, grim cast of Gerolt's profile.

He opened the gate to the garden so that she could pass through first, then drew her hand back into his arm as they started down the graveled path.

"When we were boys," he said, "Sam spent hours each day at the mews, training a fledgling peregrine to hunt. He even slept with it so that it would learn his voice and scent and touch. But when it grew time to loose the bird from its tethers, my father commanded him to surrender the peregrine to me. It did not know my voice. It did not love me as it loved Sam, but my father would not be disobeyed. Sam gave it to me with tears in his eyes. I feared it would break our friendship, and I hated my father for his command, but Sam rebuked me. He said my father did it in love for me because he wished me surrounded by men he knew would be true to me whatever the trial. 'We shall be true to one another, always,' Sam said, and we clasped arms as men do, though we were scarce ten years old."

They passed a cluster of rose bushes, and the stately hollyhocks, but Cassandry sensed Gerolt did not see any of them.

"But something changed in the East. Sam was three years a prisoner among the infidel. He will not tell me what he suffered there, but he came back with a hardness that was not there before. I have done all I can think of to help him. I cared for his children, I buried his wife, I gave him refuge beneath my own roof when he came home to his ruined lands. What more can I do?"

The note of helplessness in Gerolt's voice startled her—to hear him speak so uncertainly, when the man she had known as a girl had always been certain of everything. Or so she had thought. Had he ever battled doubt in raising her? Had he sat long into the nights, as Cassandry sometimes sat, rehearsing every scenario and its possible outcome before laying his counsel before her? She could imagine him differently now that she was a parent. A young man with a younger ward wrestling with his inexperience in how to raise her, extending guidance with a confidence he had perhaps not always fully felt, because he had instinctively known that she had needed most of all a dependable anchor she could rely on. How often had she done the same with Egelina?

Reflections of Cassandry's childhood did not lessen her intense awareness of Gerolt now, not as the brother she had once idolized but as a man who was arousing long-dormant emotions in her. The muscled arm beneath her hand, the breadth of the shoulder that tempted her to lean her head against it . . .

She forced her thoughts back to their conversation about Samson. She considered her response to Gerolt's words carefully.

"Sometimes events form us beyond our control," she said at last, stretching for generosity, not for Samson's sake but for Gerolt's. "Time changes everyone. It has surely changed Samson. You are not responsible for whatever he suffered in the East."

"No. But I can continue to stand his friend. I must do so, Cassandry."

Resolution replaced the uncertainty in Gerolt's voice. This was the man Cassandry remembered.

"Gerolt." She stopped and turned to face him. He waited, brows slightly raised. Memories rushed through her. The letters, Antony's fury, the heart pain that followed, the forced kisses at the stable. Revelation hovered on her tongue . . . and died there. No, she could not tell him how Samson had misused her. She could not destroy his friendship with Samson the way Samson had destroyed her marriage. She too had changed, but not so greatly that she could summon the spite to hurt Gerolt as deeply as she might hurt Samson.

"What did you wish to show me?" she asked.

His face relaxed. He took her hand and pulled her a few more feet down the path, then stopped beneath a chestnut tree.

"There." He pointed up into the branches.

Cassandry knew immediately where they were by the entwining letters carved into the bark. *A C.* Antony and Cassandry. She felt a twinge in her chest, but a twittering sound drew her gaze upward.

A small, plump brown bird cocked a suspicious eye at them from her nest amidst the leaves.

"Jenny Wren! Oh, but Gerolt, it cannot be. It has been over twenty-four years!"

"And every year, one of her descendants returns to this tree to nest. Shall we sit awhile and watch her?"

Before she could protest, he had his arm around her waist, pulling her down into the fragrant grass that sprang below the tree.

"Gerolt, what are you thinking? My gown. It will stain terribly."

"You never used to care about such things, Cassandry."

"Because I was a heedless girl who knew you would replace all my ruined surcotes. Oh, dear. I must have been a dreadful drain on your purse." Twenty-four years was a very long time for that thought to occur to her. What a selfish child she had been.

"Nonsense. It was mostly your mantles I had to replace, as you had the good sense to arrange them under your gowns when you sat. After the first few silks, I made sure your mantles were all made of inexpensive linens in the spring, until Jenny Wren hatched her small family and they all flew away."

Cassandry was very aware that his arm lingered around her waist. She ought to shift across the grass, but the casual embrace held her ensnared beside him. His heart could not possibly be pounding as hard as hers. All his thoughts were of the past, of stained mantles and the girlish delight that she had discovered a silly bird in a tree.

"Do you remember how I taught you to sit very still so as not to frighten her?" he asked. "I would come into the garden and think I had stumbled upon a statue, you sat so quiet and solemn when you watched her."

"And then you sat beside me," she recalled, "and pointed and whispered, drawing my attention to her tiny beak and pert, upthrust tail, and the bands along the edges of her wings."

"You could watch her for hours. I'd never seen a child so fascinated with a bird."

"I made up a poem to her," Cassandry confessed. "There was a great deal about spring and the pink dawn and birdsong. I would sit here beneath the tree and speak it ever so softly to her. And she would chitter and chatter back to me as though she understood and approved every word." Cassandry drew up her knees and wrapped her arms around them.

"Do you remember how it went?"

Cassandry shook her head with some regret. She had not yet learned how to write, and the poem, once so cherished between her and Jenny Wren, had faded with the years.

"A pity," Gerolt said. "I am sure her many-times-great-grand-daughter should like to have heard it."

Jenny Wren fluttered her wings and let out an abrupt string of rasping chirrs.

Gerolt bent his head to Cassandry's ear. "She is scolding us for being so loud. We must be quieter."

Something tickled along the back of Cassandry's throat. Laughter? It was gone again so quickly she could not be sure, banished as her gaze fell once again upon the entwined initials. She had brought Antony here to show him Jenny, years after she had discovered the bird at nine. They had sat together, just as Gerolt had sat with her as a child, just as he was sitting with her now, watching Jenny build her nest, listening to her morning song. Cassandry had had to teach Antony to whisper, as Gerolt had taught her. Antony had liked to tease her by clapping his hands and startling Jenny away, but then he would beg Cassandry's forgiveness and kiss her, and her irritation would dissolve. He had carved their initials in the tree the day he had said he wished to marry her, making this their own special place.

But before it was ours, it was mine and Gerolt's. She had a sudden impulse to draw Gerolt's arm tighter about her waist, to lean her ear into his warm breath, to turn her head, to catch his mouth . . .

She tightened her arms around her knees instead. "I cannot believe you remembered any of this absurdity of mine."

To her relief he leaned back, stretching out his long legs and planting his palms in the grass behind him to prop himself up. "I brought Fleur and Rauffe here when they were little to show them the nest. Jenny and her grandchildren were not always content with the ones from the years before but built fresh ones from year to year. I climbed up in the tree to remove the old ones. Sometimes I would perch Rauffe on one of the branches so that he could lift them down to me, but Aveline did not approve. He was thin and prone to fevers and headaches she said weakened him and might make him fall. I was always just below him to catch him, of course, but she scolded me worse than Mistress Jenny is scolding us now, so after a few times, I made him stand below to watch with Fleur."

They both sat quietly for a while, until Jenny Wren settled back down in her nest. Even as a child, Cassandry's heart had soared whenever Jenny fluttered and flew away, and had clutched with something tender as Jenny warmed her eggs, then faithfully cared for her hatchlings until they grew large enough to fly themselves.

How *had* her poem of old gone?

> *Jenny Wren, my faithful friend,*
> *How your music cheers my ear*
> *In the pink of dawn . . .*

What had come next? The part about Jenny singing to the sun? Or Cassandry yawning and rubbing the sleep from her eyes? The words had been silly and childish, her first attempt at poetry, and doubtless the world would not mourn their loss. But she wished she could remember them.

A breeze brushed along her cheeks. The sunshine ran warm along her neck. The tightness that had become so intricately woven into her breast that she had ceased to register it, registered now as it slowly released. She felt oddly youthful sitting in the sweet-smelling grass watching Jenny Wren as Jenny watched her. But not so youthful that the pull of attraction ceased to ripple between her and the man beside her.

She stole a glance at Gerolt's profile. It had grown serious again, and reflective.

"What are you thinking?" she asked.

"That Sam and I were not always so different." He kept his tones low, like she, so as not to set Jenny off again.

"You and Sam?" Cassandry could think of few statements more ludicrous. "You are nothing alike!"

"We were once. We fell into a great many scrapes together, and Sam was not always the one leading the way."

Gerolt was the most honorable man she had ever known. He must be jesting with her.

"Name one," she demanded.

"We stole into the village one night and raised the hue and cry just to see all the villagers turn out in alarm. We hid and smothered our laughter as we watched them run about in confusion in their nightclothes."

"That sounds like Samson."

"It was me too, Cassandry. It was my idea. It was Sam who suggested we frighten the dairymaid by tying fur masks over our faces and springing out at her with growls so that she dropped the bucket of milk and ran off screaming of demons who had come for her soul. But I said we should hide my father's sword in old Ned Atkin's haystack. I did not know my father would put Ned in the stocks for it. I deserved the thrashing he gave me when I confessed."

Cassandry sniffed dismissively. "Boyhood mischief. You grew out of it. Samson did not."

"I might not have. There was worse 'mischief' as I grew older. Gambling and drinking. We had begun to walk a dangerous road together, Sam and I. Do you know what stopped me?"

She shook her head, grappling with the implausible portrait he had drawn.

"You." He turned his head to meet her shocked gaze. "Had my father not died and left you in my care, I might have remained as reckless and undisciplined as Sam. But suddenly I was responsible for raising a nine-year-old girl, and I knew I could not do so if I drank away my days in a tavern. You were still grieving for your parents. Even after a year in my father's wardship, you still carried that lost, lonely look in your eyes. The day after I buried my father, I vowed I would find a way to make you smile, to win your trust, to raise you to be as fine a lady as my mother had been. I did not have a notion how to do any of it, but there was something about you that made me determined to try. It was not easy. I made a great many mistakes."

"I do not recall a one," she protested.

He grinned. "You were small, and, as you said yourself, age has dulled your memory."

She swatted playfully at his shoulder. "It is not that dull."

He laughed, sending up another scolding from Jenny Wren. He pressed a finger to his lips, signaling silence until the bird settled back down. By then Gerolt had grown sober again. He straightened, folding up his stretched out legs.

"I hoped fatherhood would steady Sam, as caring for you did me. But instead he went off on that wretched crusade."

"What, so now I was a daughter to you? Or did raising me merely make you feel ancient?"

That brought the twinkle back to his gray eyes, but another expression lurked behind it, something warm but cautious. "And what was I to you? A brother?"

Her breath caught a little. "Yes . . . then."

The twinkle faded at the little pause between her words, but if anything, his eyes grew brighter. "And now?"

She did not answer, but neither could she pull her gaze away from his. Not until he shifted his position and his face slowly drifted ever so close to her own. Then her lashes brushed against her cheeks as she closed her eyes and waited for his hand to tenderly touch her face, his breath to brush her lips . . .

"My lady! Are you here?"

Jenny Wren set up a raucous cry as Lora, Cassandry's maid, burst around the bend in the pathway to join them.

Cassandry blessed the angry, territorial bird for drawing the servant's attention away from her flaming cheeks. She could not see what Gerolt was thinking, for he had turned his head the other way. Had he truly been about to kiss her or had she drifted off into some daydream? Gerolt rose and held out his hand to Cassandry. She let him draw her to her feet, but again when she glanced at him his gaze was fixed elsewhere, this time on the servant.

"What is it, Lora?" Cassandry asked, hoping Jenny's strident reprimand would cover the huskiness in her voice.

"Lady Egelina is in the hall with Lord Rauffe and—there, you old bird, be quiet!—well, if you wish to speak to her before she can escape you again, I believe this would be a very good time."

"Go," Gerolt said, releasing Cassandry's fingers. "You will not want to lose this opportunity."

She *must* have misinterpreted his intentions for him to speak in such cool tones when her own heart still raced and the heat still lingered in her face. Cassandry walked ahead of the servant so that Lora might not see her blush. Egelina and Rauffe. Soon to be married. What had Cassandry been thinking? It was sin to covet Gerolt. She must put all thoughts of him from her mind. But the numbness of her life with Antony had been shattered, and she walked from the garden still shaking with desire.

Chapter 14

She had smiled. She had almost laughed. And he had almost kissed her.

Gerolt dropped back down in the grass and shoved his hands through his hair, simultaneously blessing and cursing Jenny Wren. The small, pert bird had brought his Cassandry back to life, and in doing so, had fanned the passion in him he had thought he could keep subdued to a simmer. He had managed to control it before, when she had been a young woman in his house, so successfully that she had never guessed how deeply he loved and desired her. But she had never gazed into his eyes then the way she had today—not with a girlhood innocence but with a woman's longing.

Why could she not have looked at him that way a month ago when he had gone to lay his heart before her? There could be nothing romantic between them now that their children were betrothed—

But they are not betrothed. Egelina crossed her fingers. His head snapped up. Jenny twittered at him.

"You wonderful, wretched bird," he said. "If you have raised my hopes for nothing, you may not find me so quick to pluck Gib Cat from the tree the next time he tries to make you his dinner."

"... and so she fell asleep beside the rippling pond,
Her hands folded against her cheek as a pillow
And naught but moonglow for her blanket.
And there in the sweet summer grass
She began to dream."

Cassandry followed the sound of Egelina's voice in the great hall, maneuvering her way through the crowd of Gerolt's knights, who all gazed at the dais. She felt the frown tugging at the corners of her mouth, but the picture that greeted her when she reached the raised platform was worse than she'd anticipated. Bad enough that Egelina draw so much attention to herself, but instead of sitting decorously in a chair, she sat on the edge of the dais as though she were a child of six rather than a young woman nearing the threshold of marriage. Cassandry knew it was the poetry. Egelina always fell into such laxity when her mind drifted into composition.

"A melodic humming roused her first,
Then a singing, as delicate as gossamer, fell upon her ears."

At least Rauffe sat beside her, albeit stiffly, cross-legged on the dais floor, saving her from complete impropriety. But the other men—Sir Ingram and Sir Fithian, among several others, sat in the rushes below Egelina as though they were boys again and not men Cassandry's own age, while several younger men lounged about in even greater informality. Sir Owen had gone so far as to sprawl on his stomach with his chin in his hands, gazing at Egelina as though fixed upon some angel. She looked celestial enough in a blue silk gown that matched her eyes, her golden hair unbound about her shoulders, and the glow of creation upon her face.

"The swans still glided beneath the mystic moonlight,
But before her gaze they began to shift and shimmer and form anew,
Until to her astonishment the gossamer song lifted the
enchantment.
The swans were but a magical incarnation of two beautiful silver
princes
Who now stood before her on the shore!"

All the men appeared enrapt by the story except for Rauffe, who rolled his eyes, reminding Cassandry of his quarrel with Egelina in the garden. They had appeared to be on increasingly good terms, but Rauffe looked anything but entranced by the poem. Had they fallen out again? Rauffe was a good-hearted boy. He was Gerolt's son and would surely grow up to learn Gerolt's judgment and wisdom. Rauffe was the only husband for her daughter Cassandry could be sure of because she was sure of Gerolt.

She could not let her desire for Gerolt blind her to what was best for Egelina. Besides, it was a mere whimsy on Cassandry's part to think that, for a moment, he had wanted her too. She had merely believed it because she had wanted it so badly to be true. Thank heaven rationality had returned to her as she had reentered the cool walls of the keep.

She was ashamed of herself for mourning the loss of her poem to Jenny Wren. She would not let anything as foolish as poetry come between Egelina and Rauffe before they were even wed. Egelina would say that verse was a very part of her nature, but Cassandry had learned how quickly the music of the soul could die.

She marched to the dais and touched her daughter's shoulder.

Egelina had apparently been so lost in her dreams that she had not seen her mother approach, for she gave a start and looked blankly at Cassandry before her face puckered in sulky resistance.

"Come with me," Cassandry said quietly.

Egelina gave an angry *hmph!* through her nose, but she stood up and shook out her skirts. Rauffe sprang to his feet alongside her. The previously lounging men all stood, looking sheepish for having been caught in such awkwardly juvenile postures. They bowed and murmured, "Lady Cassandry. Lady Egelina, thank you for your poem," as Cassandry guided her daughter firmly out of the hall.

"What did you think you were doing?" Cassandry demanded when they were alone in their chamber. "You are neither a child nor a servant to be sitting all helter-skelter on the dais like that, and in one of your best gowns!"

Egelina fretted her lower lip before she replied. "I told Sir Fithian about my poetry, so he asked me to recite one of my verses today. I did not think—I was standing when I started, but I always recite the part about the swans while I'm sitting by the pond in our garden at home, and there was no chair nearby, so I . . . I just sat where I was. No one seemed to mind. They all sat on the floor with me."

"So as not to embarrass you by looming over you. They are gentlemen, Gelli. But what they must have thought of you!"

Egelina's face went so fiery red with embarrassment that it softened her mother's heart. Cassandry drew Egelina into her arms.

"Hush, my love. No irreparable harm has been done. Just try to be less careless in the future."

Egelina nodded against Cassandry's shoulder, then suddenly

pushed out of her mother's arms. "No. I'll not apologize or let you lecture me when you have been lying to me for *years.*"

"Gelli—"

"Is it true what Lord Gerolt told me? That you know how to read and write? Do not lie to me again." Antony's blue eyes flashed at Cassandry from her daughter's face.

For a moment Cassandry recoiled, then she recovered herself. If Egelina had her father's flashing eyes and stubborn chin, her straight little nose and the curve of her lips were Cassandry's. *She was born of us both. Even her poetry came from Antony as well as from me.* Then there must be some part of Cassandry in her daughter she could reason with.

"I did not lie, exactly," Cassandry said, "though I did not tell you the truth, either. Come sit with me on the bed, and I will try to explain."

Egelina sat, but she left some distance between her and her mother and crossed her arms in a clear display of her continued anger.

Cassandry had been seeking Egelina for days, bent on this very conversation, but now that the moment had come Cassandry battled with herself not to shrink from it. It would have been easier to tell a loving, compliant, forgiving daughter than the glaring young woman beside her. She took a moment to search for the words. She did not want them to be harsh or hurtful, but the time for pretending was past.

Nevertheless, she tried to begin the story gently. "I was very like you when I was young, Egelina. Believe it or not, I too was once filled with poetry."

Egelina looked surprised, then her brows twitched down in suspicion. "I never heard you quote a single verse. Not one!"

"It is true, all the same. Your father loved poetry too. Before we were married, we would sit in Lord Gerolt's garden and compose together, your father a stanza, then me with a responding one, then he with a response to me . . . Those were among the happiest days of my life. But your father had one advantage I did not. He knew how to write, and because I feared our love poetry would be lost, I begged him to record them on parchment." Cassandry flicked away a blade of grass that had clung to her gown. "But that did not content me, either, for then I wished to be able to read the poems for myself, over and over when we were not together. I loved your father so very much, you see. So I begged Lord Gerolt to teach me to read and write as well. He said his own mother never learned to read. But he was Gerolt; he never denied me anything."

Some of the hostility left Egelina's face as she became caught up in her mother's story.

"The game between your father and me then took a new, delightsome turn," Cassandry continued. "Not only could we recite poetry together in the garden, we could now write to each other every day. We continued to create sweet poems together. Every morning I would send him the stanza I had written the night before, and every night he left a stanza of his own outside my chamber door." Cassandry felt a painful prick in her breast. Her life with Antony had begun with such sweet promise! She realized there had been a second, until now unconscious reason for her outrage at the tokens Egelina and she had found in the mornings. The discoveries had seemed a mockery of the secret game she had once played with Antony.

"I know, Mamma."

Cassandry's head cocked, puzzled at her daughter's words.

"Oh, I did not know that you could write, but I knew Papa could. He told me once that he used to write you poetry and that he left the poems outside your door. I always thought all the words that bubble up in my head came from Papa. I did not know some of them came from you."

"Your Papa told you about his verses?"

Egelina nodded. "I was little, but I remember. He told me that night you both put me to bed after you found me sitting on the steps, watching you dine. The night he called you"—she blushed—"that wicked word and lied to me about what it meant." In that quicksilver way she had of shifting her emotions, she abruptly flung her arms around Cassandry. "He did not mean it, Mamma. He did not mean to hurt you."

Cassandry was too relieved for her daughter's embrace to contradict her. She held Egelina tightly for several minutes before pushing her gently away and tucking a strand of golden hair behind her ear.

"Perhaps he did not," Cassandry said, "but I am afraid we hurt each other in the end. And it was because of pen and parchment."

Egelina's fair brows plunged down as she grew cross again. "Nothing you can say will change my mind about the nunnery."

"Gelli, I thought you were becoming fond of Rauffe."

"Oh, I like him well enough now, I suppose," Egelina confessed. "As a friend. But I do not want to marry him. I am going to be a nun and learn to read and write. I *am*, Mamma!"

"Oh, Gelli, a nunnery is the furthest thing you are suited for. Do you imagine they will let you write of young girls who fall asleep beside a pond and waken to silver princes on the shore?"

Egelina flounced up and away from the bed. She stood for several minutes with her back to her mother, then turned very slowly with her arms crossed again. "Perhaps—just perhaps—if you would not be so stubborn, I might consider a husband. Not Rauffe," she added quickly, "who has not the least appreciation of poetry. But someone like Papa."

Cassandry swept to her feet, her hand going to her throat in horror at the thought. "Oh, child, a man like that would break your heart."

Egelina looked shocked. Cassandry had not meant to blurt out the truth like that. The early tokens outside the door must have begun to turn Egelina's head. Cassandry cursed Samson for not attaching her name to the gifts earlier, allowing Egelina time to form the romantic notion that some knight—no doubt one as handsome as a silver prince—sought to court her instead of her mother.

"I must tell you the rest," Cassandry said, "and you must listen very carefully." She realized her palms had grown moist and ran them down the front of her skirts. She had never wanted Egelina to know these things, but it was imperative now that she learn the truth, for her own safety.

Still, Cassandry sought for the gentlest way to word it. "Men change after marriage. Before a betrothal, they do not like it, but they accept that many men are free to court you. But after you marry, once you are theirs alone, they become . . . possessive . . . jealous. It was not only poetry I learned to write, Gelli. After we wed, I sometimes wrote letters to old friends who lived here at Lyonstoke, to men, like Lord Gerolt, whom I had known all my life. The letters were perfectly innocent, but your father did not like it. It caused . . . problems between us. He wanted me to stop. I was selfish and did not want to. We quarreled."

The word felt a pale description of the violent verbal altercations between her and Antony.

"Everyone quarrels," Egelina said. "You and I are quarreling now, but that does not mean I love you any less."

Oh, how those words comforted Cassandry. But the stubborn set of Egelina's mouth did not soften. Cassandry knew she had been *too* gentle, wishing not to stain the memory of a father who had loved his daughter. But Egelina had to be warned.

"It grew into more than mere arguments," Cassandry said, "when a certain man of my acquaintance began to take advantage of my knowledge. He wrote inappropriate letters to me. You are old enough now to guess on what subject."

Egelina's eyes grew wide. "Do you mean like those stories of men who fell in love with other men's wives in those songs the minstrels sometimes sang before our hearth? The ones that made

Papa smirk and look at you? I thought he was just laughing at the minstrel's songs and that you only blushed because I was in the room and you thought me too young to hear them."

"You were too young. We should have sent you to bed, but I was a coward. I knew your father would not openly mock me when you were in the room, so . . . so I clung to you and kept you near me when I should not have."

"But Papa cannot really have thought you were in love with someone else?"

Cassandry took too long in searching for an answer again. She remembered the way she had clung to Gerolt. It had not been love, not the romantic kind—not then—not like she felt now . . .

Egelina slapped a hand to her lips and backed another step away. "Mamma!" The word came muffled from behind her fingers. "You could *not* have loved someone other than Papa!"

"No, Gelli, of course I did not," Cassandry said quickly. "But that man who wrote me was very cunning in his words, and one day your Papa found one of the letters, and nothing I could say would convince him that I loved only him. That was when I learned the true power—and danger—of the written word. Those letters ruined everything that was trusting and loving between your father and I. And it is why I will not allow you to repeat my mistake."

"But Papa forgave you."

Forgave me? For a sin I never committed? Had such an irony been true, Cassandry was not sure she would have accepted such "forgiveness."

Egelina must have realized how her words sounded, for she lowered her hand and added, "I am not saying you were guilty. Of course I do not think that, Mamma. But after he treated you coldly, Papa was sorry, like he was that night when he called you . . . that word."

Cassandry sighed. "I wish that were true, Gelli, but you do not understand how it was between your father and me. He could not overcome his anger, and I . . . I could not overcome my hurt. The only thing we agreed upon was that you should never know. So we did our best to shield you—" She broke off, startled by the furious blaze in Egelina's eyes.

"Well, you did not shield me. You used to sing to me at night, and sometimes you even laughed, but then you stopped. You hardly smiled at all, and you never sang anymore. And Papa—he would come to me while I was playing with my dolls and scoop me into his arms and cry into my hair and say he had been unkind to you again and he was sorry, but he knew you could not forgive him. And then I would hear him shouting at you all over again, and I would hear you crying, and you wouldn't sing me to sleep when I begged you to, and then Papa would come in and kneel by my bed and weep again. You 'shielded me' from nothing, except that I did not know *why* you were both so unhappy."

Cassandry flinched as though the vehement words had been physical objects flung at her. Her thoughts lashed out at Antony. How could he burden their young daughter with his tears? If he had truly been repentant he would have ceased to belittle and humiliate Cassandry. At least she had confined her own tears to the privacy of her chamber.

But her strong streak of honesty swiftly condemned herself as well. She had tried so hard to be everything her daughter needed in a mother—to hold her, to teach her, to guide her—but Egelina was right. Her music had died with her poetry, and although she was certain it was not true that she never smiled at her daughter, she could not remember the last time she had laughed.

A part of her thrashed herself alongside Antony that she had not protected Egelina from their conflict, as she thought she had done. But in a way it made it easier that Egelina knew.

"Then there are no more secrets," Cassandry said, "for I have now told you why. It was the letters, Gelli. If I had not known how to red and write, that man"—she would not speak Samson's name when Egelina could not avoid encountering him in the castle—"could never have stirred up such mischief between your father and me. Everything would have been different between the two of us—between the three of us."

She moved toward Egelina, suddenly needing the comfort of her daughter in her arms again, but Egelina stepped around her.

"I am sorry, Mamma. I am sorry Papa did not believe you. It is all the more reason, then, for you to let me go to a nunnery. If men are so jealous, then I will be safe from mistrustful men there."

"Or," Cassandry said with a frown, "you will not learn to write, and you will marry Lord Rauffe, and no man will ever be able to come between the two of you with a letter Rauffe knows you do not know how to read."

Egelina planted her hands on her hips and shook her golden head so hard her curls whipped from side to side. "I will *not* marry Rauffe. I crossed my fingers when I said the vows, so you cannot make me. I do not want to be like you, Mamma, someone who never smiles and who lets their poetry die. If that is the cost of marriage, then I never, never shall!"

"Egelina—"

"*No!* I would sooner learn to write sacred poetry than no poetry at all. I will be a nun or I will be a spinster, but I will never be a wife unless you let me learn to write!"

She ran past her mother, opened the chamber door, and slammed it behind her. The sound still reverberated in Cassandry's ears as she sank back down on the bed. Antony would have agreed with her refusal to teach Egelina, though he would have laid the blame for their daughter's rebellious waywardness at Cassandry's feet.

Had he really wept at Egelina's bedside? Had there truly been moments when he regretted his hurtful, spiteful words?

Why did you not speak them, then? Oh, Antony!

Cassandry found her hand at her mouth and tears in her eyes. Whatever the reason, he had *not* spoken them. Instead, he had beaten her down until her only remaining protection had been an inner deadness that had left her unable to laugh with their daughter or sing to her.

Cassandry had felt light in the garden again today, watching Jenny Wren. She had felt sunshine on her skin, the caress of the breeze on her cheeks. Sitting in the grass with Gerolt, the deadness in her that had begun ever so subtly to ebb since returning to Lyonstoke had so dissipated that she had even felt the tickle of laughter in her throat. And desire for a man she could never, ever have. Even if Gerolt wanted her in return, what would become of Egelina? A nunnery was out of the question. But to trust her daughter to any husband but Rauffe—Rauffe was young, but Cassandry saw too much of his father in him to doubt Ruffe would grow up as honorable as Gerolt. The only bit of annoyance she saw between them was Egelina's poetry, and as long as Egelina did not learn to write, she would outgrow the foolishness. Her verses would fade, as Cassandry's had to Jenny Wren, and Egelina would soon find herself too busy being a wife and mother to even miss them.

Yes, all would be well once Egelina married Rauffe. Giving Egelina to any other man was unthinkable. What if he broke her heart with impatience or abuse or indifference? What if he became jealous, as Antony had, and stripped her of all the radiant exuberance that made her Egelina? No, there was no other future Cassandry could bear to imagine for her daughter.

The one useful thing Antony might have done had he still lived would be to command Egelina to obey him and marry as he bade her. Egelina needed a father's strong hand, but there was no one to stand in Antony's place. Except for—

Except for the man who never once commanded me. Gerolt had preferred persuasion, and he had always been able to convince

Cassandry of his wisdom. Even when she had been so very eager to marry Antony at fourteen, the only time she recalled resisting Gerolt's counsel for days, but in the end he had convinced her to wait another two years. She wondered if he had put his foot down more firmly with Antony at the time, for Antony had ceased to press her to beg Gerolt to let them wed.

She would ask Gerolt to do what she could not. After all, marrying their children had been his idea. She might be Egelina's mother, but he was Egelina's guardian and liege lord. Whether by persuasion or the strength of his authority, Egelina must be made to bend.

Chapter 15

G erolt stared, startled, into Cassandry's face. "You wish me to do what?"

"Command Egelina to marry Rauffe," she repeated. "I have tried and tried to reason with her, but she will not listen to a word I say."

She could not be serious? Not after what he had seen in her eyes today? Not after she had almost let him kiss her?

He had observed the change in her, sitting beneath the tree. Her eyes had lit with pleasure while watching Jenny Wren. It had clicked in his mind that perhaps familiar objects and creatures and routines that had once brought her happiness here at Lyonstoke might do so again, easing her sorrow, luring her into feeling joy in living—and loving—once more. Rauffe's health had improved so dramatically Gerolt felt confident there would be years before his son had a need to marry. Years to find him some wife other than Egelina.

Gerolt had assigned his knights to patrol or other duties to arrange for a quieter atmosphere in the hall this evening so that he and Cassandry might play chess as they had when she was young. How often during such games had she chattered merrily away at him, freely trusting him with the things of her heart. It was too much to hope for merriment tonight. He had known it the moment she entered the hall with Egelina, Cassandry's face stiff and resolved. He had conceded to her request that a board be set up for their children to play as well, but he and Cassandry had been a half-dozen moves into their own game before Cassandry revealed why she looked so grave.

He grasped for some way to deflect the determination in her eyes.

"If Egelina is still reluctant, perhaps we should reconsider the match." *Please, Sparrow, do not cast away what we almost gained today. Give me time to heal your heart. Give me time to court you.*

"No," Cassandry said so brusquely that he thought at first she had read the plea in his mind. "She is simply being stubborn. They are too young to know what is best for them; they require us to guide them."

"Then you command her," he said, his exasperation mingling with a stab of chagrin. "She is your daughter."

"You are her guardian," Cassandry countered. "The marriage was your idea. It is your duty to see that she obeys you."

Gerolt glanced away from the chessboard and saw Egelina whispering so incessantly to Rauffe that Rauffe's attempts to reply were swiftly stifled. Egelina slapped his hand twice when he tried to move first his knight and then a rook, pointing to the danger that awaited him from her bishop and queen while scarcely pausing to draw breath in whatever she was saying.

"So that she will hate me instead of you?" Gerolt said. He moved one of his rooks forward to knock down one of Cassandry's pawns. "You will go home to Rengrave Castle, and I will be left with a daughter-in-law who detests me."

"She will not detest you. She will thank you for it one day." Cassandry made an attempt to block the rook.

"She may thank me more for letting her fall in love and marry a man of her own choosing, as you did. Perhaps I should never have suggested this match—"

He broke off as Cassandry's hand jerked and knocked over her queen, sending the figure rolling so briskly it took out her knight and his bishop and several of his pawns.

"Oh!" She quickly began to gather the scattered pieces. "Oh, we shall have to start over. I am sorry. I will reset the board while you go speak with Egelina."

He caught her hand and was surprised to find it shaking. "Cassandry—"

She looked up, a faint shimmer in her eyes. Tears? "Gerolt, I beg you. You promised me she should marry Rauffe. You gave me your word. You cannot be the man I remember if you mean to break it now."

The very idea of breaking a pledge made him recoil. He sought for another tactic. "Let us give her more time," he suggested. "No doubt she will come around on her own in the end. I am certain she takes after her mother and is a sensible girl at heart." And while Egelina was considering, Gerolt would be doing his utmost to change Cassandry's mind.

"She is her father's daughter and has not the least sense." Cassandry pulled away her hand to begin reordering the pawns.

Gerolt watched her for a few moments in silence. Did she realize how much her words revealed? Since their encounter outside the stables, he had wondered if her grief were truly caused by Antony's death or by something else she was concealing from him. He asked softly, as she set the rooks in the corner squares nearest her, "Are you ready to tell me what happened between you and Antony?"

"There is nothing to tell. And if there were," she added, raising her dark eyes to his in quiet reproof, "I should expect you to respect my privacy by not pressing me to confide what I prefer not to."

He fixed his gaze on his own pieces as he began to organize them on the board so that she might not see how her rebuff had hurt him. He hated the secrets that had fallen between them, all begun by the letter he still kept in his chamber, requesting him with chill politeness to refrain from writing further to her. *My husband is my life now. I must needs forsake the past, which I regret, includes you, my former guardian.*

Former, she had underlined twice, doubling the blow that reminded him she now belonged to another man. Had it been wrong to seek to maintain her friendship? Had it been disloyal to Aveline? His wife had never seemed to want his friendship. Aveline had appeared to find her highest pleasure in fulfilling what she claimed to be her "duty" as his wife, the mother of his children, and mistress of his castle. Nevertheless, guilt that a part of him still clung to another woman had prompted him to accept Cassandry's dismissal, however reluctantly. *She is wiser than I,* he had told himself. But all the love he had poured into his lands, and into Fleur and Rauffe, had not completely filled the empty crack in his heart that Aveline and Cassandry between them had cleft there.

"Very well," he said. He stood up abruptly, leaving half his pieces still sitting randomly on the board.

She looked startled. "Where are you going?"

"To play a game with your daughter. You said you wished me to speak with her."

Cassandry's breast rose with a quickened breath. "Are—are you going to command her to marry Rauffe?"

"Not until I have exhausted a few other methods that used to work on you."

"But if persuasion fails? You are her guardian, Gerolt. She will have no choice but to do as you bid her."

I wish I had commanded you to marry me twenty-four years

ago. But you would have hated me for it. You were so completely in love with Antony—then.

He would have the truth from her eventually. He only prayed it might not be too late when he finally learned it, for she had quite rightly perceived that his honor would not allow him to abjure a marriage between their children unless Cassandry consented to it.

He left her to join Egelina and Rauffe.

"A game, my Lady Egelina," Gerolt said, laying a hand on his son's shoulder. It was still too thin but was beginning to flesh out. "Let us see how well your mother has taught you to play."

Rauffe protested. "But we are still in the middle of our game."

Gerolt studied the board for a moment, then moved Egelina's queen to corner Rauffe's king. "Checkmate, my son. Now, go play with Lady Cassandry. Mayhap you will have better luck beating her."

Rauffe sat frowning a moment at his cornered king, then shrugged, stood up, and took his father's place across from Cassandry. Gerolt watched her smile as she welcomed the youth. For the second time since dinner today, it actually reached her eyes.

"Well, my lady," Gerolt said, sinking down into the chair his son had abandoned, "shall we set up the board anew?"

He collected the pieces and arranged them for a fresh game, aware as he did so how Egelina nervously pleated her fingers together.

"You and Rauffe appeared to be enjoying your game before I preempted it," Gerolt said.

Enjoying? She had been chattering away as cheerfully as her mother had once done with him, and while Egelina had not seemed inclined to allow Rauffe much opportunity to respond, he had not been slumping or scowling. Was Gerolt being selfish? Were the two falling in love? If so, how could he deny them a future together just to indulge a longing he should have outgrown years ago? He had passed his fiftieth year, had lived his life, had reared a family. Could he deny these children the opportunity to do the same merely because Cassandry had fallen into his life again?

Unable to speak for a moment past the lump that rose in his throat, he waved a hand over the board, indicating the first move should be Egelina's.

She nudged a white pawn forward. Her face was very pink. "I did not throw a tantrum, if that is what Mamma told you. I lost my temper when she told me she could write but that I must not—but it was not a tantrum."

He recovered his composure during this defensive statement. "She said no such thing of you." He opened up a space with a red pawn. "In fact, she has told me nothing at all about your quarrel. I have not come to scold you, if that is what you fear."

"Oh. Well, good, then. For I do not throw tantrums."

"I am certain you do not."

What he would do with her if she should, he had not the least idea. Fleur had never been so volatile, nor had Cassandry. Neither of them had prepared him for temperamental children with stormy blue eyes.

"Do *you* think it is fair, sir? That she will not let me write?"

He sought for some ambivalent answer that might satisfy both her and her mother.

"She says men change after marriage," Egelina continued before he could find one. "Is it true? Did you change when you married Lady Aveline?"

"Change? How?"

Egelina looked like she regretted her impulsive outburst. She tossed her head in too casual a manner. "Oh, I don't know. Just . . . change." She moved her pawn another square, he presumed attempting to make room for her knight to escape.

"Everyone changes, my lady." He moved another pawn of his

own. "All of us, as we grow older. You are no longer a child. You have quite grown-up thoughts now, do you not?"

She nodded her head so eagerly he had to bite off a smile.

"I am certain your parents changed too." How much? Dared he ask her? No, unworthy to take advantage of her innocence to discover what Cassandry did not wish him to know. He continued to Egelina, "What you want today will not be what you want tomorrow. This nunnery you desire, are you certain you feel a call-ing, or is it merely that you do not wish to marry my son?" He held his breath, quite ignobly hoping she would confess the latter.

She fretted her pretty lower lip with her teeth. "I do not wish to marry Rauffe," she said as frankly as she had when she and Gerolt had danced.

He released his breath slowly so as not to startle her with an explosive exhale of relief.

"I used to think . . . I used to dream that someday I might fall in love and marry *someone*—"

"Like a beautiful silver prince?" he teased when she broke off. "Sir Fithian told me of your poem."

"I know that is only pretend," she said, her blush deepening. "I like pretty words and the pretty pictures I see in my head, but I know they are not real. There are so many of them, sir. Words and pictures. I am terrified that if I do not find a way to save some of them to parchment, I will forget them when new ones flow into my mind. I almost asked Rauffe to teach me, but then I thought that might encourage him to think I had changed my mind about marrying him, so I refrained." She gave a tragic little sigh. "There really is no way other than the nunnery."

The pace of their play had picked up. Three pawns on each side had fallen. He let her slide her rook through the path she had cleared and take his knight while he struggled with his reply. He felt Cassandry watching him and cast her a glance, meeting briefly the sternness in her eyes. He had given his word. Only Cassandry herself could allow him to void it. Cassandry—or the nunnery.

Selfish. Egelina did not have the disposition to be a nun. He knew he could not encourage that, even if it would free Cassandry for him. She wanted this marriage. *He* had wanted it too, until— until he had almost kissed her. How did he know she would have welcomed that? She might just as easily have slapped his face. *You are a very old fool, Gerolt. She cast you from her life. She will not trust you with whatever hurt she carries in her. She did not love you then, and she does not love you now. Be content with her friendship, if you can win it back, and help her bind these two children together as we both said we wished.*

"You asked me if people change after marriage." Gerolt removed a threat to his queen with his rook. "Sometimes a man and a woman do not know how well suited for marriage they are until after they are wed. If you will forgive me for indulging in my son's virtues for a moment, allow me to assure you that he is honest and generous and has been taught to treat others with courtesy and consideration. I would expect him to treat his wife the same. He may not be fond of poetry, but he likely has interests you would consider dull as well."

"He is hound mad," Egelina said. "He knows every breed for hunting and what one excels at over the other, and—well, I did not much listen when he rattled on and on about it at dinner. I suppose I should no more like to listen to him talk about hounds every day than he should wish to listen to my poems. Which just goes to show," she added, making a surprise move with a pawn that took one of Gerolt's bishops, "that we are not suited for each other at all."

Gerolt took a moment to recover from the blow to his little army. "You say that because you are not yet wed. Of course you will not agree in everything, but in the things of most importance, you will soon find yourselves so intricately bound together that one day you will not be able to imagine your life without the other."

He would not embarrass her by speaking of the children that would come, but it was children, he had learned, that could bring the most disparate couple together. He and Aveline may have shared few things of the heart, but when it came to the stillbirth and the child they had lost in the cradle, they had been one in their grief, as they had been united in their joy when Fleur and then Rauffe had been born, linked in their worry for Rauffe's health, and again joined together in mourning when Fleur had died in childbed. Had Aveline filled his deepest emotional needs? No. He supposed he had not filled hers either, for she had never invited him to try. But to say that in twenty-three years he had not come to love her would not have been true. There were days he still keenly missed the sound of her voice, the scent she had worn, the tread of her footstep on the stair.

Egelina broke through his memories. "But Rauffe will not allow me to write once we are wed. So it must be the nunnery. Please, sir, will you tell Mamma so?"

"Why will Rauffe not allow you to write after you are married?" Gerolt asked.

"Because people change. *Rauffe* will change, or I will, and what if . . . what if . . . ?"

"What if what?"

"Oh, I cannot say, except that it will be terrible and I do not wish to have my poetry die and to cease to smile and sing."

"That would be terrible, indeed." Gerolt cast another glance at Cassandry, waiting for Rauffe to make his next move. *Is that what happened to you, Sparrow? Did Antony change?*

"Do not tell her," Egelina hissed. "I did not mean to say— Please! She does not want anyone to know—"

That brought his gaze back to Egelina's agitated face. "Know what, my lady?"

Egelina pushed so abruptly away from the board that her queen and king both toppled over. "I do not wish to play anymore. I have a headache . . . my stomach . . . I am feeling faint . . . Oh, I must go!"

"Wait. Let me summon your mother if you are so unwell."

Egelina looked panicked. "No! Tell her I went out to the garden for a breath of air, but that is all. I am fine."

Cassandry had caught her daughter's movement and had risen, with Rauffe, from their own board.

"Oh, please, *please* do not say anything to her of our conversation," Egelina pleaded. "She will think I said it in spite, but I would never betray her, no matter how angry I was with her. *Please*, sir—"

"Your confidence is mine, my lady," Gerolt assured her.

"Egelina!" Cassandry joined them. "Whatever is it, my love?" She placed a hand to her daughter's brow, clearly alarmed by her reddened face.

"It is nothing, Mamma. Lord Gerolt said something to make me blush—but only in fun," she added swiftly when Cassandry sent a startled look at Gerolt. "I will go cool my cheeks in the garden, and Rauffe must come with me because . . . because I wish to ask him about the white puppy in the litter that frolicked before the hearth last night."

"Really?" Rauffe went bright with pleasure. "You mean Venus? She's called a rache, a scent hound used to bring down the prey. Or she will be when she grows up. She's the runt of the litter but already very fleet and—"

Egelina took Rauffe's arm, and they went out of the hall together.

"A pity she says she will not marry him," Gerolt murmured. "She appears to have done him a world of good." He turned his head and caught Cassandry's accusation.

"You said you would convince her."

"I am still working on it." Knowing it would bolster her will against his own, he reluctantly added, "I believe she would consent very readily if you would only allow her to learn to write. I will make it clear to Rauffe that he must never mock her poetry or even roll his eyes again. What harm can there be in it, Cassandry?"

"If I wished her to know, I would have taught her myself," she said. "You must allow me to know best with my own daughter."

A week ago Gerolt would have simply accepted this, but now he shook his head. "If you have taught me anything since you have been here, it is that sometimes we are too close to our own children to know what is best for them. In seventeen years, it never crossed my mind that almonds might be responsible for Rauffe's headaches, yet in a matter of days you guessed their ill effect on him, removed them from his diet, and restored him to good health. Perhaps you cannot see the situation clearly with Egelina. Let me ask one of my clerks to teach her—"

"No."

"Why? What can you possibly fear from it? It did you no harm to learn." She averted her face a little too quickly. He inhaled sharply. "Did it?"

"What an absurd question," she said. "Shall we finish my game or yours while we wait for the children to return?"

He was not convinced by her parry. Had he stumbled across part of the mystery she held from him? But what could it possibly have to do with the written word? How could that have changed her marriage? For Egelina had clearly implied that something in her marriage had changed.

Perhaps if they resumed another game now that Rauffe and Egelina were gone, kept their conversation light and casual until Cassandry relaxed, she would let fall another clue.

"Let me see where you left off the game with Rauffe," he said. "I have not played with him for ages. Come show me what he remembered from our matches when he was a boy."

Cassandry spent several minutes pointing out Rauffe's moves, which Gerolt agreed had been quite respectably shrewd. His son perhaps played better when he did not have a pretty, gilt-haired young woman chattering away at him.

"You must admit," Cassandry said, moving her knight to block the last move Rauffe had made, "it is encouraging that they went out to the garden together, do you not think? She cannot be completely averse to him. They talk together freely at the dinner table now. I know she thinks her poetry stands between them, but that will fade as she grows older."

He slid his queen three squares to take out her knight. "Is that what happened with you? Did you outgrow your poetry?"

She pursed her lips for an instant before she replied without taking her gaze from her lost piece. "That, and a great deal of other nonsense."

"But not chess, I hope? I fear you have grown a little rusty."

"Antony did not like to play. But I only need a little practice before I have you at a standstill again, my lord."

"You, my dear, were always too busy prattling at me while you played to pay strict attention to my instructions."

"When I was little." She moved her king safely out of reach of his queen. "But I was watching you more carefully than you thought. Remember how often I learned to checkmate you in my thirteenth year? That was because I knew if I chattered enough questions at you, it would divert your concentration while you considered what counsel to give me. Into your distraction I slipped, my lord, and began to win game after game. Or have you chosen to forget because you are too embarrassed even now to confess you were outwitted by a thirteen-year-old girl?"

"A thirteen-year-old minx, you mean." He laughed and was rewarded with an almost mischievous gleam from the glance she darted at him.

They fell into comfortable conversation as they moved and

countermoved. No matters of great import passed between them until Cassandry rather absently said, "I hope you do not mind that I visited Lady Aveline's solar today? It will become Egelina's when she marries Rauffe. I was surprised to see my tapestry of the white doe and the maiden still hung on the wall. Did Lady Aveline not object to another woman's handiwork in her private chamber?"

"It was a particular favorite of hers," Gerolt replied. "Though she never knew you, she praised my 'young ward's' talent and chose to keep it when she replaced others that pleased her less."

"The balance is off."

He removed his queen from a threat by her bishop. "Balance?"

"There are one too many rabbits in the scene, and the bird on the right should be farther from the corner. It did not bother Lady Aveline?"

"I do not think she ever noticed. She never spoke of it."

Cassandry changed her bishop's direction to take his rook. "Antony would have. He did not like it when my weavings were not precisely symmetrical."

Gerolt stared at the part in her smooth, dark hair where the white of her scalp showed through. Antony—brash, reckless, devil-may-care Antony—had complained to his wife of an extra rabbit in a tapestry?

A vivacious clapping of hands brought up Cassandry's head and turned his own toward the entrance of the hall. Marion stood there with Samson at her side.

"Oh!" Marion exclaimed. "I told Father it was too soon to go to bed, even though we passed Lady Egelina on the stair on her way to retire. May we join you? I have not played chess in ever so long!"

She glided over to the board where he sat with Cassandry, Samson strolling casually behind her. Gerolt rose and bowed to her.

"Of course, my lady. There is a board there, where my son and the Lady Egelina were playing earlier—"

"Checkmate."

Gerolt jerked around to see Cassandry plop her bishop into an empty square diagonal to his king. She stood while he was still staring at the board for an escape he gradually conceded was impossible.

Cassandry's lips turned up, but this time her eyes remained unlit. "I am afraid I am too old for these late-night hours. Good night, Lady Marion, Sir Samson, my lord."

She curtsied to each one of them.

"But that will leave our numbers uneven," Samson protested. "Just one game with me, my lady."

"I do not think so, sir."

"Please." Samson lightly set a hand on her arm and guided her over to the other board while Marion sat down with a glowing smile in Cassandry's former seat.

"My husband always let me win," Marion said as she reorganized the pieces on the board. "Will you be equally chivalrous, my lord?"

Gerolt resumed his seat, resisting the impulse to gaze after Cassandry. "One does not learn by receiving easy wins, my lady."

"That is what Fleur always said you taught her. She was the one who showed me how to play, and she was quite merciless. Very well, then. Humiliate me as you please, sir." She gave him a saucy grin.

He lent but half an ear to her animated conversation as they began to play. From the corner of his eye, he saw that Cassandry and Samson remained standing beside their board. A quick, sideways glance revealed them engaged in what appeared to be an intense, low-voiced exchange.

"Marion," Gerolt said when she fell into silence to study her next move, "do you wish to marry again? Is there one of my men who pleases you? Or perhaps one of my widowed vassals? If so, I shall gladly dower you again. I wish you to be happy."

She raised her gaze swiftly to his face. "Marry—one of your men or vassals? But I thought . . . My father said . . ."

"I know what your father has likely said to you. He feared for Rauffe's health, as my wife did, as we all did. But Rauffe is well now and growing stronger. He will soon wed the Lady Egelina, and within a few years I expect I will have a grandson." He cursed Samson for the stricken look on his daughter's face. Gerolt had frankly told him he did not desire Marion to wife. How could Sam have been so thoughtless as to raise the hope of marriage in her anyway?

"I should not disappoint you," she whispered through lips that trembled touchingly.

"I am too old for you, my dear."

"You are not! I should make a very good wife."

"I do not doubt it—to someone else."

"To you! I—"

An angry voice, just short of a hiss, cut her off. "This ends now, Sir Samson. If I find one more outside my door, I will show him the letters. I swear I will."

Gerolt swiveled fully in his chair, but Cassandry was already sweeping out of the hall.

Samson pulled his chair over to Gerolt and Marion and sat down beside their board. Had his friend gone a little pale, or was it a trick of the torchlight in the hall? Surely the latter. Sam's smile was as easy as ever.

"I seem to have lost my partner. I shall have to sit here and watch the two of you."

Marion pushed back her chair and stood up. Even Samson had to see how close she was to tears. "I am afraid the game has lost its allure for one of us. I think I will follow Lady Cassandry's example and retire for the night. My lord. Father." She curtsied to them both, then departed with a dignified gait up the stairs.

"If I did not know you better," Samson said, leaning back in his chair to gaze at Gerolt, "I would think you had just done something to break my daughter's heart."

Chapter 16

Egelina looked up with a start from where she sat on the bed in her nightdress. She stood to greet her mother as Cassandry entered their chamber, but Cassandry observed how her hands slipped behind her back.

"I thought I would find you asleep again." Cassandry closed the door and embraced her daughter. She craned her neck a little to try to glimpse Egelina's hands, but Egelina wound her arms around Cassandry and returned her hug. When Cassandry released her, both hands were behind Egelina's back again.

"I was just sitting here . . . thinking," Egelina said while Cassandry wondered if, and what, her daughter might be concealing.

"About what, my love?"

"Oh . . . just about the day." Egelina pulled free the ribbon she still wore with her right hand and turned away to place it in her jewelry casket. "I like it here, Mamma. Everyone is kind to me. Sir Ingram makes me laugh, I have finally learned to understand Sir Fithian's lisp, and Sir Owen shares poetry with me. He is Welsh, you know, and says that poetry blooms in every Welshman's heart."

Egelina's hands were lost in the shadows near the jewelry

casket, but Cassandry heard the tiny click of the key as she locked it shut.

Whatever she might have placed there alongside the ribbon paled in comparison with Cassandry's alarm at her daughter's words. She spun Egelina about to face her.

"Gelli, you are not falling in love with Sir Owen? There could be nothing worse than to marry a man like him."

Oh, heavens! Was it possible that Sir Owen had left the early tokens? It was just the sort of thing a "poet" would do. Had not Antony left verses at her door? Perhaps her request that Gerolt investigate the matter had frightened Sir Owen into stopping, but by then Cassandry had accused Samson, thus giving him the idea to take up the game himself with her.

"I did not say I wish to marry him, Mamma, though I do not see why you say it would be so bad if I did. He is honest and chivalrous and clever—"

"And as handsome as a gilded prince?" Cassandry said, remembering the silver princes of Egelina's own poem.

"He is handsome," Egelina agreed, "though probably not as handsome as a prince. It was just a poem, Mamma. I did not make my princes silver to be beautiful but to be mystical, like the moon. I do not care how a man looks if he has an honest heart."

Cassandry should have been pleased by this reply, but since Egelina had just called Sir Owen "honest," she remained suspicious.

Egelina pulled away from her mother's grasp, stretched and yawned, then slipped into bed. "Rauffe is not nearly as bad as I feared he would be, since he has stopped mumbling and blushing and slouching." She settled her head against the pillow. "He has some very odd quirks, though. Did you know he cannot tell colors?"

Cassandry was considering how to ask Gerolt to rebuke Sir Owen while concurrently rebuking herself for feeling so downcast at the sight of Gerolt playing chess with Marion, but this statement snapped her attention back. "What do you mean, he cannot tell colors?"

"With his clothes. I asked him why he sometimes wears that garish green surcote to dinner, and he looked surprised and said, 'It is not green, it is yellow.'" Egelina yawned again. "So I asked him what color my gown was, and he said it was yellow, too, when you know, Mamma, that I wore red tonight. I asked him what color his tunic was, and he said, 'Blue, of course,' but he thought the shocking green embroidery on it was yellow again. So he can see some colors, but I think he cannot see greens and reds. He said I could test him in the morning with the flowers in the garden. It was too dark to see their colors clearly tonight, even with a full moon." She rolled on her back and appeared to stretch her toes beneath the sheets. "I think it is very unkind for people to laugh at him for something he cannot help. Good night, Mamma."

She shifted again, with her back to Cassandry, and from her deepened breathing, fell asleep almost instantly.

Cassandry mulled over this new information about Rauffe as she moved to the door to call Lora to help her undress. The poor boy. As if his life were not already difficult enough. She would have to tell Gerolt about his vision problems tomorrow. If Gerolt could tear himself away from Marion long enough to listen. She wondered how late they would sit together in the hall, if Samson would leave them to play alone, if their conversation would grow warm, if their night would end with kisses—

She paused, her hand on the latch, her cheeks hot, and leaned her forehead against the still-closed door. *Shame on you, Cassandry! Shame on you for coveting a man's kisses at your age, especially Gerolt's. Marion will make him happy, while you hold only blame in your heart.*

Blame, but love and longing, too, so strong that it made her ache clear to her core. *Are you angry because he taught you how to write, because he did not stop your marriage to Antony, because he did not come racing to save you instead of letting you cut him off, or because he is in love with a merry young woman instead of you?*

The answer did not matter. Egelina was clearly softening toward Rauffe. If Cassandry could head off the temptation of Sir Owen, she was certain it would not be long now ere Egelina dropped her objections to the marriage. And once she did, once they were wed, there could be no future for Cassandry and Gerolt, even if Cassandry found a way to let her hurt and anger go.

Cassandry was not surprised when she awoke alone again. She presumed Egelina had taken Rauffe out into the bright morning sunlight to quiz him on the colors of the flowers. Yes, their courtship was proceeding very nicely.

Cassandry had slept surprisingly ill again, considering it was the first night she had not tossed and turned worrying about Egelina. She sat up, scrubbed her hands through her tangled hair, found a silver thread in the strand that fell over her eyes, and plucked it out. She studied the felon between her fingers. Gerolt was ten years older than she, with a great deal more sprinkling of salt in his hair than she yet possessed. By the time Marion grew old enough to find her first gray hair, Gerolt would be too old and blind to see it. The thought brought Cassandry a dismal sort of jealousy.

Wicked. What harm has Marion ever done to you, save to bring her joyous spirit into Gerolt's life?

Joy. The memory had felt a vague illusion when Cassandry had first returned to Lyonstoke, but yesterday in the garden, watching Jenny Wren, struggling to remember her girlhood poem, the sensation had returned to her vividly. And last night, while she had sat playing chess with Gerolt, another long-lost emotion had settled over her—contentment. Until Marion had joined them, stirring up all of Cassandry's old grudges as a defense against the hurt that had surged in her at seeing the young woman take her place at the chessboard.

Cassandry shook herself and climbed out of bed. She would be no more suited for the nunnery than Egelina if she continued to harbor worldly thoughts like these. She exchanged her nightdress for a fresh chemise, combed and pinned her hair, rinsed her face in the basin of water on the table near the wardrobe, selected her gown for the day, and set it on the bed. She found herself drawing a slow, tense breath then. Would there be another token outside the door when she called for Lora? Or had the threat she had made last night to show Gerolt Samson's letters finally frightened Samson into desisting with his wretched game? If it had not, she did not know what she would do, for she had no actual letters to carry out her threat.

She pulled open the door, her gaze riveted to the spot where the tokens had repeatedly appeared. As she had dreaded, there lay a new one. She bent to pick up the tiny basket with a polished red apple lying on a bed of straw. A bit of parchment was tucked in alongside it. If only her name would appear in Samson's handwriting instead of this simple script that disguised his identity, she might at least have shown *this* to Gerolt—

She paused. This time there was no sign of her name, and the parchment was folded. She set the basket on the bed alongside the gown, unfolded the parchment, and read.

"A word fitly spoken is like apples of gold in pictures of silver."
Let this small gift remind you how dearly you still lay on my
heart.

Her own heart nearly vaulted out of her chest. The apple was red, not gold as in the proverb, but the apples had always been red at Lyonstoke, and he had never been one to boast of his wealth. *Oh, saints. Gerolt, have you gone mad?*

Perhaps it was a mistake. Perhaps her memory had faded and she mistook his distinctive script.

I could sooner forget my own name than this bold, beloved hand.

She grasped wildly for another explanation. She had told Gerolt of the gifts, and it had put the romantic idea in his head to try it for himself. The apple had surely been meant for Marion, but Egelina's suitor—nay, Cassandry's suitor—had seen it outside Marion's door, deemed it better than his own, and moved it to Cassandry's threshold.

Surely, *surely* that was what had happened? Gerolt could not possibly mean—could not possibly be the one who—

Do not be absurd, Cassandry!

But was it any more absurd to think that Samson had swiped and exchanged the gift?

She would have to find Gerolt, she thought between pounding heartbeats, and ask him. No, she would have to sound him out first, in case the apple had truly been meant for Marion.

But what if—*what if*—he had meant it for Cassandry?

Saints, Cassandry, you are shaking like a fourteen-year-old girl again. Think of Egelina. You must not love him. Think of Egelina. You must not let him love you. Think of Egelina! Where else will her future be safe but with Gerolt's son?

Oh, Gerolt, what can you be thinking?

She could not know until she asked him.

"Good morning," Gerolt said when she joined him.

It had taken her some time to locate him in Lady Aveline's solar. Twice as spacious as Cassandry's solar at Rengrave Castle, she had once freely plied her embroidery here in the sunlit mornings.

"I hope I am not disturbing you?" she said. Had she intruded upon some private memory of his late wife?

"I came to study your tapestry." Gerolt stood with his hands clasped behind his back as he perused it. It draped the wall between a pair of velvet-cushioned chairs that stood near a hearth.

Anxiety gnawed at her stomach. "I was very young when I wove it," she reminded him. "Not yet fourteen. I became more skilled with practice. Never truly proficient—I was not disciplined enough to achieve the proper symmetry, and my judgment of colors often erred—" Colors? What was it she was supposed to tell Gerolt about colors? She could think of nothing but Antony's cutting disparagement of her tapestries. Her body tensed, bracing for the accustomed criticism.

"I was just thinking," Gerolt said, "that it has exactly the right number of rabbits."

"Oh, no. There is one too many. Look. Three beside the doe and three beside the lady. There should not be a seventh one peeking out from beneath the rose bush, here."

She moved to the tapestry to point out the error. The other rabbits gamboled about the central figures, but that seventh one— what had possessed her to sneak him into the scene and throw it all off balance?

"It adds a touch of charming whimsy. And your 'misplaced' bird"—his finger pointed to the right corner—"looks as though she is about to fly off the weaving and soar about the room. Jenny Wren was most certainly her inspiration. There is mischief in that bright eye of hers as she watches us watching her. I think because there was mischief in the weaver."

He turned on the words and grinned at her. Half of her wanted to continue to draw his attention to her mistakes—an errant thread there and there and there—but memories of a young girl playfully "hiding" the seventh rabbit and honoring the little bird who had brought her so much joy by weaving her portrait in the corner were seeping through the other half.

Cassandry shook the crowding thoughts away like an old, tattered blanket, once beloved but now worn-out and useless.

"I'm afraid someone else attempted a bit of mischief this morning that may have gone awry," she said, forcing a smile.

"Oh?" He raised his brows and waited.

She could not come straight out with her question, for she might not like the answer. "There is an apple missing from the kitchen." Surely he would catch the hint?

"An apple?" Now he looked puzzled. "Do you mean there is a shortage for dinner? Then send a servant out to pick some more. The orchard is full of well-ripened fruit."

She moved away to another tapestry, one that had not draped the wall when she lived here. "I mean a very particular apple. Deep red and well shined. Lady Marion will regret that it went astray."

"Marion?" He came to stand beside her. "Has she been in the kitchen?"

Clearly he did not wish to betray himself to Cassandry. She smothered a sigh. She would have to pretend the same ignorance as he, then.

"She never showed a personal interest in the preparation of meals when she was growing up here as Fleur did," he continued, maintaining his façade about the apple. "Aveline taught them both how to manage the kitchen servants with a firm but general framework of expectations. Fleur liked to sample the dishes, though, to smell the spices, occasionally even to bake me an elderflower pie, like you did." He paused before adding, "She was a loving, generous-hearted girl, like you, Cassandry."

Without quite knowing how, Cassandry suddenly knew that the tapestry they gazed at together had been woven by Fleur.

Maybe it was the sudden catch in his voice or the sad way his eyes lingered on the handsome young knight with the thick-maned, fish-tailed sea lion on his shield—Gerolt's emblem—as he bowed over the hand of a golden-haired lady in a gown very similar to the one on Cassandry's weaving.

He must have caught her glancing back and forth between the tapestries.

"She always admired your pattern," he said. "As Aveline did. I hope you do not mind that Fleur copied your lady? At least it should please you that she included an equal number of rabbits on either side."

His bantering tone could not conceal the sadness she heard beneath it. Without thinking, Cassandry impulsively slid her fingers into his and squeezed them. "I am sorry you lost her."

"Not a day goes by that I do not miss her still." The heartache vibrated clearly in his voice now.

Cassandry remembered how emotionally painful her miscarriage had been. She could not imagine the anguish of losing a living daughter, one cherished through childhood and grown to womanhood. *If I ever lost Egelina . . .*

How it happened, she did not quite know, but suddenly she was in Gerolt's arms, her own wound tightly about his waist. Did she seek to comfort him or the other way around?

"I am so very sorry, Gerolt." How inadequate the words! She leaned her head against his broad shoulder and allowed the tears to roll down her cheeks.

"We cannot control the fates, Cassandry. All the years I feared it was Rauffe I would lose, but it pleased God to take poor Fleur instead." His hand, so gentle, brushed against her wet face. "Do not fear for your daughter," he said with a tender perception. "I will take care of Egelina. I will love her as though she were my own. Whatever lies in my power to protect her, you may be assured I will do. Beyond that, we must hope for heaven's mercy upon her and Rauffe when they are wed."

She nodded, knowing he was right. He was always right. Almost always. *Except for Antony.*

But that was not what made the tears sting anew in her eyes. *When they are wed,* he had said. He was again committed to the marriage between their children. As she had suspected, the apple had not been meant for her. She swallowed her unreasonable disappointment. She would have to find a way to restore the gift to its intended recipient. Perhaps she could have Lora set it outside Marion's chamber while they dined today. Without proof that Samson had filched it, it was useless to accuse him to Gerolt.

She really should break free of his embrace. He loved another woman. But his hand continued to rest for several minutes against her cheek, holding her bound as though with a spell. She tried to think of the nunnery, the peace she would find there, but the palm of Gerolt's hand was too warm against her skin. Egelina and Rauffe —soon they would be married. To covet Gerolt would be sin.

But they were not married today. Antony—he had failed her with Antony and let her sink into despair. But she moved her head just a fraction and found the beating of Gerolt's heart, and this one present, vital moment swallowed up all the hurt and anger and despair of the past.

She felt a small pressure against the top of her head. A kiss? 'Twas not possible. But whatever it was set her trembling as sweetly as though the caress had fallen upon her lips.

"Why must we bother them? I tell you, it was only too much sun."

The voice, drifting too near to the solar's door, startled them into breaking apart. Cassandry whirled again toward Fleur's tapestry, knowing her face to be a flood of color, while Gerolt turned to greet the speaker.

"Is something amiss, my lady?"

Had Cassandry needed any proof that she had been thoroughly lost in a fantasy, she heard it in Gerolt's cool, self-possessed tones. His embrace had only been one of comfort, no different from the hundreds of times he had held her when she had been a little girl.

"It is nothing," Cassandry heard Egelina say. "I took him out to quiz him about the flowers without thinking about how bright the sunshine was. It gave him a small headache, but even he protested it was nothing like the ones he had suffered before."

"He is very pale. I think we should be concerned."

Marion. Cassandry had no choice but to turn about, but her gaze was snagged by the other woman's before she could look at Egelina. Cassandry could only hope the color had faded from her face.

"Are you speaking of Rauffe?" Gerolt asked. "Why were you quizzing him about the flowers? Your mother is well versed on every bloom in my garden if you need help to identify them. I suspect Rauffe does not know a columbine from a gillyflower."

"I was testing him on their colors," Egelina said.

"Their colors?"

"He has difficulty identifying some hues. Specifically—"

"It is his illness," Marion interrupted, turning her full attention to Gerolt. "Lady Aveline always worried that the fevers he suffered when he was a boy had affected his brain. I confess I have feared the same, my lord."

"There is nothing wrong with his brain." Egelina looked so indignant Cassandry knew her fears about Sir Owen had been foolish. Her daughter was clearly falling in love with Rauffe. The realization should have filled Cassandry with satisfaction and relief. Instead, she suffered a little sinking sensation.

"Well, there is something amiss with him," Marion countered, "for he has gone to bed, has he not?"

"The sun was too bright. It gave him a headache. Just a *small* headache. But he said the dark sometimes makes him feel better, so he went to his room. Truly, my lord," Egelina said to Gerolt, "I do not think it is serious."

Marion looked disdainful at this reply. "It is always serious with Rauffe. I have known him much longer than you. Or you, for that matter, my lady." She attempted to rob any disrespect from these words to Cassandry by bobbing her a curtsy. "'Tis a pity you dismissed his physician, my lord. But Lady Aveline confided much to me about Rauffe's condition. I believe I know a potion that will help him. I would have tried it with him before, but Lady Cassandry—well, I am certain she thought she was being helpful, but she is a stranger to Rauffe and could not truly know what was best for him."

Cassandry struggled against her own indignation now. She had not the least doubt that she had identified the source of Rauffe's headaches correctly. But she had not known then that Gerolt intended to make Marion his wife. If she had, she would have stepped aside and allowed Marion to take charge of the kitchen and the inventories, and even Rauffe's health. No, that would have been a mistake. If she had been trained by Aveline—

"No almonds," Cassandry said.

"I am not convinced they ever did him the least harm."

They both turned toward Gerolt, Marion with her arms crossed, Cassandry with a toe tapping while she awaited Gerolt's support.

To Cassandry's dismay, he looked uncertain. "He did suffer from a great many fevers as a boy." His gaze slid from Marion to Cassandry, then back to Marion. "Prepare your potion. But let the Lady Cassandry assist you. She has wisdom and experience, Marion."

"So had your wife, my lord, and she taught me all I need to know to care for your son."

Cassandry suspected Marion viewed this as a chance to prove her worthiness to Gerolt as his future wife. Much though she wanted to argue with the younger woman, she had no wish to diminish Marion in Gerolt's eyes. Cassandry need not embarrass her here or make Gerolt choose between the loyalty his attempt at compromise showed he felt to them both.

"I beg your pardon, Lady Marion," Cassandry said. "I did not intend to question your skill. I will leave Rauffe in your care." *For now.*

"But, Mamma—"

"Hush, Egelina." She took her daughter's hand and patted it, hoping to press home her message for silence. "If you will excuse us, my lord, it is time I showed my daughter how to inventory your wine. I do not doubt your butler keeps all in perfect order, but Egelina will be chatelaine here one day, and the responsibility to oversee all matters of the castle will rest upon her shoulders."

Cassandry stated the fact simply and hoped Marion would not take offense. Gerolt, like Cassandry, was in the autumn of his life. Heaven had shown her with Antony how unexpectedly it could snatch one's soul, and when it snatched Gerolt's—though she fervently prayed 'twould not do so for a very, very long time!— Marion would be left a young dowager, her role usurped by the wife of Gerolt's heir.

Marion raked them both with narrow-eyed dislike as they left the solar. Cassandry would have to try to arrange an accord between Marion and Egelina before Cassandry retired to the nunnery—and out of Gerolt's life forever.

Chapter 17

Egelina said the roses were red, but they all looked sort of yellowish to me. I knew the violets were purple, though, and the periwinkle and columbines, and all the yellow ones—the marigolds and daffodils—she said I named those colors all right, too"

Cassandry watched Rauffe closely, encouraged by the animation in his face. Despite the headache he claimed continued to nag him, he had let her light several candles, insisting they did not hurt his eyes as usual. In fact, he sat cross-legged on the bed instead of reclining and talked in easy tones.

"I did not think you so interested in flowers as to have learned all their names," she said from the chair where she sat beside the bed, remembering how Gerolt had said Rauffe would likely not know a columbine from a gillyflower.

"Fleur taught me when she would take me out to watch the bird in its nest. Father said that all wrens are called Jenny, so we named her so. She was a quaint little thing, but I had not been out to see her since Fleur died. It made me too sad to watch her alone." His shoulders drooped a little but then lifted again. "Egelina and I watched her a little today, though, until she scolded us so badly we moved away."

Cassandry could not resist the impulse to tease him. "Now that you have come to know my daughter better, the thought of marrying her is not quite so dreadful as you thought at first." She did not realize she'd spoken with a smile until Rauffe grinned back at her.

"She is quite clever, and kind, too. She never once laughed at me when I got the color of the flowers wrong."

It warmed Cassandry's heart to hear praise of Egelina. Perhaps she had not failed as much as a mother as she sometimes feared.

"Can you not see red at all?" This condition of Rauffe's was quite curious.

"I suppose I never have," he replied. "I always thought it was just another shade of yellow—like this." He sprang out of the bed, diving for the scarlet surcote he had tossed across the back of a chair before he had climbed onto the bed, but he staggered before he reached it.

Cassandry jumped up and caught his arm just as the door cracked open.

"I'm fine," Rauffe said, though he sounded somewhat out of breath. "I got . . . a little dizzy, is all. It must be the headache. It's starting to throb a little more."

Marion entered in with a goblet in her hands. "Then I have come just in time." She saw Cassandry. "What are you doing here?"

If Marion suspected that Cassandry had come to inspect her potion before Rauffe drank it, she was correct. Still, Cassandry had prepared a less provocative explanation for her presence.

"Lord Rauffe is betrothed to my daughter. I merely wished to see how he was feeling."

"Anyone can see he is feeling dreadful," Marion replied. "Look how pale he is. And you heard him say his head is throbbing. You must get back into bed at once, Rauffe, and then drink this."

"But—" Rauffe began.

"No 'buts.' I have prepared this exactly how your mother would have, and you know how very diligent she was over your health. She always knew what was best for you. Now back into bed."

Rauffe skulked over to the bed, looking like a sulky little boy. He muttered as he sat down on the edge, "She did not know best about the almonds."

Marion gasped aloud. "How dare you be so disrespectful, not only of your mother but of a divine food that would have returned you to health if you had only the patience to endure a little discomfort in the meantime."

Cassandry saw Rauffe's consternation and remembered his fear of the nut's divinity. She said, "His headaches were more than 'a little discomforting,' they were completely disabling, Marion, and not all almonds are divine. Most are just almonds. And I hope there are none in that goblet you are holding."

Marion's chin went up. She might be cheerful and lively when she was with Gerolt, but she stared at Cassandry with clear dislike. "They would not have done him the least harm, but Gerolt told me very firmly that I might not use them in the drink, so of course I have honored his request."

Cassandry understood the young woman's affront to have her knowledge and authority challenged, but she could not forget how drastically wrong Lady Aveline had been about her son's diet. Every time Marion quoted Rauffe's mother as her mentor, it raised warning hackles on the back of Cassandry's neck.

She stretched out a hand. "If you do not object, I will take just a sip."

The goblet trembled in Marion's hand, evidence of her anger. "You are not chatelaine here, to command me, my lady."

"Nor are you, Lady Marion. But I am the mother of Lord Rauffe's betrothed, and for now that gives me some precedence. The goblet, please."

"Don't drink it," Rauffe said. "It's foul."

Marion thrust the goblet into Cassandry's hand as though spurred to spite by Rauffe's warning. Cassandry sipped the contents, then scrunched her nose, barely resisting the impulse to spit the mouthful out. She knew she must not judge it by taste. Many efficacious medicines tasted horrid. Marion had attempted to mask the unpleasantness with a generous dosage of honey, but it could not conceal the rank taste of valerian. Cassandry detected no almonds in the smooth, herb-infused wine. Though decidedly less pleasant than the remedies she had applied to Rauffe, she acknowledged that valerian might ease Rauffe's headache and help him to sleep.

She handed the goblet to Rauffe, who groaned.

"Do I have to? I told you it's foul."

"Just drink a little—"

"He must drink it all." Marion marched over to the bed, rudely shouldering Cassandry out of the way. "Every drop of it, Rauffe."

Marion stood with her hands on her hips until Rauffe reluctantly obeyed her, though not without several choking and gagging sounds between gulps.

"There. Now lie down."

"But I'm not sleepy," Rauffe said.

"You know Lady Aveline always sent you to bed and wrapped you up warmly—"

"But I'm not cold, either."

"Oh, Rauffe, when did you become so quarrelsome? You never used to speak to Lady Aveline this way."

"You are not my mother," Rauffe pointed out. "You are only just as old as Fleur."

"That does not matter," Marion said. "I may be as good as your mother someday, and when I am, you will treat me with respect as your father's wife."

"Father's wife?" Rauffe looked stunned. "Father would never marry you!"

"He will when he sees how I have made you well. He will be so grateful he will *beg* me to marry him. I will make him happy, Rauffe, happier than even Lady Aveline did."

The expression on Rauffe's face went from stunned to appalled. He started to surge to his feet but must have been struck by another wave of dizziness, for Marion, who has half his size, had no trouble pushing him back onto the bed so hard that he fell over backward.

"I will leave you in Lady Marion's capable hands," Cassandry said, hoping to pacify the young woman's resentment. "I promised your father I would teach Egelina how to inventory his wine cellar today."

"Wait," Rauffe called as she moved toward the door. He had recovered enough to sit up again. "Lady Cassandry, I was hoping— that is, I thought perhaps—perhaps you would help me pick out some clothes to wear to dinner today."

His face turned a little ruddy in the candlelight as he made the request. Gerolt had said Rauffe had always been stubbornly independent on the matter of his clothing. She counted his request a touching sign of the affinity that had grown between them.

"I should be happy to," Cassandry replied. "Give Lady Marion's potion a little time to take effect while I work with Egelina, then I will return—and bring Egelina with me, if you do not mind," she added. "She has always had the most excellent taste in attire. Sometimes I even let her dress me."

Rauffe laughed as if he did not believe her. Cassandry went out, puzzled at how easily a smile now came to her lips.

Now that their quarrels appeared to lie behind them, Cassandry looked forward to a pleasant hour with her daughter, introducing her to the origins of Gerolt's many wine barrels. But she could find Egelina nowhere—not in their chamber, not in the hall, nor in the kitchen or garden. Cassandry disappointedly assumed she had gone riding with one of Gerolt's knights again.

Cassandry left word with Lora to call her as soon as her daughter returned, then stood debating what to do while she waited. At length she obtained a freshly cleaned shirt belonging to Rauffe from one of the laundresses. Cassandry had given up embroidery years ago, leaving it to servants with skill to stitch more perfect patterns than she. But she had loved embroidery once, and it occurred to her that Rauffe might be more forgiving of her clumsy stitches than Antony had been.

She would like to have sat in the solar, where the light this time of day was the best, but she would not be comfortable there knowing it had come to belong to another woman and would soon belong to Marion. She settled for a chair near the window in her bedchamber and began a pattern of racing dogs around the shirt's cuffs.

In dipped her needle, out it drew, in, out, in, out . . . Over and over until the rhythm began to beat in her mind and gradually words began to form.

> *They fly, they fly, fleet over the ground,*
> *The hounds chase the doe through the forest green.*
> *The trumpets blare and arrows speed,*
> *A bound and a leap, and the doe soars free.*
> *The huntsmen mourn their quarry's loss,*
> *But the fawn greets his mother 'neath a dappling tree.*

"Whatever are you thinking of, Mamma?"

Cassandry looked up, startled. "Where have you been?" she

asked her daughter.

"About the castle. You look very dreamy, Mamma. How long have you been sitting here with that shirt in your lap?"

Cassandry glanced down to discover her hands had, indeed, fallen lax. Great heavens! She had been lost, like Egelina, in the composition of a poem!

Egelina crossed the room and picked up the shirt, studying the row of hounds Cassandry had stitched on the left sleeve before her mind had wandered.

"How pretty!" Egelina exclaimed. "Is this for Rauffe?"

Cassandry welcomed the diversion. "How did you guess?"

Egelina held up the shirt to the light of the window. "He is hound mad." She lowered the shirt. "It is almost time for dinner. Rauffe is feeling well enough to join us, isn't he?"

"Oh!" Cassandry stood up. "I quite lost track of the time. I promised Rauffe we would help him pick out his wardrobe for dinner."

"We? Pick out his wardrobe?"

Cassandry took the shirt and folded it to finish later. "You were quite right that he cannot see some colors properly. He asked us"—she saw no harm in inserting the plural—"to assist him in sorting out colors that would match." She smiled at her daughter. "A week ago he would have been too proud to ask any such thing. You have made a wonderful change in him, Gelli."

"Oh . . . well . . ." Egelina blushed and swiveled her toe against the floor, as though her mother's praise embarrassed her.

She went with Cassandry so meekly that Cassandry decided to raise the subject of the betrothal again after dinner, and this time she expected a willing acquiescence from her daughter.

Upon reaching Rauffe's bedchamber, to her dismay—and apparently to Egelina's as well—she found Rauffe asleep.

"We must wake him," Egelina said, but Cassandry stayed her.

"Hush, Gelli," she whispered. "Leave him be. Lady Marion

gave him a draught to help his headache. There must have been something stronger than I knew in it to make him sleep so long."

Cassandry wondered how many other ingredients the valerian had covered? Whatever they were, the single mouthful she had swallowed had left her unaffected.

Egelina followed her mother back out of the room, looking surprisingly cross. Would she miss Rauffe's company so much at dinner? Cassandry's hopes mounted for a betrothal sealed before nightfall. She did not speak her thoughts to Gerolt as they ate, for he looked as worried as Egelina seemed disappointed by Rauffe's absence at the table. Cassandry spent the meal reassuring Gerolt and seeking to distract her daughter's boredom while into every lull of conversation slipped the refrain, *They fly, they fly, fleet over the ground, The hounds chase the doe through the forest green.*

She tried to push the verses away, but round and round they ran through her head, as swift as the hounds of her poem. She knew what they wanted. Release. Not to the insubstantial air, where they might float away and be forgotten. *You want me to write you down. Well, I will not. Chant and roll and whirl in my brain as you will, but I will not indulge what I have forbidden Gelli. I will not be the hypocrite she thinks me.*

Rauffe was still asleep at the meal's end, so Cassandry dragged her reluctant daughter down to the wine cellar.

"Why must we inventory all these stupid barrels?" Egelina dealt one of them a little impatient kick. "Does not Lord Gerolt have a butler?"

"Of course he does," Cassandry said. "But sometimes servants grow careless or even dishonest. You must learn which wines your husband favors the most and see that those are always replenished before the barrels run dry. If the butler grows neglectful, it will be your duty to nudge him along."

"Papa never had so many barrels. Why must Lord Gerolt be so greedy?"

"He is not greedy, Gelli. Lord Gerolt maintains a much larger household than your father did. You will have a great deal more responsibility as chatelaine here than I had at Rengrave Castle."

Egelina lagged about the cellar at first, making no effort to conceal her initial boredom, but as Cassandry began to explain the various regions each barrel of wine came from, her daughter's interest gradually perked up.

"Have you been there, Mamma? To Gascony and Bordeaux and Sicily?"

"No," Cassandry replied, "but Lord Gerolt has. He told me about each one when he taught me about the wines. I had no mother to teach me as I am teaching you, Gelli, and Gerolt's mother had died by the time I came into his care. Of course, he might have assigned a servant to instruct me in the duties I would need to know as a wife, but I think he enjoyed telling me about his travels and used these casks as an excuse to do so."

"Did he also teach you to embroider and spin?"

Cassandry laughed at the expression of awe on her daughter's face at the thought. "No, there were a few domestic skills he thought best to leave to other women. The wife of one of his vassals taught me, though I was never very talented with the needle."

"Papa thought your work was pretty." Egelina brushed away the dust on one of the barrel's labels and traced her finger over the letters that identified its origin.

Cassandry's laughter choked off, a wedge of sour, contradictory memory rising in its place.

"He gave me a piece of linen once, with some golden apples embroidered on it," Egelina continued. "He said you had used the wrong colored threads so that he could not wear it on the surcote you made him, but your stitches were very tiny and delicate, and he thought I might like to have it, so he cut up the surcote and gave me a piece."

Antony had cut the surcote up? Belittling Cassandry's work to her face had not been sufficient?

"Can you not tell colors either, Mamma?" Egelina asked. "Is that why you used the wrong threads?"

"I see colors fine, Gelli. I used the nearest colors I could find to match the emblem of your father's house, but your father was very particular over many things in his life."

Egelina sighed. "I know. But I think he was sorry. He said he hated losing his temper with you, but you were so pretty he could not help himself. He said he wished he had not cut up his surcote, for the colors were only a little off, but he had done it and he knew you would not forgive him, so there was no use asking you to. I told him he should count before he said unkind things to you, but he frowned terribly at me. I did not like it when Papa frowned, so I did not say anymore."

"I am sorry if he frightened you, Gelli." A little twig of anger burned in Cassandry to think that Antony had done so.

Egelina shrugged. She moved to another barrel and dusted off another label. "His frowns did not frighten me so much as when he would yell and you would weep. Sometimes . . . sometimes I would sneak into the passageway outside your chamber door and sit on the floor and listen. I could not hear the words, but I heard the shouting and the crying. Then horrible thoughts would come into my head. *What if Papa becomes so angry that he leaves us and never comes back? What if he sends Mamma away and does not let her come back?*"

"Oh, Gelli!" Cassandry wrapped her daughter in her arms, ashamed and horrified that they had unknowingly brought such anguish to Egelina. "Why ever would you think such a thing? Your father and I were married, and married couples do not separate however difficult things may be between them."

Egelina pressed her face into her mother's shoulder and spoke in muffled tones. "I know it is against the law of the Church. But

Queen Eleanor was married to the king of France before she married King John's father. The Church let them separate when Queen Eleanor did not give the king of France a son, and you never gave Papa a son. And he was so cold and angry with you all the time. He told me he was sorry, but he never changed, and I was afraid that he . . . only then he died. *He* was the one who went away, Mamma, and I am glad that you do not weep anymore, but I miss him."

Cassandry kissed her brow. "Of course you do, my love."

She held Egelina while her daughter cried softly. A smothering guilt rose up in Cassandry. Had she not been so immersed in her own despondency, she would have seen her daughter's distress and comforted it. Antony had reproached her for many things in the course of their marriage but never for not bearing him a son. He had doted too entirely on Egelina and had begun to speak of choosing a husband to care for her and her inheritance after his death.

None of them had known how near that day lay. Nothing would infuriate Antony more than Cassandry allying his precious daughter with Gerolt's son, but Cassandry remained convinced it was the best solution. Why, Rauffe had never once complained about Egelina riding so frequently with the knights of the castle, not even with the young Sir Owen. Jealousy had been the poison that had destroyed Cassandry's marriage, a trait Rauffe did not appear to nourish. And he and Egelina were coming to such a warm accord between them.

Friendship. That was what had always been missing in her life with Antony. There had been excitement and passion but never something as simple as friendship. It had not seemed important at sixteen. But it meant everything to watch it grow between Egelina and Rauffe. Now, with the maturity of years behind her, there was nothing Cassandry cherished more than a friendship that had grown into love.

"I did not mean to make you sad, Mamma."

Cassandry did not realize that Egelina had leaned away from her until her daughter spoke. She thrust Gerolt's face out of her mind. If only she could so easily cast him from her heart.

"I am not sad, Gelli. Only that your father and I hurt you—for that, I am so very sorry."

Egelina stared a little too deeply into her mother's eyes. "I miss Papa," she repeated, "but I like to see you happy. You have been happy here the last few days, have you not, Mamma?"

"I suppose," Cassandry said.

Egelina smiled and blinked away the last of her tears. She sat down suddenly on a small barrel of wine, ignoring her mother's quick protest that she would soil her gown in the dust.

"Rauffe showed me the dearest bird in the garden today. He said its name was Jenny. I made up a poem to her in my head, but I did not say it aloud to Rauffe because he would have rolled his eyes. Would you like to hear it?"

Cassandry felt a frown begin to tug at the corners of her lips, but she caught it and forced her mouth into a line. She must not encourage Egelina in this foolishness. Next she would be begging to learn to write again.

They fly, they fly, fleet over the ground, The hounds chase the doe through the forest green . . .

She shook her head briskly to dispel her own poem from her head and saw Egelina's face fall. *That gesture was not aimed at you, child.*

Egelina had suffered enough hurt from her parents' selfishness. Tomorrow Cassandry could be stern and wise again, but for today she could bend and listen.

She found a barrel her own height and lowered herself onto it. If she could not smile in genuine welcome of her daughter's verse, she found she could smile at her daughter in tenderness.

"Yes, Gelli. I would like to hear it."

Chapter 18

Cassandry flung back the shutters and whispered into the morning air, "They fly, they fly, fleet over the ground, The hounds chase the doe through the forest green . . ."

She released the words into the air and let them float away. It brought her a pang to give them up, but it was for the best. They had woven themselves in and out of her dreams all night, until she had woken once again exhausted. She refused to take up the pen again. Now that she had given them voice, she trusted they would cease to nag her. She had forgotten all her other poems after Antony had burned them.

The chamber door opened slightly, and Egelina peeked around it. "Oh, you are up." Egelina looked hesitant, then came the rest of the way into the room. "I suppose you will not like it, but I found this outside our door."

Cassandry tensed. "Another token?"

"Yes, Mamma. This one has some kind of note."

She extended her palm to reveal an intricately worked metal ball tied to a ribbon. A pomander, such as a lady might wear around her neck or tie to her girdle to carry a religious keepsake in.

Cassandry recognized the script on the slip of parchment in Egelina's other hand.

"Someone has misplaced it," Cassandry said. "It should have been left at Marion's door."

"Marion's? Why would someone leave it there?"

It was not Cassandry's place to speak of Gerolt's romantic gestures toward another woman. "Her name is on the note," Cassandry lied, knowing with Egelina's ignorance of the written word she could not contradict her.

"Is it?" Egelina brought the gift to her mother. "Where? Oh, forgive my curiosity, Mamma. I know you do not wish me to learn to read and write, but you showed me all those barrels of malmsey wine yesterday because you said they were Lord Gerolt's favorites. *Malmsey* begins with the same sound as Marion, but I do not see the symbol on this parchment that I saw on the barrels yesterday."

Cassandry took the note and read it. *Dear One, may this keep you close to heaven when I cannot be there to guard you.*

She took the pomander from Egelina and opened it. An exquisite rosary of sandalwood beads with a silver crucifix lay coiled inside. Before she could stop it, the thought sprang to her mind: *It is too late now. Where was this—where were* you—*when I needed you and heaven to guard me from Antony's reviling?* She cut off the useless censure, reminding herself that these words were not meant for her.

Egelina stepped beside her to gaze at the parchment. Cassandry closed the pomander and temporarily tied it to her girdle.

"There," she said, pointing to the word *may* on the parchment. "You missed it because the word was so small. That letter is called an *M.* 'Tis the same letter *malmsey* and Marion begin with."

Egelina's finger moved to touch the word. "But that is only three letters, Mamma. Marion's name has more sounds in it than that. Or does each letter make a longer sound? Mare"—her finger touched the *m*—"ee"—her fingertip moved to the *a*— "un"—and glided to the *y*. She lowered her hand. "Is that the way it works?"

Cassandry squirmed inside. Lying felt shameful, especially with a crucifix hanging from her girdle.

"No, it does not work that way," she confessed reluctantly. "I misread it. Forgive me, Gelli."

"What does it say, then?"

"That I will not tell you. You will not trick me into teaching you how to read. I know you think me hard, but you will thank me one day."

Egelina's mouth gave a quirk her mother recognized as annoyance. But she only said, "If Marion's name is not on it, then why do you think it was meant for her? It was left at *our* door. It must have been intended for you or me. All the other tokens were."

"I am certain it was a mistake," Cassandry repeated firmly. "I will speak to Lord Gerolt about it." Or more precisely, she would speak to Samson. She folded the parchment and slipped it inside the pomander with the rosary. "Do not worry about it, Gelli. I promise I will put a stop to it today. Now tell me, have you visited Rauffe this morning? How is he?"

"He is up," Egelina replied. "I hope you do not mind that I went to help him choose his clothes? Garin went with me, and Rauffe was half dressed when he let me in, so there was nothing inappropriate with my visit."

Garin? Ah, yes, the red-haired squire. Why could Cassandry never remember his name? "That was kind of you, Gelli."

"I like picking out clothes, as you know, Mamma. Rauffe will look very handsome today, and no one will make fun of his hose. But I am worried about him."

"Why, love?"

"He said his head still aches, and his eyes looked a little foggy, but he insisted on going down to train with the squires. I do not think he is well."

"I will check on him, my love. What are your plans for the day?"

"Would you mind if I finished the shirt you started with the racing dogs? I found a tower chamber that has very good morning light."

Cassandry gave her daughter the shirt and embroidery threads with a subdued breath of relief. The pattern had caused enough mischief yesterday. She feared if she resumed the rhythm of the stitches, another poem might slip into her mind like the one she had just released.

They fly, they fly, fleet over the ground, The hounds chase the doe through the forest green.

Egelina looked up from the embroidery basket at Cassandry's tiny gasp. "What is it, Mamma?"

"Nothing, love," Cassandry said quickly. "Go along to the tower chamber."

When she was gone, Cassandry hurried back to the open window and threw her poem, a little more loudly this time, back onto the wind.

Cassandry watched Rauffe with concern from the edge of the training area. Sir Payne had set a makeshift fence around it with points called foul for any squire who stumbled into the barrier. All had stayed sufficiently clear of it that Cassandry felt secure in standing just outside the perimeter. Rauffe successfully blocked two blows before a third one fell with such force on his sword's blade that he landed in the dirt. He rolled and found his feet again, but Egelina was right. His movements seemed slow and heavy.

"Do you think Gerolt will not discover what you are doing?" she said to the man beside her.

"And what is that?" Samson asked. He had seen her observing the squires and joined her near the fence.

"Robbing your daughter to play your futile game with me."

"I, rob Marion? You will have to be more clear on exactly how and why I would do such a thing."

How dare he make such sport of her. Did he take her for a fool? "I was not seduced by your salacious letters twenty-three years ago, I'll not be so now by an apple or a pomander." She had left the former in her chamber, having forgotten to return it to Marion when Rauffe had fallen ill again yesterday. The pomander she untied from her girdle and slapped into Samson's hand.

After a moment of gazing silently at the object, he flicked it open and took out the parchment.

"Did you think I had forgotten either his script or yours? That is Gerolt's writing. Give it back to your daughter. What sort of father are you that you would spoil her happiness to further your own lewd ends?"

He glanced up from Gerolt's note at that. "I asked you to marry me, Cassandry. I do not see what was lewd about that."

"You forced kisses on me that I neither invited nor desired. And your letters to me—" It all flowed back. Not only had Samson ruined her life, his actions had inflicted pain on Egelina as well. Her fury returned. Had they not been standing in so public a place, she would have slapped him again.

She turned to leave before temptation overwhelmed her and saw Gerolt strolling toward them. "Give me the pomander," she said to Samson.

"Why? I thought you wanted me to return it to Marion."

"So you admit you took it from her door?"

He shrugged. "I will see it safely into her hands."

He slipped the object into his sleeve before Gerolt reached them. Had he guessed her intention to reveal his dishonorable theft of the token by showing it to Gerolt?

"Quarreling again?" Gerolt asked, studying Cassandry's heated cheeks.

Cassandry had never nourished spite in her heart, not even against Antony, but it tripped off her tongue like bitter venom at Samson. "Your gift went astray, my lord. Twice. If Lady Marion has not thanked you for your devotion, I suggest you ask her father why."

There, she thought as she swept back toward the keep. Let him explain his actions to Gerolt. Samson's behavior with Cassandry had been reprehensible enough, but to misuse his own daughter in his attempt to indulge his selfish lusts! It was time to open Gerolt's eyes to the depths of his friend's despicable nature.

Even knowing how Samson watched him, Gerolt could not tear his gaze from Cassandry's retreating form. This was torture, having her beneath his roof, watching her slowly come to life again, seeing her smile, hearing her laugh, dancing with her, playing chess with her, sitting in the garden watching Jenny Wren, glimpsing in her eyes what he had dreamed of for so long with such little hope of ever receiving—the welcome when his mouth had drifted toward hers in the garden grass before Cassandry's maid had come upon them.

Then all snatched away again with her stubborn insistence that he hold to his word to marry their children. He cursed himself for ever having allowed the thought to cross his mind, and cursed again that he had spoken the thought aloud to her. It had seemed, at the time, the only way to bring Cassandry back to Lyonstoke and keep her near him after she had stated so emphatically her antipathy to marrying again.

Had he known that here, beneath the familiar roof of her childhood, she would slowly thaw from the frosty, distant, empty woman who had rejected him at Rengrave Castle, that she would grow again into his own warm, generous, laughing Cassandry, that she would gaze at him in the heart-stopping way she had in the garden . . .

It could not be too late, whatever she said, whatever promises he had made her. She had given Gerolt time by healing his son. Time to court her, whether she willed it or not, time to find another husband for Egelina and another wife for Rauffe.

A hand gripped his shoulder. "It could never have worked, Gerolt," Samson said. "She was too much in love with Antony. She would have hated you if you had denied their marriage."

"She is not married to him now," Gerolt replied, unable to keep the longing from his voice.

"It would be sin between you if the children marry."

"And if they do not?" He could find a dozen other men eager to marry Egelina. He would select one who was kind and honest, handsome and young, shrewd enough to govern her inheritance but gentle enough to never govern her. Everything Cassandry wanted for her daughter, *anything* she wanted for her, he would find.

"Egelina is her only child, born fifteen years ago. I remind you again that Cassandry will bear you no heirs, and though I know you will rebuke me for saying it again, you must face the harsh reality that Rauffe will likely not live to give you heirs either."

"He is better." Gerolt's gaze remained where Cassandry had vanished from view. "Cassandry has made him better. You have seen him yourself, training with the squires, eating everything in sight, the way you and I did when we were his age. The color is back in his face. Why, he even came down to breakfast dressed with impeccable discrimination."

"Gerolt." Samson's hand tightened on his shoulder. "Look."

Gerolt resisted for a moment. Rauffe was better. So what if he had missed yesterday's meal? If he had been a little pale again this morning? He had eaten breakfast, girded on his sword, and come out to the bailey to train . . .

"Gerolt."

He turned his head slowly, fearing what he would see before he saw it. Rauffe sitting inside the fence with his back against the temporary planks, his sword lying in the dirt beside him, his face in his hands. Gerolt made a sharp gesture in the air that caught enough of the squires' eyes that they backed away from the circle they had formed around Rauffe to let his father reach him.

"What happened?" Gerolt asked Sir Payne.

"I don't know, sir. One moment he was wielding his sword effectively, if a little sluggishly, the next he just stumbled and landed on his knees. Thomas helped him over to sit by the fence."

Rauffe pulled up his head. "I'm all right. I just got a little dizzy. It's this curst headache—"

"Headache?" Gerolt cut him off. "I thought you said you were better this morning?"

"I was. Well, I wasn't any worse than when Marion's potion put me to sleep. It's different from the ones before. I thought I could fight my way through it."

Gerolt reached out his hand to help Rauffe up. Rauffe cast a glance at the other squires, and Gerolt caught their quickly concealed smirks. He knew what they were thinking. The same thing Gerolt would have thought during his own proud, healthy, impatient youth. *This weak, sickly boy will one day be our lord. How are we to follow a man who lies about all day groaning in his bed over a twinge here and there in his temples?*

Rauffe ignored his father's outstretched hand and managed to scramble to his feet on his own. He bent and picked up his sword, but Gerolt saw the way he shuffled his feet to maintain his balance.

"I can fight, Sir Payne."

Gerolt admired the stubbornness in his son's voice. He hated to embarrass Rauffe before the other squires, but fear had clenched his belly. So many fevers in Rauffe's early youth. So many headaches. So many times Gerolt had stood watching his son's shallow breathing while he slept, afraid to leave lest he return to find the thin chest grown still.

He took the sword from Rauffe's hand. "Go to bed," he said as softly as he could. "I will send Cassandry up with something to help you."

Rauffe's pale face managed a dull flush. "I don't need to go to bed," he muttered with another narrow glance at the now sober-faced squires who still watched him.

"Did you fall at a blow from one of their swords"—Gerolt cocked his head very slightly toward the squires—"or did you simply fall?"

Rauffe clamped his mouth tight on the answer, but he had already confessed to the dizzy spell.

"You are ill. Go to bed. It will be worse if I drag you there than if you obey me on your own. Or can't you—?"

"I don't need your support," Rauffe snapped.

Gerolt withstood his son's glare, the embarrassment and shame in his eyes, and the resentment his father had cast both upon him. Rauffe marched away from the training field, his long strides undoubtedly intended to prove his father's concerns absurd, but he wobbled three times before he reached the keep.

Gerolt handed the sword to Sir Payne, then turned to follow his son, murmuring to Samson as they walked, "I must find Cassandry. She will know what to do."

"She did not know last time."

Gerolt paused and swung around in surprise. "She removed the almonds from his food and his headaches went away."

"And they have now returned. The almonds were clearly not the cause. Her remedy, at best, conveniently coincided with a recovery that would have occurred anyway. Send Marion up to him again. You heard him say her potion helped him."

Had he? Gerolt tried to remember Rauffe's exact words, but he had been too worried to listen. But Marion had treated his headache last night, and Rauffe had come to breakfast this morning, and, at least for a while, had trained successfully with the squires. Something in her potion must have worked. He ran a distracted hand through his hair. His instincts told him to call Cassandry, but reason reminded him that Aveline had dragged Rauffe successfully through every illness and that Marion had learned her healing knowledge from Aveline.

Gerolt gave a curt nod and resumed his course until Samson caught his arm and stopped him again.

"Gerolt—it may be that no one can help him. I will add my prayers for him to yours, but if heaven determines to claim at last what we have all feared from his youth—you will need a wife who can give you sons. I ask this not only as her father but as your friend—do not close your mind and heart to Marion."

"It is just a headache," Gerolt said. "He has had them before. He always recovers. Rauffe will be fine. You will see."

Chapter 19

Cassandry left the kitchen, dusting flour from her hands. She had needed something to occupy her thoughts besides worrying about Gerolt's reaction when he learned that Samson had stolen his gift to Marion. He would be angry, of course. How angry? Enough to place blame where blame was due—at Samson's selfish, lecherous feet?

Or would Samson cast the blame on Cassandry, accuse her of luring him into temptation the way Antony had accused her with Samson, with Gerolt's men, with Gerolt himself? She did not think she could bear to see condemnation in Gerolt's eyes. Oh, why had she allowed herself to be provoked into challenging Samson today? Why had she not counted and counted first? Why had she not simply left the pomander at Marion's door and pretended a dignified ignorance of his wretched, maddening game?

She had sought to distract herself by helping with the pork tarts for dinner, but Emma Cook had become annoyed when Cassandry suggested that Gerolt would like more cheese. She held her tongue thereafter, but silence allowed so much apprehension to creep back into her mind that she had welcomed the reemergence of the chasing hounds and the bounding deer drumming through her head. She was thankful for it now, for anything but visions of Gerolt's disappointment and censure when he saw her again.

Perhaps Samson will say nothing. Had he not slipped the pomander into his sleeve before Gerolt joined them?

They fly, they fly, swift over the ground—

Between the poem and her agitation, she had grown careless with the tarts and allowed flour to bespatter the front of her gown as well as her hands. She crossed the hall and started up the circling stone steps to change but found her pathway blocked when she reached the top.

"Rauffe?"

He sat slumped on the steps, his fingers working through his hair. He looked up when Cassandry spoke his name.

"I was waiting for you," he said. There was a blurry note in his voice that matched the haze in his eyes. "I hoped you'd come . . . before Father found me here. I was on my way to your chamber, but . . . this is as far as I made it before my knees suddenly turned to water."

"Let me call for help." She took a step back toward the hall but felt a tug on her skirts.

"No, please. I don't want Father to know."

She hesitated, then sat down on the step beside him. "What happened?"

"My head. It hurts again, only—not like before."

She gently swept back the hair that had tumbled over his brow and found his forehead moist. That was not necessarily alarming. He had been practicing swordplay with the other squires. As for the headache, there had been no almonds in Marion's potion, Cassandry was sure of it. "How is this different?"

"They usually come on fast and hard and I can't bear the light and my stomach flops . . . and then I'm sick. But this one . . . it only nagged a little at first. And the light didn't hurt my eyes, and I wasn't sick. But I have these bouts of dizziness. The pain . . . is not so bad that I should be dizzy, but . . . one moment I'm fine. The next . . . my eyes go blurry and my head spins. But if I rest . . . a moment, I'm fine again."

How long had he been sitting here? "Are you feeling better now?"

He nodded. "I think so. Father told me to go to bed, but that will just prove me the dismal failure Mamma always said I was. I thought . . . I was well. I was trying so hard to prove her wrong to Father."

Cassandry remembered how he had wept when he had repeated his mother's cruel words. His eyes remained dry now, but the skin stretched taut over his pallid cheeks—with illness or with determination not to succumb to weakness? Perhaps both.

She stood and held out both hands to him. "Let me help you up. Do as your father says for now. Go rest. I will bring up some fresh herbs to ease your head again. And then—do you think you can remember everything you have eaten for the last two days? It may be that it is not only almonds that fail to agree with you."

Rauffe ignored her proffered assistance and leveraged himself up with one fist against the steps and his other hand against the wall. He swayed a bit, then steadied. "I have eaten so many things I do not know if I can remember them all. Everything has tasted so heavenly since you banned boiled chicken and almonds from my diet. But I will try. I hope it is not pork or venison or cheese or pepper. I especially like pepper, even when it makes me sneeze. Or onions or pears or—"

"Make me a list," she interrupted before he could rattle off any more. "Do you need me to call you a scribe?"

He shook his head. "No, I have some parchment and pen and can write myself."

"Good. You cannot possibly be averse to every food. We will try eliminating them one by one."

"Let's start with peas. Cook sprinkles them into a great many dishes, and they're boring."

Cassandry laughed. "I think you are feeling very much better, but go to your room for just a bit anyway."

Rauffe gave a grin so like one of Gerolt's that it made Cassandry's heart trip a little. Rauffe mounted the last few steps, then turned around again.

"I almost forgot. I was looking for Egelina. That was why I was on my way to your chamber. Can you find her and send her to see me? It probably isn't important, but I'd like a word with her anyway."

"Of course," Cassandry said. She trusted Egelina would be amenable to keeping him entertained while Cassandry dealt with prickly Emma Cook, who would likely not be pleased to remove peas or anything else from dinner today.

Cassandry decided to eliminate first the likelihood that Egelina had gone riding, and was pleased to discover that her mare was still in the stables. She tried the kitchen next, in case Egelina had slipped in after Cassandry left, and was surprised to encounter Marion just exiting with a familiar goblet in her hands.

"Is that for Rauffe?"

"Gerolt asked me to prepare it," Marion responded with a smile Cassandry could only describe as smug. "He has complete faith in my wisdom to know what is best for his son."

"What is in it?" She caught the disdainful rise of Marion's brows and added, "So that I might tell Egelina. It will be her duty to care for Rauffe when they are married."

"Oh, she need not worry about that for a very long time," Marion said. "As Gerolt's wife, I will take care of his son. The Lady Egelina need worry about nothing more than embroidering Rauffe's shirts and sitting prettily at his side at dinner. And, of course, giving him an heir. If I deem her clever enough, then I shall share with her my secrets—in time."

Marion glided off on the words with the goblet held high in her hands.

Cassandry hesitated outside the kitchen entrance, her hackles bristling at this dismissal of her daughter's future role at Lyonstoke Castle. She should not be disappointed that Gerolt had turned to Marion instead of herself to help with Rauffe. She needed no further evidence that he and Marion had reached a serious understanding. But she wished, just a little, that the numbness that had encased the heart Antony had broken had not dissolved so completely amidst the safe, happy, contented memories bestirred by her return to Lyonstoke. Numbness was a blessing, a welcome cocoon against pain. She tried to pull a bit of it back around her but failed. Gerolt had made life too real once more.

She peered around the doorway just long enough to be sure that Egelina was not in the kitchen. Cassandry suspected Marion's potion would send Rauffe to sleep again before he could join them to dine, so she saw little point in wrangling with Emma Cook over peas. Best to find Egelina before Rauffe was unable to say whatever it was he wanted to say to her.

It took some time of fruitless searching before Cassandry remembered the tower chamber where Egelina had taken Rauffe's shirt to embroider. Cassandry supposed the morning light would be best in the east tower, so that was where she chose to look first. There were several chambers in the tower, most of them storage for armory. Swords and bows, daggers, lances, and other weaponry cluttered the first level chambers. Shields, gauntlets, helmets, and coats of mail were spread around the chambers on the second floor. Cassandry could not imagine any of these areas being comfortable premises for embroidering. Unless Egelina had taken her stitchery to the top of the tower itself, directly into the sunlight and open air.

Up another flight Cassandry climbed, reaching a third chamber along the way. She nearly passed it, assuming it also brimming with items of war, when voices caught her ear. The door stood slightly ajar. Some of Gerolt's knights must have come up on an errand. Should she disturb them to ask if they had seen her daughter? She peered through the crack. A man sat on a barrel with his back to Cassandry. She instantly knew the blue round cap as it sat slightly angled on his curly brown hair. He had worn it multiple times to dinner, each time with a different colored band tied around it.

"I tremble like a hawthorn branch when I think of you, more gloriouth than the thun, fairer than a midthummer day."

Oh, dear. Had Sir Fithian fallen in love? Whatever lady he had brought here to confide his heart to, Cassandry had no business eavesdropping. She began to ease softly back toward the stairs.

"... fairer ..." a feminine voice repeated, low and a little husky "... than a ... midsummer ... day."

Cassandry whirled and slammed wide the door with a *crack* against the inside wall. Sir Fithian jumped, and so did the slight, golden-haired girl who had sat just outside of Cassandry's sight. Cassandry stared at them both, speechless for a moment.

"M-Mamma," Egelina stammered.

Cassandry's gaze whipped from her daughter's mussed hair to Sir Fithian's scarlet face. She stepped slowly into the chamber. Dread chilled her spine. Besides a cluster of barrels, there were stacks of canvas fabric piled about the room such as might be used for tents, together with pallets and bolsters—some of which had tumbled from the stacks into disarray on the floor.

Egelina, so innocent—and ignorant—of men.

Cassandry knew her eyes must have flashed when Sir Fithian tried to step back a pace and knocked the apparently empty barrel over.

"L-Lady Cathandry," he stammered.

Cassandry had rarely felt so betrayed. Her eyes stung a little, for she had been fond of Fithian as a boy. But he was no boy now, and she had never thought to ask his adult reputation with women. Everything snapped into focus. The origin of the original favors—

"How could you?" Cassandry's voice vibrated at the terrible vision of what she had stumbled upon. "Seducing not only an innocent girl but the betrothed of your own lord's son! I thought you an honest man, Sir Fithian, from the way Gerolt commends you, but when he learns of this!"

"Mamma, we were just—"

Cassandry cut Egelina off with a jab of her hand, but the protest reminded her of her daughter's presence. She tamped down the scream of fury rising in her throat and made a desperate attempt at control. *One, two, three . . .*

"Sir Fithian"—*four, five six*—"if you have"—*seven, eight, nine*—"dishonored my daughter . . ."

Sir Fithian sent a wild look over her shoulder at Egelina. "My lady, I would not—

. . . *Ten, eleven twelve . . .* Cassandry's hands balled so tightly she could feel her nails dig into her palms. *Thirteen, fourteen . . . Do not flail at him . . . fifteen, sixteen . . . not in front of Egelina.* She counted up to twenty, hoping she could speak steadily again, but her words still came out with a tremor.

"Let us go below stairs, Sir Fithian, and discuss this matter with Lord Gerolt."

The color that had stained Sir Fithian's face drained away. "My lady, I thwear I have not—I beg you not to tell Lord Gerolt that the Lady Egelina and I— "

"Mamma!" Egelina rounded her mother and planted herself between Cassandry and Sir Fithian. She fluttered something in Cassandry's face. "Sir Fithian has been teaching me how to write. Look!"

She pushed the sheet of parchment so close to Cassandry's

nose that Cassandry's eyes nearly crossed at the black marks there. She snatched the sheet from Egelina's hand.

Someone had written in a stark, strong hand—*I tremble like a hawthorn branch when I think of you, glorious as the sun, more fair than a midsummer day.* The same words ran below, this time in a wobbly, tentative script.

"It is one of my poems," Egelina said. "The squire says it to the maiden after the silver princes mist back into swans. It is at the very end when they fall in love."

"She thaid you were too buthy to teach her," Sir Fithian added quickly. "She thaid that you would not mind if I thowed her how to record her poem. It is thuch a pretty poem, Lady Cathandry."

His gaze lingered a little too warmly on Egelina. He appeared to realize it and swiftly snapped his attention back to her mother.

"But I would never, ever harm her, my lady. I am not thuch a villain. Nor would I betray my friendthip with you, or my loyalty to Lord Gerolt."

"Mamma, please, you must not be angry at Sir Fithian," Egelina begged. "He has only been kind to me, and so very much a gentleman. You must not think wicked things of him, and you *must not* say wicked things of him to Lord Gerolt!"

Cassandry's suspicions remained unsatisfied. "Writing poetry does not normally muss a woman's hair." How many times had she and Antony paused in their verses to indulge in a few heated kisses? She glared again at Sir Fithian.

"I did not know learning to write would be so hard," Egelina said before Sir Fithian could stammer out a defense. "I kept throwing down the pen and shoving my hands through my hair when I grew frustrated. But, each time, Sir Fithian set the pen ever so gently in my hand again and promised it would not be long before the words flowed as smooth as sweet molasses if I would only be patient and keep practicing." Egelina took the parchment back from Cassandry and stared down at the wobbly letters with a sigh. "They are very far from becoming as smooth as molasses, but they are better then yesterday, so I have hopes that he is right."

Could this rendezvous be so harmless? Cassandry sent another searching glance about the room and observed a few things that had escaped her in her initial panic—another barrel with a few sheets of parchment spread on top, together with an inkwell and a discarded pen. A large stack of canvas piled up beside the barrel, just tall enough for someone to sit atop and reach the pen. True, Rauffe's shirt and the embroidery basket both lay abandoned on the floor beside the canvas stack, but so, too, did several balls of scrunched up parchment. *I should have taught her how expensive parchment is before her exasperation wasted so many of Gerolt's pennies.*

Harmless . . .

She looked again at Sir Fithian. He watched Egelina as she studied her imitation of his script. There was something worse than warmth in his eyes now. There was tenderness. The alarm that had begun to ebb away swirled back around Cassandry.

She retrieved the parchment from Egelina. "You knew that I expressly forbade this. It stops, Egelina. Now." She crumpled the sheet and tossed it to join the others on the floor.

Egelina's face went stormy. "It is too late, Mamma. I have learned every letter of the alphabet. I shall continue practicing, with or without Sir Fithian. I even know a few words on my own, though I do not know how to spell *glorious* or *midsummer* or *hawthorn* when I am not copying the way he wrote them, but I will learn them, with or without him. I swear that I will. And then I shall write down *all* my poems."

Like a flash of lightning, she suddenly turned pleading again. "*Please*, Mamma. There are so many new ones trying to crowd in every day. My brain does not have room for them all. But Sir Fithian helped me to write down a very small one, and now it no longer nags me." She stamped her foot when Cassandry stood silent. "How can you not understand?"

They fly, they fly, swift over the ground—

Oh, Gelli, I do understand, and that is why I must be so cruel.

Sir Fithian started to say something, then fell quickly silent again. If Egelina had hoped he might come to her defense, he clearly disappointed her. Her eyes flooded with tears before she turned and ran from the chamber.

"I did not know," Sir Fithian said when Egelina was gone, "that you had forbidden it, my lady. She did not tell me."

"Oh, I have no doubt of that, Sir Fithian," Cassandry replied. "I am quite certain this trysting was entirely Egelina's idea."

Sir Fithian's eyes grew round with horror. "Not trythting, my lady. I thwear on my honor ath a knight that I have not, and would never, dithhonor the Lady Egelina!"

Cassandry studied him long and solemnly. "No," she said at last, "I do not believe you would. We were quite good friends once, were we not?"

"You were alwayth kind to me, my lady. When I was a thcared and lonely page boy, you gave me gingerbread when no one wath looking and errandth to run for you that made me feel important and kept me too buthy to remember that I was thcared and lonely."

Because she had remembered how lost and frightened she had been when she had first come to Lyonstoke, bereaved of her parents, cast upon the mercy of strangers.

"Then we may speak frankly to one another now, may we not?"

"Of courth, my lady," Sir Fithian said, though he looked rather wary.

"Lady Egelina is betrothed to marry Lord Rauffe." So thought the entire castle, and it would be true enough ere long.

"I know that, my lady."

"Egelina is very young—very innocent—and I fear her poetry

has made her very romantic. She has little experience with men. A cunning one might know how to turn her head."

She thought a sad and somewhat bitter curve settled over his mouth. "Not a man ath old ath I, my lady. Not when there are handthome young knight like Thir Owen about the cathtle." He appeared to catch a wandering thought and straightened. "But she ith betrothed to Lord Rauffe, ath you thay. All of Lord Gerolt'th knight will honor that, even the young, handthome oneth—and if any of them do not, they shall have my blade to contend with, for I will guard her for my lord ath I would guard hith own life."

A gleam of martial challenge sparked in Sir Fithian's eye as he spoke.

Cassandry said softly, "Will you guard her for duty, or for love? Or both?"

Sir Fithian bit his lip. He struggled to meet Cassandry's eye, but his gaze shifted and fell. He was not so old. He was only three-and-thirty. The difference between his age and Egelina's was smaller than that between Marion and Gerolt. But years of silence had stretched too long for Cassandry to fully know his character, nor would Gerolt give an heiress of Egelina's standing to a man of Sir Fithian's modest status, however faithfully he had served him.

Friendship was growing between Egelina and Rauffe. So long as nothing—and no one—disrupted it, Cassandry hoped for a long and contented marriage between them.

"You must teach her no more," she said to Sir Fithian. "And should she ever find a way to learn, you must swear to me that you will never write to her, not even in friendship, as you and I once did."

Sir Fithian protested, "There wath no harm in our letterth to one another. I found great pleathure in your correthpondenth after you left Lyonthtoke."

"This is different, though, I think. Can you swear to me that your affection for her would never slip into a word or a phrase?

That however careful you strive to be, she would never, ever guess your heart?"

That bitter turn descended on his mouth again. "She would not thee it, if it did," he muttered, admitting what Cassandry had feared.

"But her husband might."

Rauffe was young and inexperienced too. He might feel threatened by a man of Sir Fithian's age and accomplishments, especially if Rauffe's health did not improve. She did not believe it in Rauffe's nature to be cruel, as Antony had become, but he might lash out in a moment of insecure anger, and Egelina's impulsive nature might rebel. Their marriage could founder and collapse in its own way. Cassandry loved Egelina and had grown to love Rauffe too much to allow that to happen.

"No more writing," she said to Sir Fithian.

Sir Fithian's broad shoulders sank a little. "No, my lady."

She held out a hand to him and said more gently when he took it in his, "Thank you, Fithian."

He kissed her fingers and gave a small smile. But when she paused in the doorway and glanced back over her shoulder, she saw that he had picked up one of the crumpled parchments and was smoothing it out on top of the barrel with slow, caressing strokes.

Chapter 20

"Is he asleep?"

Gerolt turned at the voice behind him. He had been pacing the passageway outside Rauffe's chamber for the last hour, too restless with worry to content himself with sitting beside his son's bed. Cassandry moved to answer her own question by looking through the doorway Gerolt had left ajar.

"He said he was feeling better," she murmured.

"When did you speak with him?" Gerolt asked.

He thought she hesitated. "We met on the stairs. I was coming down as he was going up to rest. Marion mixes a very powerful potion. He looks to be sleeping soundly."

Gerolt did not know why he grew defensive. Her tones, like her words, were perfectly mild, yet he replied a little too quickly, "Aveline taught her. You must understand how frequently we feared for Rauffe's life through the years. Aveline always made him well again." Cassandry turned away from the door, her lips tight. "What is it?"

"'Tis nothing. I do not suppose Egelina has been to see him?"

"I have not seen her. Why?"

"Rauffe said he wished to speak with her, but we had another quarrel and I forgot to tell her."

"Another quarrel? About the marriage?"

"No, about the pen."

Gerolt knew better than to question her judgment on that matter again.

"Marion's potion made Rauffe better before," she said. "There is no reason to think it will not do so this time."

Had the potion made Rauffe better? He had still been pale at breakfast. He lost his balance at sword practice. And Rauffe admitted that his head still ached. Yet Gerolt clung to the only hope that had sustained him through Rauffe's precarious seventeen years.

He repeated, "Aveline always knew what to do. She always made him well. And Aveline taught Marion."

Was it concern that he had offended Cassandry by turning to Marion instead of her that lent him this sickish sensation as he said it? Or was it fear that he had made a mistake in doing so?

"What would you have done?" he asked her.

"I cannot know for sure because I do not know what Marion put in the potion. I do not think I would have sent Rauffe to sleep. But I am sure there is little harm done in that, except that we shall miss his company at dinner."

He thought she smiled, but he could not be sure in the dimness of the passageway. He scrubbed a hand across his forehead. "I'd hoped—I prayed—that you were right about the almonds, but—"

"I *was* right. Rauffe said that this—illness—felt different."

"You do not think it is an illness?"

"I do not know. I should like to have talked to him more about it, to watch him to see if this would pass on its own or grow worse over time. I meant to review his diet again. But I can do none of these things until he awakens."

Gerolt shoved his fingers through his hair. "I should have consulted with you before I asked Marion. But I panicked when he confessed he fell on the training field. All I could think was *What would Aveline do?* And Marion—"

"'—was taught by Aveline,'" Cassandry finished his refrain. "Do not berate yourself, Gerolt. I do not know that my methods would be any better than hers."

There. It was in her voice clearly that time. A soft but discernible note of skepticism. And his gut clenched over it. Aveline's methods had always been strong and certain—but what if they had also been wrong? He tried to push the thought away. Rauffe had always recovered, hadn't he? The fevers had ceased by his tenth year. But Gerolt recalled that Aveline's treatments had never varied over the early course of Rauffe's life. From the smell that greeted Gerolt whenever he entered Rauffe's chamber, she always employed the same herbs in his baths and teas and in the ointments she had smeared on his chest. She had allowed the physician Hyll to bleed Rauffe so many times that Gerolt had grown alarmed at his weakness and finally commanded them both to stop. The fevers waned and returned and waned and returned, then finally had simply ceased. Aveline had triumphantly proclaimed the virtue of patience, but eight years seemed a long while for a remedy to work.

The headaches had continued to plague Rauffe long after the fevers had left him. But they too had ebbed beneath Aveline's wisdom. Or had they done so because the potions had made him sleep through dinner after dinner, depriving him of the almonds she ordered Emma Cook to sprinkle lavishly in all their food, including Rauffe's dishes?

Gerolt did not know what to believe. Rauffe had not eaten almonds for days, and the headaches had returned. And now so had the fever.

He caught Cassandry abruptly by the hand and pulled her into Rauffe's chamber.

"Oh," she whispered. "I do not think we should wake him."

"I doubt that we could."

Gerolt picked up the candle from the table near the door. Rauffe had laid his dagger on the tabletop and leaned his sword on the chair beside it. Both blades shimmered in the candlelight before Gerolt carried the candle over to the bed and held it so that Cassandry could see the flush on Rauffe's cheeks. She bent down to touch his face. So gentle. Almost caressing. Aveline had always pressed a brisk palm to Rauffe's forehead, then wiped her hands with a cloth as though she found the moisture there distasteful.

Cassandry brushed her fingers lightly over Rauffe's cheeks and brow. "He is warm," she said, "but his flesh is not burning. I do not think we need be alarmed just yet."

Gerolt had seen Aveline fight ferociously for Rauffe's health. But he had never seen her tender with their son. Cassandry tucked a stray curl behind Rauffe's ear, then straightened.

"Let him sleep awhile longer. I will check on him again after dinner. That is, if you wish me to."

Gerolt nodded. He found that a lump had clogged his throat. They left the chamber, but when she would have closed the door, he stayed her with a touch to her hand. He was not ready to leave his vigil in the passageway quite yet.

She slowly withdrew her hand. "I must go. If I do not make peace with Egelina again, you and I may have to dine alone on the dais." Her tones were playful but also a little breathless.

"Wait," he said when she started to turn away. "There is something I must say."

She waited, but the rest remained lodged beneath the lump that had become a dry boulder in his throat. Hope. So cruel a cheat. It had reared its beautiful head exhilaratingly as he had watched Cassandry come back to life again. All shattered once more with the same exquisite sting as the day she had confided to him her love for Antony. Two thoughts had drummed in Gerolt's head as he'd paced, one placed there by Samson, the other borne of desperation. Either would crack his heart apart a second time, but somehow he had to speak them.

"Sparrow, you know that I must have an heir."

A moment of silence pulsed between them. He waited for her to chide him for the childhood name that had slipped out before he could catch it. Or to remind him in surprise—or rebuke—that he already had an heir.

But when she spoke, she only said quietly, "I know."

Even in the dim light of the passageway, he could not bear to face her. He turned to lean his back against the wall. "Rauffe has been ill for so many years. I have prayed for him in the chapel until my knees were raw and stood hours beside his bed, watching him toss with fever. Other times he lay so pale, his breathing so shallow, that I dared not leave him lest he be alone when his chest grew still."

He closed his eyes, reliving those episodes with a terror he could never speak aloud, for he was Lord Gerolt of Lyonstoke Castle and must stand strong before his men, whatever the pain and grief and fear in his heart.

"Oh, Gerolt." Cassandry's soft voice broke.

He tightened his jaw. He did not wish even Cassandry to see his weakness, but confessing it was the only way he knew to try to win her understanding so that she might forgive his plea.

"I thought when you removed the almonds that the nightmare might finally end, that Rauffe would at last be well. More than well, that he might actually grow strong and vigorous. But now . . . there might not be time, Sparrow. I know I promised you a year, but if Rauffe makes another recovery"—*Please, heaven, grant him one more reprieve!*—"I should like him and Egelina to marry now."

He heard Cassandry's startled breath. "Gerolt, they are too young!"

"You were only a year older when you married Antony."

"*I* was too young. You should never have allowed it."

He opened his eyes, but she had already averted her face. He found her hand and drew her a step toward him. "Cassandry, what happened between you and Antony?"

She answered again with silence.

A sound from the chamber drew Gerolt to the door. 'Twas only the creak of the bed as Rauffe shifted from his side to his back, raised a hand to scratch at his hair, then sank back into slumber.

Gerolt felt Cassandry's hands on his shoulders, drawing him back into the passageway.

"Come away, Gerolt. Let him sleep. You can do nothing for him here, and he is quite likely to feel better again when he awakes."

"If he does not—" Gerolt's voice rasped hoarse. "Oh, saints, Cassandry, if he worsens and dies—"

"Gerolt, it is far too early to worry about that."

"You have not been here, Sparrow. I have worried about that for seventeen years." He leaned against the wall again, feeling the need of its solid support. "I could do nothing but pray while Aveline lived and was my wife. But she is gone, and I have a duty to my name to ensure that I leave behind an heir. I pinned too many hopes on Rauffe, blinding myself to the truth because I could not bear the thought of losing him the way I lost Fleur." Gerolt sought for Cassandry's gaze, but he could not tell in the murky light if he found it. "Sam has urged me to marry again and have more children. Marion is eager and willing to wed me and has proven herself capable of bearing healthy sons."

"You should wed her, Gerolt. Whatever the future holds, more children will bring you comfort, and Marion will make you a cheerful wife." Cassandry's voice carried low and a little husky, surely so as not to disturb Rauffe.

Her words of approval cast a shaft through Gerolt's heart, crushing his final dream. But he had known it must be so from the moment he had come to Rauffe's chamber and seen the flush returned to his son's cheeks.

"Aye," he said. "It is the sensible thing to do. But . . ."

Cassandry laced her hands together in front of her. "But . . . ?"

The ache that seized Gerolt's breast each time Samson prodded him to wed Marion at last spilled out in words. "But marrying again will leave me nothing to remember Rauffe by if heaven chooses to take him. At least I have the letters I exchanged with Fleur. They bring her back to me, however briefly, when I read her words. But Rauffe—I will have nothing but perhaps a toy, a scrap of his mismatched clothing, but nothing of *him*." Gerolt's breath suspended for a moment. "Unless he and Egelina marry and give me a grandson, or even a granddaughter. Then—" He closed his eyes and let the picture flood his mind. "Oh, Cassandry, then the child's hair might curl as Rauffe's did, his eyes might be brown like Rauffe's, or I might catch a glimpse of him again in a granddaughter's smile. He will not be gone, vanished from me like smoke. A part of him will still live in his child. Marion can never give me that."

A beat of stillness before Cassandry spoke. "But Egelina can."

He pushed away from the wall, desperation strengthening the weakness in his knees. He tried again to seek her gaze. "You said you wished for this marriage. They have clearly grown fond of each other. I do not wish him to marry a stranger, but neither will I force my will upon you. If you cannot grant me this marriage now, then I will wed Marion. Either way, I dare not wait any longer." He ran a hand over his hair, this time feeling the coarseness of the gray that grew amidst the brown. "I am growing old, Cassandry. I must have some influence in my heir's rearing for as long as heaven will grant me."

"You must not speak that way," she said roughly. "You are

healthy and strong. Many days will remain to you yet to see your sons grow." She paused. "Or your grandchild."

"Then you will at least consider my request?"

"I do not like it. They are too young. You must trust me to know that, regardless of what the Church decrees. But I understand." Her hand found his arm and pressed it. "Gerolt, I do understand. And I cannot say that if our fears were reversed I would not wish for a grandchild to remind me of Egelina." She squeezed his tight muscles again, then released him. "I must think on it, at least for tonight." She paused as though debating. "Gerolt, if I agree, then you must know it is only because you will be here to guide them. To teach them both, as you taught me, to be kind and patient with one another, and never to let either hurt the other."

She must have known the question this would raise again. "Cassandry—what did Antony do?"

Gerolt did not know how much longer he could bear the wondering.

"It does not matter now," she said in a dull little voice.

"It matters to me." He reached out to brush a thumb along the silk of her cheekbone. "You were so in love with him. You glowed with it so brightly I feared you might shatter into a thousand joyous shards. And Antony loved you. I would never have let you marry had I not been absolutely convinced of that."

His hand rested on her cheek for a long moment before he felt the wet sensation of tears.

"Egelina says he loved me too," Cassandry whispered. "But Gerolt—he was not the man I thought him. Why did I not see it? Why did *you* not see it?"

"Cassandry—"

This time, *she* paced away, running her hands up and down her sleeves. "It was my fault. I should have been a better wife. I had no sense of symmetry in my weavings, I used the wrong shades when I embroidered his shirts, I wrote wicked letters, but they did not seem wicked. I was only lonely. Lonely for Lyonstoke. Lonely for you."

For me? His heart jammed, even as he struggled to make sense of her nonsensical words.

"Do you mean the letters you wrote my men and me after your marriage? They were not wicked, Sparrow. They were generous and loving toward men who counted you their friend. Antony objected?" Was this why she refused to teach Egelina to read and write?

She swiveled on her heel and paced the other direction, holding herself as if seized by a chill. "He was jealous, though I never gave him reason to be, I swear I did not. If Samson tells you otherwise, you must not believe him. Please, Gerolt, you must not believe him!" Her voice rose, almost on a note of panic.

"What has Sam to do with this?"

She hesitated. "I cannot say. He is your friend. Perhaps I merely misread—or misunderstood—" She moved away, sweeping down the passageway again. "Antony thought there was something between us. There was not! But Antony—I thought it so flattering before we were married when he glowered whenever Sir Ingram joined us to walk in the gardens, or when Sir Payne came riding with us, or when he found me sitting in conversation in the hall with Sir Edward or Sir Samson or with you."

The words rattled out of her as though they had been pent up so long she could not keep them dammed up any longer.

"But I was equally at fault, for I teased him with the wreath you wove me when I knew it made him frown, and I danced with you when he did not like it. I think he was even jealous of Jenny Wren because he knew I had sat beneath the tree with you before I did with him."

Another swing to pace the opposite way. She wrung her hands against her gown.

"I told him he was being ridiculous, but a part of me—oh, such a naïve part of me!—thrilled to think that he wanted me to be so entirely his alone. But after we married, after I had given myself to him completely and he should have trusted in my love, he still glowered and frowned. Even after he burned the letters, even after he made me write that degrading response, even after he made me cut you off—"

"Wait." Gerolt caught her by the shoulders. "*Antony* made you cut me off? Antony was jealous of *me?*"

Perhaps it was the same shadows of the corridor that had released Gerolt's emotions about Rauffe that had at long last loosed her reluctant tongue.

"He was jealous of everyone, even his own young knights. I must not smile at them or wear attractive gowns or even ask after their health. He dismissed them, one by one, until we were surrounded with nothing but graybeards. But still he was not satisfied. I could do nothing right. My weavings, my embroidery, my dinner selections, the way I managed the household—the only thing I ever did that pleased him was bear him Egelina." Her shoulders hitched beneath his hands, but he heard only a thin breath where he expected a sob. "I stopped feeling, Gerolt. I shut off my heart to try to shut out the pain. I was not the mother I should have been to Gelli. I could not laugh with her or sing. I have done naught but fail. Fail Egelina, fail Antony—"

"Hush, Sparrow, hush." He cupped her face between his palms and found her silent tears. "You have raised a lovely young woman. Intelligent and bright, and I think with a heart as warm as her mother's."

"She is tempestuous," Cassandry said, "and headstrong and rebellious—"

"And Rauffe is moody and stubborn and mumbles so that sometimes I fear I have gone prematurely deaf. They are both young, as you say, and perhaps neither of their childhoods was ideal. Aveline coddled Rauffe too much, and the setbacks to his health prevented him from participating in the discipline the other boys his age learned as pages and squires. Antony's—" Gerolt bit off the word *abuse*, and substituted "—flaws undoubtedly affected Egelina as much as your bewilderment and pain. I have also seen her show Rauffe great kindness. That, I think, she learned from you."

Her hand slid up to his. He thought she meant to pull his touch away, but then it simply rested against his fingers. "Rauffe wants so much for you to be proud of him. He has no comprehension of how much you love him. Why have you never told him?"

The question surprised Gerolt. Speak to Rauffe of love? His own father had never spoken of love to him. Gerolt stretched back in his mind. His father had not been a man to show emotion, but Gerolt had felt his support in his words of praise—when Gerolt had learned to wield his sword with skill, when he had mastered his first destrier, when he had learned to outwit the quintain, when he'd brought down a deer in the woods. Perhaps that was why Gerolt had courted Cassandry with praise as a girl, instead of speaking to her frankly from his heart, permitting Antony to beguile her away from him with the endearments that fell so easily and passionately from his lips.

If Gerolt's praise of his son had been sparse, it was because Aveline had kept Rauffe at such a distance, refusing during the boy's spans of health to allow him to ride or hunt and dragging Rauffe back to the fire whenever Gerolt tried to smuggle him into the yard to show him how to use a sword. Rauffe could not know, when sick, how fervently his father prayed for him, the hours Gerolt stood at his bedside while he tossed with fever or slept.

"Perhaps we both have failed in our own way," Gerolt said, his throat thick with regret. "I should have found a way to reassure Rauffe. I should have found a way to tell you . . ."

Her fingers curled around his as he trailed off. Again he feared she was about to pry his hand away. Again her touch lingered against his.

"Tell me what?"

He could not say it. He *dared* not say it. He had just begged her to hasten the marriage of their children. If she refused, then he must wed Marion. He could not be false to her any more than he would have allowed himself to betray Aveline. *But Marion is not my wife yet, and Egelina is not yet Rauffe's.* Would it be sin in this moment before either commitment was made to kiss Cassandry?

You will never have another chance. If not now, then never.

But a variant voice stole into his mind, checking his mouth as it drifted toward hers. *What if you shock her with your passion? What if this smoldering ardor of yours destroys the trust she has always held in you? Will you throw away all you have ever meant to one another for a moment of selfish pleasure?*

He could see the gleam of Cassandry's eyes now in the dimness of the shadows, but he held his mouth aloof from hers and uttered softly, "Sparrow . . ."

"Is that who I am to you?" she whispered. "The little sparrow you raised? The child . . . the sister . . . ?"

"Sister?"

He caught his breath at the absurdity of the thought. He had never thought of her as a sister. As his ward at first, aye, but how swift the years had flown and blossomed her into a shining young woman.

"Cassandry—if you wish things to remain as they have always been between us—then let go of my hand. Otherwise—I am very much afraid—that I am going to kiss you."

The fingers that curled around his did not so much as twitch, but her free hand slid around the back of his neck, ever so lightly nudging his mouth the final distance to hers.

In twenty-three years of marriage, Aveline's lips had never welcomed his so eagerly. Even passion had been mere duty to her.

Gerolt had not realized how large the void she had left in him until he felt the emptiness flooding with Cassandry's warmth and zeal. How he had fought the dreams through the years of a moment just like this. How he had struggled not to betray Aveline and Antony in his thoughts. But he poured it all into Cassandry now, dreams and thoughts and passion and all the pent up love in his soul.

Her arms twined around his neck, drawing him closer, as his fingers caressed her face, her throat, sought out the pins in her ever-bound-up hair and released her tresses. They tumbled over his hands like a fountain of silk, his last conscious thought before he surrendered himself to the flames of a radiant, blinding love that threatened to consume him. He lost count of how many times they kissed, how many times her mouth reached for his, clung to his, and how repeatedly and urgently his did the same.

He did not know which was worse, the physical or emotional wrench, when she twisted her head away and refused to allow him to capture her lips again.

"Gerolt—"

He could barely hear her through his pounding desire. He pressed a kiss to the softly pulsing vein at the base of her throat. She sagged a little, as though her knees were giving way, but he wound his arms around her waist and held her clasped tight to his breast.

"Oh, Gerolt, we must stop. This is madness!"

"Stop?" He buried his face in her hair, praying as hard as he had ever prayed for Rauffe that reality might remain at bay. *Do not wrest her from me. I have waited twenty-four years for this. Nay, I have waited a lifetime!* So it felt, all the years since she had wed Antony. He had been loyal to Aveline, he had even loved her—but not like this. Not with a love that set every particle of his being exultantly alive. He lifted Cassandry off her feet and spun her around with so much vigor that it swirled her hair across her face.

He set her back down, swept her hair away with a laugh, and kissed her again.

She reciprocated his energy for several more exhilarating minutes before she pulled away again.

"Gerolt, we must not. Marion—Egelina and Rauffe—this cannot be between us!"

No. I cannot think of them. I will not think of them! But the names rolled through his elation, his passion, crushing the breath and hope alike from his lungs and his heart.

She stroked his face before pushing him gently away. "You know—we both know—this must never happen again." Her fingers stole to his lips, which still held the heat of her kiss. "But—may heaven forgive me—I am glad it happened once."

Her voice broke, and he was certain she whisked away a tear. 'Twas a noise from Rauffe's room that turned his head and allowed her to slip from his arms. She was gone before he could stop her. He stared in her wake, the void she left throbbing like a rough, raw wound.

Again the sound. The creaking of a bed. Gerolt moved to the door of Rauffe's chamber and saw his son sitting up. He sat cross-legged atop the bed, his shoulders slumped, rubbing at his eyes. Gerolt pushed the door wide and strode in, snatching up the candle to better view his son.

"Rauffe, what's the matter?" His voice was husky from his passionate exchange with Cassandry.

Rauffe looked up. His eyes were red-rimmed in the candlelight and, Gerolt thought, a little too bright.

"Nothing is wrong." Rauffe's voice sounded a little thick. "That is, my head still hurts and my stomach feels a little . . ." he paused as if searching for a word, then shrugged ". . . hot. I do not think I can go to dinner, but—"

"There is no need," Gerolt said swiftly. "Shall I ask Marion to fix you another potion?" He could not ask Cassandry now.

"No. I do not want to sleep again yet."

Gerolt waited in the silence that Rauffe let fall, with the same helpless feeling that always seized him when he stood by his son's sickbed. Cassandry's words floated into his mind. *Rauffe wants so much for you to be proud of him. He has no comprehension of how much you love him. Why have you never told him?*

"The hounds miss you," Gerolt said abruptly.

Rauffe pulled his gaze from the candle's flame. "What?"

"The hounds that romp in the hall at night, and the ones in the kennel. You have a rare gift with them. Even the recalcitrant ones, the ones the huntsmen despair of and would have me destroy—I have seen how they come to you, how they obey your commands."

"You would not drown them?" Rauffe looked alarmed. "Venus and Bragge. They will be fine hunting dogs one day. If I could only rid myself of these headaches long enough to train them—but they are good dogs, sir. Please don't—"

"They shall await your recovery, my word on it. I would not waste a good hound when I have a son I am confident can teach them to hunt swift and sure."

Rauffe's already ruddy cheeks deepened with a flush of clear pleasure in this reply. Gerolt moved to return the candle to the table, thinking its distance might help Rauffe grow drowsy again.

"Father?"

"Yes?"

"Will you sit with me awhile and tell me the story of Iconium again?"

Rauffe had not asked for that tale for nearly four years, since he had begun to slump and mutter and roll his eyes and generally exasperate Gerolt to the limits of his patience. It would soon be time for dinner, and if Rauffe demanded the tale from beginning to end, as he used to do, Gerolt would be here a very long time.

He snagged the chair beside the table and drew it up alongside his son's bed. Let the diners wonder where he was. No moment felt more important to him than this did now.

"It was a beautiful spring dawn. The sun was just beginning to shimmer along the trees and clouds rolled like small clusters of wool in the sky when I kissed your mother good-bye and rode off for the lands of the East to ransom Sir Samson from his Saracen prison . . ."

Chapter 21

Cassandry and Egelina dined alone on the dais. A servant brought word to the company that Gerolt had chosen to dine with his son, reassuring Cassandry that Rauffe not only had awakened but must be feeling better again. Her heart rejoiced for Gerolt, but almost immediately the former weight of her spirits extinguished the emotion. For the first time, she welcomed Egelina's cold silence. It spared Cassandry the necessity of engaging in conversation when she could barely drag out of her anguish the words to tell Egelina that she should go speak with Rauffe at the meal's end, before Marion administered another of her potions to him. Egelina gave one curt nod and returned to her lamb stew.

Marion, at one of the tables below, appeared to be ignoring her father nearly as stiffly as Egelina was ignoring Cassandry. *You should thank him. 'Twas Samson who put the idea of marrying you into Gerolt's head, when he could have his pick of any of the young women in the realm.* Unless Cassandry agreed to marry Egelina quickly to Rauffe. Either way, the bliss she had tasted in Gerolt's kisses had already withered. All of her longings had been stilled in his embrace, only to be snatched away by one cruel truth—she was too old. She would not bear

Gerolt the heir he needed. Likely she could not. He knew it too. Then why had he kissed her? She knew the difference between love and lust. The former she had learned with Antony, when their marriage was still new and fresh and trusting. The latter had brimmed over in Samson's coarse letters and in his assault at the stable. Gerolt's embrace had engulfed Cassandry with love. It had been all her wounded heart had yearned for. But it remained just as forbidden as it had when she thought he would never see her as anything more than his Sparrow.

Egelina pushed her empty trencher away. "May I go see Rauffe now?"

"He may still be with his father," Cassandry replied.

"Lady Marion is looking impatient. See how she keeps glancing from you to the stairs? You know no one can leave the hall before you rise, save you give them permission. If she carries another potion to Rauffe and he falls back to sleep, I will never know what he wished to say to me."

Cassandry had, indeed, observed Marion's behavior. She had observed a great many things in her attempts during dinner to distract herself from the too-familiar despondency trying to settle over her. She needed to make a clearheaded decision about Rauffe and Egelina marrying sooner rather than later. Cassandry had struggled to keep her attention keen by watching the covert glances Sir Fithian cast at Egelina and by frowning at Samson, who gazed boldly at Cassandry when he was not placing tidbits on Marion's trencher and murmuring into the ear she kept turning away from him.

"Yes, very well," Cassandry said to her daughter, "you may go. Beg Lord Gerolt's pardon if you interrupt them and withdraw until they are finished. But do not go to the tower."

"No, Mamma," Egelina replied in arctic tones. "I will bring my embroidery here to the hall when the tables have been cleared away and work in full view of Lord Gerolt's household so that none might suspect me luring men aside to seduce me."

Cassandry flinched. "Gelli, I never thought any such thing of you."

"But you thought it of Sir Fithian. I do not know how I can ever face him again."

Given the poorly concealed affection Cassandry still saw in Sir Fithian's eyes, she thought that might well be for the best.

"Go to Rauffe," she said. "You and I will talk of all this later."

"No, Mamma, I do not think we shall. You know my determination. I do not think there is anything left between us to discuss." Egelina rose with great dignity, her eyes like blue chips of ice as she departed the dais, her chin lifted high in the air.

Cassandry forced herself to finish her meal, even though every bite felt like dust on her tongue. She hoped it would give Rauffe time to say whatever he wished to say to Egelina.

Cassandry had just taken her last bite of roast pork when she saw Gerolt descending the stairs. A servant approached him quickly and gestured at the dais, but though Gerolt threw an unreadable glance Cassandry's way, he shook his head and moved down the tables toward where Samson sat.

Oh, saints, oh, saints! Gerolt was going to confront him over— what? Cassandry could scarcely remember what all she had babbled in the passageway. She knew that she had prattled far more than she had meant to and that some of it had to do with Samson and the letters, but then Gerolt had kissed her and sent everything but her urgent need for him out of her head. Now he had his hand on Samson's shoulder and Samson was rising from his chair. Gerolt's precedence outweighed Cassandry's, and when he began to withdraw Samson from the hall, the rest of the company took it as a signal that they might be dismissed as well.

Cassandry fled to her chamber to formulate her defense against whatever lying, sordid accusations Samson intended to lay against her. In her haste, she nearly trod upon the little cluster tied by a ribbon outside her chamber door.

Another token? But they had never been left this time of day. She thought they were twigs with a bow wound around them, but when she picked them up the aroma of cinnamon coiled through her senses. Three sticks of it, neatly tied together, with a piece of parchment attached. Cassandry had restocked all the spices in the kitchen, but she had had the servants grind the cinnamon. Then where had these sticks come from? They had not been outside her door when she went to dinner, and Samson was in the hall the entire time. But Gerolt had not been, and could easily have set this token before Marion's door. It hurt to think he had done so, so soon after kissing Cassandry, but she had agreed frankly with him that he should wed Marion. Cassandry's eyes had no right to fill with tears.

Samson must have left one of his servants to watch Marion's door and remove the gift to Cassandry's. Marion clearly needed no wooing from Gerolt, and Samson had proven himself a selfish father before.

Voices sounded, and footsteps. Other diners retiring to this part of the castle. Cassandry opened her chamber door and slipped inside. Her action dislodged the ribbon from where it lay across a word on the parchment. Her breath caught. Once again her own name stared up at her in the same simple script that had accompanied the hair ribbon and hairpin.

So Samson had reverted to tokens of his own. She would have thrown the gift in his face if he had been standing here. Instead she threw it on the bed with a force that made it bounce three times across the blankets. When it rolled to a stop, the parchment had flipped over. There was more writing on the other side. Even from this distance she recognized the hand, so distinctive from the script of her name. She moved to pick the parchment up with suddenly trembling fingers.

How you have been missed! May this bring you warm memories of home.

Gerolt. What could he mean by such a gift? She flipped the parchment back over to see if she had only dreamed her name there, but it stood out as clearly as before. Not Marion. Cassandry. An impossible thought jarred her.

"Were they *all* meant for me?" The apple and the pomander? The shell, so like the one he had tied around her neck at twelve? And the wreath he had woven for her at fourteen? Was it possible Gerolt had been showering gifts on her all this time and never said a word? "Gerolt, you know I cannot—*we* cannot—"

She read the words again. *May this bring you warm memories of home.* She had lived longer at Rengrave Castle as Antony's wife than she had as Gerolt's ward at Lyonstoke.

But this is where I learned to laugh again after my parents died. This is where I learned to trust and hope again. It was here that I left my pony to ride that gentle brown mare with you beside me, to dance with my hands in yours. I learned to sew and embroider and weave, to sing, to play chess, to be kind and patient, to count so that I might not lose my temper, to be strong so that others' cruelty might not hurt me . . . This—this truly was my home.

She had not realized how much her sadness with Antony had begun to dim until the memory of all she had lost as his wife washed over her. She dropped suddenly to her knees beside the bed and wrapped her arms around herself. Antony's golden face and Gerolt's dark one battled before her, but it was Gerolt's that finally surged to the fore, and it was to him she turned her plea.

"I tried so hard when I left. So hard to do everything you taught me, to remain the woman who brought pride to your eyes when you gazed upon me. But I was not strong. I was too weak to fight Antony's anger and jealousy. He tore you from my life, and I crumbled. Why did you not come after me? Why?"

The conviction of Gerolt's love robbed her of her bitterness, but her confusion lingered. Then through it cut another question. If Gerolt had come, what would she have done? Run into his arms and confessed her mistake? That she should never have left Lyonstoke, should never have married Antony?

She could not have done that. Gerolt had given her a gift few women were allowed—the gift of choice. She had used it to wed Antony of her own free will. Pride, if nothing else, would have held her silent. That, and the love that all of Antony's beratings and belittlings had never quite completely slain.

"Forgive me," she whispered. "Gerolt, forgive me for blaming you. If you had come, it would have changed nothing, for I could never have confessed the truth to you."

She wiped her eyes and gazed again at the parchment. And now, what did this mean? Why leave the gifts first in secret? Why pretend ignorance when she told him of their appearance?

"I expect such games from Sir Samson. But from you, Gerolt?"

It did not make sense. The man she knew—the man she loved would not dishonor their children or her conscience by pursuing an illicit relationship with her.

But Egelina had crossed her fingers at the betrothal.

The first token had appeared the next morning. And the night they had played chess, when Rauffe was returning so vigorously to health, Gerolt had been reluctant to press forward with Rauffe and Egelina's marriage. Had Gerolt, in truth, been courting Cassandry all this time? Was it possible—she gasped aloud, stunned at the thought that flashed into her mind. Was it possible that the day he had come to talk to Cassandry of a second marriage, he had been speaking of himself?

Her hand flew to her lips. *I did not know. Oh, Gerolt, I did not know!*

And now it was too late. He had proposed the marriage of their children when she had refused him, and however he might have wavered afterward, Rauffe's relapse had cemented his commitment to his son's union with Egelina. Then why leave this token and speak of home?

A parting gift. It could be nothing else. To remind her how dearly she had once been cherished here, how dearly she might still have been cherished had she not been so blind.

She leaned against the bed and wept. Surely heaven would only condemn her tears *after* she took her vows at the convent? She had buried her love for one man in her life. She would bury this love, too.

"Just give me time," she prayed. "I did not know Gerolt loved me until this day. Just give me a little time to grow empty again so that You may fill me with Your grace." *Please, please, let me find grace and peace. It has been so long since I have known either.*

When her tears were spent, she wiped them away, kissed Gerolt's note, then rose. She went to place the token in her jewelry box, where she had placed the others she had kept, save for the ones she had given to Samson.

Samson. Would Gerolt repent of his kisses if Samson succeeded in convincing Gerolt that Cassandry had tried to seduce his friend while she was married to Antony? Would Gerolt be glad to grant her boon, to cast her from his sight and finally from his heart? The thought sickened her, but there was naught she could do to head off the blow if Samson chose to deal it.

She opened the door to her wardrobe and reached for the carved wooden casket on the shelf, the gift Antony had given her to celebrate their first year of marriage. Because the shelf stood above her head, she pulled down Egelina's jewelry box by mistake, as she often did. Cassandry was about to return it and reach again for her own when a sudden memory stirred. The night Egelina had appeared to be concealing something behind her back, when Cassandry had wondered if . . . and what . . . Egelina had slipped surreptitiously into this box.

Antony had given this jewelry casket to Egelina, too, on her tenth birthday, but he had been surprisingly responsible enough to give a matching key to Cassandry. Cassandry had never used it before, but she felt suddenly filled with misgivings. So many of Gerolt's men had gazed admiringly at Egelina—Sir Owen, Sir Ingram, the redheaded squire, Sir Fithian. Cassandry did not like to suspect any of them of giving her daughter inappropriate gifts when they all thought her betrothed to Rauffe, but sometimes men did foolish things. Gerolt's tokens locked away in her own casket lay evidence of that.

She retrieved the key, set the casket on the bed, and unlocked it. She was not certain what she expected, but it was not a feather peeking between a chain with sapphire studs and a ruby brooch. Why would Egelina have tucked something as common as a feather amidst her jewels? Cassandry lifted it out. She recognized immediately the shaved point at the end. A pen. And where there was a pen . . .

She tossed the quill on the bed and dug deeper beneath the jewelry. She discovered a small, stoppered inkpot. Cassandry's lips tightened, but her heart did not trip into a double beat until she pulled out three pieces of parchment. *Please, oh, please,* she prayed as panic surged past disapproval, *do not let these be love letters!*

She unfolded the first with unsteady hands that quickly steadied again. Someone had traced out a line of thin, wobbly *E*'s across the top. Below it ran a line of *G*'s in the same tentative hand. Below that a line of *L*'s, then *I*'s, *N*'s, and *A*'s, then, finally, at the bottom, the letters put together. EGELINA. She was learning to write her name. Cassandry could not quite call it harmless, but at least 'twas not a love note from some clandestine suitor.

She hoped the second piece of parchment might be equally innocuous. Perhaps, in its own way, it was. This time Egelina had written a very small poem, four lines only, though some of the words had been crossed out and rewritten because errant letters had stolen in here and there. Against her will, Cassandry felt her mouth soften a little. She had been fourteen, only a little younger than Egelina, when she had learned to write so that she could share her poetry with Antony. She remembered the labor it had been to learn to form the letters correctly and arrange them in ways that Gerolt had said made sense—into words, like the ones that flowed oh! so easily from her tongue. How many times had she thrown down her quill in frustration? How many times had Gerolt picked it up again and gently set it back in her hand? She remembered his eyes sometimes twinkling at her mistakes. Had Sir Fithian smiled over these errors of Egelina's? Or was he too besmitten with her to give her aught but earnest encouragement?

"Oh, Gelli, this *must* stop."

Her hand hovered over the last piece of parchment, her mind filled with the vision of Sir Fithian's devoted gaze on Egelina. Tensing for the love note she expected at last to find, Cassandry pulled the sheet open—and found it blank. She looked from the first to the second to the last. Perhaps Egelina had taken this one to practice on when she was not with Sir Fithian in the tower?

With her fear removed, Cassandry sat down on the bed. She pulled the second parchment over to her again and this time read the words. The poem was simple, like a child's poem, nothing like the complicated verses Egelina had been weaving for Gerolt's company in the hall or the youthful but sophisticated poem she had shared with Cassandry in the wine cellar. Egelina must have carried this poem around in her head a very long time before Sir Fithian showed her how to write it down. Cassandry tried to remember just one of her old poems, but they were all gone. Blown away like mist . . . or burned in the fire of Antony's anger. Except for one . . .

They fly, they fly, fleet over the ground,
The hounds chase the doe through the forest green.
The trumpets blare and arrows speed,

A bound and a leap, and the doe soars free.
The huntsmen mourn their quarry's loss,
But the fawn greets his mother 'neath a dappling tree.

A few days ago, Cassandry had tried to toss the poem out of her head by shouting it into the wind. But suddenly she did not want to forget it. Poetry had once been like living breath to her. She had found life again here at Lyonstoke Castle. 'Twas no wonder she had found her poetry here, too.

They fly, they fly, fleet over the ground . . .

It would be hypocritical of her to pick up that pen and write it upon the empty piece of parchment. But it would be the last time, unless she chose to bend her mind to holy verse in the convent. She had never written a poem for Gerolt. She had chattered to him an innumerable number, but her writings had been for Antony only. Would it be so very wicked to leave Gerolt just one to remember her by?

The scratch of the pen against the parchment felt odd at first, dragging and slow. But by the third line the words began to flow. The pen moved faster, her pulse beat quicker, her sorrow and heartache dulled until joy itself felt as though it were spilling out of her along with the words. How had she forgotten this? It was not Antony who made writing poetry so rapturous. It was the act of writing itself, the choosing of each precise word and knowing that the ink on the page would bind her verse to the parchment forever and ever.

"Mamma!"

Cassandry's head snapped up to see Egelina in the doorway. How long had she been there? Had she seen—?

"Oh, Mamma!" Egelina ran across the room and flung her arms around Cassandry's neck. "You understand! I see it in your face. You finally understand!"

Cassandry swayed beneath the force of Egelina's hug, but

Egelina quickly braced her with her arm around Cassandry's waist as she sat down on the bed beside her mother.

"What does it say? Will you read it to me?" Egelina pled. "Oh, wait, I know these words!" Her finger moved beneath the first line of the poem. "'They fly, they fly . . .' What is this one, Mamma?" Her finger paused beneath the fifth word.

Cassandry hesitated, but Egelina's excitement and the tug to share her verse now that it was on the page overwhelmed her.

"Fleet," Cassandry said.

"'Fleet over the . . . '?"

"Ground."

"'. . . ground. The . . .'"

"Hounds . . .'"

"Hounds? Like this one, only with an *h*?" Egelina pointed at *ground*.

"Yes, Gelli. If you remember that they sound alike, you may remember that they are spelled the same too."

Egelina's finger returned to the first line, pointing to each word as she read it. "'They fly, they fly, fleet over the ground, the hounds chase the doe . . .'"

"Through . . ."

"'Through the forest green.'" She grinned at her mother's surprise. "I am composing a poem about a doe and green forests too. I asked Sir Fithian to teach me those words especially."

Cassandry's doubts began to swirl back at the mention of Sir Fithian's name. She almost withdrew the parchment and folded it up, but Egelina slipped it from her fingers before she could.

"Mamma, your writing is so much prettier than Sir Fithian's. I'm afraid my letters will never look like these if I learn from him. Will you teach me, please? To make pretty letters like these?"

Cassandry felt a familiar chill. How could she give her daughter such a dangerous tool? Yet, for the first time, her heart lay divided. *Poetry was once the breath of life to me. Egelina breathes of*

*the same air. Will you stifle her very being? Will you suffocate her,
as Antony suffocated you?*

As though anticipating her mother's reply, Egelina said swiftly,
"I will never, ever open a note that any man writes to me. If I
receive one, I will burn it in the fire. I promise, Mamma! Just show
me how to write down my poetry so that I do not forget it, please! I
will be ever, ever so good if you will. You will not even recognize
me, I will be so good." She gave a nervous little laugh on the words,
but she watched Cassandry's face with an almost painful anxiety.

Cassandry gazed down at the pen still between her fingers,
remembering the joy she had been lost in only moments before.
Fear and heartbreak had made her forget. She wanted desperately
to protect Egelina from every means the world could form to hurt
her, including this. But *she* was the one who was hurting her
daughter the most by refusing to let Egelina be Egelina.

*Antony took your poetry, your whimsy, your music, your very
worth, and left you empty. Do not set Egelina down the same road.
Let her breathe. Let her fly.*

"We will need more parchment. And more ink than this tiny
inkhorn holds." Cassandry smiled at her daughter.

"Oh!" Egelina bounced up and whirled about the room, then
returned to catch Cassandry by the hands. "There are more of
both in the tower. Oh, Mamma, thank you. *Thank you!*"

As the hours waned and the piles of poetry grew around them,
Cassandry felt their hearts knit together with a poignancy beyond
anything her love for her daughter had conceived before this day.
It would wrench her very soul to leave this newfound camaraderie
they had found! She wanted to stay to witness the glowing,
talented woman Egelina would become. She no longer wanted
Egelina trapped in a safe, mundane marriage but luminescent in a

marriage of mutual, nurturing love, the sort of wonderful, bolstering love Gerolt had always given Cassandry and that Rauffe would surely learn from his father how to impart as well.

I want to see and hold my grandchildren.

But these thoughts were more dangerous than any letter Samson had ever penned to her. She had tasted Gerolt's kisses and could never be content to be near him and not want him to kiss her again and again—and again. The nunnery was her only safety from the fire of temptation that burned in her bones.

Chapter 22

Gerolt took Samson to his own chamber, the only place he could be certain they would not be interrupted without at least a warning knock on the door. Samson did not wait for an invitation to seat himself but threw himself into a negligent sprawl in the large, carved chair beside the bed.

"I have always envied you this," Samson confessed. "This fine carving." He ran a finger along the tufted mane of the sea lion's head, then traced the detailed scales of the fish tail that formed the chair's armrest. "These jewels." He flicked at the rubies winking in the lion's head for eyes. "Those velvet curtains with their gold embroidery." He nodded at the bed curtains before returning to rub his hand almost caressingly over the polished wood of the chair. "I never had anything so fine as this at my castle, not even before my wife wasted my inheritance while I languished in that Saracen hellhole."

Gerolt watched him from where he stood at the foot of the bed. He saw the familiar bitterness at the corners of Samson's mouth, but for the first time he felt no pity for it.

"What else did you envy, Sam? Antony's wife?"

Samson glanced up swiftly. "Ah. So she has told you of our little—interlude."

Gerolt linked his hands behind his back. He scarcely knew what to make from Cassandry's distraught ramblings in the passageway outside Rauffe's chamber, and yet he had an almost overwhelming urge to drag Samson out of his smug posture in that chair.

"I should like to hear your version of that 'interlude.'" Did Samson know him well enough to take warning from the intense calmness in his voice?

Of course he did. Samson straightened a little, but he did not rise. "It was a jest, Gerolt, nothing more. You know how often Cassandry wrote to us all after her marriage. It is dangerous to teach women to write. Did I not warn you it would lead to trouble when you gave in to her entreaties?"

"What I remember is how downcast you looked when Antony joined my household and she fell in love with him. Until then, I had not realized that you admired her. I chose to overlook it at the time. You were not the only one of my men whom I suspected hoped I might one day grant her hand. She was lovely and warm and with such innocent fervor trusted each of you as her friends."

They had all grown fond of her, his knights, his squires, even his pages, following Gerolt's lead at first in helping her adjust to her new home, then falling under the spell of her bright, merry spirit. It was inevitable that a few of them would covet her as she grew toward womanhood. Saints! Gerolt had done so himself. But despite allowing a degree of familiarity with his men, he had always enforced most strictly the line of respect he'd laid down for Cassandry's treatment. No one had ever dared cross it, not even Samson, who spent more time than any other man in Gerolt's company, and therefore also had greater access to Cassandry than any of his other knights.

"Whatever your desire for her, you cannot have spoken your thoughts to her then," Gerolt said. "I would have seen the change in her behavior toward you if she had grown wary of you."

"She was your ward. Our friendship meant more to me than whatever desire she might have stirred. I honored that, Gerolt. Our friendship."

Some significance Gerolt could not discern hovered about the words Samson let hang in the air. Though Samson did not move or change his expression, Gerolt felt a shade fall between them. Was Sam falling into the doldrums again?

"And after she wed Antony and left Lyonstoke . . . ?"

"Well, then, she was not your ward anymore, was she?"

Gerolt stared at Samson, taken aback for a moment before his heart began a slow acceleration.

"What did you do, Sam . . . when she was no longer my ward?" He spoke with the same warning calm as before. 'Twas the tone he had used when he'd dismissed Sir Miles from his service. Samson had stood at Gerolt's shoulder that day, where he had stood all their lives.

Samson leaned back in the chair again, stretching his legs out before him and crossing them at the ankles, but Gerolt knew Samson as well as Samson knew Gerolt. Tension had entered Sam's casual posture.

"There were letters between us," Samson said, "all long since destroyed to protect her modesty. She was young. She was newly wed and newly acquainted with passion. It spilled over into the words she wrote to me. I may have allowed a mild flirtation to ensue between us, but I assure you it was all harmless."

Gerolt snared Samson's gaze and held it hard. "Was it, Sam? Harmless?" Cassandry's ramblings about Antony's jealousy had implied otherwise.

"Has she shown you any evidence that it was not?"

"I did not ask her. Shall I do so?"

Samson sat up again. "Whatever she says, I swear that it never went beyond words between us."

"What sort of words?"

"I have told you. She grew hot for me. She wrote to me boldly. Perhaps she wrote so to all your men—"

Gerolt rarely lost his temper, but it snapped now. His hands whipped from behind his back and dragged Samson to his feet. "You expect me to believe a slander like that? Of Cassandry?"

Samson knocked away his grasp and backed away, breathing hard. "But you will believe her slanders of me? You have known me for over forty years. She lived in your house a mere eight before she scorned you for Antony. You saw in her what you wanted to see, Gerolt, a sweet, guileless lamb. But she grew up to be a woman, a passionate woman. If you could read the last letter she penned to me—"

"Then show it to me, and perhaps I will believe you."

"That was twenty-three years ago. I told you I burned it to spare you knowing how wanton she had become."

Gerolt's fist snapped out, catching Samson on the chin and knocking him into a stagger across the room. Samson regained his balance before he fell. He pressed a hand to his jaw, staring at Gerolt in shock.

Gerolt struggled to control his anger at hearing the word *wanton* coupled with Cassandry's name. "Cassandry never had eyes for you, Sam. She never had eyes for anyone but Antony."

"Antony was a boy," Samson flung back, "and a pathetically insecure one at that. He covered it with bluster and bravado, but he must have quickly grown wearying as a husband. Do not blame me if she became disillusioned and looked among her old friends for 'comfort.'" Samson's lips curled into a sudden sneer. "I see what it is. It wounds you that she turned to me instead of you."

It would—were it true. Gerolt relocked his hands behind his back before he hit Samson again. He strode across the floor, struggling against rage and a reluctant doubt. Cassandry had admitted to being lonely, while Antony's jealousy had clearly cut her sweet, trusting soul to the quick. But turn to Sam for consolation when she had not shared one hint of her troubles in the letters she wrote to Gerolt? Even if he could accept that—even if he could forgive her—how could he reconcile such behavior with the candid, honest kisses she had shared with him mere hours ago? *I will not believe them less than honest. Not unless I have some proof.*

He swiveled on his heel to catch Samson's gaze again. "When did this alleged 'affair of words' happen?"

Samson was opening and closing his mouth, as though testing the soundness of the jaw Gerolt had struck. He ran his hand along the beard that fringed it before he answered.

"A year or so after she wed Antony. You had married Aveline by then, but I was still a bachelor."

"So you were, one who did not scruple to seduce married ladies if they caught your eye."

"Only willing ones, Gerolt. And I never had to seduce a one of them."

Another slur against Cassandry. Gerolt laced his fingers tighter before they found their way around Samson's throat, but the ugly doubt still throbbed against his temples. Whatever had happened had been sufficiently serious for Antony's anger to extinguish her light and leave her the empty shell Gerolt had discovered at Rengrave Castle. Had Antony been justified? Had she brought her misery upon her own head?

He strode toward the door.

"Where are you going?" Samson said.

"To ask Cassandry if it is true."

"You think she will admit to it? She will try to cast the blame on me, to say that I initiated our letters."

Gerolt swung about again. "Did you, Sam?"

"Gerolt—"

"Why did she choose you? Why not Ingram or Payne or Tobias? They were her friends as well as you. They admired her, too, and sighed equally when I gave her hand to Antony. Why you,

Sam?" Samson held himself a little too still. "Or did you choose her?"

"Are you calling me a liar? You have known me for more than forty years."

"Have I? Have I ever known you, Sam?" Gerolt's heart resumed its steady, puzzled drumbeat. The roguish but loyal features he had loved from boyhood dissolved into the face of a stranger. "I raised Cassandry, I taught her right from wrong. When she wept, I comforted her. She came to me—*to me*—with her every joy and burden. I did not merely feed and clothe her, I poured my very soul into her. I *loved* her, Sam. And you knew it. If she was hurting so much from her marriage, why would you keep it from me? Worse, why would you encourage it?"

The only movement now from Samson was the bob of his Adam's apple.

Gerolt walked around him slowly. "You say you have always honored our friendship, but it was not honor to pursue her behind my back, knowing what she had always meant to me."

Samson revolved to follow him. Gerolt paused when he reached the bed. He stood aghast for a moment at a possibility he had never entertained before. He had thought Samson spoke either playfully or beneath the influence of one of the dark clouds that had dogged him from the East. What if that cloud had loosed a long-buried truth?

"Was it because of this?" Gerolt stretched out the bed curtains with their lavish embroidery of gilt threads. "Or this?" He dropped the curtains and walked to the chair, touching the carved sea lion head with the ruby eyes that Samson had stroked so reflectively. "Or perhaps these." With a fresh rising heat, Gerolt stripped off the rings on his hands and tossed them at Samson, then jerked a cloak foaming with fur from its peg and flung it, too, while Samson was still fumbling to catch the rings.

Samson glanced up for one unguarded moment, and Gerolt

saw the truth.

"Envy? You did it for envy of me?"

"Gerolt—"

Gerolt silenced him with a jabbing finger that stopped just short of the quick rise and fall of Samson's breast. "One lie, Sam—just one—and you can return to your own castle as the pauper your wife left you." Gerolt stood as rigid as Samson until convinced that Sam understood him. He lowered his hand very slowly before he asked, "Who wrote first—you or Cassandry?"

Samson's tongue darted out to wet his lips before he answered. "I."

Relief, anger, and betrayal all melded together in a molten lump in Gerolt's gut. He had to force out the next question, for one of two people whom he held dear would slip further away from him in its aftermath.

"These letters of hers, her 'hot' replies to you, the ones you say you destroyed—did they ever exist?"

Another pause. "Only one."

It was not the answer Gerolt had hoped for, but he forced himself to withhold judgment until he heard the rest. "And it said?"

A smirk stole at the corners of Samson's lips. "It would have burned your eyes to read it, Gerolt. She thanked me in the most lurid tones for our amorous trysts."

"Trysts?" Gerolt's stomach clenched. "You said your 'jest' never went beyond words."

"It did not, but I suspect Antony saw one of my letters and thought otherwise. She cut it off, Gerolt, our 'affair' that never existed, in the only letter she wrote to me after I sent her, oh, a dozen letters or so—rather warm ones, I confess. After she had received the others with a freezing silence, I can only presume she finally penned her impassioned reply to me under some sort of duress."

What was it Cassandry had rambled in the passageway? "Even after Antony made me write that degrading response . . ." Gerolt gave a silent groan as it rushed back. "He was jealous of everyone. I could do nothing right. I stopped feeling. I shut off my heart to try to shut out the pain." *Oh, Sparrow, Sparrow* . . . Guilt bubbled up like scalding acid. But how could Gerolt have guessed that Samson, the man he had trusted before all others, would set such a chain of tragedy in motion?

Gerolt fell to pacing to try to harness his fury before he gazed again at his 'friend.' "When were these 'trysts' Antony suspected you of supposed to have taken place?"

"Do you recall how often you took it in mind after her wedding to visit your manor in Hertfordshire? Rengrave Castle lay along the road, conveniently positioned to require a vassal of yours to grant you hospitality for a night or two as you journeyed to inspect your lands. I think that was no coincidence—was it?"

Gerolt had never confessed to anyone the whisper of misgiving he had smothered on the day of Cassandry's wedding. Antony had been young, impulsive, and immature, but he had loved Cassandry and never, to Gerolt's knowledge, had treated her disrespectfully. Gerolt had kept a discreet but keen eye upon Cassandry as well, so that he might catch the slightest trace of distress upon her face if trouble fell between her and Antony. Gerolt would have ended the courtship in an instant if he had glimpsed it, but he never had. Nevertheless, he had determined to reassure himself that their happiness would continue into their marriage, and so had used his manor in Hertfordshire as an excuse to call upon them with some regularity that first year. If anything, Cassandry had only glowed more brilliantly than before, while Antony beamed with pleasure in his new wife. At every visit, they had appeared as much enwrapped in their poetry and love as they had at Lyonstoke.

Samson continued on in Gerolt's silence. "Of course, you never traveled there alone. You always took a retinue of knights with you. While Antony rode out with you to show off his lands, some of us always stayed behind to entertain Cassandry. I was never alone with her, none of us were, but once Antony discovered my letters, he either did not believe that or he chose not to. I told you he was insecure. I am amazed that you did not see it too."

Gerolt *had* seen it. But Cassandry had so often drawn out Antony's better traits that he had convinced himself they would mature together in their marriage. And perhaps they would have, had Samson not chosen to meddle.

Gerolt turned toward Samson again. He had forced him to admit what he had done and when. Now Gerolt had to ask the most devastating question of all.

"Why, Sam? What harm had Cassandry ever done you to make you torment her?"

"It was not my intention to torment her. I hoped to seduce her."

His gaze flicked to Gerolt's balling fist, but this time Gerolt caught himself and counted silently until he managed to relax his fingers.

"Why?" he asked again. "Why this betrayal of her? Of me?"

"I thought you already guessed. Because of this. And this." Samson tossed the rings and cloak back to Gerolt.

Gerolt flung them onto the bed. "Enough of your games," he snapped. "Tell me straightly. You owe me that."

Samson crossed to the bed and rubbed a corner of the fur-lined cloak between his fingers. "You are so smug in your wealth you cannot even conceive what it might have been like for me, can you? Velvets and silks and furs. Well-stocked fortresses, manors that prospered, men to serve you, vassals who respect and fear you."

"All of which I shared with you. When did you lack for any extravagance of clothing you wished? When did you not sit in my hall and eat the same fine dishes as I? Even my vassals knew to honor you."

"They did not honor me, Gerolt. They feigned to please you, but after my father died, when I remained at Lyonstoke instead of leaving to take control of my inheritance, they smirked and muttered that I was a malingerer sponging off your wealth."

"I kept you with me gladly because I could not imagine my life without you by my side."

"Nor I without you, then. But that did not change the fact that everything you gave me, the clothes, the jewels, the food, the wine, the very roof over my head, all belonged to you. My father's keep felt so paltry beside all this." Samson swept out his arm, engulfing Gerolt's chamber in his gesture, and by extension, Lyonstoke Castle itself. "You even secured my wife for me. I told you I could not afford the marriage price Herleve's father demanded for her hand—"

"—and I made up the difference," Gerolt finished. "You did not ask that of me; I offered because you desired her. You never asked any of it from me, Sam. I *wanted* to share it with you. You were not a sponge or a malingerer. You were my brother, as dear to me as if we had in truth shared flesh and blood."

"I knew that. And I was grateful, because you were as blood and flesh to me too. But it was all still yours. Just once, Gerolt—just once I wanted something of my own, something you had not given me, something I won for myself, something that with all your wealth and privilege could never be yours, even if it was only because you were too honorable to take it."

"Cassandry? Sam, had you succeeded—"

"I know. It would have broken our friendship if you'd learned we were lovers. But I did not need you to know, Gerolt. I did not *want* you to know. It would have been enough to love her in secret, for *me* to know that the one thing you wanted more than your own life, if not more than her happiness, belonged to me."

For over forty years Gerolt had thought his friendship with Samson as immovable as the earth upon which he trod, when all this while a poison had been cankering in Samson's breast. Gerolt wrestled to understand, to find some part of him that could forgive the man who had been true to him in so many other instances, but he could only think of Cassandry's hollow eyes. The emptiness in her had never lain in her grief for Antony's loss but in the death of their love—the venomous spike driven into their marriage by Samson's selfish "envy."

"Did you know?" Gerolt said roughly. "Did you even care what your actions would cost Cassandry?"

Gerolt saw more truth than he wanted to in Samson's face.

"If anything, I hoped his jealousy might drive her into my arms."

Gerolt's battle for sympathy vanished. He narrowed his eyes, trying to reconcile the viper before him with the man he had loved. "Antony was not the only one who was 'pathetically insecure.' I am not to blame for the wealth and responsibilities my father left me. You had other choices than to attempt to shame Cassandry. If you wanted something of your own, your father left you lands, however modest, for you to manage and make prosper. You might have married a wife within your means, reared a family that did not require my assistance to sustain. You did not need to ruin Cassandry's life because you were so insecure you felt a petty need to spite me."

Samson flushed. "I made a mistake. I knew it as soon as I read the letter she sent me. I regained my senses in that moment and regretted my rashness. I burned the letter so that you would never know."

"This is not the story you first told me. You slandered her to my face."

"And deserved the blow you struck me for it. I was afraid if I told you the truth, you would turn me out of your house, just as you threatened. If my father's keep felt paltry when I inherited it, it is little more than a hovel now. But, Gerolt"—Samson spread his hands as if in an appeal—"I tried to make amends. Oh, not with Cassandry. Antony would never have let me near her after what I did. But I tried to change, to become the man you just described." His fingers curled back into his palms. "'Tis true, I coveted Herleve d'Aufai's dowry and let you help me obtain it. But I left your shadow after we married. I took her to my father's castle and tried to improve the lands he left me. But after a time I grew bored with Herleve's witless prattle, and then I grew restless. Another kind of independence beckoned me, the glory of battle in the cause of the Holy Cross. There, at last, I thought I could make a name for myself that was all my own. But then came the disaster of Hattin, the shame of defeat, the humiliation of captivity—"

Samson's eyes darkened with some haunted memory, then they flashed with a rage so raw it startled Gerolt back a step.

"—and your abandonment," Samson finished on a snarl.

"Abandonment?"

"Three years, Gerolt." Samson's voice went savage. "Three years you left me in that hell before you bothered to bestir yourself to ransom me. Had it been you, envy or not, I would have flown to your side faster than the wind."

Gerolt had heard this complaint before, always spoken in a dark, jesting tone, never with such naked animus. He answered as he always did. "I came as soon as your messenger reached me."

Scorn twisted Samson's mouth. "Did you? I sent five men to you with my captor's terms. Even he agreed, after the fifth, that I had been forgotten."

Gerolt protested, but Samson shouted over him.

"Do you know how many of our men were cut down at Hattin? Our foot soldiers fell by the thousands, Gerolt. Only a handful of the twelve hundred knights who rode into battle escaped. The rest were taken prisoner. The wealthiest were treated with honor and ransomed. The luckless surviving foot soldiers disappeared into slavery. And the fortuneless knights, like me—we were cast into prison while our captors decided how to deal with us. But not before they demonstrated what fate could befall us anytime they wished to inflict it."

Samson's hands were fully formed fists now, and Gerolt saw how his friend's strong, burly body began to shake.

"After the battle, our Saracen masters executed every knight of the Templar and Hospitaller orders who had fought with us. Two hundred men, Gerolt." Samson's voice sounded strangled. "They cut off their heads and made us all watch as they did it." He dropped suddenly, white faced, onto the bed, as though buckling at the vision. "I used to wake up screaming in the night, dreaming that my head would be next. When you did not come, when my captor eyed me with increasing disdain and impatience—" He shuddered. "Had I had access to a sword, I would have thrust it through my own heart sooner than endure the horror of the Templars and Hospitallers. How I prayed for you to come! And how I hated you when you did not." He dropped his white face into his hands and shuddered again.

Horror ticked up Gerolt's spine as the details of Samson's ordeal at last poured out. "I did not know. Sam, how could I know? None of your messengers reached me except the last. By then you had been over two years a prisoner. You must have told your captors of my wealth, for they demanded a high price for your freedom. It took me time to raise the sum, time to travel so far a distance, time to find your prison, for they had moved you. But I swear, once I learned of your dilemma, I came as swiftly as I could."

Gerolt moved to place a hand on Samson's shoulder, trying to brace him, but Samson struck him away and rose, still trembling, to his feet.

"I have tried to convince myself of that a hundred times," he said. "But things have been strained between us ever since I returned. You cannot deny it."

No, Gerolt could not, but it had not been by his choice. He sensed, however, that Samson would reject any blame. Perhaps his long terror had left him too deeply scarred to do so.

Nevertheless, Gerolt insisted, "I did all I could for you. I cared for your family while you were gone. I ransomed you. I brought you back to Lyonstoke. I have done all in my power to help you since then. I do not know what more I can do."

"You can give me Cassandry's hand."

Gerolt almost gasped. "What?"

"My lands are ruined, but her dower lands are fat. She remains a desirable woman, as you know full well yourself. But you are still too principled to take her dishonorably, and when you wed Marion . . ."

"I am not going to wed Marion. I have asked Cassandry's consent for Rauffe and Egelina to marry now. I trust they will soon give me a grandson. Rauffe seemed much recovered when I left him a few hours ago."

"We have both seen how quickly Rauffe's health can backslide. He may well not last the year. Wed Marion. And let me wed Cassandry. You owe me that much, Gerolt."

Gerolt shook his head. "No, Sam. I am sorry for what you suffered in the East. I would have 'flown to your side like the wind,' had I known. Fate was cruel, but I did all I could for you then and have done all I can for you now. I will not give Cassandry's hand to the man who robbed her eyes of joy."

Samson's gaze narrowed. "I was right. Our friendship died in that Saracen prison."

"Sam."

But Samson strode from the room, shutting the door behind him with a ringing slam.

Chapter 23

Cassandry kissed every token she had retained before setting each one tenderly back into her jewelry box. This morning she would give Gerolt her consent for Egelina to marry Rauffe. Rauffe had been on his feet again, pacing restlessly in his room, when Cassandry had looked in on him before bedtime. He had slept so much from Marion's potions that he was wide awake and abominably bored. Since everyone else had retired, he latched onto Cassandry's company and chattered cheerfully with her until long past midnight, when she at last roused a sleepy page boy and sent him off to find a book for Rauffe to read. Rauffe had protested a bit sulkily that he was not in the mood for a book, but he acquiesced when she gave the page permission to bring up the puppies Venus and Bragge to keep him company.

By tomorrow Cassandry was certain Rauffe would be well enough for a wedding. And then she would reveal to Gerolt her boon and he was honor bound to grant it. At last she would retreat to the convent she had longed for since Antony's death, the one place she had thought she might at last find peace—until Gerolt had kissed her. In that incandescent exchange, the wounded wife, the benumbed mother, the broken woman had all burned away in the brightness of Gerolt's love. For the first time in twenty-three years, Cassandry had felt whole again.

Until reality had crashed back in upon her, fragmenting her soul once more. They could never be together. She wished she could take these small gifts to remember him by, but one did not retire to a convent to cling to the world, even one so precious and fleeting as she had found in Gerolt's arms. She would return the gifts to him after she talked to Egelina. Her daughter had risen early, as she so often did here, and already gone to breakfast when Cassandry awoke. They had not spoken of the marriage yesterday. Though almost certain Egelina would at last profess her willingness for the match, Cassandry had nourished just a faint enough trace of worry that she had not wished to spoil their happy hours spent over yesterday's poetry.

She returned the jewelry box to the closet, then opened the door to seek her daughter.

"Egelina!"

Egelina sat on the floor, slumped so far over that her face was nearly buried in the lap of her gown. Her shoulders shook on a series of broken sobs.

Cassandry dropped to her knees beside her in alarm. "Oh, my love, what has happened?"

Egelina flung her arms around her mother.

"Oh, Gelli! Are you sick? Are you hurt?"

"It is not me; it is Rauffe," Egelina wept.

"What about Rauffe?"

"He is sick again. Oh, Mamma, he is so sick! He tried to tell me not to worry when I went to get this, but—"

Another sob choked off the rest. Cassandry felt the movement of her daughter's arm in unison with the word *this*. She managed at last to nudge Egelina to a sufficient distance to allow her to see the parchment Egelina held.

"A poem?" Cassandry asked. And then she saw, dangling from

between the fingers that clutched the parchment, a fine gold circlet inset with twinkling diamonds and emeralds, such as a lady might use to secure a veil in place over her hair. "What is this, Gelli? Where did you find such a thing?"

She took the circlet from Egelina, and when her daughter did not answer but sat gazing at her mother with wide, watery eyes, Cassandry took the parchment, too. Her breathing froze. The parchment was filled not with Egelina's still tentative letters but with Gerolt's strong, beloved strokes.

Cassandry

Her name was no longer masked in an indistinctive script but stood out boldly in Gerolt's own hand.

You are much mistaken, dear Sparrow, if you think to turn me so easily away from you. You know that your happiness has been the one desire of my life, to see you lit with joy. Our years together were dear to me, as I am convinced they were to you. That is why I cannot believe you would toss away the remnants so utterly from your memory. I will not believe it, Sparrow, until you tell me to my face. Aye, tell me, when next we meet, that no corner of affection remains for me in the chambers of your heart, for you have filled mine to overflowing.

The words abruptly stopped.

Everything inside Cassandry trembled. She did not care how impossible, if Gerolt had stood before her now she would have hurled herself into his arms and wept out her love for him as fervently as Egelina was weeping now. Yet as strongly as his words stirred Cassandry, something about them felt off.

"Gelli"—Cassandry's hand shook along with her voice— "where did you get this? Did you find it here outside the door?"

Egelina started to nod, checked herself, gave a half shake of her head, then burst into tears again.

"Egelina."

Egelina gave another sob before stammering out, "R-Rauffe gave it to me."

"The letter?"

"A-and the circlet. H-he told me yesterday that they were h-hidden beneath his bed, in case he was asleep when I came to fetch them this morning. O-only he was not asleep when I came. He was moaning and feverish and s-said his head hurt like when he ate almonds. But he said I must bring these anyway, b-because you and Lord Gerolt are going to make us m-marry."

Cassandry patted her daughter's hand. "I meant to tell you this morning. You have grown fond of Rauffe, have you not? You will like to be his wife. Whatever Lady Marion has been giving him, I will make her stop and he will be well again in no time." Cassandry prayed it might be so, that there was merely something in Marion's potions that disagreed with Rauffe, as his mother's almonds had. "You are very grown up now, and so is Rauffe. There is no reason to wait another year for a wedding. As soon as he is feeling better, you and he—"

Egelina gasped again, but this time the sound was one of shock. "Oh! I did not think he could be right. Marry Rauffe *now?* No, no, no! I will not marry him now, and I will not marry him ever!"

Her eyes flashed between the tangles of tear-dampened hair that had fallen over her face.

Cassandry stared at her in stunned perplexity. "But you have been spending so much time together with never a quarrel. I thought you had grown fond of one another. And all this weeping—"

"Because I do not wish to marry him does not mean I wish him to die!" Egelina dragged her sleeve across her eyes, which were growing moist again. "Oh, Mamma, I *am* fond of Rauffe. But I do not love him, and he does not love me. But Lord Gerolt loves you."

It took all of Cassandry's willpower not to look at the letter she still clutched in her hand. The answer to its "offness" had slowly begun to unravel itself in her mind. "I take it you have read this?" She gestured at the parchment. "It is not what you think, Gelli. It was written a very long time ago."

In answer, she suspected, to the letter Antony had made her write, frigidly severing Gerolt from her life. She knew why Gerolt had never sent it. They had both been married, and he must have feared he had come too close to crossing the line of loyalty to his wife and her husband. The thought took her breath away again. She did not need to look at the letter to remember his words. *You have filled my heart to overflowing.* Written twenty-two years ago. He had loved her so long without her knowing? He had been her friend, her guardian, her rock—but in all these years, she had never thought of him as a lover, until these last few precious weeks.

I wish I had known. Oh, Gerolt, I wish you had told me! I might never have wed Antony!

But that was foolishness. The signs of Gerolt's affection had always surrounded her. Antony had blinded her from recognizing the depth of its source. Or perhaps it had been her youth. Or maybe her love for Antony had been true. It had felt true and might have remained so had Samson never written those hateful letters.

Egelina drew back her attention with a sniffle and another swipe of her sleeve, this time beneath her nose. Cassandry smoothed the tangled hair from her daughter's eyes.

"You are mistaken, Gelli. This letter does not mean at all what you think."

"It is not the letter," Egelina said. "I could not read all the words of it. I know from the way Lord Gerolt looked at you the very first day we arrived, and how he looked at you when you played chess, and any number of times when we sat at dinner. So I thought if I could make you love him too, then I should not have to marry Rauffe. If you and Lord Gerolt marry, then Rauffe and I will be brother and sister and it would be sin for us to wed."

"Yes, Gelli, I know that, which is why Lord Gerolt and I are *not* going to marry."

"But you love him too, Mamma!"

"Gelli—"

"I did not think it at first," Egelina rushed on, "but I thought you might find his tokens romantic and fall in love with him. And you have! I have seen you smile again, really, truly smile from your heart, and I have even heard you laugh. You are happy again. You admitted to me that you have been happy here."

Cassandry dodged a direct response by addressing a question raised several times now by Egelina's impassioned words. "Gelli, what did you mean when you said Rauffe gave you this letter and this circlet. Where did he get them, and why did he give them to you?"

Egelina drew a rasping breath. "Oh, I will tell you all about it later, but you must come, Mamma, and see him. He is so very sick!"

Cassandry rose as Egelina scrambled to her feet. "Rauffe has been sick many times since we came to Lyonstoke. You have never been so urgent over a headache of his before."

Egelina scrubbed the tears from her cheeks and bounced on her toes impatiently. "It is more than a headache. When I entered his chamber, he was feverish and moaning and his brain was muddled—he did not even know who I was at first. I had to say his name several times. Then he seemed to remember me and tried to sit up, but he clutched his stomach and fell back on the bed. I said I would run for help, but he stopped me. He said I must bring you the letter and token because he would be well again in a trice and then you and Lord Gerolt would make us marry . . . but I do not think he is going to be well, Mamma. His face was so very red and hot, and when I looked back from the doorway, he had curled up, groaning, on the bed."

"Oh!" Cassandry handed the letter and circlet to Egelina. "Go lock these in my jewelry casket for now, then come join me in Rauffe's chamber. I may need you to run errands for me." If Rauffe was as sick as her daughter implied, Cassandry would not like to leave him to go in search of herbs and medicines.

Egelina nodded and rushed through their doorway while Cassandry hurried to Rauffe's chamber.

"Drink it." The woman's voice issuing from beyond Rauffe's open door sounded irritable. "Stop thrashing around and just drink it."

Cassandry quickened her pace and entered the chamber. Marion stood by the bed with a familiar goblet in one hand while her other attempted to lift Rauffe's head, which kept whipping from side to side. Cassandry marched to Marion's side, startling the young woman into dropping Rauffe back onto his pillows.

Cassandry held out her hand. "Give that to me."

Marion's fingers tightened around the goblet's stem. "This is none of your affair, Lady Cassandry. Lord Gerolt gave Rauffe's treatment over to me."

Cassandry dropped her arm, concealing her frustrated fist in her skirts. "What is in it?" She nodded at the goblet.

"Herbs to make him well. Go away. You are not needed here."

Marion reached again for Rauffe's chin, but he rolled his head away. Cassandry caught a glimpse of his eyes before he did so. Glassy. She suspected unseeing. And his hair lay matted against his forehead as though with sweat. Marion managed to scoop up Rauffe's head and swiftly pressed the rim of the goblet to his mouth.

"Stop!" Cassandry said so sharply it made the other woman

jump. "Before you give him one drop, you will name me every herb and spice you have put in that wine."

"I do not answer to you, Lady Cassandry," Marion said coldly. "I will soon be mistress here. Lady Egelina will fall under my care then, and when I say the word, you will be gone."

A new voice spoke from the doorway on a deep, tense rumble. "You are not mistress here yet, Marion. And when Lady Cassandry asks you a question, you will answer."

Marion released Rauffe again to dip a curtsy to Gerolt as he joined them in the room, but she kept her chin at a defiant tilt. "My lord, I have done as your late wife taught me. She said that patience and persistence would make him well. Did not my first potion enable him to return to the training field?"

Gerolt hesitated before giving what looked like a reluctant nod. "But he got dizzy again and could not finish his practice."

Cassandry added, "Nor could he finish climbing the stairs without sitting to catch his breath."

"It takes time for these things to work," Marion said, "which you would know, my lady, if you had the least skill." She turned back to Gerolt. "I came to check on him before dinner yesterday and saw through the doorway that he was sitting bright-eyed on the bed, asking you questions about your days in the East. Was he not feeling much better then?"

"He appeared to be," Gerolt admitted again, "though he still complained of a headache and that his stomach did not feel steady enough to join us at dinner."

"Time," Marion repeated, "and rest. My potions help him sleep, and while he slumbers, the herbs work to restore his humors to balance and thus his health."

Marion could not have given him something to sleep last night, Cassandry thought, or Rauffe would not have kept Cassandry up talking past midnight.

"Did you visit him this morning?" Cassandry asked. "Early? Perhaps near dawn?" Before Egelina had come.

Rauffe moaned, turning Marion and her goblet toward the bed, but Cassandry moved quickly between them. She ignored Marion's cry of indignation and bent to feel Rauffe's cheeks and forehead. He was burning up!

She snapped over her shoulder, "Well, did you?"

"Answer, Marion."

Gerolt's voice sounded tight. Cassandry glanced at him as he came to stand beside her, but his gaze, dark with dread, was fixed on Rauffe's flushed face and staring, glassy eyes.

"Marion!"

Even Cassandry had never heard Gerolt bark like that. It broke the young woman out of her sullen silence.

"Yes, I came to see him. He was dozing with those wretched puppies of his asleep at his feet. They growled at me when I tried to drive them off the bed, which woke Rauffe. He said he would not drink my potion unless I left the dogs where they were. I agreed, so he drank, but as soon as he fell asleep, of course I chased the dogs out. Filthy, wicked beasts. They will never be tame. You should let your hound master drown them."

Gerolt muttered a curse, but whether at Marion or the absent hounds, Cassandry could not tell. He repeated Cassandry's gesture and laid his palm against Rauffe's face. Some flicker of awareness registered in Rauffe's eyes. He rolled onto his side, curling up in a ball, and groaned out, "It burns. It burns."

Cassandry bent over him swiftly. "What does, Rauffe?"

His head stirred when she touched the hot nape of his neck. "Lady Cassandry?"

"Yes, I am here. What burns?"

"My stomach. It is on fire." He gave a muffled, rasping sob and curled in tighter upon himself.

Cassandry swung around on Marion. "Tell me what you put in that drink, and tell me now."

Marion cast an imploring look at Gerolt, but he returned an implacable stare. "Tell her, Marion."

"Nothing to bring this on," Marion said, clearly defensive. "Marjoram, buglass, centaury . . ."

All harmless, Cassandry thought.

". . . lovage, feverfew, rue, and lemon balm . . ."

For headaches.

"And valerian," Cassandry added, remembering the taste that had wrinkled her nose when she had sampled the potion before, "which is why Rauffe called it foul, but coupled with the lemon balm, it would help him sleep."

"I used some camomile, too. And honey, to try to sweeten the mixture."

None of these ingredients would bring on stomach pains or fever. In fact, some of them should do the very opposite.

"What else, Marion?"

"That is all."

Cassandry gazed uncertainly at Rauffe. If 'twas not a reaction to some ingredient in the wine, then he must be ill from some other cause.

"She is lying," Gerolt said.

Marion gasped. "I am not! How dare you—?"

"Fleur said the corner of your mouth always twitched when you told an untruth. I saw it, just now, Marion. What more did you put in the wine?"

Marion looked defiant, but something else gleamed in her eyes as well. Fear. The sight of it jolted a sudden realization in Cassandry.

"You must have given Rauffe some of that drink before Gerolt gave you leave to mix it. How else would Rauffe know to warn me that it tasted foul before I sipped it?"

Gerolt took a step closer to Marion, allowing his height to tower over her. His brows drew together in the most terrible frown Cassandry had ever witnessed upon his face. "What did you give my son, Marion?"

Marion cowered, actually drawing closer to Cassandry as she did.

"Marion." His voice was perfectly even this time. Dangerously even.

"'Twas—'twas something my father gave me."

"Samson?" Gerolt's face paled. "What was it?"

Marion cast a glance at the door as though wondering if she might be able to dash through it.

Gerolt caught her by the shoulders and shook her. "What was it, Marion?"

Alarmed, Cassandry reached out a hand to his arm. "Gerolt—"

But he shook her off in the same motion that shook Marion a second time.

"I do not know what was in it," Marion said on a pant of fear. "It is something he brought back from his journey to the East. He said it would make you marry me."

"Make me marry you? A love potion should go into my wine, not Rauffe's."

"It was not a love potion. I do not know exactly what it was, except that it made Rauffe sick. Only a little sick!" Marion added quickly. "Father said to use it sparingly, to increase it little by little so you would suspect a natural illness as Rauffe grew worse. Father said it would frighten you into thinking that Rauffe might die, and if he died, then you would have to marry me to get another heir."

Marion gasped, then cried out as Gerolt's hands went so rigid on her arms his knuckles turned white.

"Let her go," Cassandry said. "Gerolt, let her go!"

Gerolt did so with a sudden shove that sent Marion flying

across the room. She stumbled against the table near the doorway where the candle burned, jostling both before she regained her balance.

"Rauffe is not 'a little sick' now!" Gerolt shouted. "Where is this poison? Perhaps Cassandry can discern what is in it."

"It's gone," Marion said hoarsely. "I gave him a little, like Father said, but Rauffe kept recovering too quickly. Father told me last night that you had decided to wed Rauffe to Lady Egelina as soon as he was well. He said to pour all of the poison into the next cup of wine. Lady Cassandry was with him half the night, so I came early this morning and gave it to him. I just thought it would make him sicker faster so that he could not marry Lady Egelina. I thought it would make his head hurt, like the almonds did, and make him too dizzy to rise from his bed, just sick enough to frighten you into marrying me quickly. I did not know it would do *that* to him."

Rauffe was whimpering now, still curled tightly into a ball, tears streaming from his clenched eyes. Whether the sweat pouring down his red-mottled face was from pain or fever or both, Cassandry could no longer tell.

"Describe it to us, Marion," she said, trying to keep her voice calm. "Was it a powder? A liquid?"

"A liquid. Clear, like water, without any scent. I threw the container away in the moat so that no one could trace it back to me."

Gerolt groaned as if *he* were the one who had been poisoned. He strode across the room and back, his hands plunging into his hair and twisting there. "What are we to do? Cassandry, what are we to do?"

She stopped him, pulled down his hands, and held them in hers. "The first thing we are *not* going to do is panic." She turned to Marion. "Where is Sir Samson now?" Perhaps he would know what was in the poison.

"I passed him in the hall on my way to bring this to Rauffe." She motioned at the goblet she still held. "Father said he was leaving."

Gerolt pulled his hands away from Cassandry's. "Leaving? Where was he going?"

"He said it was time for him to face the demons of his past and prove he was still a man. He is returning to the East."

Gerolt's face went stark with desperation. "I cannot search all the roads to the coast. We will never find him in time."

Cassandry crossed the room and plucked the goblet away from Marion's grasp. Marion attempted to grab it back, but Cassandry held it out of reach.

"If you poured all the poison into the cup you gave Rauffe at dawn," she said, "then why were you trying to make him drink this?"

"I grew afraid when the first cup made him so ill. I was trying to negate the effects."

"Another lie," Gerolt snapped. "You had better learn to cover your mouth when you speak them."

Marion's fingers flew to her lips, but this time Cassandry had seen the twitch too.

"It does not matter," Cassandry said. "Rauffe did not drink from this cup." She handed the goblet to Gerolt. "Put this somewhere safe. I will check the ingredients later. And I think you should secure Lady Marion someplace where she can neither do more harm nor flee. She looks terrified enough to bolt if we let her."

Gerolt nodded. "I will set guards outside her chamber door." His gaze went once more to his son's tightly coiled body. "What about Rauffe?" Gerolt's voice came raw and hoarse.

"I cannot guess at an antidote if I do not know the poison." Cassandry sent a glance at Marion's frightened face, but Gerolt stood between her and the doorway. "The best I can do is try to purge the poison out. You will have to fetch me some herbs from the kitchen."

"I am not leaving this room while Rauffe lies writhing like that."

Rauffe was not writhing precisely, but he had begun to rock his body a little from side to side, as though the pain had grown too great to lie still.

"Gerolt, I have no one else to send," Cassandry said. "Egelina said she would join me, but something has clearly detained her. You are not suggesting I trust Marion to fetch the herbs, are you?"

He looked at first as though he would argue, then said roughly, "I will call a servant." He pulled open the door.

She supposed it would do him good to vent his anxieties by shouting down the passageway. She let him go and turned back to the bed. "Rauffe," she called softly, "can you hear me?"

She pushed the damp locks from his forehead and continued to speak his name, trying to draw him to some consciousness other than his pain. The fourth time she did so, his eyes scrunched open. She saw first the tears that still swelled there, then the way his lids drew wide. His lips parted and he croaked out a word.

"Marion."

That was when Cassandry saw the shadow.

Chapter 24

Cassandry felt a rush of wind as she whirled about. The dagger's blade plunged down into the pillow so near to Rauffe's face that even in his pain he flinched, then rolled. Cassandry cried out and grabbed for the hilt, but Marion jerked the dagger free and swung it at Cassandry. Cassandry flung an arm up to ward off the blow. The steel bit into her flesh before a voice rang from the doorway.

"What the devil—?"

Gerolt strode back into the room. The shock of the dagger's impact buckled Cassandry's knees and dropped her onto the bed, but she struggled back up with a scream as Marion flew toward Gerolt, Cassandry's blood red on the blade.

Gerolt blocked more nimbly than Cassandry had and tried to catch Marion's wrist, but she wrenched it away. While he was distracted with the dagger, she slapped the goblet of wine out of his hand and sent its contents spewing through the air. Somehow she managed to dart around him. She spun in the doorway and brandished the blade in warning.

"Do not come after me," she panted, then dashed into the dimness of the passageway.

Gerolt took a step to follow, then pivoted and crossed to Cassandry. "Let me see it."

She dazedly held out her arm. Blood seeped through the slash in her sleeve. The cut stung, but she sensed it was no more than a flesh wound, and a shallow one at that. The speed of her deflective movement must have kept the dagger at a glancing angle.

"Where did she get the blade?" Cassandry asked.

"It was Rauffe's. He left it on the table over there."

A groan came from the bed, but fainter than before. Cassandry glanced over her shoulder. Rauffe had curled into a ball again, but his body had grown more slack. If he ceased to fight the pain, if he succumbed to the refuge of full unconsciousness, Cassandry did not know if she would ever be able to rouse him from it.

"There is no time to hunt for bandages," she said as Gerolt moved away, presumably to do just that. "Here, tear a strip from my chemise and bind the cut for now. Then listen very carefully while I tell you what I need from the kitchen. Do not argue with me! We cannot wait on a servant. They may have gone chasing after Marion."

Gerolt cast a tortured look at his son. Something in Cassandry's voice must have convinced him that every moment was critical. She set a hand to his cheek, then stretched up to kiss him.

"Rauffe needs you to be strong for him, as you always were for me."

She had never seen Gerolt so white, so terrified. But he knelt when she held up her skirts, and ripped off a length from her chemise. He wrapped her arm with steady fingers and a gentle touch, then stood back and said with quiet but disciplined urgency, "Tell me what you need."

Cassandry opened the shutters to air out the room after the servants had cleared away the bowls and chamber pots. Others had bathed Rauffe, weak, listless, and ashen from the purging, then dressed him in a fresh linen smock and withdrawn, leaving only Gerolt and Cassandry at his bedside once more.

"Do you think we got all the poison out?" Gerolt asked, a tremor in his voice.

Cassandry wished she knew of a certainty. Rauffe's breathing remained very shallow and a bluish tint stained his closed eyelids.

"We must pray that we did, for I have done all I know how to do for him."

Gerolt's hand hovered near enough her own to clasp. She longed to entangle her fingers with his, to feel his strength quiet her doubts, even as she fought to quiet his, but she did not know if she had earned the right to his touch. If the purging had not been enough, if Samson's poison had been too strong or Rauffe had been too far lost to it . . .

"Sit with him," she said. "Watch him and call me if his breathing does not improve soon. I must go look for Egelina. As distressed as she was over Rauffe, I do not know why she did not join us hours ago."

Cassandry started to turn away, but Gerolt caught her lightly against him and pressed a warm kiss between her brows.

"Thank you," he murmured.

He hid his face against the curve of her throat, and before she could stop herself, she wrapped her arms around his neck. They clung together in simple silence for a long while. They did not need words. Gerolt's love embraced her so completely that every heartache fell away. She was his. A part of her always had been. Now she felt her whole soul pour into his, and his into hers. They stood as much one in this moment of compelling union as any rush of heated passion could ever make them.

But it could not last. She knew it before he kissed her softly and sweetly on the mouth. She allowed herself to reciprocate for a handful of heartbeats before she drew her lips away and felt herself crack apart again.

"Cassandry—"

She stilled his words with her fingers. "Nothing has changed, Gerolt."

He pulled away her hand. "How can you say that? There is no question of my marrying Marion now."

"But you still need a wife who can give you heirs. What if Rauffe had died? What if—?" She broke off, unable to speak what they both must still face. *What if he does not recover?*

Her gaze darted to Rauffe, lying so still on the bed, his chest barely rising and falling. When she looked back at Gerolt, his gaze was fixed on his son.

She slipped from his arms and out of the room.

Mamma, I have gone to see the standing cross. Join me and I will explain.

Egelina had obediently placed the circlet alongside Gerolt's unsent letter inside the jewelry casket before setting the casket on the bed and leaving her note sitting on the lid.

Cassandry remembered the cross, erected before the Conquest, marking for travelers the halfway point between where Gerolt's castle now stood and Woburn Abbey. Gerolt had brought her to see it as a girl, a great stone monolith with a circle enclosing the intersection of the crossbar. The stone had been decorated with elaborate knot-work carvings, ancient Celtic, Gerolt had told her.

The hairs on Cassandry's arms chilled up. Egelina had been

distraught about Rauffe. Why would she go riding off to view the cross without knowing the end of his illness? She would not—unless she had been lured or coerced.

The latter seemed unlikely, Cassandry reassured herself quickly. Someone, a servant, one of Gerolt's knights, at the very least a stable hand, would have seen a tear-stricken girl being forced from the castle and come to report it. Lured, then. How? And by whom?

Cassandry asked in the stables. The groom who had saddled Egelina's mare said she had been accompanied by the squire Garin but was otherwise alone. Cassandry commanded that her own mare be saddled. At Rengrave Castle, she had galloped hard to whip her emotions away in the wind. She urged her mare into the same pounding pace, but now she was keenly aware of everything around her—the thudding of the horse's hooves against the wooden drawbridge, the lapping sound of water from the moat, the fresh, sparkling scent of spring air, the snap of her mantle. Gerolt's fields blurred where his villeins plowed their spring crops. She rode past the village with its mix of neat and dilapidated cottages, between the smear of greenery soaring skyward on either side of the forest road.

Cassandry strained her eyes for sight of the great stone cross, knowing it stood around the next bend in the road.

Her vision was hazy with wind-blown tears when she saw the rider waiting beside the cross. She slowed her mare and tossed her head to clear her gaze. Her back went stiff. She shot a look past the horseman, searching behind him, then to the other side of the cross, but saw only empty road. She threw her gaze wildly into the trees that spanned to the left and the right, but no bright, golden face stared out at her. Where was Egelina?

She rode up to Samson. "What have you done with my daughter?"

"She is perfectly safe, I assure you," he replied. "She is exactly where she always said she wished to be."

Cassandry's nervous fingers caused her reins to flick a little, making her mare prance in reaction. She leaned forward to calm the horse with some soothing strokes to its neck, her mantle falling over her arm. She must not let Samson see her alarm, but her heart pounded nearly as hard as her mount's racing hooves had done. A few hours ago, she would have suspected mischief from this wretched knight, but no evil. That was before he had poisoned Rauffe.

"I am in no mood for your games, sir." Fear for Egelina made Cassandry snappish. "Answer me straightly for once."

Samson nudged his mount alongside hers so that he could hold her gaze. "She is at Woburn Abbey, up the road. The monks will escort her to Elstow Abbey in the morning, where she will profess her desire to become a nun."

Cassandry weighed the odds as she looked down the road past the cross. Could her mare outrace the larger mount he sat astride?

"Go ahead," Samson said. "I will be happy to accompany you. In fact, I intend to do just that. Only I would remind you that the Lady Egelina is of age to make her own choice. The monks have no obligation to return her to you against her will."

"I am her mother. Of course she will come with me." But Cassandry knew a qualm of doubt. Even through her tears for Rauffe, Egelina had repeated her refusal to marry him. Did she still think a nunnery was her only escape?

Samson quieted his horse as it sidled a little. "I think you will find her mind quite made up to the contrary," he said. "As I trust yours will be when we stand before the abbot to exchange our vows of marriage."

"Is that what this is about? You kidnapped my daughter and hold her hostage to force me to marry you?" But why should

Cassandry be surprised at so low a stratagem? A man who attempted to poison an innocent boy would not balk at abducting an equally innocent young girl to blackmail her mother. "You are detestable!" She spat the word at Samson. "I knew you base twenty-three years ago when you destroyed my marriage for a selfish whim. But this, Sir Samson! Your crimes this day against a man you called your friend, and now this!" She could not finish he so disgusted her.

"My friendship with Gerolt has been dead for fourteen years. We were neither of us honest enough to admit it until yesterday. I asked him then for your hand. He denied me. Well, guardian or no, we will see what power he has to deny a holy sacrament of the Church once you are my wife and our union consummated."

Samson reached out a gloved hand and, before she anticipated his intent, slid the reins from her grasp. He clicked his tongue, and his horse fell into a walk, drawing her own along with it.

"The abbot is expecting us, and then we must be off to my shambles of a keep. I regret subjecting you to such inhospitable surroundings for a wedding night, but I suspect wherever Gerolt chooses to look for you, it will not be there. Even if he guesses you are with me, I trust that Marion has convinced him to look in another direction."

To the coast, on his way to return to the East. How deeply in league with one another had they been? Had Marion known Samson's intent to abduct Cassandry when she had poured Samson's poison into Rauffe's wine?

"I suppose I should not be surprised that you raised such a sly, scheming daughter."

Samson grimaced. "I did not raise her at all." Their mounts' hooves clopped hollowly against the road. "I abandoned her to seek adventure. I thought parenthood an empty, restrictive burden until I returned from the East and saw how Rauffe dogged his father's heels when he was well, his eyes alight with an admiration bordering almost on idolatry, while Fleur laughed with Gerolt, and teased him, and so clearly adored him. My children welcomed me home as a stranger."

Cassandry tightened her hands on her pommel and tried to remain disdainful of Samson's prattle, but something in his dark, somber voice impelled her to listen.

"My sons are polite and dutiful, but it is Gerolt they respect and honor for providing them with futures when my wife squandered their inheritance, then died. He provided for Marion as well, wedding her to a knight who claimed he loved her. But what does love serve when the husband dies and his dowager mother takes the rearing of her children from her, saying she is too young to know how best to raise her late husband's heirs?" The murky cloud over Samson's face grew darker. "Marion blamed me. I was her father yet had no power or wealth to fight for her rights. Gerolt advised her to be patient, to prove to her mother-in-law that she could be a kind and capable mother. But she did not wish to be a patient mother and widow. She wanted to remarry, and as soon as Aveline died, I knew whom she wished to wed."

"Gerolt." Of course. Why not? Samson was Gerolt's closest and most trusted friend. That, coupled with her upbringing in Gerolt's house, must have made the pathway to becoming Gerolt's new wife appear as smooth as glass.

"It should have been easy enough to maneuver," Samson said, "except that Antony died and Gerolt set his eyes anew on you."

"Our children are bound. Gerolt and I could never marry."

"I know that. Gerolt knew that. But still, he could not bring himself to think of any woman but you. Whether you willed it or not, you held him blind to Marion. He convinced himself that Rauffe would live to marry and sire children, relieving him of the responsibility of siring any more of his own. Thus he could subdue his conscience while continuing to weave his dreams around you. But if you marry again"—Samson slid a meaningful glance at Cassandry—"he will be forced to admit that you are truly beyond the reach even of those dreams. The same honor that withheld him from you when you married Antony and turned him to marry Aveline, will at last open his mind, if not his heart, to Marion."

Cassandry gave a soft, scoffing snort before she remembered that Samson did not know how Marion had exposed a part of their plan.

"So it was all a lie at the stables," she said. "All the hot things you said to me, your kisses—it was only a scheme to part me and Gerolt."

Samson drew their mounts to a standstill and shifted toward her in the saddle. The simmering gaze he ran over her belied her accusation. "Nay, everything I said to you was true. You are still a desirable woman, Cassandry. Give me time, and I will bring fire to those condemning eyes of yours. The fire of passion, not anger."

"And what makes you think I will give my consent to marry you when we stand before the abbot?"

"The same thing that brought your daughter out to meet me." He reached into a pouch at his belt and drew out a vial of ruby liquid. "The antidote to make Rauffe well. Or at least restore him to the dubious state of health he possessed before I gave Marion the Bane of Fire." He shrugged when Cassandry cocked her head, puzzled. "'Tis what my Eastern captors called the contents of the other vial, the clear one, that kindles a blaze in the belly."

Cassandry recoiled, remembering Rauffe's anguished groans. Samson did not seem to see it. His gaze shifted over her shoulder, hazing briefly, before he returned his attention to her.

"I told Garin to deliver my message to you and the Lady Egelina as soon as he found you alone, to meet me at the standing cross, but he said she would not wait for you and left you a note to follow. I sent him ahead to escort her to the abbey. Once I explained to her how Rauffe's recovery depended on her answer, she went willingly with him and agreed to make her request to the abbot to join a nunnery. I heard her tell Rauffe it was her desire that day I came upon them in the garden, when he laughed at her poetry. So I am actually doing her a service, you see."

Samson's utter indifference to his own depravity nauseated Cassandry. "You bribed her with Rauffe's life, and now seek to do the same with me. You are contemptible, Sir Samson."

He looked unmoved by her scorn. "I thought it best to remove temptation lest Rauffe's recovery nourish false hopes in Gerolt of a grandson again."

Cassandry gazed at the vial, wondering if there were some way she could draw it close enough to seize it. If she offered Samson a kiss . . .

She shrank at the thought, remembering his hot, unpleasant assault at the stables. Besides, what would she do if she snagged it? He still held the reins of her mare, and Egelina was still at the abbey about to commit herself to a life she was drastically unsuited for unless Cassandry could stop her.

"How do I know that is not merely wine in that vial," she asked, "or water dyed red?"

Samson held it up to the sun as if studying its ruby contents. "I cannot say, of a truth, what is in it, anymore than I know what was in the bane I gave Marion. But I saw them both used in my prison in the East. One day my captors cast into my cell a slave who apparently refused to tell them something they wished to know. I watched while they forced the bane down his throat. It cast him into such paroxysms of agony that he begged them for death. When they dangled the antidote before him, he told them what they wanted to know. Then they gave him this" —Samson swung the vial gently back and forth between his thumb and forefinger— "because they said he might prove a useful spy. And he lived."

Samson slid the vial back into his pouch. "My captors thought it amusing when I begged them for a vial of the bane. They mocked me as a coward, for I confessed I would sooner poison myself than lose my head to one of their swords, as they took delight in threatening."

Samson looked away, but not before Cassandry saw him quiver as if a remembered nightmare passed over his features.

"They said I would not have the courage to do it. They gave me the antidote, too, convinced I would prove myself too weak to submit to the agony of the poison. They were right. However they taunted me with their swords, I could not bring myself to drink the bane, even after I had despaired of Gerolt ever coming to deliver me from that hell." Samson's shoulders shuddered a little. "By the time Gerolt finally came, my captors had forgotten I still had the vials. I do not know why I did not pour them out on the ground before I left, but I did not. I brought both back with me."

Cassandry saw the remnants of a tortured past in his eyes when he looked back at her, but she had only to think of the suffering of the innocent young boy at Lyonstoke for her heart to harden again.

"And now you have used your 'bane' most vilely," she said. "I am sorry for what you suffered in your prison, but that cannot excuse what you have done to Rauffe."

"Rauffe has always been sickly. He will not live to see his twentieth year. Aveline repeatedly said so to me, though she dared not say it to Gerolt, for Gerolt loved his children beyond what Aveline thought was seemly. Ironic, is it not? I envied Gerolt his clothes and his jewels and his privilege—but when I came home from the East, I found it was the love of his children that I envied of him the most." Samson's mouth gave a sardonic twist before settling into a grim line of bitterness. "My sons have simply forgotten me as they advance along the paths Gerolt has set them on, but Marion—I do not understand why my leaving should have wounded her so, yet she remains cold as ice to me. And I find it haunts me, Cassandry, nearly as much as my dreams from the East. I *will* make things right with her before I die. She will warm to me, she will even forgive me, when Gerolt learns to love her and honors her as the mother of his heir."

"And to accomplish that, you had to remove the heir he has now."

"Sicken him was all. Time and Rauffe's own naturally paltry health will do the rest. Gerolt only needed to be jolted into accepting the inevitable. With you gone and a fresh reminder of how fragile his current 'heir' is, he will do the responsible thing for his title. He will wed Marion."

"I do not think so, Sir Samson." An insect buzzed past Cassandry's face. She raised her hand to swat it away.

"What happened to your arm?"

Her motion had caused her mantle to fall away from her sleeve, exposing her makeshift bandage. Cassandry saw a dark stain beneath the winding cloth. Even shallow wounds could bleed copiously, and her vigorous ride to the standing cross had evidently caused hers to do so. She extended her arm toward Samson.

"Your precious Marion panicked and came flying at me with a dagger after Gerolt and I exposed your scheme to murder Rauffe."

"Murder?"

"You wish me to use a softer term? 'Sicken,' as you said? When a boy lies unnaturally at the point of death, placed there by the deliberate application of your 'bane,' I can find no kinder word for it than murder!"

Samson abruptly grasped her upper arm, dragging her upward from her saddle. "What do you mean? I did no such thing."

She pried at his fingers. "But Marion did at your orders. I have thought you a knave, Sir Samson, but never such a coward that you would hide your crimes behind your daughter."

He dropped her back into her saddle. His cheeks blanched. "I told her to increase the dose, aye, but I warned her to be careful. Killing was never the object."

Cassandry rubbed her arm where his fingers had grasped her so fiercely. "You expect me to believe that after you have confessed so much? Abducting my daughter, abducting me, speaking complacently of an early death for Rauffe, giving your poison to Marion, all to salve your conscience as a failed parent by tricking Gerolt into marrying her?"

"I would not kill his son."

She gave a brittle laugh at his pathetic denial. "You said your friendship with him was dead."

"I would not kill Gerolt's son!"

Samson shouted it now with such a wild look in his eyes that she almost believed him.

"What has Marion done?" he demanded.

Cassandry stared at him, trying to discern if the throb of horror in his voice was real.

"*What has she done?* Cassandry!"

"She emptied the entire contents of the vial you gave her into Rauffe's wine. She said you told her to."

Samson dropped the reins of Cassandry's mare as he swayed a little in his saddle. His pallor turned almost gray. "Then Rauffe is dead?"

For the first time, uncertainty began to grow within her. "No. I tried to purge the poison out of him, but—but I do not know if it was enough."

Samson's hands gave a jerk, making his mount retreat a few steps. Then Cassandry glimpsed a swift hardening of his mouth before he whirled the horse so abruptly in the road that it shrilled a harsh neigh. A crack of his reins, and a cloud flew up from the flying hooves that carried him down the road toward Lyonstoke Castle.

Cassandry wavered in indecision. Should she follow Samson

or go after Egelina? Her daughter was safe enough in the abbey for now. Samson had said the monks would not escort her to a convent until morning. What did Samson intend to do? Was that truly an antidote, or would it negate the effects of her purging and push Rauffe over the threshold of death? She flicked her reins and drove her heels into her mare's flanks to send it flying in Samson's wake.

Chapter 25

What was taking her so long to return? Twice Gerolt had sent a page to find Cassandry. First when Rauffe's shallow breaths had not improved after half an hour. Again a few minutes ago when the light from the window revealed that the blue tinge of Rauffe's eyelids had spread to his cheeks. Though his lips remained palely pink, Gerolt had a plummeting sensation that the color was slowly draining from them, too. Both times the page had returned without Cassandry or any knowledge of where she might have gone.

What could she be doing? How could she desert him at a time like this?

"Rauffe." Gerolt bent to touch his son's hand, hoping to stir him into consciousness. The fingers twitched and grasped Gerolt's briefly, then fell still again. So cold. "Cassandry, where are you? *Where are you?*"

The door banged against the wall, sending a reverberating shudder through the silent chamber. Gerolt spun, a shout of relief on his lips that died when he gazed into the eyes of his son's murderer.

"How could you think I would do this?" Samson said on a

snarl. "After all these years, after all we have shared, how could you think—"

Gerolt lunged across the room and clamped his hands around Samson's throat. They staggered together, Samson clawing at Gerolt's tightening fingers, but Gerolt's superior height gave him leverage to ram Samson against the wall and press until Samson's eyes began to bulge.

Cassandry appeared beside them. "Stop! Gerolt, stop! He says he has a cure!"

Gerolt felt her dragging at his arm, trying to free his stranglehold. Her words made him hesitate through his rage. He eased his grasp just enough to allow Samson to speak, but his hands remained encircled about Samson's neck, ready to crush his former "friend" to his knees if this were some sort of trick.

"It was a mistake," Samson croaked. "Marion must have misunderstood me. Gerolt, I would not do this. Let me help him."

Gerolt sought Cassandry's gaze, desperate for wisdom greater than his own. "If he lies—"

Cassandry cast a glance at Rauffe. Gerolt saw the alarm that flared in her eyes before she lifted her hands, then dropped them in a helpless gesture. "I do not know that we have a choice."

Gerolt reached for Samson's dagger and pulled the blade free before he let Samson go. "You said our friendship died in a Saracen prison," Gerolt said, "but *you* will die here if this 'cure' of yours fails to revive my son."

Samson rubbed his bruised throat before he moved to Rauffe's bedside and pulled a vial from the pouch at his belt. Gerolt watched, hand clenched on the dagger's hilt, as Samson opened the vial, lifted Rauffe's head, and touched the small container to the paling lips. Samson stood for a moment, unmoving. Gerolt knew from the vial's angle that no liquid had yet poured into Rauffe's mouth.

"Where is Marion?" Samson asked.

"She seized Rauffe's dagger, attacked Cassandry, and fled," Gerolt answered coldly. "We have yet to find her."

"But she is still in the castle?"

"My knights are searching for her, and the stables have been warned to watch for her. Aye, she must still be somewhere in the keep."

Samson turned his head to meet Gerolt's gaze. "What will you do to her when you find her?"

"She poisoned my son. What do you expect me to do with her?"

Samson set Rauffe's head back down and turned, the vial still full of its blood-red liquid. "It was a mistake," he repeated. "I was not clear in my instructions to her. I only wanted to make Rauffe sick, not kill him. Marion must have misunderstood when I told her to be sparing with the dosage."

Gerolt shook his head. "Cassandry and I caught her with a fresh cup at Rauffe's lips *after* she had administered your poison."

"We do not know what was in it," Cassandry said. "It may have been harmless, Gerolt."

"Then why did she slap it out of my hand before we could test it? And why did the maid who cleaned it up after you left say she had seen Marion in the kitchen grinding up some monk's-hood root?"

Cassandry gasped. "Monk's-hood? Where would she get so dangerous a plant as monk's-hood?"

"Aveline kept some in the infirmary garden. She used it to make an oil to rub into Rauffe's joints when he was a boy and complained that they ached when he suffered from his fevers."

"If she put monk's-hood in Rauffe's wine—" Cassandry's eyes shone with shock and horror. "Oh, but Gerolt, we cannot be sure now."

"The maid was frightened enough to wrap a cloth around a cut on her finger before she wiped up the spilt wine. She said she saw Marion grinding up the roots and asked her about it. Marion told her she was making an ointment, as Aveline used to do, but the maid said when Marion left the kitchen she carried only a goblet of wine and all traces of the monk's-head root were gone." Gerolt turned a grim glare on Samson. "What do you think, Sam? She confessed that she had been using the poison you gave her for days. Perhaps there was not enough left in the final dose to kill Rauffe as quickly as she wished. Monk's-hood would have finished him off within hours. She is your daughter. If anyone would know her mind, it would be you."

"No, Gerolt," Samson said, an edge to his voice. "I have never known her. But you are right about one thing. She is my daughter. I abandoned her as a child. I failed her as a young widowed mother. But I can save her from this." He gestured at Rauffe.

"Then do it," Gerolt ground between his teeth.

A footstep sounded in the doorway. "My lord, we have found her."

"Marion?" Samson said sharply before Gerolt could respond to Sir Ingram.

Sir Ingram glanced at Samson before turning back to Gerolt. "Aye, sir. She was hiding in the armory tower where the empty storage barrels and tents and such are stored. We tried to corner her, but the barrels are so erratically arranged it is like a maze in there. She escaped and ran up the stairs into the open air of the allure."

"And so?" Gerolt snapped. "Why have you not taken her?"

"She has a dagger."

"And you all have swords. If my men cannot disarm a woman with a dagger, then I have surrounded myself with incompetent bumblers rather than the expert knights I thought you."

Sir Ingram looked hurt by the insult. Gerolt never berated his men so. He tried to rein in his temper but had not time to stand here counting before he spoke. Rauffe's life hung by a thread, and

Samson's stiff posture suggested he meant to do nothing about it until he learned the fate of his daughter.

"You do not understand, sir," Sir Ingram said. "She is not threatening us with the blade, she is threatening herself."

Samson took a step toward him. "What do you mean?"

"She is threatening to kill herself if we come near her. What shall we do, my lord?"

Samson started for the door, but Gerolt caught his arm. "Where do you think you are going?"

"To get Marion."

"Not before you save Rauffe, you won't." Gerolt shoved him back into the room.

"What do you intend to do with her?" Samson demanded again.

"Do not worry," Gerolt replied. "I am not an executioner. She will stand trial before the royal courts for her deeds. Sir Ingram, return to the tower and see that she does not harm herself."

"Gerolt, give her to me," Samson pled as Sir Ingram left the room. "I will take her away from here. You will never see either of us again."

"She is a murderess, Sam, or as good as one. I cannot simply set her free to wreak more havoc wherever she will."

"She is my daughter!"

"And Rauffe is my son! Now either pour that 'cure' of yours down his throat, or give it to me so I can do so." Gerolt leveled Samson's dagger at his old friend's breast.

Samson stood as hostile as a bristling wolf. "Swear Marion's safety to me first. Let me take her away unharmed. Swear it, Gerolt."

"You forget which one of us holds a blade."

"Swear it!" Samson shouted, raising the fist that closed around the vial. "Or I will smash this against the floor. If Marion stands trial, you know she will die. And if she dies, then so does Rauffe."

Cassandry had moved to the bedside, but she turned at this, her face flushed with indignation. "Rauffe is innocent!"

"And so might Marion have remained," Samson said, "if I had not abandoned her and her mother. Choose, Gerolt."

Gerolt knew he could not reach Samson before he followed through with his threat. He stared at this man he had once counted as a brother and wondered if his own enraged face looked as vicious and foreign to Samson as Samson's did to him. But what choice did he have? Neither vengeance nor justice would bring Rauffe back from the dead.

He lowered the dagger. "Go. Give me the vial and go."

Samson remained in his wary, wolfish pose. Even the teeth he bared looked savage. "You must swear in the presence of your men lest they try to stop me."

Leave this room before Gerolt knew whether the contents of that vial worked or not? What if it contained more poison? What if it contained a cure, but the cure was too late?

"No, Sam. I cannot swear before I know what that vial does."

They stood at stalemate until Cassandry appeared so suddenly between them that Gerolt wondered if she had conjured herself from one spot to another.

"Gerolt," she said softly, "give me the dagger." He did not obey so much as he allowed her to pull it from his hand. "Sir Samson, give me the vial, then go to the tower with Gerolt. Hold Marion there. If your antidote works, I will come and tell you both. Gerolt *then* will swear before his men to let you and Marion go. If your antidote does not work . . ."

She trailed off, but Samson finished for her. "Then I will confess my crime to the royal courts." He slapped the vial into Cassandry's hand.

Gerolt saw in Samson's haunted eyes the lie he would tell if Rauffe died. He would take as much of the blame as he could from his guilty daughter. In that moment, Gerolt knew that Samson's hands remained unstained of the crime he would confess to. Then the remedy would work. He knew that, too.

If it were not too late.

"Do not come any nearer! Step back! *Step back,* or I swear I will do this!"

The shrill warning greeted Gerolt as he emerged onto the allure of the armory tower behind Samson. Three knights, Fithian, Ingram, and Owen, had formed a loose half circle around the wild-eyed woman cowering against the crenellated tower wall. All three men had their swords drawn, but Gerolt could not see Marion clearly until he reached Sir Fithian's side. Her hair fell tangled over a white face streaked with tears. She had the point of Rauffe's dagger poised only inches from her stomach.

"Marion!" Samson said. "What are you doing? Put that blade down."

Her head jerked at her father's voice, then her gaze caught Gerolt's.

"No," she whimpered. "No, no, no."

She dropped to her knees and with shaking hands nudged the blade's tip until it touched the fabric of her gown. Gerolt watched with horror the struggle on her face for resolve to complete the deed she threatened. What had she seen in his eyes? The same violence he had felt pounding through him when he and Samson had confronted one another in Rauffe's chamber?

"He is dead," she moaned. "Rauffe is dead." She began rocking back and forth so hard Gerolt feared she might pierce herself in her throes of despair. "I should have waited. I should have waited for the poison he gave me to work." She cast a glance of hatred toward Samson before a sob rose as her gaze returned to Gerolt, "Then you would never have known what I did."

Gerolt motioned his knights to move back toward the tower door. Samson tried to draw closer, but she shook her head in so brusque a warning that he stopped. He crouched down so that his eyes were level with his daughter's.

"Marion, Rauffe is not dead. Put the blade down."

Doubt flickered in her eyes. "But I emptied the vial you gave me into his wine. I thought it would act quickly, but instead it threw him into so much pain, and he lingered and lingered—I could not bear to see him like that. I did not know he would suffer so."

"I warned you to be careful, to increase the drops by only a few."

"But Rauffe kept getting well. He would have married the Lady Egelina, and they would have had children, and *he* would have had no need of me."

Gerolt knew Marion spoke of him, though she appeared too ashamed to meet his eyes. He dared make no reply. He knew it would have been cold and harsh, for nothing but blazing anger pulsed inside him.

"I told you to be patient," Samson said. "Rauffe's health was fragile all his life. You knew that; you saw it for yourself as a girl. Even Lady Aveline did not believe he would live to marry and sire children. You only had to be patient."

"I could not. *She* changed everything. Lady Cassandry. She made his headaches stop. She made him thrive. And she was suspicious of my potions. She might have found a way to counteract them or simply make me stop, then Rauffe would be well all over again, and what would happen to me?" She sent another reviling look toward Samson. "*You* put the idea into my head. When Lady Joan humiliated me by taking my sons away, when you caught me alone and weeping. You said Lord Gerolt would marry me and I would never be at another woman's mercy again. As Lord Gerolt's wife I could command Lady Joan to give me back my sons. I could humiliate *her*. All of his vassals would bow down to me—to *me*, the daughter of a graceless pauper knight."

Samson colored at her dig but repeated, "Patience, Marion—"

"I did not want to be patient!" Marion screamed at Samson. "I *could* not be patient, not after *she* came. He looked at her in ways he never looked at Lady Aveline. Warm and passionate and with so much love I knew it made him ache inside." Marion's eyes flashed suddenly at Gerolt, filled with baffled rage. "How could you want her so? She is old! Her hair is full of gray threads! Her brow is furrowed, and there are cobwebs at the corners of her eyes."

It was a vast exaggeration of Cassandry's features. Gerolt knew only the myopic young with their still callow charms could fail to see the beauty of a silver strand of hair, the wisdom in a creased brow, the compassion in crinkled eyes.

"I do not expect you to understand. Your judgment has been that of a selfish child." Gerolt's voice came out as stark as he'd feared it would. If this had been her behavior as a wife and mother, no wonder Lady Joan had removed Marion's children from her care. "I took you into my own house. I reared you alongside my own children. Fleur and Rauffe both looked on you as a sister, Aveline as a daughter. And this is how you repay us? By murdering Rauffe to marry me?"

"Gerolt," Samson said sharply.

Gerolt belatedly remembered the menace of the dagger she held. To his relief, it tilted at a less-ominous angle as Marion dragged one hand through her tangled hair.

"It was mad of me, I know. *He* jumbled everything in my head." Another caustic glance at Samson. "He told me you were going to hurry Rauffe's marriage to Lady Egelina. I panicked that I would lose you. I was not thinking clearly when I poured all the poison into the wine. But I did not want Rauffe to suffer, not like that! That is why I crushed—"

"Marion, hold your tongue," Samson tried to cut her off, but the rest of the words tumbled out.

"—the monk's-hood root and stirred it into his wine. He was dying. I knew he was dying, but it was so horrible I thought it would be merciful to end it swiftly!" Her eyes widened, dilating with frenzied terror as the weight of her confessions suddenly appeared to crash into her awareness. "Oh, saints, oh, saints!" she gasped and brought the dagger back up. "I cannot bear what they will do to me. They will hang me or strangle me or b-burn me. I would sooner end it now. Quick, quick—"

There was no reason in her eyes, only distraught hysteria. Her hands went still, the skin stretched taut over her cheekbones, bracing for the blow.

"Marion!" Samson screamed on a dragging sob. "Stop! *Stop!* Gerolt, please!"

Fury and the sting of betrayal pummeled against Gerolt's ribs, but through his rage slipped the pinched, white face of the child he had called her and the hoarse, anguished cry of a friend.

"Marion." It took all of Gerolt's self-mastery to speak her name quietly, but with a force he hoped to pierce through the madness of her fear. "Rauffe is not dead. There is no need for this. Put the dagger down."

She knelt immobile as a statue, her face still bleak, the blade still poised. "Did she save him?" Marion asked, her voice almost eerily calm now.

"Your father brought a cure. So you see, there is no need—"

"But I am still guilty." Tears spilled down her cheeks again. "If you give me to the courts, there will be prison, and waiting, and trials, and more waiting, this time for a scaffold. I would rather end it like this. Now." Gerolt saw her mouth the silent word: *Quickly.*

There was no reaching her before she could do the deed. Gerolt searched with a rising desperation for words to deflect the purpose she looked chillingly reconciled to.

A stirring sounded, a rustling behind him, then a hand touched his. He glanced down at Cassandry. Her eyes looked moist, but she smiled.

Gerolt almost swayed with relief. He clamped a hand on Samson's shoulder, sustaining them both with her silent news.

"No trials, Marion," Gerolt said, his voice gruff. "No prison. Your father has bought your life. Put the dagger down and you may walk out of Lyonstoke with him, a free woman."

Her head turned. She searched Gerolt's face as if looking for a trap.

"I have given your father my word, and you know I do not swear falsely."

Her gaze shifted to Samson, as tear-streaked as she, still on his knees, his hand outstretched to her. There was no gratitude in her eyes as she rose slowly to her feet. She crossed with halting steps to him. Samson rubbed a hand over his wet face before he stood. He reached for the dagger she still clutched, but she twitched it away.

"If I did not fear the punishment so, I would thrust this through your heart," she hissed. She flung the dagger with a clatter at Samson's feet. "I hate you. I will always hate you."

Samson's breath shuddered from his chest before he replied, "That may be, my dear. But right now I am the only escape you have."

He started to guide Marion toward the tower door, but Gerolt stopped him.

"A word," he said quietly, then called to his knights, "Escort the Lady Marion to the yard to wait for her father."

When they were gone, Cassandry murmured, "Rauffe is sleeping, Gerolt. Truly sleeping this time." She hesitated, then reached out a hand to Samson. "Thank you."

Samson cast Gerolt a sideways glance before he took her fingers. "I will not ask your forgiveness. What I have done is unpardonable. I deserve to have that dagger thrust through my heart. If it could undo the damage I have done to Marion and to you . . ."

He dropped her hand as though his own had grown weighted with the regret that filled his eyes.

Cassandry's lashes fluttered down so that Gerolt could not read her expression. "I must return to Rauffe," she said and turned back toward the tower door.

Her rebuff seemed to drain Samson of all but a wearied resignation. A too-familiar gloom stole in alongside the dejection.

"You should have left me to rot in the East," he said to Gerolt. "None of this would have happened had I not returned. I would never have known how I ruined Marion's life, would never have become obsessed with healing our breach." He paused, then jerked his shoulders abruptly back, though the effort looked almost to exhaust him. "I swear to you, Gerolt, when I set her on this path, I had no comprehension of the lengths she would go to. Nevertheless, the blame is mine, and I will not shirk it. Thank you for your mercy. As I promised, you will not see either of us again."

Gerolt caught Samson's shoulders and held him. "Do you think that is what I want?"

"I should think you would want me in hell."

Gerolt supposed he should, indeed, recoil from all his friend had done, but the past ran too deep between them—the shared boyhood larks, their youthful striving together to earn their spurs, the man who had always stood at Gerolt's back as loyal and as inseparable as a shadow, and the wrenching pain Gerolt had felt when that shadow had ripped itself away to ride off to the East. Samson had not come back the same man. Even now, with the revelations Samson had finally shared with him, Gerolt knew he could not fully comprehend all that his friend had suffered in that Saracen cell. Samson had said their friendship had died there, but it had not for Gerolt. He felt the bond of it acutely stretched but still unbroken.

"I cannot condemn you for loving your daughter, Sam. Marion made her own choices. The guilt is hers, not yours."

Samson shook his head. "I bequeathed her my deceitful, selfish blood, and then I abandoned her. She had no choice at all, Gerolt."

Gerolt shook him, frustrated, as he had felt for years, at not knowing how to break through Samson's black despondency. "She had a mother, too. A frivolous, impulsive, imprudent mother whose influence she undoubtedly felt more than yours in your absence."

"But it was I who planted the idea of marrying you in her head. It was I who gave her the poison—"

"And it was you who rode hell-bent to save my son when she used it against your counsel. I will not forget that. If you had not sparked her mischief"—Gerolt carefully chose the softer word to spare Samson—"something else would have."

Some sound prompted Gerolt to turn his head as he said it. He saw Cassandry lingering by the door. Their gazes caught. She looked almost surprised, but even as he raised his brow in question, she vanished into the tower stairwell.

"Here." Samson's voice called his attention back. "I must give you this before I go." He pulled something from the pouch at his waist and dropped it into Gerolt's palm.

Gerolt gazed down at the pomander, the gift he had given Aveline on their twentieth year of marriage. He remembered how she had given a rare blush of pleasure and how pretty she had looked and how he had thought, *These have been good years. Perhaps not as full and passionate as I had once dreamed of with another—but, nevertheless, good years.*

"Open it," Samson said.

Gerolt did so. A piece of parchment lay across the crucifix inside. He recognized his own writing instantly. *Dear One, may this keep you close to heaven when I cannot be there to guard you.* The words jarred him as he recalled another crucifix sent with these words, ivory with mother-of-pearl inlays, strung on a red silk ribbon.

His throat abruptly constricted. "Where did you get this?"

"Ask Cassandry when I am gone."

Gerolt looked up, puzzled, then set the question aside as another more imminent one confronted him. He felt Samson waiting, as if reluctant for the parting they stood at. Gerolt felt the pain of it too. It had been one thing to see Sam ride off to the East, not knowing when he would return yet somehow certain to the soles of his feet that he would. This, Gerolt knew, was different.

"Where will you go?" he asked.

"East," Samson replied. "I bade Marion tell you so to cast you off my trail with Cassandry, but I think there was truth in the lie. I have cowered too long from my demons. The only place to slay them is where they first rose up to haunt me."

In a younger, freer day, Gerolt would have insisted on riding at Samson's side to battle those demons with him. Such days as those, alas, were long past them both. He prayed that Sam would find some peace at the end of his lonely road.

"And Marion?" Gerolt said.

"She will come with me, of course. The sharp desert air may clear her head and perhaps humble her heart. I shall take great care of her"—Samson's mouth went slightly grim—"whether she wills it or not."

Gerolt extended his arm. Samson hesitated, then grasped it in a tight, parting gesture. It was not enough. Gerolt pulled him into a rough embrace.

"Come back, Sam," Gerolt growled into his ear. "And when you do, you will find welcome here, as you always have."

Samson said nothing as they broke apart, but Gerolt saw him swallow hard. A moment later he was gone.

Gerolt stood alone on the tower. The sun bathed his face in its warmth. He glanced behind him. His shadow had never looked so empty.

He felt the pull from the chamber below, the promise of her comfort. He fought it. Marion was gone too, but she had left the same impasse in her wake. *Either Rauffe and Egelina must marry, or I must wed a young wife.*

But neither must happen today. He crossed to the tower door, ran down the stairs, and strode with a quickened pace through the galleries and passageways until he opened the door to Rauffe's chamber and fell into Cassandry's arms.

Chapter 26

A half dozen highly charged kisses passed between them before Cassandry came to her senses. One moment she had been sitting beside Rauffe's bed, watching him sleep, the next Gerolt had come charging through the door, his face stricken and hungry all at once. He had dropped to his knees before her, and without even thinking, she had wound her arms around him and met his urgent lips.

"Stop," she murmured against his mouth and tried to push him away. "Gerolt, stop. We cannot do this."

"I know," he said and kissed her again.

It was only a sound from the bed that finally broke them apart. Cassandry continued to stroke the hair at the nape of Gerolt's neck as his head turned, her lips smiling at the knowledge of what he would see.

Samson's antidote had worked surprisingly quickly. Rauffe's breaths had deepened first, then the blue tinge had faded from his cheeks and lids. He remained pale, but a slight blush of pink had risen beneath the pallid skin. Still, it had not been until Cassandry saw his stiffening muscles begin to relax that she had called the page to sit with him while she ran to the tower to tell Gerolt. When she returned, Rauffe had shifted onto his side, one hand drawn up loosely beside his pillow, the soft drone of restful, healing sleep humming from him.

"He will be well now, Gerolt," she said. "It will take time, but I am certain he will be well."

She continued to fondle his hair while he studied Rauffe. She wished to remember the texture—straight and slightly coarse and sprinkled with salt amidst the brown. She knew now that she could never entirely cast aside the sweet, worldly memories of these last few weeks. She would still go to the convent when Egelina married, but it would not be as a nun. She could not in honesty vow away the memory of Gerolt's kisses or how complete and healed she had felt in his arms. But nuns needed lay sisters to attend to daily, menial tasks so that they might be free to study and pray. The work would help keep the sting of Cassandry's loss at bay while allowing her to reminisce as she wished without sinning. She could dream, too, when work was done and she lay in her hard, narrow bed, dream of the gray eyes that were patient and wise, dream of the shape of his nose, the curve of his mouth, the strong jut of his chin, and of all the little moments between them, from girlhood to earlier this day when they had stood clinging to one another, so utterly at one.

She sighed and smoothed down his hair. "What time is it?" she asked.

Gerolt rose and moved to look out the window. "I'd say we are yet a few hours from sunset. Why?"

She stood. "I must fetch Egelina. Sir Samson sent her to the monastery with instructions for the monks to conduct her to the convent of Elstow Abbey in the morning. Something is not right with her. I thought her reconciled to marry Rauffe, even happy to do so, but she told me this morning she is still against it, and I do not know why."

Gerolt looked startled. "You mean she's renewed her request to become a nun?"

"It is absurd, I know. She is ludicrously unsuited for a religious life. Do not worry," she said, anticipating his concern that the marriage to Rauffe might be frustrated. "I will bring her back, and by the time Rauffe is well again, I will have sorted it all out with her. She confesses she is fond of him."

"Hardly fond enough if she fled to a monastery to avoid him. What if she will not come back with you?"

Were her doubts so easy to read? Of course they were, for Gerolt.

"She will have no choice if I send one of my men," he said. "I am her guardian and make generous contributions to the abbey. The monks will not wish to displease me." He called the pageboy who waited outside the door. "Fetch me Sir Owen—" he began.

But Cassandry said, "Send Sir Fithian. Egelina trusts him." And however smitten with her daughter he might be, Cassandry trusted him too.

"Very well," Gerolt said. "Find Sir Fithian and tell him I want a word with him."

The page bowed and left.

Cassandry would go with the knight, of course. She started to say she must change her gown when a voice spoke from the bed.

"Father?"

Gerolt returned at once to the bedside. "Rauffe?"

Rauffe's eyes were barely slitted open. "I thought I heard your voice."

His words slurred, Cassandry hoped from sleepiness and not a return of pain. Already his eyes slid shut again.

Gerolt sank into the chair Cassandry had vacated. "Are you feeling better?"

Cassandry heard the tension beneath the soft question.

Rauffe's head moved in a slight affirmation against the pillow. "I got so cold . . . but it is better now."

"Your stomach?"

A pause. Then, "Aches. But the fire is gone. I thought Marion's potion was foul, but it was nothing to the stuff Lady Cassandry forced down my throat." He gave a faint shudder, then said on a mumble, "It saved my life though, didn't it?" Cassandry and Gerolt exchanged a glance. Rauffe could not have seen it with his eyes still closed, but he continued, "When Bragge got into the hall at Christmas and ate some ivy, I had to make him retch to get the poison out. Did Marion poison me?"

Cassandry touched Gerolt's shoulder. However curious, this was no time for lengthy explanations. Rauffe needed rest.

Gerolt nodded his understanding. "We will tell you everything later. Go back to sleep for now."

Rauffe mumbled, "Fleur always said . . . there was . . . something . . . aslant . . . in her . . ." The last word fell away with his lips still parted, replaced with the droning breath of slumber.

"I must go," Cassandry murmured. Before her hand slid from Gerolt's shoulder to his hair again. Even with the urgency of retrieving Egelina, the temptation to stand here caressing him was nearly overwhelming.

He caught her fingers before she could withdraw them. He kissed them, then frowned. "Have you not attended to your arm?"

He had seen the stain on her bandage. There had been no time to redress it since his original bindings.

"I will do so before I leave." She paused, then added, "I cannot go while you are holding my hand."

His grasp only tightened. They gazed a little too long into each other's eyes. Cassandry saw too much in his. The love he found so hard to speak but so freely showed. His dread of losing her. His resignation that he must.

"One last kiss," he pled.

But she shook her head. "I am afraid I am not strong enough to give you only one."

He released her with obvious reluctance just as a footstep sounded and Sir Fithian appeared in the doorway.

Brother Hildebrand, the monastery guest-master, showed Cassandry and Sir Fithian into a neat, clean little chamber within the guesthouse that held a narrow bed with a blanket neatly folded at the foot, a small hearth with a pile of firewood for brisk spring evenings, and a table where a young girl with golden hair and red, swollen eyes was sniffling between bites of soft cheese and bread.

Egelina dropped the crust she was holding when she saw her mother. "Mamma, what are you doing here?"

"I have come to rescue you, child, what else?"

Egelina rubbed at her ruddy nose but said, "I do not need rescuing. Brother Hildebrand, please stay."

The guest-master paused in his retreat through the doorway.

Cassandry said, "You know I cannot let you do this, Gelli. Besides, there is no need. Sir Samson's antidote has worked, and Rauffe will be well in no time. And Sir Samson has gone far, far away. So you see, there is nothing to keep you here."

"It was not about Sir Samson. Well—" Egelina dragged her sleeve beneath her nose this time "—only inasmuch as he suggested the very thing I desired most in exchange for giving you the antidote. But I do not want to go back to Lyonstoke. And you cannot make me." A familiar flash challenged Cassandry from her watery eyes. "Father Bartholomew has promised an escort for me, to take me to Elstow Abbey tomorrow."

Cassandry studied her daughter. For someone on the verge of obtaining what she "desired most," Egelina looked very close to bursting into tears. Cassandry turned toward Brother Hildebrand, and in the process caught the deep anxiety in Sir Fithian's gaze. His affection for Egelina could not have been more obvious if he had blurted it aloud. Cassandry smothered a sigh. As fond as she was of Sir Fithian, if he could not conceal his emotions better than this, he could not stay at Lyonstoke once Egelina and Rauffe were wed.

"Sir Fithian," she said. "I believe you carry a message to the abbot from Lord Gerolt? Brother Hildebrand, will you please show him the way?"

She held up a silencing finger to Egelina, cutting off her protest. Brother Hildebrand bowed his obedience. Sir Fithian sent a guilty glance at Cassandry and left the chamber with a blush on his cheeks.

When they were gone, Cassandry sat in the empty chair across the table from her daughter. "Now tell me what this is about, Gelli."

"I have, a thousand times. I wish to be a nun." Egelina dabbed at her eyes with her sleeve, broke off a piece of cheese, and popped it in her mouth.

Cassandry had had nothing to eat all day and gave in to the temptation to nibble on a little of the bread. She waited until she had swallowed before saying, "If this is about your poetry, you may write it to your heart's content. They won't let you do it in the convent, you know. Or, at least, you may only write about sacred subjects. No more swans that turn into silver princes or odes to Jenny Wren."

The corners of Egelina's lips drooped. "I know. I will be very good and only write about the Saints and the Holy Spirit and—and pious subjects like that."

Cassandry had thought all this nonsense at an end when she'd capitulated on the poetry and the pen. Something was seriously amiss if she could not lure Egelina back with her first love. Cassandry took another bite of bread while she tried to read her daughter's face.

"I am glad Rauffe is better," Egelina said while her mother ate.

"Sir Samson promised his antidote would make Rauffe well. It scared me ever so much when he said it, for I had not even thought the word *poison* until then. How did it happen, Mamma?"

"Sir Samson's daughter poured a dangerous draught into some of Rauffe's wine."

"Lady Marion?" Egelina looked shocked. "Why would she do such a wicked thing?"

"So that Rauffe would die before he could marry you. Lady Marion thought Lord Gerolt would marry *her* if he did."

"Wed Lady Marion? But he is ever so much in love with you!"

"I do not know what makes you think that," Cassandry said, trying to still the way her stomach fluttered at her daughter's declaration. "Lord Gerolt and I are good friends, that is all." Then she remembered. "You are thinking of that letter he wrote to me? That was years ago, Gelli. It meant nothing. He was my guardian once, and, of course, affection grew between us, but it was never romantic." *Not then. Not for me. Because I was too blind to see.* She pushed the bread away and said as gently as she could, "He is your guardian now, too, and he wants your return to Lyonstoke."

Egelina's lower lip quivered. "To marry Rauffe?"

Cassandry reached across the table to take her daughter's hands. "The two of you are better matched than you know."

Egelina pressed Cassandry's fingers. "Please, Mamma. I like Rauffe very much, but I do not want to marry him."

"You must marry someone. Yes, my dear, you must," Cassandry said when Egelina shook her head. "You are heiress to four castles. That is not a responsibility you can run away from, even to a nunnery."

Egelina pulled her hands away and sat back in her chair, her posture stiff with resistance.

Cassandry hated to ask the question. She did not know what she would do if Egelina answered as she feared. "Is this about Sir Fithian?"

Egelina blinked. "Sir Fithian?"

"He has been very kind to you. It was wrong of him to teach you to write behind my back, but he . . ."

"He what, Mamma?" Egelina said when Cassandry trailed off. Then her body stiffened indignantly. "You are not going to accuse him of seducing me again?"

"No, child, I am not," Cassandry said quickly. "But if you . . . if he . . . It will not do, Gelli. Even if Lord Gerolt did not wish you to marry Rauffe, I do not think he would—"

"Oh!" Egelina's cry cut her off. "*Oh!* Sir Fithian and me?" She sprang up from her chair, her face aflame. "No, Mamma! I do not wish to marry Sir Fithian. I do not wish to marry *anyone*." Her fingers twisted together in distress. "I am sorry about the castles, but cannot Lord Gerolt just take them for himself? If I enter a nunnery?"

Cassandry rose. "He might, if this were truly a matter of conscience on your part. But I do not believe that. Look me in the eye and tell me I am wrong."

Egelina's gaze shifted everywhere but to her mother's. Cassandry caught her by the chin, but Egelina's lashes fluttered to hide her eyes.

"Please, Mamma," she whispered. "Please do not take me back to Lyonstoke. Please do not let Lord Gerolt force me to marry."

"Rauffe?"

"Anyone!"

This time Cassandry asked simply, "Why?"

Egelina's lips trembled for what felt like an eternity to Cassandry before she answered.

"Because he will change—or I will change—or maybe we both will change. And then it will be like you and Papa. He will be angry and then be too proud to apologize, or maybe that will be me. You know how hasty my temper can be. Oh, please, I do not want to change, and I do not want to hurt someone, and I do not want to be hurt, and I do not want my poetry to die!"

Cassandry flinched. She had let her wounds from her marriage and her fears for Egelina destroy her daughter's confidence in men and Egelina's faith in her own nature. *I only wanted to keep you safe, child. I never imagined you would jump to such conclusions!*

"Gelli, Gelli." Cassandry used both hands to wipe away the tears now flowing freely down Egelina's cheeks. How to heal this damage she had unwittingly caused? *With the truth, Cassandry. Speak the most essential one first.* "You are not like your father, child. Yes, you are impulsive because you are young. But you are also compassionate and kind. Think how clever you were to recognize how Rauffe could not see colors the way we do, and how you did not laugh at him or mock him for it but helped him instead."

Egelina sniffled. "It would have been cruel to mock him for something he could not help." Her mouth wobbled again and more tears flowed. "I am sorry, Mamma. So sorry that Papa was cruel to—"

"That is in the past," Cassandry interrupted firmly. "You must not doubt your own goodness. And you must forgive me for the times I was cross, for I am proud of you, Gelli." She drew her daughter into a fervent hug.

Egelina returned the embrace, but still wept into her mother's shoulder. "I was cross too, and I too am sorry, for I love you so much, Mamma! I wish—I wish—"

"What do you wish, child?"

Egelina gave a sob but only answered with a shrug.

"You do not really wish to be a nun, do you?" Cassandry said softly. Egelina shook her head. "You would like some silver prince to sweep you off your feet someday."

"No," Egelina answered in a muffled voice, "that is not real. I—I want someone to . . . love me . . . someday. But how could I trust him? You said that men change after marriage. What if he—?"

Cassandry quieted the rest with her fingers to Egelina's lips, then led her back to the table. She put the chairs together so that they could sit face-to-face, with Egelina's hands in Cassandry's.

"I was wrong to tell you that, Gelli. All men do not change."

"You said Papa did."

Gerolt's words to Samson came flying back to Cassandry. She saw now what she could not during the pain of her marriage. The seeds of Antony's jealousy had always been there, waiting for an excuse to spring forth. If Samson had not sparked them to their abusive flowering, something else eventually would have.

"Your papa did not trust me as he should have. But all men are not like your papa. I do not think Rauffe would ever hurt you on purpose. And I am quite sure he would apologize if he did."

"How can you be sure?"

"Because he is Lord Gerolt's son, and Lord Gerolt has never hurt me. You see, Gelli, Lord Gerolt did not change." Cassandry paused and reflected. "No, that is not true. Everyone changes. But some people change in good ways, Gelli. You say that Lord Gerolt loves me. Why do you think that?"

"Because of the way he looks at you."

"Is that all?" Antony had once looked at Cassandry with love too.

"And the way he treats you."

"How is that?"

"Like . . . like he thinks you something precious and dear in his life. And—" a little light of understanding suddenly flickered in Egelina's eyes "—and like it would hurt *him* if he were to hurt you."

Cassandry's heart warmed and splintered all at once. "So you see, Gelli, Rauffe—"

"Rauffe does not look at me like that. Maybe he would be kind and not change—but I do not love him, Mamma, and he does not love me. Besides, if we marry, you cannot marry Lord Gerolt."

"I cannot marry him anyway, Gelli."

"Why not? You love him too, do you not?"

Because sometimes love is not enough. And sometimes love comes too late. Cassandry could not speak these hard truths to a daughter still so precariously on the edge of faith and fear.

"Come back to Lyonstoke, and we will talk about it there."

"Not if you are going to try to make me marry Rauffe."

"Gelli—"

"No! I would be bored to death with all his talk of hounds, and he will be bored to death with my poetry. He said he would have to marry me if his father insisted, but that he would really rather not, which is why he was so relieved when I told him what I was doing and said he would help me—"

Egelina pulled her hands away to slap one to her mouth, then laced them in her lap and stared at her mother defiantly.

Cassandry forbore to remind her daughter of her incoherent disclosures when she had come in a panic to Cassandry for help with Rauffe's "illness" this morning. Cassandry had not understood half of the disjointed tale, but she had understood enough to say, "I think it is time you told me where you found that letter Lord Gerolt wrote to me. Yes, and the gold circlet, too."

Egelina's mouth quirked sulkily. "They were Rauffe's idea. He will have to tell you."

"He cannot do so just now. He is still sick."

"Then when he is well."

"Will you leave him to take the blame himself? For something you confess you began?"

Egelina's gaze fell to her hands. Cassandry watched as the skirts of her daughter's gown moved with the back-and-forth swing of her foot.

"No," Egelina mumbled at last. "That would not be fair."

Oh, how Cassandry loved this strong streak of honesty in her daughter. "Then you will have to come back with me, won't you?"

There was still too much fear in Egelina's face. Cassandry leaned forward to tuck a strand of hair behind her daughter's ear.

Egelina tossed her head. "Why are you always doing that?"

"Doing what?"

"Playing with my hair."

"Am I?" Cassandry laughed. "Because you are my daughter and I love you. I cannot explain it better than that. You will do the same with your daughter when you are a mother."

This time the quirk on Egelina's lips turned upward. "I like it when you laugh, Mamma. It is such a pretty sound."

Cassandry's heart wrenched that she had failed to do so more when Egelina was small. Gerolt—dear Gerolt!—had given Cassandry back the gift of herself. Would she bury the gift away in a nunnery so soon, rather than share it longer with her daughter? *I lost too many years with you, Gelli. Too many years lost to my own confusion and hopelessness and grief.*

Gerolt. All her life, she had trusted his wisdom and judgment, but this time she knew he was wrong. However grounded his urgency for a grandchild was in his love for Rauffe, Egelina and Rauffe were too young to marry. It was unfair to place such a burden upon their shoulders. Perhaps in time they would both change their minds toward one another, but for now—for now, Cassandry wanted to take Egelina back to Rengrave Castle and laugh with her and write poetry with her and teach her to look to the future with optimism rather than doubt. She wanted to nurture a secure, joyful daughter.

"I will ask Lord Gerolt to delay the betrothal with Rauffe," she said. "And I will ask *you* to give it more time before you reject Rauffe entirely. But if you do not change your mind in a year or two, then I will not insist you marry, and neither will Lord Gerolt."

He would have no need to. He would not wait that long before he took a young wife for himself and sired a brother or two for Rauffe—just in case. The thought took a bit of the glow off her future with Egelina, but Cassandry had been reconciled to that inevitability for a long while now.

"Ever?" Egelina queried.

"Ever what?"

"Ever marry. If I don't marry Rauffe—"

"I cannot promise that. Your father and I very thoughtlessly bequeathed you those castles," Cassandry said with a smile she hoped looked more teasing than as strained as it felt, "and they must have an heir. And you would regret it very much one day if you did not have sons and daughters to love as much as I love you."

She twitched Egelina's hair again, which made Egelina laugh, but a hint of misgiving returned to her eyes.

"You promise it will not be for a year or two? And may I at least choose for myself?"

"With my guidance," Cassandry said, remembering how flawed her own young judgment had been, "and consent to your choice by Lord Gerolt. He will remain your guardian until your marriage."

A discreet cough sounded, turning both their heads to the doorway. Sir Fithian kept his gaze fixed firmly on Cassandry.

"I have thpoken to the abbot, my lady. He underthandth Thir Gerolt'th pothition regarding the Lady Egelina. If we thtart for Lyonthtoke now, we can thtill arrive before thundown."

Cassandry thanked him and told Egelina to fetch her cloak. The happy years she envisioned with her daughter dimmed a little more, for that joy could not come before she walked through the sorrow of painful good-byes.

Chapter 27

Go? How could he let her go? Everything Gerolt had done for the last six weeks had been to keep Cassandry near him.

Yet he knew she was right. It had been selfish—aye, selfish—however well-meaning, for him to push for marriage between their children so soon. For in truth, that was all they still were. He had seen it clearly in Rauffe's pale, pinched face during the days of his recovery. He was just a boy, in no way prepared to become a father. Gerolt had let fear and grief overpower him, or he would not have needed Cassandry to remind him of that.

Marion's poison and Cassandry's purging had left Rauffe's stomach so raw that he had been unable to eat anything other than gruel for the next three days. Cassandry had nursed him tenderly the first day, then turned his care over to Gerolt. Rauffe appeared flattered by his father's tending. He sat propped against his pillows, demanding between slurping spoonfuls every detail of Marion's assault upon him, then revealing tale after tale of the little acts of maliciousness Marion had performed while growing up with him and Fleur.

"Mostly she would take things that weren't hers," Rauffe said, "then blame the thefts on a scullery maid or a page. Mostly just little things. The last bit of honey in the kitchen, or the bells from one of the squire's shoes, or a ribbon from one of Mamma's ladies. One time she stole a silver ring, though, with an amethyst in it. But Fleur took it away from her and snuck it back to its owner before she noticed it was gone."

Gerolt listened from his chair beside Rauffe's bed, appalled. "Fleur knew? Why did I never hear any of this?"

"Fleur was too soft hearted to tell. She knew Mamma would switch Marion if she knew. Fleur said Marion's life was so sad she could not bear to cause a rift between her and Mamma."

"What did Marion have to be sad about? Your mother loved her as if she were truly your second sister."

"*I* did not think Marion was sad at all; I just thought she was shameless. But when Fleur asked her why she took things, she said her own parents had cheated her." Rauffe studied the gruel in his spoon and tilted out a few peas before he continued. "Her mother was higher born than her father, but she married Sir Samson because he was your friend and her father thought it might win him influence with you. Marion's mother resented it when Sir Samson had not enough money to buy her all the gowns and jewels she wanted. Marion remembered her saying so, even though Marion was just a little girl." Rauffe swirled his spoon in the gruel, clearly trying to avoid any more peas. "After he left them to join the crusade, her mother told Marion they both deserved better than Sir Samson had given them. She ruined Sir Samson's lands trying to raise her family back to the status of her own birth, and then she died, leaving Marion and her brothers with nothing. Marion said if her mother had not married Sir Samson, *she* would have been born a highborn lady worthy of a rich husband instead of being a near pauper forced to marry a middling knight."

"That 'middling knight' adored her. Quit picking at your gruel."

"Cassandry could not possibly have made this. She knows I dislike peas."

"They do not give you headaches, so eat them. They will do you good."

Rauffe obeyed but with a scrunched-up face. "Fleur felt sorry for Marion because she was so bitter. Marion never showed it to you or Mamma, though. Especially with Mamma, she was always smiling and sweet and eager to please because she thought Mamma was grooming her to become the wife of someone like you. Until you betrothed her to Sir Gregory. Well"—Rauffe shrugged as though he'd grown bored with Marion's past—"I knew she was willful and a little 'aslant,' as Fleur used to say, but I never thought she was devious enough to poison me. Thank heaven you didn't marry her."

Thank heaven, indeed! Gerolt felt a fool for not recognizing what Marion had been, but in truth, she had never appeared to him anything other than a laughing, good-hearted girl who mostly kept close company with his wife.

Rauffe's rallying spirits encouraged Gerolt for his full recovery. But for how long? He had relapsed too many times over too many years. Marriage to Egelina was out of the question, at least for another pair of years or so. But Gerolt knew he could not wait that long for himself. Marion was gone, but his own dilemma remained. He needed more sons in case fate chose to be cruel and snatch Rauffe away. And Cassandry was right, though Gerolt hated it. She could not remain at Lyonstoke while he took another wife.

After informing him of her decision for herself and Egelina, she'd avoided him, perhaps wisely, to give them both space to brace for their inevitable separation. She had agreed to stay until Rauffe was well enough to leave his chamber, but she and Egelina did not even join his household at dinner. Gerolt caught glimpses of her here and there as she flitted with her daughter through the castle, but somehow she managed to never quite cross his path. Nevertheless, the comfort of her continued presence was all that held Gerolt's aching parts together. He feared he might shatter when she left. His next wife might find herself with a husband as hollow as Cassandry had appeared the day she had ridden back into Lyonstoke's courtyard.

The morning that Rauffe felt up to eating some cold chicken for breakfast, Cassandry sent Gerolt word that she and Egelina would be starting for Rengrave Castle. But she wished to speak with him and Rauffe first, in private. Gerolt sent back the page who bore her message with an invitation to Rauffe's chamber, then went to see that Rauffe made himself presentable for their visit.

"Shall I assist you in matching your clothes?" Gerolt crossed to the large chest that held Rauffe's garments. Rauffe had confessed to him his challenge with perceiving colors.

"There is no need," Rauffe said. He dropped with an encouraging spryness to one knee beside the chest before lifting up the lid. "Egelina has laid out all the colors for me. Look. All the clothes in this pile are red"—he pointed to the neat stack of folded cloth with a strip of parchment pinned to the top item with the word *red* printed out in Rauffe's hand—"the clothes in this pile are blue, and these are all green." He rather unnecessarily went through each hue before glancing up with a grin.

"Egelina did that for you?"

"She put the matching colors together, but I wrote their names out because she was still learning to form her letters."

Cassandry had asked Gerolt not only to stay the marriage but to delay the betrothal between Egelina and Rauffe. Gerolt had agreed, but he wondered now if the latter had been necessary. Egelina would clearly make Rauffe an excellent wife one day.

Gerolt waited beside the window while Rauffe dressed, watching the morning sun dart playfully in and out of the clouds. He felt the small bulge of the object he had tucked inside his belt so that Rauffe could not yet see it. Gerolt wished he could speak of it to Cassandry alone, but he knew she would refuse if he asked such a moment of her. He wanted too much to hold her, to kiss her, to beg her to stay, but since he could offer her no status other than mother to his future daughter-in-law, he knew it was more prudent to part at arm's length. His next wife, whoever she might be, deserved better than a husband who could not conceal his longing for another woman.

A light rap fell on the door just as Rauffe finished slipping on his shoes. Gerolt crossed the floor to let Cassandry and Egelina enter. The stern cast of Cassandry's mouth startled Gerolt, but it softened as she moved to take Rauffe's hands.

"I heard you ate well this morning. You are feeling better?"

"Yes, my lady, thank you," Rauffe said, then blushed when Cassandry reached up to kiss his cheek.

She laughed. "I think I am allowed to do that after all you and I have been through together."

She tousled his hair as though he were an impish boy and not a gangly youth who stood half a foot taller than she. Rauffe's blush deepened, but Gerolt saw the reciprocal affection in his son's face. Her gaze moved a little too quickly past Gerolt as she turned toward Egelina. Her daughter held a small wooden casket clasped to her breast, her eyes fixed warily on her mother as Cassandry's frown returned.

"Close the door, Gelli, then come over here and stand by Rauffe."

Her daughter obeyed, dragging her steps with clear reluctance.

"They have been at mischief together," Cassandry said. "Egelina refused to tell me the whole of it until Rauffe was well

again. Well, child, you see Rauffe on his feet with the flush of
health on his cheeks, so there will be no more dallying."

She opened the casket Egelina held and pulled something out.
A red-and-white-rayed seashell dangling on a leather thong. The
one Cassandry had worn her first morning back at Lyonstoke, so
similar, save for its color, to the one Gerolt had given her when she
was twelve.

"Oh," Rauffe said abruptly and sat down very suddenly on
the bed.

Cassandry's eyes narrowed. "What do you know about this,
Rauffe?"

"Nothing, I swear! That is, only what Egelina told me after
she—"

Egelina kicked his ankle. "Hush!"

"Yes," Cassandry said. "I am certain she started this game
alone, for she did not know you well enough that first day to enlist
you as her accomplice."

"Accomplice to what?" Gerolt broke in.

"To try to trick me into thinking—" Cassandry cut herself off.
"Someone left this outside our chamber door the first morning we
were here. I thought one of your men left the trinket for Egelina,
but you put it there, didn't you, Gelli? For me."

Egelina refused to meet her mother's eyes, but after a moment
she nodded.

"Where did you get it?" Cassandry asked in tones Gerolt
suspected even her headstrong daughter would hesitate to ignore.

"Papa gave it to me."

The answer clearly took Cassandry aback. "Your papa? I never
saw you wear it. When did he give it to you?"

"After you lost your gray one. Papa showed it to me"—Egelina
nodded at the red-and-white shell—"and said he had found you a
new one to make you smile again, but then he sighed and said it
was pointless because you would never forgive him, so he gave the

shell to me instead. He told me to keep it secret so that seeing it would not make you sad."

Cassandry stared at the shell for a long moment. The sternness slid from her face, but Gerolt could not interpret the expression that replaced it. She finally dropped the shell back into the casket.

"And the wreath?" A softer note had entered her voice. "I presume that came from you, too?"

Egelina traced a silken-slippered toe in a circle on the floor. "I ran down to the gardens early and made it while you slept. You were always sleeping late because you tossed and turned so much at night."

An inkling of comprehension pierced Gerolt's puzzled brain. "A wreath? You said it was for Egelina. I queried all my men."

"I am sorry if it caused awkwardness," Cassandry said. "It never crossed my mind that Egelina and Rauffe might be behind it."

"I had nothing to do with any wreath," Rauffe said swiftly, "or the tart Egelina made and had served to you at dinner. What?" he asked when Egelina glared at him. "You told me all about it when you said you had run out of ideas and asked for my help."

Egelina gave an exasperated huff. "Fine. I made the tart the day you took me to the kitchen to make bryndon cakes, Mamma, while you were attending to Rauffe's headache. And yes, I ran out of ideas after that, especially when you kept insisting the tokens were for me, even though *you* were the one who had once had a shell necklace, and *you* were the one who loved sweet woodruff and periwinkle, and custard tarts were *your* favorite dish, not mine. So I went to Rauffe and told him again that I did not wish to marry him. He said he did not wish to marry me either but he did not know what to do about it because his father was determined. So I told him of my plan. He, of course, was too slow-witted to see that there was anything between you and Lord Gerolt—"

"I wasn't slow-witted," Rauffe objected. "I was distracted with my headaches. It's true, though," he added, "that I didn't believe her at first. But I was willing to try anything to get out of the betrothal." He cast his father an apologetic look. "I'm sorry, sir. I know you wanted us to marry, but she was so annoying at first with all her silly poetry, and when I tried to change the subject to hounds, she said that she liked dogs well enough but describing how they were trained for the hunt was simply tedious." He returned Egelina's glare. "I could not think of anything worse than to have to spend the rest of my life with someone who constantly spouted verses with words I couldn't even understand and who wouldn't let me talk about hounds—"

"I never said you could not talk about them," Egelina interrupted. "I just said—"

"So when she came to me the morning after Lady Cassandry banned further almonds from my food," Rauffe continued speaking over her protest, "I was feeling so much better that I said I would help her find another token."

However excellent a wife Egelina might make Rauffe in the future, they were quarreling like children now. Gerolt bristled with impatience, coupled with dismay when he recalled which "token" had followed the custard tart. He counted—swiftly—before confronting his son.

"You stole your mother's mirror?"

Rauffe went very red. "It wasn't stealing. You said I could choose some of her trinkets to keep someday. But, yes, I took Egelina to your chamber, and we looked through her jewelry casket with the broken lock. When Egelina saw the mirror, she exclaimed that it would be the perfect thing, for she remembered that you had once given Lady Cassandry one very much like it before she lost it, like she lost the seashell."

Cassandry raised surprised brows at her daughter. "How did you know about the mirror? I lost it before you were born."

Egelina's gaze again dropped from her mother's. "It was one of the quarrels I overheard between you and Papa. Papa was reproaching you for—well, many things—and he mentioned a mirror Lord Gerolt had sent you one Christmas. You told him it had just been a trinket, the mirror no bigger than Papa's thumb. When I saw the one Rauffe showed me, it looked just like the one you described to Papa."

She moved to sit down beside Rauffe on the bed.

"Mamma never wore it," Rauffe said, "for she told Fleur to do so would be vain. She did not even like Fleur looking at herself in water. I thought after all these years you would have forgotten about it if you saw it again, sir."

"But I knew you would not, Mamma." Egelina looked at her mother now, sharing a silent message that Gerolt felt himself shut out from. "What did you do with it? It is not in the casket with the other things we left. The pomander isn't here either."

Gerolt slid a thumb into his belt near the little bulge beneath it.

"I thought the mirror came from Sir Samson," Cassandry said, "so I gave it back to him." She threw a worried glance at Gerolt.

"And Sam gave it back to me," Gerolt reassured her. "Of course I recognized it, Rauffe, and so did he. I thought a thief had stolen into my chambers."

"I'm sorry," Rauffe mumbled, but Egelina's toe gave a sharp tap against the floor.

"Why would Sir Samson give you a gift just like one Lord Gerolt had given you?" she asked Cassandry. "You were so frustrating, Mamma! I could tell by your manner that you were still refusing to see what was right under your nose. That is why Rauffe and I attached your name to the ribbon and the hairpin, so that you could not pretend anymore that you thought the tokens were meant for me. Rauffe wrote it, but still nothing was happening between you and Lord Gerolt. So we finally had to take drastic measures."

Cassandry crossed to the bed and pulled a small, folded piece of parchment from the casket. She flicked it open and held it under Rauffe's nose. "By 'drastic,' I presume you mean forging your father's handwriting?" Rauffe recoiled, but before he could reply, she turned back to Egelina. "And what did you think would happen when I showed this to Lord Gerolt and he said he never wrote it? He would have been embarrassed, and I would have been humiliated."

Gerolt joined her to look over her shoulder at the parchment. *"A word fitly spoken is like apples of gold in pictures of silver." Let this small gift remind you how dearly you still lay on my heart.* Inside the open casket lay a small apple, alongside a ribbon, a wooden hairpin, and a gold circlet—the latter three he recognized as also having belonged to Aveline—and three sticks of cinnamon tied together with a slim red ribbon.

"Rauffe did not forge that," he said of the parchment. "That is my writing."

Cassandry turned her head to stare at him, her mouth slightly agape. Oh, saints, how he longed to kiss those lovely, startled lips.

"You sent me the apple and the pomander?"

"No. But I wrote that. And this." He pulled the pomander from inside his belt, opened it, and drew out the slip of parchment that lay across the crucifix. "I wrote them both to Fleur." He heard a small gasp from the bed but did not look to see whether it issued from Rauffe or Egelina. He fancied he could guess, though. For now, he held Cassandry's bewildered gaze. "I missed Fleur after she married, so we sometimes wrote to one another, as you and I once did. And sometimes I sent her gifts, once a miniature painting of an apple, done in gold leaf, set inside a painted silver frame. Another time this pomander. This, though . . ." He lifted out the parchment that lay beside the cinnamon sticks. *How you have been missed! May this bring you warm memories of home.* He finally looked at the couple on the bed. "I do not know how you knew I sent her this one with a small cask of cinnamon."

Rauffe had gone into a defensive slouch, his head down, as was Egelina's, to avoid Gerolt's eyes.

Egelina looked a little apprehensive but confessed, "Some of the spice must have spilled on it. The scent still clung to the parchment. It is what gave me the idea."

Gerolt lifted the parchment to his nose. She was right.

"But there were no cinnamon sticks in the kitchen for you to take," Cassandry said.

"I know. During one of our rides, Sir Fithian took me to a market town and I bought them there."

"You would not, however," Gerolt said to Egelina, "have known where I kept Fleur's letters." He waited, watching from the corner of his eye, for Rauffe to lift his head.

His son finally did so. "I knew where they were. I remembered that Fleur's husband gave them back to you when Fleur died, but I didn't know you still read them."

Only a hundred times or so. "And thus you thought I would not notice if you cut them up." Gerolt had checked the stack of letters after Samson had given him the pomander and found sections from three of them removed with what looked like some very careful knife strokes.

"Gelli!" Cassandry exclaimed. "How could you and Rauffe desecrate something you must have recognized as precious to Lord Gerolt?"

"Don't blame her," Rauffe said. "Cutting up the letters was my idea."

"But only after I said that we needed something so obvious from your father that Mamma could no longer mistake or ignore it." Egelina drew a deep breath, then stood, her face filled with determination. "You see, my lord, I saw what Rauffe and Mamma did not at first . . . that you were in love with her. I thought the tokens would help *her* see it. At first I wanted you and her to marry so that Rauffe and I should not have to, but then I saw her grow happy again in your company, and I am certain that she has grown to love you too. So please, will you marry her so that she does not have to be sad anymore?"

Gerolt felt his own breath suspend. Relentless desire warred with clear-eyed reason. He sought Cassandry's gaze and caught her answering yearning behind the pain and regret there. But she turned back to her daughter and spoke firmly.

"That is not possible, Gelli. This phantom courtship you and Rauffe devised was impossible from the first. And it is completely unnecessary to urge Lord Gerolt to play out your game, for we have promised you shall not have to marry Rauffe if you do not wish to. Now, we have a long ride ahead. Return the items Rauffe gave you and say good-bye to him while I speak a word to Lord Gerolt, then we must be on our way."

"But, Mamma, it is not about me and Rauffe anymore." Egelina turned, pleading, to Gerolt. "My lord, you know what I say is true! Tell her!"

Cassandry set a firm hand on Gerolt's arm and drew him over to the window. They waited until Egelina sat down once more in apparent defeat beside Rauffe, rummaged through the jewelry casket, pulled out the hairpin, and gave it to Rauffe.

"She is right," Gerolt murmured then. "I do love you."

"I know." Cassandry's voice broke a little. "I love you too. But it is too late to change the past, and I cannot provide what your future needs."

She drew something from her sleeve and pressed it into his palm. A sheet of folded parchment. Gerolt opened it and read the reply he had written when Cassandry had cut him out of her life. The one he had never sent.

"Sparrow," he whispered, falling into the name of affection he had prefaced the letter with, "I—"

She silenced him with fingers that trembled slightly against his lips. "I know. You were right not to send it. But thank you for wanting to." She glanced at the bed, where Egelina was extending to Rauffe the ribbon, then stretched up to kiss the corner of Gerolt's mouth. She dropped her hand, her eyes moist. "You were right about Antony, too. If it had not been Sir Samson, it would have been something else."

Gerolt did not care if Rauffe and Egelina saw. He grasped Cassandry's elbows and would have drawn her to him, but she resisted stiffly.

"I do not know how he could love me," she continued of Antony, "and say the hurtful things he did to me, but Gelli said he used to kneel by her bed and weep at night. He told her he was sorry that he hurt me—but then he did it all over again."

And again and again. Cassandry did not need to say it. Gerolt saw it in her still-wounded eyes.

"So why did he search out that shell for me after he—after I lost yours?"

Gerolt knew better than to press her for the story of his lost shell. Too much pain lingered in the confused gaze she raised to his.

"Fleur told Rauffe when they were all growing up that there was something 'aslant' in Marion. Perhaps there was something aslant in Antony too, something he did not know how to control." Gerolt brushed a stray strand of hair away from her temple with his thumb, then gave her a crooked smile. "It may be there is something a little aslant in all of us if we had courage to look deeply enough into our souls."

It took a moment before she nodded. Her eyes went hazy, as though focusing on some inner memory. "He told Gelli that I could not forgive him. But he was wrong."

Gerolt knew she was thinking again of the red-and-white-rayed shell. He felt suddenly an intruder on her privacy and turned his attention to the young couple on the bed. They were embracing! Well, at second glance, Egelina was embracing Rauffe, while Rauffe returned her hug awkwardly, looking embarrassed, flattered, and lonely all at once.

Gerolt felt Cassandry's fingers press his tightly, but even as he looked down at her again, she slipped away from him.

"Come, Gelli," she said so crisply that Egelina sprang up from the bed.

Egelina's face was wet with tears, but Gerolt did not know how to answer the imploring look she sent him. Cassandry gave one final embrace of her own to Rauffe, then swept her daughter out the door.

Chapter 28

"Aren't you going after her?" Rauffe said.

Gerolt clamped his pain down as tightly as he could before he answered. "No, Rauffe, I am not."

"Why?" Rauffe rose from the bed, looking alarmed. "Father, why? Egelina was right. You love Lady Cassandry. I own it took me awhile to see it, but once Egelina told me what to look for—"

Gerolt thought a lie would be wisest but found he could not when he met his son's eyes. "It is true that I care for her deeply. But there are reasons why we cannot marry. I will explain them to you another time."

"You do not need to explain them." Rauffe spoke bitterly now. "I know why you cannot marry her. It is because of me."

The words landed with a small punch to Gerolt's stomach, knocking the air briefly out of his reply. "No, Rauffe, of course it is not."

But he knew from Rauffe's face that he had hesitated too long.

"You think I am going to die and leave you without an heir."

Gerolt shook his head.

"I heard you!" Rauffe shouted. "Talking to Lady Cassandry outside my door. It is why you wanted to marry me to Egelina *now* instead of waiting a year. It was that and hope for a grandson, you said, or marry Marion." He took a sudden step toward Gerolt, then halted. His cheeks had gone pale again, causing his eyes to burn darkly in his thin face. His voice moderated, but it shook a little now. "Mamma always told me that you were ashamed of my weakness and headaches. But that night I woke up and heard you and Cassandry talking, and I slipped out of bed to listen. You told Cassandry you wanted a grandson to remember me by if I died. You wanted—to remember *me*." He spoke as if the thought awed him. "I never knew until that night, until I heard Cassandry ask you—" He broke off and rubbed his eyes.

The same way Gerolt remembered Rauffe rubbing them when he had found Rauffe sitting up in bed after Cassandry had left Gerolt that night. Rauffe's eyes had been red-rimmed and bright.

"She asked me why I never told you that I loved you." This time when Rauffe looked up, Gerolt recognized tears in his eyes. Guilt rose in Gerolt's throat. "Rauffe, I did not know how. My father—your grandfather—"

"You don't have to explain," Rauffe said. "I don't need anything more than I heard that night." He gazed at Gerolt with a misty gratitude before he took another step, close enough for Gerolt to lay his hands on his shoulders. "Sir, I promise I will not disappoint you. I promise I will not die before I give you an heir. Just please marry Cassandry."

Before he had witnessed Cassandry's tender caressings of Rauffe in his illness, it had never occurred to Gerolt to share the same physical affection with Rauffe that had come so easily to him with Fleur. Now he pulled his son into his arms.

"I have never been disappointed in you, Rauffe. And I pray you will not die. But you cannot promise—"

"I can if you marry Cassandry." Rauffe drew away, his tears replaced by a stubborn set to his face. "She made me well. I never felt so vigorous in my life as I did after she removed the almonds from my food and drink."

"But then you relapsed," Gerolt reminded him.

"Because Marion poisoned me. Which she could not have done if you had married Cassandry to begin with."

Gerolt opened his mouth to argue but found he could not. Rauffe had made too truthful a point.

"There were reasons we could not marry before," Gerolt tried to explain. "She was not ready."

"But she is now. Egelina and I both saw her kiss you right there by the window when you thought we were not looking. Even I can see that she loves you now. She will keep me in better health than any silly young wife you can wed."

Gerolt felt a tug in his chest as powerful as if a physical cord sought to jerk him from this chamber into the yard below. Did she still linger there? Was it too late?

Aye, too late. Twenty-four years too late. "Rauffe, you are young, but I have taught you of our duty to our inheritance. It is no light thing for a man with my lands and responsibilities to die without heirs. I am content with you. I am proud of you. But fate is fickle. It took your sister. If it yet takes you, too—"

"Fine," Rauffe cut him off. "Then I will marry. I am well. I can take a wife and get you a grandson. Now. I will marry anyone you choose—except Egelina."

Gerolt gazed into his son's earnest face, stirred to the heart by his offer. But Gerolt had learned his lesson. "I'll not ask that of you." *Even for Cassandry.*

"You don't have to. I am willing. Just bring Cassandry and Egelina back."

Gerolt did not miss the urgent coupling of Egelina's name with Cassandry's. "I saw you too, Rauffe, embracing Egelina. She will make you an excellent wife in a pair of years or so."

"I don't want her for a wife. We are not at all suited to wed. But"—Gerolt saw him swallow hard—"I should rather like having her for a sister. I have missed Fleur too."

Guilt struck Gerolt a second time. His grief for his daughter had been so deep he had not thought of Rauffe's loss. He recalled the lonely look on Rauffe's face when Egelina had hugged him good-bye.

The invisible cord jerked again, more forcibly than before. Gerolt planted his feet hard against the floor. However remorseful for his mistakes as a father, he had a duty to fulfill, to his lands, to his ancestors.

Rauffe must have seen his determination.

"I will marry anyone you choose," Rauffe repeated, his voice edged with desperation.

"You are too young. I will not allow that yet. Do not argue with me."

Rauffe's shoulders slumped. He returned to sit on the bed, then dropped his head into hands. "Then I wish I *were* dead. Every time I look at you, every time I look at whoever you wed, I will know it was my fault that you are not with Cassandry."

"Rauffe, no." Gerolt grasped again those sunken shoulders and pulled his son back to his feet. "This is not your fault."

"I won't die."

"You cannot promise that."

"I can! I am well. Cassandry made me well."

"And what if you relapse again?"

"What if I don't? What if I live to marry and have a dozen sons? You will have spited yourself for duty, for fear . . . for nothing." Rauffe's hands encircled Gerolt's wrists in a grip that was reassuringly strong. "Father . . . go get Cassandry."

Gerolt searched his son's impassioned face. A stubborn vitality had always shone in Rauffe's eyes, however ill he had fallen. It blazed there now.

What if . . . ?

Gerolt had focused on fate's unlucky whims for so long. Did he dare hazard all the future that this time it would be kind?

"Twelve grandsons, eh?"

Whatever doubt still challenged Gerolt, none flickered in Rauffe's lightning grin. "Not one less."

Gerolt allowed the cord of love to yank him all the way to the door before he hesitated again.

"It would be selfish," Rauffe said before Gerolt could turn back into the room, "to deny me a mother wise enough and skillful enough to help me keep my promise. Who knows what havoc with my health a young, careless wife might cause? The one thing you have never been, Father, is selfish. Don't begin today."

Gerolt could not stop himself from laughing at his son's deft chiding. He felt hands on his back, pushing him firmly through the doorway. Nevertheless, "what if" drummed through his head as he strode down the passageway.

What if Rauffe dies?

What if he lives?

What if I need more sons?

What if a young wife dies in childbed, as Fleur did, or bears me no children at all?

What if . . .

Too many what-ifs. There was only one certainty. His need for Cassandry.

She turned in her saddle as the ground around her and Egelina shook with the reverberating thunder of horses' hooves. A bend in the road behind them hid the hurried rider from her traveling party's view, but Cassandry motioned them to draw their mounts and the baggage wagon to the side of the road. Their escorts, Sir Fithian and Sir Ingram, along with the maid Lora, obeyed. After a moment of hesitant curiosity, Egelina followed. Cassandry joined them there to allow room for the rider to pass. He took the curve in a cloud of dust cast up by the frantic gait. Cassandry welcomed the distraction, however brief, from the dull, weary thudding of her heart. Her attempts to engage Egelina in cheerful-toned conversation while Cassandry felt so heavy and dismal inside had already exhausted her nearly past bearing, and they had not traversed more than a couple of miles from Lyonstoke.

"Cover your face, Gelli," Cassandry warned, "or that cloud will cast grit in your eyes."

Egelina obediently drew her cloak across her face to shield herself from the dusty onslaught. Cassandry started to do the same, but just before the rider reached them, his horse reared and shrilled. Its fore hooves flailed for a moment in the air, then hit the ground with such a sharp clip that it sent bits of the road flying up. Cassandry lowered the edge of her cloak, startled. The man dismounted and strode out of the dissipating cloud with such familiar, purposeful steps that Cassandry's breast gave a lurch of befuddled hope.

She determinedly squelched it before he reached her. Only something dire could have brought Gerolt pounding after her like this.

"What has happened? Has Rauffe fallen ill again?"

Gerolt tossed his response at the knights. "Sir Ingram, Sir Fithian, escort Lady Cassandry's maid back to the castle. And take the wagon with you."

The knights exchanged glances but obeyed without question.

The curtness of his orders frightened Cassandry even more. "Gerolt, what is it this time? More headaches? A fever? Why are we lingering here? Egelina, come, we must return to Lyonstoke for the night."

"Wait." Gerolt grasped her mare's bridle to restrain her when Cassandry tried to turn her mount in the road. "There is nothing wrong with Rauffe." He grinned. "In fact, he has never been so right."

Cassandry tried to still her heart as it tripped again. "Then what are you doing here?"

He led his horse over to Egelina and gave her the reins. "Hold these for me. I have a word to say to your mother."

Egelina looked puzzled, then her face, so dolorous since they left Lyonstoke, went suddenly radiant with one of its quicksilver smiles.

Gerolt returned to Cassandry's mare and stood, hands raised, waiting to lift her to the ground. A violent trembling seized her. Oh, saints, if she misread the intent in his eyes—

"Let go," he said softly, nodding at her tight grip on the reins.

She pried her fingers loose almost painfully, set her shaking hands to his wide, strong shoulders, and with a flood of doubtful tears blurring her eyes, surrendered herself to him.

Her feet had barely brushed the ground when he whispered in her ear, "Marry me," and kissed her.

Impossible! But she melted into him all the same.

"Oh!" Egelina squealed. "Mamma!"

Cassandry tore her reluctant lips away from Gerolt's fervent caress to see what had upset her daughter. Egelina had her hands over her eyes.

"What is the matter, Gelli?"

Egelina cracked open her fingers, then lowered them with an expression of relief. "Must you do that standing right here in the road? What if someone rides past and sees you?"

"What?" Gerolt said. "You mean this?"

He dragged Cassandry back against his chest and kissed her again.

"Yes!" Egelina cried. "Stop it!"

When Cassandry and Gerolt broke apart, she had covered her eyes again.

Cassandry caught Gerolt's wide grin before he leaned his chin against the top of her head, presumably to gaze at Egelina.

"I thought you wished me to marry your mother."

"I do. I just did not think you would do—*that*—in front of me."

Gerolt roared with laughter until Cassandry, still clasped in his arms, found herself joining him in a fit of unmatronly giggles.

"Well!" Egelina said, her voice very prim. "Thank goodness you have both at last come to your senses." Her face was still quite red as she moved her mount forward and extended Gerolt's reins to him. "Let us go back to Lyonstoke."

"I must first help your mother remount," he said.

But Cassandry sobered when his hands moved to her waist. "No, wait. Egelina, give us another moment."

Egelina's brows twitched together, but she rode a few steps away, leading Gerolt's horse with her.

Cassandry stood then, in the circle of Gerolt's embrace, rubbing her hands against the breast of his tunic, feeling the hard muscles beneath it. Egelina was wrong. She and Gerolt had both slipped very, very far from rationality. It took all her strength not to lean her cheek against his heartbeat, to remind him instead of the painful truth.

"I cannot, Gerolt. Marry you. You should not have ridden after me this way." She almost said it was cruel but knew he would never intentionally hurt her. She added instead, "It was hasty. You know that I can give you no sons."

"You do not have to."

She frowned up at him. "You said yourself you need more heirs. In case Rauffe—"

"Rauffe has promised to live and give me a dozen grandsons. So you see, there is not the least reason why I cannot marry you."

Her mouth popped open in surprise. "A dozen—?"

Gerolt silenced her with a third kiss. "You've no notion," he murmured after a tender but very thorough assault, "how tempting your lips are when they are all agape like that."

She relished the heat that lingered on her mouth, but his

pronouncement was absurd. "Rauffe cannot possibly guarantee you any such thing!"

"He assures me that he can. In time, when he is older, he is more than welcome to try." Gerolt cupped her cheeks between his palms, holding her with the strength and authority that had so often quelled her childish fears, but the light in his eyes was very different now. "He said something else, much more sensible. What if, Cassandry? You and I have not even considered that. What if it is not Rauffe who dies? What if it is me, or you?"

"Oh! Why would Rauffe say a thing like that?"

"He did not, exactly. He only got me thinking. How old were your parents when they died?"

"Mamma was twenty-four, Papa thirty. The fever took them both within days of each other, you know that."

"My mother died when she was thirty-five, my father at forty-four. Six years younger than my own fifty years. What if, Cassandry? What if it is not Rauffe who has few years left, but you and I? What if I die tomorrow, or the next day, or the day after that? I do not want to spend whatever time I have left on this earth regretting what I lost—again."

The thought of his death cast a streak of terror through her heart.

"Nor do I," she whispered.

"Then come home with me." He scattered kisses, light as butterfly wings, all over her face, sending delicious tremors to her fingertips and toes. "Come home with me to stay."

"How long are you going to keep doing that?" Egelina demanded.

Cassandry followed Gerolt's twinkling eyes to her daughter. This time Egelina was staring with a fixed determination at a fleecy white cloud directly over her head.

"If your mother does not concede to my demands, I shall have to do it a great many more times," Gerolt replied. "I am her liege lord, you know. She cannot continue to defy me without some sort of punishment."

Egelina lowered her gaze to her mother's face. "Then you had better change tactics, for it looks to me like she would be quite happy to stand here in the road being 'punished' till sundown." She rode over to them both and shoved the reins of Gerolt's horse into his hand. "Really, Mamma!" Her face shone scarlet, but a giggle escaped her. "May I at least ride back to Lyonstoke and tell Rauffe that you are coming . . . eventually?"

Cassandry gazed into Gerolt's laughing, patient, smoke-gray eyes. Her guardian. Her friend. Her rock. Her love. "Yes, Gelli."

Egelina did not wait for Cassandry to change her mind but gave another squeal, this one of happiness, before urging her mare into a gallop down the road that led to the castle.

This time it was Cassandry who stretched up to kiss Gerolt before murmuring to her now-absent daughter, "Tell Rauffe I am coming . . . home."

Medieval Glossary

Allure – the walking space on top of a tower or castle wall

Bailey – the courtyard of a castle

Butler – official in charge of a lord's butts of wine and beer

Chatelaine – wife of a lord, in charge of the domestic upkeep of his castle

Canonical hour – one of seven prayer times observed by the Catholic Church during the Middle Ages; the hours were announced by the ringing of bells which assisted people in determining the time of day

Chemise – a woman's loose undergarment

Citole – a medieval stringed instrument; the citole had four strings with a body that was often described as a "holly leaf" shape

Crenelated – a wall with gaps for firing arrows, etc

Dais – a raised platform in the castle **hall**

Destrier – medieval warhorse

Dinner – during the Middle Ages, this was the midday meal, generally starting between noon and 1 PM

Dispensers – sub-official under the **butler** in charge of dispensing the wine or beer

Drawbridge – a bridge that can be raised or lowered to permit access across a ditch or moat into a castle's **bailey**

Fortnight – two weeks (from "fourteen nights")

Feudal contract – Feudalism was a military system in which a man of lower standing (the **vassal**) swore fealty (from the Latin word for fidelity) to a man of higher standing, who became his "lord (or **liege lord**)". The two men thus entered into a contract in which the vassal promised to fight for his lord when called upon, in return for which the lord promised to protect the vassal from all external threats and forces.

Gallery – a balcony; also a long passageway open on one side that connects various parts of a castle

Gatehouse – the heavily fortified entrance to the castle complex

Girdle – a belt worn around the waist

Kirtle – a long gown worn by women

Liege lord – see **feudal contract**

Mail – a flexible armor made of small, overlapping metal rings

Manor – agricultural estate owned by a lord; sometimes attached to a castle, sometimes attached to a fortified manor house

Matins – the first **canonical hour** of the Catholic Church; in 13th century England in the spring, the church bells rang around 5 AM for matins.

Merlons – the part of a fortified castle wall that juts up between two crenels (gaps or open areas)

Mews – a birdhouse designed to house one or more birds of prey for medieval hunting

Moat – a broad, deep ditch filled with water that formed a defense around a castle

Pantler – the official in charge of a lord's bread and pantry

Parchment – material made from animal skin used for pages of books or other writing

Quintain – a device for squires and knights to practice fighting on horseback. A quintain consisted of a revolving post with an object (like a shield) on one end and a sandbag on the other. The squire or knight would attempt to ride at the object and strike it with their sword or lance and then get out of the way before the sandbag could whirl around and hit them.

Rebec – a bowed stringed instrument with 1-5 strings and a narrow, boat-shaped body

Saracen – term used by medieval Christian writers for Arabs and Muslims during the Crusades

Sea lion – in medieval heraldry, the sea lion had the head of a lion, webbed front feet, and the tail of a fish

Shawm – a double reed instrument of the Middle Ages

Smock – a loose, blouselike garment

Solar – a small, well-lit room, usually the domain of the lady of the castle

Spurs (to earn one's spurs) – when a squire became a knight (around the age of 21) he received a pair of golden spurs, hence the phrase "to earn one's spurs" meant to earn a knighthood

Surcote – also known as the surcoat or super-tunic; a secondary tunic worn over an under **tunic**, usually more elaborately decorated

The hall or great hall – the central living space of the castle inside the **keep**; the ceremonial and legal center

The keep – the central tower and main residence area of the castle

Token – a small gift or keepsake

Trenchers – large slices of stale bread, cut either round or square, and used as "plates" for medieval dining

Tunic – a sleeved, loose-fitting outer garment worn by both men and women; could be worn alone or under a **surcote**; for a man, could be knee or ankle length

Vassal – see **feudal contract**

Vows of future consent – what differentiated a betrothal from a marriage; vows of future consent ("I will") created a betrothal, while vows of present consent ("I do") created a marriage

Wall-walk – the walking space behind the fortifications (**merlons** and **crenels**) on the **battlements**; also known as the **allure**

I hope you enjoyed reading **Courting Cassandry**. If you did, would you please consider ~

Recommending this book to a friend.

Leaving a review on the website where you downloaded this book. Just a few words about what you liked about the story will help other readers find and enjoy this book too.

Subscribing to my newsletter at joycedipastena.com so we can keep in touch about future releases and follow along with new books I'm writing. Turn the page to learn more!

Thank you so much for reading ***Courting Cassandry***!

Join Joyce's
Medieval World

JOYCE DIPASTENA
Illuminating the Middle Ages
Timeless Tales of Love

Visit joycedipastena.com to sign up for Joyce's newsletter and receive a free copy of her medieval romance, **Loyalty's Web**. Her newsletter is sent out three times a month and includes announcements on new releases, special promotions and offers, periodic giveaways, historical trivia, and more! You are free to unsubscribe at any time.

About the Author

Joyce DiPastena illuminates the Middle Ages for modern readers through heartfelt historical romance. However many changes a few centuries may bring, she believes that stories of love can unite people across time.

Joyce grew up in southern Arizona and can easily withstand summer temperatures of 115 degrees, as long as she's sitting in a restaurant, movie theater, or under a ceiling fan—inside an air-conditioned building. She can be bribed with chocolate chip cookies and enjoys attending the Arizona Renaissance Festival every year. She holds a degree in history, specializing in the Middle Ages, from the University of Arizona. Joyce currently resides in Mesa, Arizona with her black cats, Nyxie and Calypso, who bring her good luck every day.

Joyce loves to hear from her readers. Email her at joyce@joycedipastena.com, visit her website at joycedipastena.com. join her newsletter, or connect with her on Facebook, Twitter/X, Amazon and BookBub. (Just search for "Joyce DiPastena." She's the only one there is!)

www.ingramcontent.com/pod-product-compliance
Lightning Source LLC
Chambersburg PA
CBHW060818120726
47909CB00006B/1981